Burn the Breeze

JUNE LARK

ISBN: 979-8-9904659-7-8
Published by June Lark Books
www.junelarkbooks.com

Content Warning

Explicit language, drug use, drug abuse, attempted drug-facilitated assault, child endangerment, abduction, assault, firearms, BDSM.

I hope you enjoy the world of Thornbrush Ranch, but first and foremost, take care of yourself.

Author's Note

Although I have been fortunate not to grow up around addiction, I've known people in my adult life who have struggled and have even lost their lives to their illness. The hurt and grief I and the people I love experienced because we love them (and will always love them) may eventually become a dull ache, but we will always miss the best parts of them. The guilt and regret we carry that we didn't do more to help can sometimes be overpowering. It's okay to let go of that because, in the end, it was their illness and it was always up to them to find the clarity they needed to get clean. It was never up to you to do it for them.

If you or someone you love is struggling with addiction, know there is help.

The support at Narcotics Anonymous focuses on helping people who are addicted to drugs, including alcohol, find a new way to live. They provide resources, meetings, and support from others in recovery to access tools to aid in recovery and living clean.

Support is one click away.

Narcotics Anonymous.

To those who have been told they are too much.
Well, let me just say—fuck 'em!
We like you just the way you are.

And to Tabi, the Lina to my Sage.

Playlist

"You Look Like You Love Me" by Ella Langley (feat. Riley Green)

"Good News" by Shaboozey

"Good Horses" by Lainey Wilson (feat. Miranda Lambert)

"She's Trouble" by Don Louis (feat. Sophia Scott)

"I'm the Problem" by Morgan Wallen

"Boot Scootin' Boogie" by Brooks & Dunn

"Cowboy Killer" by Blake Tyler

"Drunk (And I Don't Wanna Go Home)" by Elle King (feat. Miranda Lambert)

"Cowboys and Angels" by Jessie Murph

"Change My Mind" by Riley Green

"Play Something Country" by Brooks & Dunn (feat. Lainey Wilson)

"Chicken Fried" by Zac Brown Band

"The Way I Wanna" by Max McNown

"Lasso" by Jake Banfield

"Tennessee Whiskey" by Chris Stapleton

"You For a Reason" by Warren Zeiders

"Bless the Broken Road" by Will Dempsey

"Never Til Now (Wedding Version)" by Ashley Cooke, Brett Young

"Make Me Wanna Smoke" by Ella Langley

"Touch Me Like a Gangster" by Jessie Murph

"Just in Case" by Morgan Wallen

"Wasted on You" by Morgan Wallen

"I'll Set the Table" by Nic D

"Rome" by BRIM

"Burn It Down (717 Tapes)" by Warren Zeiders

"Fire and Gasoline" by Shaboozey

"Rock My World (Little Country Girl)" by Brooks & Dunn (feat. Marcus King)

Barrel Racing Terminology

Alley/alleyway—the entrance into the arena where the horses and their riders begin to run.

"On deck"—you're the next rider in the ring.

"Be thinking"—when you hear this at a competition, you're the fourth rider in line.

"Up"—it's your turn to enter the arena.

Bottom of the ground or bottom of the draw—after five runs, they rake the grounds. If you are bottom of the ground, you are the last to go before they re-rake for the next run.

Dash Ta Fame (DTF)—an all-time leading barrel racing sire.

"Drug his butt around the barrel"—horse got low in its hind quarters using its muscles to work hard at turning the barrel efficiently.

Free runner—naturally running son of a gun (won't have to ride aggressively but may be more difficult to turn).

Jackpot—a barrel racing event where a portion of the entry fees are given as prize money.

Lina's Columbia River Circuit Schedule

May Week 1: Joseph Round-up

May Week 2: Augustus Stampede

May Week 3: Molliville Showdown

May Week 4: Big Basin Buckeroo

June Week 1: St. John Rodeo

June Week 2: Salmon Ridge Rodeo

June Week 3: Prineville Fair & Rodeo

June Week 4: Homedale Stock Show & Rodeo, Frontier Days

July Week 1: Willows Rodeo

July Week 2: Big Buckin' Showdown

July Week 3: Washington State Rodeo

July Week 4: Lakeview Round-up

August Week 1: Puyallup Stampede

August Week 3: River Valley Round-up

September Week 2: Hermiston Fair & Rodeo

September Week 4: Columbia Valley Rodeo

October Week 1: Columbia River Circuit Finals

PROLOGUE
Lina

One Year Earlier

He was fucking me—*with his eyes*. Eyes that were dark and shadowed beneath a black cowboy hat. The rowdy Saddle Room bar at the Joseph Round-Up pumped classic country music over the inebriated shouts and laughter of the crowd. The bass reverberated through the soles of my boots, traveling up my bare legs until it settled in my core. It almost felt like the cowboy who bit at his lip while he watched me was humming right into my cunt. Thick hands picked up the glass of whiskey off the bartop, bringing it to his lips. Hands that I could imagine wrapping around my throat. He sipped, his gaze locked on me. And it felt as if he were sipping *me*.

"Are we getting a tattoo or what?" Viv asked, nudging my shoulder. Snapping me back to reality.

"You're seriously going to do that?" Kale Pardy questioned, reaching over me to slam his token on the bar.

"How do ya want it?" the bartender asked.

"Neat," Kale stated matter-of-factly.

Vivian Kelly—my only barrel racing friend because the

rest were competition—was always up to getting trashed with me. Kale was a bull rider from my hometown who often came out to party with us.

"Actually," I said, eyeing my cowboy on the other side of the bartop, "give that to me." I held out my hand, and Viv slapped the temporary Saddle Room logo tattoo into my turned-up palm.

"Oh, I see." Viv smirked, taking in what I was seeing … Mr. Tall, Dark, and Handsome. I wasn't ashamed to admit I was gawking at the man.

Even among the bustling rodeo crowd, he seemed large. Wide-set shoulders, corded arms that proved he was used to throwing calves over his shoulders. I'd let him throw me around. Hell, I wanted him to do more than just throw me around. A trim, dark beard covered his chiseled jaw. He looked a lot older than what I typically went for—rugged and edgy. My heartbeat picked up a notch. I bet he had more experience than any of the boys I'd ever been with. I'm so sick and tired of playing with *boys*. I needed a *man*. A man who could show me a thing or two, match my energy, and bring all my darkest desires to the surface.

His tongue darted out to lick a droplet of whiskey off his fuckable lips. Oh, how I'd love to be that drop of whiskey.

Neon beer signs on the wall behind him glowed like a beacon, pulling me in with an uncontrollable force. I felt like a moth being drawn to the fire, but I didn't care if I got burned. I'd let myself burn to ashes just to have that man touch me.

The bartender set Kale's whiskey on the bar, but before he could even grab it, I snatched it and knocked it back until

every last drop slid down my throat. The burn was so good …
coursing down my throat, spreading its warmth to my limbs,
my breasts, my belly, and then between my legs, until even my
toes tingled in my boots.

"Hey! You fucking serious?" Kale exclaimed, looking
aghast with his mouth agape.

I stifled back a giggle, shoving the glass into his chest. "I'm
in love, Kale. I needed that, okay?"

I looked back across the bar at my mystery man. His
smoldering eyes were dimmed by the brim of his black cowboy
hat—eyes that were luring me in and tracing the swell of my
breasts in my tight tank top. It felt as though he was trailing
a finger over my skin, dipping into my cleavage and circling
the hardened peaks. I could feel my heartbeat in my stomach.
His gaze traveled over my long legs as I stepped away from
my friends and pushed through the crowd. I felt as if I were
swimming through a current, floating in thin air, moving in
slow motion toward him while his eyes continued to devour
me.

I stepped into his space, demanding his attention. All of
his attention. The shadows gave way to a handsome face, with
dark, chestnut-brown eyes that were warm and full of desire.
A straight, strong nose and full, delicious lips that tipped in a
lazy smile. *What I'd give to suck that bottom lip into my mouth.*
My heart thrummed as I felt a blush creeping up from my chest
to my cheeks.

Oddly enough, his cologne smelled like something I've
known my whole life. Familiar scents like sandalwood and
leather mixed with undertones of cherry hit me like a brick

wall. My breath hitched as music pounded in my ears, and everything seemed to fade into the distance.

So is this what love at first fucking sight feels like?

I took a bold step closer, my toes bumping his boots, then another step until I was nearly pressing my body against his.

"You new here, cowboy?" I asked peering up at him, my hand going to his belt buckle to draw him closer. The heat and hardness of this very large man felt so damn good against my soft skin.

"I've been around." His voice was husky and deep, a rasp to it that was fucking sexy, and it weakened my knees. What I wouldn't do just to hear this man tell me to "beg for it" and "be a good girl" in that voice. I'd be a goner.

I brushed my fingertips down the cold metal of his buckle and over the zipper of his jeans. I could feel the stiff bulge in his pants. *Good Lord! This man was packing!* I swallowed hard.

Just as the Saddle Room tradition demanded, I wrapped my hand over his dick, gripping it through the denim. A faint smile ghosted over my lips as I claimed him as mine.

He hissed through his teeth, his cock twitching in my grasp. I smirked, feeling powerful and in control. This man was going to be mine all night long.

"I was hoping you could help me with something?" I asked coyly, holding up my other palm with the temporary tattoo.

"Yeah?" His fingertips trailed up my arms, sending shivers in their wake. "Where do you want it?" I brushed my wavy, brown hair off my shoulder and pushed my breasts forward, revealing the top of my cleavage. His gaze followed my movement.

"I was thinking it should go right above my heart."

His smile grew slightly. A mischievous glint mixed with desire flickered in his dark orbs.

"Well, we're gonna need to get it wet first." His voice vibrated through me.

I pressed my tits against his chest, offering myself to him.

He set his hat on the bar beside his drink. I could smell the smoky sweetness of whiskey on his breath, and I wanted nothing more than to drink him in. His eyes held mine as he wrapped his large hands around my waist, holding me still while he dipped his head. I arched my back to give him better access. His lips brushed against the sensitive skin of my breast, his beard scraping deliciously across the swell. My lungs sucked in air while his fingers dug into my hips, as if to keep me from floating away.

Slowly, torturously, his tongue swirled along my skin, his mouth opening to suck me in. God, I hoped this man fucking bruised me. I hoped he left his mark beneath the tattoo. His mouth suckled on my skin, drawing me in. Each pull of his mouth was like a fucking tether to my clit. Each sweep of his tongue shot waves of electricity directly to my center. I closed my eyes, the heady buzz of the whiskey making this feel like he was fucking me right here under the hazy, red glow of the neon. I rocked my hips toward him, his cock bucking into my stomach as my fingers laced themselves in his hair.

I panted, my pussy pulsed. His mouth sucked. I heard him groan, and that was nearly enough to send me over the edge. It felt as if he were sucking me dry—sucking all of the air from my lungs.

"I want you to fuck me," I managed to breathe out. I couldn't quite tell if I actually thought it or said it out loud. Everything was blurry, and the only thing I could see straight was Mr. Whiskey Cowboy in front of me.

But I must have said it aloud because he answered with another rock of his hips so I could feel the outline of his hard-on. His tongue darted out to soothe the skin he most likely bruised.

He pulled away, making me frown. Cool air danced across my now damp and sensitive skin, leaving goose bumps.

His eyes found mine, now almost black with need. No longer that sweet, brown color. They were filled with hunger.

I shifted in my boots.

Fuck, I did say it out loud.

He let go of my waist, but he did not peel himself away from me. Separating the plastic from the tattoo, he pressed it with his palm against my skin. My chest heaved beneath his hand, which was nearly large enough to cup my whole breast. His deeply tanned skin complemented my golden hue—his rough and calloused, mine soft and supple.

His gaze flicked back to mine, holding me there, piercing into my very soul. All I could hear was our heaving breaths, my blood pumping in my ears, and the subtle hum of the bar disappearing into the distance.

"Come back to my place."

He didn't have to ask or demand it. I would have followed him anywhere. He could have led me into the bathroom, and I would have gladly spread my legs for him.

We stumbled into his dark apartment above a workshop. It was located on a farm on the outskirts of Joseph. I gripped onto his shirt for dear life, keeping him flush against me. He tasted so fucking good. I couldn't get enough. I was greedy for him. Needing more of him. My tongue stroked against his, our lips molding together. If the man fucked the way he kissed, I was going to be in trouble.

The living room was dark, except for the stream of moonlight that came in from the window. A single couch and coffee table faced a flat-screen TV. A few boxes were piled against the wall. *Perhaps he just moved here or he was moving?* He pulled at the hem of my shirt, his fingertips dancing across my skin.

"Off. Now," he growled.

I fisted his shirt, not wanting him to pull away, while I toed off my boots and shimmied out of my shorts as quickly as I could. I lightly nipped at his bottom lip before breaking away to pull my tank top over my head.

His chest heaved as he drank me in. I watched his eyes skim slowly over my white lace bra and panties.

"Fuck. You're a goddamn smokeshow," he said as his hand cupped my jaw and his thumb brushed over my bottom lip.

I never needed reassurance from a man to tell me the obvious, but for some reason, coming from him felt different. I tried to brush it off with a quick laugh, but it came out low and sultry.

My hand went to his belt, pulling him back into me. I

needed him closer. Now. I didn't want to stop touching him. Not even for one second. I slammed my mouth to his, his teeth scraping against my swollen lips until he sucked in my tongue.

Fuck. This man was going to be my undoing.

And I didn't even know his name.

I tugged on his belt, unclasping the buckle and unbuttoning and lowering his zipper. His cock strained at his boxer briefs, and my pulse pounded like a drum between my legs. I could feel my panties already soaked. I pressed my thighs together, subconsciously desperate for any form of friction.

I tried to steady my breathing as I watched him lean down to tear off his boots, then quickly pull his shirt over his head. He looked almost as desperate as I was.

Goddamn. The man was a fucking god. Every muscle was shredded. Ridged lats, strong pecs, abs chiseled right down to his cut V. Muscles that only hard work and cowboying could create. Saliva pooled in my mouth. I'd be drooling if I kept ogling him this way.

"How do you want me, cowboy?" I asked, watching him step out of his jeans.

His strong, thick thighs dusted with hair reminded me that he was very much a *man*. My heart pounded erratically, anticipating what he had in store for me. I'd try anything once, and I was quickly growing obsessed with this cowboy. I'd do anything he asked of me.

"Spread yourself out on the couch," he instructed.

I lay down across the plush, gray couch, unclasping my bra and letting the straps fall off my shoulders. The cool evening air teased my now-exposed skin, making my nipples pebble.

He bit his lip, just as he had in the bar, and hummed in appreciation.

"Panties off," he demanded. "Spread those pretty thighs for me, sweetheart."

I shimmied the lace over my hips, down my legs, and over my feet until I could kick them off. Who cares where they landed in the dark? I did as he asked, allowing my knees to fall open so he could see how wet I was for him.

The moon cast shadows across his face, but his eyes blazed with need.

"See something you like?" I teased.

"Fuck, you're drenched."

"Just for you, baby." I ran a hand up the inside of my thigh, my fingertips dancing over my pussy lips, spreading the moisture up and over my clit. "Do you have a condom?"

He stood still for a moment, his gaze jolting back to mine. A moment of what looked like doubt—or was it guilt?—washed over him as he hesitated. My brows pinched together, concerned. Did he not want to do this? Did I take it too far? Was he regretting bringing me home?

He turned around, walking away and disappearing behind a door, which I assumed was his bedroom. I sat up. Maybe this wasn't going to happen after all? *Shit.* Where were my panties?

I scanned the dark floor, looking for where my underwear could have landed. I squinted, not being able to see much. I did, however, notice a toy tractor lying on its side on the carpet. Did this guy have a kid?

Before I had too much time to spiral on that, he strode back out into the living room. Having shed his briefs, he was now on full display—every chiseled, rock-hard, tan muscle. I wanted to lick this man. Everywhere. It didn't matter where as long as my tongue was on his body. His hand flexed as he rolled the condom onto his *very* large cock.

"Holy shit!" I said, before I could even think. "How in the hell do you walk around with that thing?"

I'd seen men in pornos that big, but I didn't think it actually existed.

Now sheathed, he glanced up at me, his face dark and determined. Not even answering my question, he stalked toward me, his cock bouncing as he approached. I scraped my teeth over my bottom lip, contemplating how in the world he was going to fit. Hell, I was wondering if I'd even be able to sit straight in my saddle tomorrow. That was a problem for tomorrow, though.

He knelt on the couch, pushing me back, wedging himself between my legs. His strong, steady, calloused hands went to my knees to guide them open. Positioning himself between my hips, he ran his tip through my wetness, flicking and teasing against my clit. I bucked my hips, urging him on. He did it again, coating himself in it.

"Fuck me," I pleaded, wrapping my hand around his neck, drawing him down to brush a soft kiss across his lips.

"This sweet little cunt hungry for my cock?" he whispered.

I hummed in agreement. I loved a man who talked dirty. "Fucking starved for it." I arched toward him, rocking against his hard cock that was mere inches away from where I needed it.

I gripped his dick and positioned the tip at my entrance.

"I want to feel how deep you can go," I told him. I had no idea how much I could fit, but I was desperate and willing to try.

He inched forward, the thick tip stretching me. My breath hitched.

"You can take me," he encouraged. "I can feel how much your pussy wants to suck me in. Now breathe, and let me take care of this needy little cunt."

I inhaled through my nose, smelling the scent of whiskey on our breaths and the sweet musk of my arousal that mingled with his. My head swam with desire and liquor as he pressed farther in.

"Fuck," I gasped, attempting to push air from my lungs.

I spread my knees wider, opening for him as he stretched my walls, pushing torturously slow until he bottomed out. It was intense, almost too much. Pain mixed with pleasure.

"It's too much," I whimpered, pushing on his abs. Not knowing whether to push him away or force him to move.

"No, baby. You're taking me so well. I bet this pretty pussy hasn't been properly filled until now, has it?"

My heart pounded. He was right. This was beyond anything I'd ever felt before, and I fucking wanted it. I wanted him to pound me into this couch until all I felt was the ghost of his cock in me for days to come.

"Then fucking move, cowboy," I said through gritted teeth, my hips squirming beneath him.

He started to pull out, and I watched with rapt attention between us as he slammed back into me.

"Oh my God!" I screamed as he hit that sensitive spot deep inside.

He paused then, looking over my head, away from us. I stared at him. His eyes grew dark and murderous, but he didn't stop.

Thrusting hard against me, he asked through gritted teeth, "Does that feel good?"

"You feel so good," I somehow managed to say.

What was he looking at?

He pounded harder, nearly to the point of pain. His eyes were glued to something over my head.

"Oh, so you've resorted to being a fucking slut because you can't have your way?" A woman's voice pierced through our heavy breathing.

"What the fuck?" I stilled. There was someone else in the room with us.

I pushed at his chest.

He thrust again, harder this time.

"Fucking shit, get off me." I pushed at him again.

He froze, as if he remembered I was underneath him. He let me push him off, and I scrambled out from beneath him, turning to see the redheaded woman standing in the dark, her arms crossed over her chest. She tapped her slippered foot, a smug look on her face.

"What the fuck is this?" I asked again, grabbing a pillow off the couch to cover myself while I stumbled around, picking up my clothes.

Irritation seemed to waft off her. "Is this some tantrum you're throwing because I'm taking our daughter? You could at least fuck whatever pussy you find in the back seat of your truck, instead of bringing it here where your wife and daughter will hear it."

"You're fucking married?" I yelled at him, quickly shrugging on my shirt.

"Ex-wife," he said so quietly, I barely heard him over the blood roaring in my ears.

"But she lives with you?" I ran a hand through my hair in frustration. I needed to get the fuck out of here. I yanked my cell phone out of my shorts as I scrambled to put them on. "You have a fucking kid?"

"Better pipe down, doll, or you'll wake her, too," the woman said with a smirk, but her eyes were burning into the man I felt vibrating beside me.

"This is so fucked up." Suddenly, that little tractor toy made sense. I no longer cared where my panties were at this point. I donned my shorts, zipping them up before pulling my boots on.

"I'll drive you back to the bar," he offered, but he still hadn't looked at me.

"Don't bother. I'll call for a ride."

I pushed past him, the heat of his skin scorching me as I walked out the door. The whiskey rolled in my stomach, telling me I was too drunk to walk back to the rodeo grounds, but I was too pissed to even think straight. The last thing I wanted to do was call Kale or Viv to come get me. I didn't want anyone to see this walk of shame.

The next day, I froze in my tracks when I walked out of the stables. *He was fucking here!* The man had no fucking class. If I were him, I wouldn't be caught dead showing my face around after the shit he pulled with me.

What the fuck did he think he was doing?

He was gathered in a group of cowboys and trainers, most of whom worked with the other barrel racers—my competition. What were they doing? My gaze narrowed as I watched the flash of green transfer between hands. Were they betting?

"Looks like Hank's at it again." Viv sighed, coming up beside me, her saddle and blanket over her arm.

"Hank? Paige's trainer?" I asked. Paige Gibson was my biggest competition. She and I were always going back and forth, setting new records. I didn't particularly like her, either, or her trainer, for that matter. I watched Hank, a big, bulky man with a thick beard, gather money in his hands.

"They're betting on our runs?" There was no way in hell I was going to put up with this shit. Not when I was already feeling the shameful burn of last night … or the fact that I was about to race last in the bottom of the draw, especially against a son of a Dash Ta Fame barrel racing stallion.

I stomped toward them, fuming. I hoped my eyes burned into the fucking side of these men's heads.

"Oh, shit," I heard Viv say behind me.

Oh, shit, was right. They were about to get a fucking mouthful from me.

"What the fuck do you think you're doing, Hank?" I asked him, watching as he took the money from the men around him.

"Just a little friendly gambling," he boasted. "Lina, it's really nothing to worry about," he said nonchalantly, pocketing the rest of his cash. I hoped he felt the fucking fire in my eyes.

Seeing this as their cue to leave, the other men turned and walked away. Everyone, except *him*. He hovered behind me. I could practically feel the heat wafting off him, like a sunburn on my fucking back.

"What's the bet?" I demanded. I needed to know.

"Reed, here." He gestured to the man towering behind me. *Reed.* So that was his fucking name. "He and I bet with the others that Paige beats you today by one whole second."

"Fuck that! Mushu's a free runner who drags his butt around those barrels." I was seething, my chest heaving.

"That may be so, but you're in the bottom of the draw today. Paige races first."

I clenched my hands into fists, keeping my thumb on the outside just like my cousin Jude showed me. I wasn't going to deck him, but I also wasn't afraid to use them if I needed to. His eyes skipped down to my hands, his smirk growing, as if he fucking knew he was getting into my head.

"May the best racer win," he said, tipping his hat and walking away.

"Wow! You're a real fucking winner. Betting against me, *Reed*?" I asked before I turned around, emphasizing his name. I hope to God my voice sounded scary enough he would shy away from me and crawl back to whatever fucked-up hole he crawled out of.

But he didn't. He held his ground when I turned to face him, stuffing his hands into his pocket as if none of this was a big deal to him. His face was a mask of smug indifference, and I wanted to pound my fist right into his skull. I imagined those handsome features caving in until they were just an ugly pit of pulp.

"She has a badass stallion," he said, shrugging like it didn't matter to him. Like none of this mattered to him. Like he wasn't balls deep in my pussy only hours ago.

If I couldn't use my fists, I'd use my hands. I shoved his solid chest as hard as I could, nearly pushing him off balance. But the man was built like a fucking tank.

"Fuck you." I pushed him again. This time, he braced himself enough only to rock on his heels. "Double fuck you." I stepped into his space, my chest brushing his. "You're fucking disgusting." I nearly spat in his face. "If you think you can fuck me and then fuck me over, you have another thing coming."

His mask seemed to drop just for a moment, a look of disappointment and regret washing over him. He could feel guilty and live with his dirty conscience for all I cared. And to think my drunk ass thought it was love at first sight!

"You're fucking dead to me!" I roared.

His eyebrow cocked. "Is that so? Makes no difference to me, *Lina*, but thank you for helping me give Mrs. Ownstead a show."

I slapped him then. Right across that smug-ass face of his. Then spat, watching my spit land right on his mouth. *Good.*

"That's the last you'll ever taste of me. Fuck you, Reed Ownstead!"

I turned on my heels, leaving him in the dust of the stable while I stormed to Mushu's stall. I needed to get my head on straight if I had any chance of running the fastest time. If this was Reed's attempt to throw me off my game … to show me that last night meant nothing … well, I'd have to show him that *he* meant nothing to me.

CHAPTER 1
Reed

Present Day

She was lying. It had taken years for me to figure it out, but now I could spot it instantly. Her eyes jumped back and forth between mine, the green nearly hidden by her heavy lids and dilated pupils.

"He better not be fucking in there, Lis." I towered over Elise Ownstead. She still refused to change her last name because she claimed she wanted to have the same last name as our daughter, despite the fact she was engaged to the man she'd had an affair with. She hovered at the door of the little, blue house on the outskirts of Willows, refusing to open it all the way. "I don't want him anywhere near our daughter."

Elise stuck out her chin in defiance, her eyes even heavier as she stared me down. "I'm her mother, so I'll determine who she can and cannot be around."

"Jesus Christ! I don't think you're in any position to make sound judgments right now." I splayed my hand on the door, willing her to let me in. The last time I forced myself in, it turned into a yelling match, scaring Penelope. If I could shield her from our poor attempt to co-parent, I'd do it in a heartbeat.

The least I could do now was protect her from seeing her mother this way. Elise and I had barely been in recovery for a year when Penelope was born. We both wanted kids, but after a traumatic birth led to an emergency surgery and postpartum depression, it didn't take long for her to relapse on painkillers and anti-anxiety drugs. I tried everything in my power to help her, to love her, to be there for her, to take on the load of parenting duties, but it wasn't enough. Instead, I failed her, and in turn, I failed our daughter.

"Penn's coming with me," I growled, leaning my weight against the door.

She scoffed. "Like the bunkhouse is any place for a child."

"I'm working on that," I snapped.

Now that Jude and Romy had just moved into the house they'd built on the ranch, the double-wide was now available. My employer, Chuck Larsen, offered to let me move in there, but I didn't think it was fair to take it since I wasn't family. I assumed his daughter Lina would want it. But now I was seriously considering it.

"I don't want her around that Larsen slut, either."

At her insult, my hand reflexively balled into a fist and smacked the door hard, causing Elise to jump. But now she seemed more alert. *Thank God.*

"Don't fucking talk about her."

Elise quickly regained her composure, her lips curving into a knowing smirk. Damn her! I was really trying to stay levelheaded, but she always found a way to snake those emotions out of me.

"Looks like she's more than just some ass, isn't she?" She clicked her tongue at that.

"I *said*, don't fucking talk about her." The words came out a whisper in my attempt to keep my anger in check, knowing Penelope could come around the corner at any moment. But there was venom laced with every syllable, and I hoped she heard it as the warning that it was.

"Fine." Elise threw up her hands in acquiescence. "You're a testy asshole this morning."

"Just tell Penn I'm ready to go."

She unfolded her arms, holding out her palm, and let out a deep sigh. As if she was the one who was on the verge of losing her temper.

I rolled my eyes, stuffing my hand in my pocket to pull out the folded check to give to her. "This is for her new boots and school lunches. Nothing else." The fact that I even had to say that was frustrating as hell.

She swiped the check from my hand and shoved it into her back pocket without a reply. "Penn!" she called over her shoulder. "Your dad's here."

"Daddy!" I heard her sweet voice cry from down the hall. The sound of her pudgy little feet pattering across the carpet tightened my chest.

Elise finally widened the door, letting me have a clear view of five-year-old Penelope running toward me. Her dark-blonde pigtails bounced as she ran, her toothy grin brightening her round face. I crouched down, spreading my arms to catch her. I was barely a foot off the ground when she launched herself into my embrace, nearly knocking me over as I scooped her up into my arms. My heart immediately felt calm and centered, the anger and frustration with Elise melting away after just a moment with my daughter in my arms.

"Do we get to see the horsies today?" she asked, pushing off my shoulders to peer into my face. Her brow pinched in a quizzical look, but her hazel eyes shimmered with hope.

"That's the plan, princess. You could help me dish out the flakes, too." She was my best little helper, mucking stalls and doling out their feed.

"Mushu's my favorite."

I grimaced hearing the name of Lina's barrel racing stallion. "He's not there today, princess, but there are plenty of others that need your snuggles." Lina was back out on the circuit, but ever since last August, she'd made a concerted effort to avoid me at all costs. Even when she was home, she was out dating every Tom, Dick, and Harry or hanging out at her cousin Jude's place.

"Have her back by dinnertime. It's a school night."

I side-eyed Elise. She looked like she was two steps away from falling over asleep. "I'll feed her and make sure she's back for bedtime."

Elise sighed and shrugged, obviously exasperated with me but too strung out to care. "Fine. Just call me when you're on your way." Her words came out slurred.

I looked past her down the hall, expecting to see her fiancé walk by, but it was nothing but a dark family room. I hated the thought of my daughter being around him. Being alone with them. He better fucking hide because if I ever caught him around Penn or anyone I cared about again, he was going to be a dead man. I gave one last glance at Elise before grabbing my daughter's hand and adjusting her little cowgirl hat so it sat just right atop her head.

"You ready, princess?" She giggled and clapped her hands together while doing a cute little dance at my side. *I guess I had my answer.*

With Lina going back and forth while on the local rodeo circuit, I half expected to see her truck and trailer blocking my parking spot beside the stable when I pulled in. When she wasn't avoiding me these days, she was blocking my truck. I'd gotten used to parking in a ditch on the dirt road and walking to the bunkhouse because of her.

She'd been a pain in my ass since Day One when I arrived and pulled into Thornbrush Ranch for my new job.

Another truck and trailer pulled in as soon as I stood waiting to meet my new employer, Chuck Larsen. Leaning against my door, I could see there was a woman with a long, brown braid behind the wheel. She looked awfully familiar.

She tapped the horn before rolling down the window, giving me a clear view of who was in the driver's seat. Oh, shit! Larsen from Willows … *I should have known.*

"Hey! You're going to need to move " Her eyes went wide with recognition at the same time my heart started to pound. "You!" Her gaze narrowed on me. "What the fuck are you doing here?" She enunciated every word as if each word were a dagger.

I crossed my arms over my chest. It had barely been two days since she'd slapped me across the face, and I could still feel the sting of her palm. I savored that burn as long as it lasted, wishing I could have that last hit again if it meant having her hands on me. Making me feel something. Anything. My pulse quickened.

Truthfully, I was surprised she hadn't kneed me in the balls. I certainly deserved it for how I treated her.

Maybe it was fate that I ended up here, looking for work. It felt like a chance for redemption—to prove that I wasn't such a fucking terrible human.

"I work here," I called over the rumble of the engine.

"The fuck you do! I'm going to have my dad un-hire *you."*

I shifted on my feet as my pants tightened. My lips tipped in amusement. Lina Larsen had a fucking mouth on her. I was reminded how she just came up to me at the bar in Joseph and told me to give her a tattoo. She was so alluring, undeniably confident. She was bold, beautiful, and determined. Everything I wanted.

From the moment I watched her ride—the way her horse inhaled those barrels—I was mesmerized. There was something about her that made my breath catch. My stomach twisted in a knot when she lost against Paige Gibson. I tried to convince myself the hookup meant nothing other than my own selfish need for revenge against Elise, but I immediately regretted it all. The primal need that zipped through my veins when I pressed my mouth to her skin was like taking a hit—an addiction I'd never experienced until now. It was a gut punch to see her face fall when she exited the gate. She knew she'd lost before she even looked at her time, and I was the asshole who did it to her.

"Now move!" she yelled, leaning farther out the window.

"I'm not going anywhere, Lina." Not now.

I needed this job. I needed it to be able to provide for Penn so I could get her out of her mother's house. I needed to be able to be close to her. And now, knowing that Lina was here, I could feel myself slowly coming alive again, like my whole body was thawing after a long, brutal winter. I was tired of just aimlessly wandering through life and making it by. I wanted to feel *something. Lina was the first one to make me feel more than I had in years. I was determined to have Lina's strong, tight legs wrapped around me again. I'd lost enough. I wasn't losing anymore. Not this job. Not this girl.*

"That's my fucking spot! It has been for years."

I put the truck into park as Chuck came out of the stables to greet me, just like he'd done that first day.

"I want to see the horsies!" Penn hollered from her booster seat behind me.

"Hold on, princess."

I hopped out of the truck, slamming the door.

"How's our littlest cowgirl today?" Chuck asked, heading toward me.

I pressed my lips together and sucked in a breath through my nose.

"That bad, huh?" Chuck's warm eyes held mine.

He knew about everything—maybe not to a certain extent, but he knew what I was dealing with and just how bad things were with Penn's mom.

He wasn't thrilled about the fiancé, either.

"It's not getting any better." I clenched my jaw.

Chuck grasped my shoulder, giving it a good, sympathetic squeeze. "I'll talk with Jude about getting you and Penn set up in the double-wide."

"I appreciate that."

He gave me a final pat on the back before opening the back door. "Is there a cowgirl back here?" he asked in a sing-songy tone.

Penelope's eyes immediately brightened at seeing Chuck. "Is Mushu here?" she asked hopefully, as if she didn't believe her ol' man was telling her the truth.

"No, darlin', not right now. But there are plenty of other horses waiting for you." He scooped her up out of her car seat and turned to me. "We'll figure it out, Reed."

I nodded. I'd do anything for my daughter, and Thornbrush Ranch was right where we needed to be.

CHAPTER 2
Lina

Turning off the highway, I rolled down the windows of my truck. Cool, fresh, country air wafted through, immediately lifting my spirits.

I sighed. "Home sweet home." I leaned my head out the window as I turned down the gravel road, passing the Thornbrush Ranch sign, and sucked in the deepest breath my lungs could hold before releasing a long exhale. Breathing in all that fresh dirt and grass.

"We're almost home, boy," I said, as if Mushu could hear me from his trailer.

Sticking my arm out the open window, I rolled my arm like a wave through the breeze, feeling it energize me. I loved being on the open road, the excitement and high energy of the rodeo, but there was nothing like coming home.

I took in the expanse of fields, the canvas of ponderosa pines, the rush of the distant Deschutes River, the bawling of cattle. If I could envision heaven, this was it. This was where my heart was. Home was never at my mom's place in Portland. She had another family to enjoy that with anyway.

I spotted Dad in a far field on top of Gus, and I gave him

a big wave. He whooped, spinning his hat in the air. I laughed, giving him the most exaggerated wave I could muster.

He was probably out checking on the new calves. Spring in Oregon was always full of new life. Another reason why I was dying to come home. I had a baby to hold and a bachelorette party to plan. As soon as I unloaded and cleaned up, I was heading straight to Romy and Jude's.

I pulled up in front of the stable, beside Reed's Dodge Ram. *Fucking Reed.* Nothing could spoil my mood, though, not even him.

Hopping out of the truck, I slammed the door, coming around to open the trailer. Mushu's ears twitched, his head turning and his nose sniffing the air.

"I bet you're as eager to be home as I am, huh, boy?"

Taking his lead rope, I led him out of the trailer, walking him in a couple circles to help him stretch his muscles. I needed it as much as he did after that four-hour drive from southern Oregon. My body ached and I could use a soak.

"Let's get you rubbed down and find you some nice oats. You did a good job, boy." I caressed his neck as I praised him. Mushu snorted in response. I smiled, shaking my head at him. We entered the stables, my eyes adjusting to the dim light.

I almost stumbled in my steps because I had a clear shot down the center of the stable to the wide-open doors at the back. The golden dusk glimmered off his wide, muscular back, bare and glistening with moisture. I bit my lip before my tongue could dart out, imagining licking up the beads of water that dripped down his spine.

Shit! Why did he have to be so … so much *man*?

He hadn't seen me come in, too busy hosing down one of the horses. I watched with rapt attention while his large hands ran down the shoulder and legs of the mare, rinsing the suds from her coat. My eyes zeroed in on those hands. They were strong and calloused, probably more than capable of squeezing the life out of someone, yet so gentle and tender.

My treacherous mind flashed back to our one moment of weakness during another evening. One that had us on the far end of the ranch arguing about … I don't even know what it was about now. Something to do with me going on a date. I wanted to challenge him, to test him, to prove to him that he did nothing to me—until he'd lost his temper and pushed me against a fence post.

He had grabbed my throat to land a punishing kiss, while his other hand squeezed my ass. My hips ground against his, needy for him. Without a word, I unbuttoned my jeans, bringing his hand to my waistband. I remember he'd tried to break his mouth away from mine to say something, but I bit his lip. I didn't want to hear what he had to say. I just wanted one thing from him. I pushed his fingers beneath my panties until he was right where I needed him. I rode that fucking rough hand until I was moaning into his mouth.

I cringed now, bringing myself back to the present. That was also the night Frank Miller, Romy's piece-of-shit father, let the horses out, and Junior Matheus pulled a gun on Romy. If Reed hadn't been following me around the ranch arguing—if I hadn't been so weak-willed—we would have saved ourselves a lot of heartache. Just another reminder why I should stay the fuck away from him.

Reed still hadn't noticed me entering the stables, so I turned away, heading to Mushu's stall.

The man was fucking poison. It didn't matter that he had a body that could wreck me. He was a dangerous distraction, one I couldn't afford. Not this time. Thank God he had a shitty personality. At least that's what I told myself. I wasn't planning on giving him the time of day to show me differently, either. I had to focus on breaking this year's record. This was my year to win the finals, and nothing was going to stand in my way.

"We'll have music, dancing, a bonfire, booze. It will be like a good ol' fucking barn raising," I told Romy, who sat in the corner of the couch.

Her lips twitched. "Are you sure this is *my* bachelorette party? I mean, I can't really drink, and it will just be Sage, you, and me." She bobbed her head at baby Charli, who lay across the crescent-shaped pillow on her lap, nursing.

"Oh, you'll know when it's my bachelorette party. I'll be going to Vegas."

"You're going to Vegas?" my cousin Jude asked when he walked into the large, open living room.

The house was something straight out of a *Country Living* magazine. All glossy and beautiful. Two-story, floor-to-ceiling windows opened up to a view of the ranch, right out to the patio and firepit. From where I sat on the large sectional facing the stone hearth, the open-concept kitchen led to the back, facing out over the bluffs toward the river and mountain range.

As soon as Jude retired from his championship MMA

career, he went right to work building his dream home with the girl he'd been hung up on since they were kids. He'd outdone himself with this one, but knowing Jude, he wouldn't have had it any other way if it meant creating his forever with his best friend.

"Not anytime soon. I don't plan to get married for a long-ass time—if ever. I mean, is there really a guy good enough for all this?" I gestured to myself.

Jude chuckled, bracing his hand against the back of the couch to lean down to kiss Romy. Her face lit up, smiling into the kiss.

"How are my favorite girls?" he asked, his lips still brushing against hers.

"Great. It's so good to be home," I told him.

His eyes cut to me, a scoff releasing through his nose. I loved poking the bear. I always had. Ever since we were kids, growing up together on the ranch.

He pressed his lips to Romy's forehead before plopping down beside her, his tatted arms stretched out across the back of the couch. She leaned into him, a soft smile on her face. For someone who had fought this tooth and nail a year ago, she looked more and more as though she belonged here. Even with the extenuating circumstances of her sister's arrest, which brought her home in the first place, I was thankful she stayed. I was happy for them, and it made my heart melt to see them so in love. I wanted that for myself, too, but if it meant leaving the ranch, giving up any part of myself—*no thank you!*

"How long are you home for this time?" Jude asked, kicking his socked feet up on the oversize, leather ottoman.

"Just a couple of days. The Joseph Round-Up is this weekend." I fidgeted in my seat, remembering the last time I was in Joseph. I hoped they didn't notice the flush creeping up my neck because I was sweating just thinking about it. It didn't help that I had to be graced with a view of Reed's muscular back earlier—and those hands. *Shit!*

Romy was staring at me with a knowing look, and it made me uncomfortable. I cleared my throat. "Can I hold her?"

"Sure. She's not even eating anymore anyway. I've become a pacifier." Romy pulled Charli from her nipple.

"She has the right idea," Jude said with a lopsided smirk. "Your tits pacify me, too."

"They're off limits to you right now, buddy." Romy covered herself back up, adjusting to hold Charli against her shoulder.

Jude rolled his head back against the couch and literally whined. Romy patted his thigh, consoling the poor bastard.

"Sounds like a good time," I grumbled. "I'd much rather have a man on my tits."

"*Lina*, Jesus Christ. Can you not—" Jude chastised.

I smiled, pleased to get a rise out of him.

"So fun." Romy rolled her eyes. "I'm a walking milk bag. Here, grab that burp cloth for me." She gestured to the floral fabric on the ottoman.

I picked it up, throwing it over my shoulder. "Come here, little angel."

I uncrossed my legs from beneath me, standing up to take Charli from Romy's arms. The little cherub was sound asleep. Her rosebud lips pursed and milky. Her legs curled up when I held her beneath her arms. It had been a long time since I'd been around newborn babies. The last time, I was twelve, and they were my twin half brothers. I knew enough to support her neck as I brought her to rest against my shoulder.

"She hasn't burped yet. Pat her back. Otherwise, you'll end up with baby puke all over you," Romy advised.

I took a whiff of her feather-soft, dark hair. Babies always smelled the sweetest. "She looks like a Larsen." I smirked, proud.

Jude beamed at that. Proud papa. It looked good on him. "But she has her mama's mouth. You should hear the screams that come out of her."

"Oh my God." Romy elbowed Jude in the ribs.

"Ouch." He laughed, holding his side as if she'd bruised him.

I patted Charli's back, waiting to hear those little burp bubbles. "I can't imagine her screaming. She's so sweet. You two did good. I can't wait to teach her how to ride."

"Of course, she'll be taught by the Columbia River barrel racing champ," Jude confirmed.

"*Almost* circuit champion," I nearly whispered. My record last year was ruined before it even started. Thanks to fucking Reed. Literally.

"This will be your year, cuz. I can feel it," he encouraged.

"Shit, I hope so. The Joseph Round-Up ruined my chances last year. I need to win my event if I'm going to have a fucking chance, and I'm *stressed*."

"You'll do it. I have no doubt in my mind. And will you quit cursing in my daughter's ear."

I rolled my eyes at him, holding back my laughter. "She

doesn't understand a word I'm saying. I gotta say, fatherhood has changed you."

"I'll take that as a compliment. After all, she's my daughter. She'll pick things up fast."

"Okay, protective asshole."

"Hey!"

I snorted a laugh. "She's my niece. She's going to end up cursing like a sailor and fucking like a rabbit."

"Over my dead body," Jude growled.

I laughed again. "Relax, *Dad*. I'm sure she'll be a perfect angel growing up surrounded by cowboys."

Jude glowered.

Romy giggled, giving me a hidden wink. "She already has him wrapped around her little finger. Pretty sure he's in for some trouble." She raised a hand, scratching the stubble on his cheek. "Did you find the lost cattle?"

"Yeah, but one has a nasty laceration on her chest."

I stopped patting Charli's back, sitting up straighter. Genuine concern overtook my entire body. I gently bounced Charli up and down, setting a rhythm for her so she could doze off. When I glanced down, she was already asleep. "From what?"

"Barbed wire, probably. Someone's been cutting the fence lines."

My mouth went dry. "What? Why didn't Dad tell me?" I shook my head in disbelief.

Jude shrugged. "He probably didn't want to worry you. Besides, we're handling it. I just ordered some extra game cameras to set up around the ranch."

"Dad's been letting you do that? Pay for things?"

"I stopped asking for permission months ago. Hired a couple extra guys, too. Marshall and Jace are out with Reed right now, repairing it."

At the sound of Reed's name, I gulped, attempting to loosen the feeling of an electric current going straight to my chest.

I *could* go talk to Dad, but I already knew I wouldn't get anywhere with him. He never wanted me to worry while I was out on the circuit, and he'd just tell me what he wanted me to hear. Jude would be honest with me, but he was too preoccupied with a new baby and planning a wedding. He was doing his part getting the cameras, but I needed to know more.

"Um … here." I needed to go. "It was so nice to hold her." I handed baby Charli back to Romy. "I need to go find Dad."

I did need to talk to Dad about what's been going on at the ranch while I've been gone, but I also couldn't sit still. It felt like my muscles were vibrating, and if I didn't move, I'd go crazy.

"We'll talk more about the party later, Romy. Thanks for the baby snuggles!" I called, shoving my feet into my boots by the big-ass double doors.

"Stay away from the southwest fence line!" Jude called after me.

He knew me well, but what he didn't know wouldn't hurt him. I needed to go talk to someone. Someone who was a straight shooter and would be honest with me, even if I had to piss him off to do so. I'd have to go talk to the one person I really didn't want to talk to. And I think I knew a way to get him to tell me exactly what I needed to know.

CHAPTER 3
Reed

I dropped another spool of steel wire beside the fence line. "This should be enough to rewire what's broken, but I'll have to talk to Chuck about getting more."

We'd have to make sure we had backstock, especially at the rate the vandal was cutting wire. Hopefully, once Jude set up those extra game cams, we'd catch the culprit. In the meantime, I was already planning on running night shifts with the other hired hands. Chuck couldn't afford to lose any more cattle.

I brushed my gloved hands off on my worn Wranglers. The spring sun blazed, causing sweat to run down the sides of my face, my shirt sticking uncomfortably to my back.

For May, it was as hot as Satan's ass crack. We hadn't had rain in over ten days, and already, we were below average rainfall for the season. It was shaping up to be a drought year, which led to poor ranching conditions. Which meant Chuck was going to have to rent grazing land to keep the cattle fed.

"Let's get busy, boys. I don't want to still be out here when the sun sets." I'd be back out anyway on the first watch. Marshall and Jace were staring beyond me into the glaring sun, their hands shading their eyes.

"What?" I turned to look in the direction they were looking and froze. My breath caught in my throat, and my blood rushed to all my extremities, including my dick.

What the fuck does she think she's doing?

Lina Larsen was picking her way around the sagebrush in nothing but a swimsuit, fringed jacket, and boots. She had a towel flung over her shoulder and the neck of a bottle of Jack in her grasp. Her long, bronze legs disappeared into brown cowboy boots, begging to be wrapped around my waist. It was a one-piece, but it was the sexiest one-piece I'd ever seen. A plunging neckline framed her perfect tits, and the high cut accentuated her perfect, wide hips. *Shit!* Was that a thong? Her firm, tan ass was out for all to see.

"Get to work!" I barked at the men. Like fuck was I going to let these dickheads get an eyeful of Lina.

"Who's that?" Marshall asked, appreciation in his voice.

"The boss's daughter and none of your fucking business," I said a little too harshly, but I hoped each word sounded like gravel in their ears. "Now get to work."

I whipped off my gloves, slapping them on the fence post. What in the hell did she think she was doing?

I stormed toward her, hoping my broad back cast enough of a shadow to shield her from their prying eyes.

She skipped over a large rock, holding tightly onto the bottle, her fringe and wavy, brown hair swaying in the breeze. Did she walk all the way out here?

"What the fuck do you think you're doing?" I seethed through gritted teeth. I could feel my body tightening up, preparing for the tongue-lashing she was bound to give me, and my inevitable, rock-hard cock that would ache for hours until I could take care of it. *Fucking shit!* I was in for one painful night now.

"Coming to talk to you," she said matter-of-factly. Her golden-brown eyes narrowed, telling me that this wasn't going to be a pleasant chat. But it was never a pleasant chat with her.

My eyebrows raised all the same. She had avoided me for months, barely exchanging a few words here and there, and now she was seeking me out.

"In *that*?" My eyes trailed along her exposed skin until I felt my dick twitch, causing my eyes to flick right back to hers. *Lock that fucking eye contact*, I told myself. Otherwise, my dick was going to start leaking at just the sight of her.

She glowered at me, her hand going to her hip. She was all fucking sass, and as much as she raised my blood pressure, she made my heart pound even harder.

"Yes, in *this*, asshole. It's ninety fucking degrees out, and I'm doing the one thing that helps me de-stress after being on the road. Why should you care what I wear to do it?"

"I care if you're distracting my ranch hands."

"At least I'm wearing a jacket. You're welcome." She peered over my shoulder, giving a little wave hello, and I followed her gaze. Marshall and Jace were both gawking at her despite the sun in their eyes.

"Fucking shit. See what I mean. I don't have time for this. We have fences to repair and a long night ahead of us."

I turned back to look at her. Her mouth curved in a flirty smile, fluttering her fingers at those two fucking bastards.

"*Lina.*" Her name came out rough and scalding, like a cattle brand being plunged straight down my throat. Shit! Why did her name have to feel so fucking good and painful all at the same time?

The brat rolled her eyes at me. "Fine. Come with me."

She turned away then, which was a big fucking mistake. Her bare ass cheeks flexed and bounced as she walked. I swallowed the thick lump in my throat and quickly adjusted myself in my pants before following her.

Lina walked over to the stock tank beside the fence line. The tank was bone dry thanks to the arid weather. Setting her bottle down on the ground and throwing her towel over the fence, she turned on the spigot to the well line. Air sputtered and thumped through the pipes before water spewed from the faucet into the tank.

Without even looking at me, she toed off her boots, her bright-purple toenails digging into the dirt. *Fuck.* Even her toes were tan and sexy. I was not a foot guy, but Lina could convert me. I was still very much an ass man, though, and she still hadn't turned around to look at me as she shrugged off her jacket and draped it over her boots.

I hated that I wanted her to look at me. To *really* look at me. I wanted her eyes, her words—anything. The last few months were torture … watching her come and go, dart the other way whenever I entered the stables, or see her hopping into some douchebag's truck when she went out.

Growing impatient, I cleared my throat. "What's this about, Lina?"

She turned around then, her warm, brown eyes watching

me. She arched her back, her perky tits straining against the nylon. I bit the inside of my cheek to keep myself from groaning.

Pointing her toes, she stepped into the water, submerging her body into the tank as it continued to fill. She sighed in relief as soon as she touched the cool water.

My eyes flicked to hers. She had one eyebrow cocked in amusement, continuing to stare at me while she picked up the bottle of Jack, twisting off the cap and bringing it to her full lips. She took a swig before setting it back down beside the tank.

"Jude just told me about the cut lines," she said. "By the sounds of it, it's been happening for a while."

My own eyebrows rose at that. I didn't even think she'd be concerned about the fence lines while she was away from the ranch. "Chuck didn't tell you?"

She scoffed, picking up the whiskey again and taking another pull, this time keeping it in her grasp while she rested it against the lip of the tank.

"Dad doesn't want me to worry, so he tends to keep things from me. How long has this been happening?"

"Three, maybe four months now." I shifted on my feet, trying to look anywhere but at her tits as they rose and fell, the water splashing across them as the tank continued to fill.

"Dad won't call the cops or the livestock commissioner unless he loses the herd. Are they stealing cattle?"

I shook my head. "We've been able to recover them each time. Whoever is doing it is just cutting wires and creating more work for us."

Since coming to Thornbrush Ranch, I'd learned Chuck

was a proud and private man. He took care of his own—land, horses, and cattle included. Lina was right. He wasn't going to involve law enforcement unless it was absolutely necessary, especially after everything they went through last year with Hazel Miller and Jesse Matheus. *More reason for me to station myself out here tonight.*

"I don't think this is just some kids fucking around." She brought the bottle back to her mouth. My eyes couldn't help following her movement, watching her plump lips wrap around the top of the bottle. My cock was growing uncomfortably hard by the second. Her throat bobbed, swallowing it down. I involuntarily gulped.

"I don't think so, either," I managed to say. "The guys and I are going to take shifts until we get more cameras up."

Her mouth popped off the bottle. *Goddammit!* Why was she torturing me? At this point, it felt like she was doing it on purpose. A bead of whiskey slipped down her plump bottom lip, her tongue darting out to catch it.

Fucking hell! "Are we done here?" I snapped, impatient.

Her eyes dropped to my pants. She had to see the hard-on behind my zipper. I needed to move, to get away from her. Otherwise, I was going to combust.

"Are you staying out here tonight?" she asked.

"What's it to you?" I knew I sounded like an asshole, but I needed to be done with this conversation before I did something I'd regret. Why did she care what happened on her dad's ranch while she was away? We were handling it.

Her brows pinched, her mouth pressing into a firm line. "It's my family ranch, you dick. I think I have a right to know what's going on here. And if there's anything I can do to help, I'm going to fucking help!"

She took another gulp of the whiskey like it was her lifeline. Like it was the only thing keeping her from jumping down my throat.

"You going to be out here all afternoon?" It was already getting late in the day, and I couldn't have her distracting the guys while we had a job to do. I couldn't have her distracting *me*.

"For as long as it takes me to cool down. Are *you* going to just argue with me and give them a show?" She pointed the mouth of the bottle toward Marshall and Jace. "Or are you going to do your job?"

I scowled at her. "Only if you let us do *our* fucking job," I said, turning away and marching back to where the guys quickly pretended they were busy at work.

My hands balled into fists. I wanted to storm back over there and either climb into that tank with her and have her grind that wet pussy against my belt buckle until she came, or pull her out of that water and tie her to a fence post until she begged for my cock.

"I'm taking the first shift!" Her voice rose behind me.

"The hell you are!" I hollered, my shoulders going rigid to keep myself from turning back around to face her. Of course she'd demand to help with the night watch.

"Try to stop me, cowboy!"

Shit! I was going to have to fight her over the first watch, wasn't I? Maybe tying her to a fence post wasn't such a bad idea.

Lina

The water might have cooled my heated skin from the hot sun, but it did nothing to lower my body temperature. I knew he felt my eyes on him. He kept lifting his cowboy hat to wipe his brow, casually checking over his shoulder to see if I was still there—pretending that he wasn't looking. His T-shirt clung to his back, and his muscles flexed and bulged while he rolled out the wire across the fence posts.

The new ranch hands were more blatant about their perusal. I winked at one of them—the handsome blond one with the mustache—when his lips curved in a grin.

Sipping the whiskey, I could feel my stress melting away. I wouldn't drink enough to get tipsy, especially if I was coming out here later tonight. Just enough to relax and not feel as though my brain were going ninety miles per hour all the fucking time.

Dad wasn't going to like that I volunteered to work a night watch, but he wouldn't demand I stay away, either. He knew once my mind was set on something, he shouldn't waste his breath.

I turned off the spigot and let the water wash over my chest. My nipples pebbled beneath my swimsuit, peeking up over the waterline. I took another swallow of the bottle, savoring the burn down my throat, but all it was doing was making me hotter and building this insufferable arousal Reed stirred in me. I needed relief.

I rubbed my thighs together in the water and ran my hand

down my chest, feeling the stiff peaks while I watched them repair the fence.

I smirked when the blond hand stopped to stare. Reed barked at him to get back to work and then turned to glare at me.

Running my hand up and down my chest, over my cleavage and neck, letting the water cool my heated skin, I let him see where my fingertips traveled.

His eyes grew dark beneath the brim of his hat while he glowered at me.

I raised the bottle to him before taking another sip.

Why hadn't he found another job yet? This had to be as miserable for him as it was for me. To see the person I hated with a passion every time I came home. To watch those hands mend fences, wrangle cattle, and train colts, all the while knowing exactly how those calloused fingers felt between my thighs.

"Ugh!" None of this was helping me de-stress. If anything, it was making me horny as fuck.

I capped the bottle and stepped out of the tank, letting the water slosh over the sides. Grabbing the towel off the fence, I dried off, wrapping it around my waist before I stuffed my feet back into my boots.

"Fucking shit," I grumbled, feeling my swimsuit cling between my legs. It wasn't just wet from the water, either. Now I needed more than a shower.

I could feel everyone's eyes on me when I scooped up the liquor bottle and jacket before walking away, my toes squishing in my boots.

Reed thought I had no business helping with night watch. Well, fuck him. This was my ranch.

Chapter 4
Reed

She beat me. I thought I'd get out to the pasture early enough, but she fucking beat me.

"Took you long enough," she chided, her saddle creaking when she turned to look my way. "You cowboys eat four-course meals now or something?"

She was such a smart-ass. My mouth twitched, fighting a smile.

I pulled up on the reins, stopping Warrior, my gray roan stallion, beside her in the dark, overlooking the eastern fence line where we'd moved the herd. Some of the cattle were still lumbering around while others were settling down for the night. It was a clear evening, the full moon and stars casting silver light across the pasture.

"Does your dad know you're out here?" I asked, my eyes dropping to her lap where a shotgun rested across her thighs. "Know how to shoot that thing?"

Lina huffed. "Any more questions, *daddy*? Who do you think I am? I don't need anyone's permission to be on my ranch, thank you very much."

She turned away from me, the moonlight glowing off her

profile. She looked like an angel with a halo, but there was nothing angelic about her. And fuck, her calling me daddy instantly made my zipper tight, even if she was being a smart-ass. *Especially* when she was being a smart-ass.

"But I told him anyway. He reminded me to bring the shotgun."

I chuckled.

Her head whipped back to me, her features shadowed by her cowboy hat, but I could see the whites of her eyes, and she was looking at me weird.

"Did you just laugh?" she asked.

"Yeah, why?"

"I've never heard you laugh before. I didn't think you even knew how."

I scoffed and shook my head in disbelief. "I laugh."

"No, you don't," she argued.

Of course she was fucking arguing with me about whether I laugh or not. I could say the grass was green, and she would say it was blue.

"All you do is grunt." Lina flipped her long braid over her shoulder.

"I'm a man of few words. What can I say?"

"You could start by saying you're fucking sorry."

Oh, here we go again. I rolled my eyes. The last time I tried to apologize for what happened back in Joseph, it turned into an argument and then my hand went down her pants. We didn't get very far because that was the night Frank Miller and Junior Matheus let the horses out.

"I've said I'm sorry. How many times do you want me to

say it?"

"As many times as you need to until I believe you. Or you fucking leave."

"Lina." I reached over and gripped her reins above her hands, bringing her horse closer. Close enough that she could see my eyes in the dark. With the sun gone, the high desert night had chilled the air enough that our breaths mingled in puffs between us. Our eyes locked, and I could see the flare of her nostrils as if it were painful to be this close to me. "I'm so fucking sorry. You have to know that I never meant for any of that to go down the way it did."

"You fucked me in front of your wife, and then you fucked up my run."

I heaved a deep sigh. She didn't mince words. How could I explain it all and hope she'd understand? How could I explain that I set out to hurt Elise because she hurt me? That in my twisted head—and inebriated judgment—I thought that if I could make my ex jealous enough, she wouldn't leave and take Penn with her? I hadn't set out to find someone whom I was so attracted to … someone who could flip my whole world upside down and make me grateful that my ex was leaving. To end up kissing someone who caused my gut to twist and my heart to clench.

I'd lost my ever-fucking mind that night. I hadn't expected to feel anything. I thought I could win some cash to follow Elise wherever she went and prove to myself that the wild barrel racer had meant nothing. That was the only reason I ended up making a bet against her run. How could I explain any of that to her when I didn't totally get it myself?

"Ex-wife," I corrected. It was the only thing I thought I could say. *Dumbass.*

Lina's eyes narrowed. "You're an asshole, you know that?"

"I've been told that a time or two."

Lina pulled on her reins, causing Mushu to shift away, and I let go.

"Tired of it yet?" she asked.

"Tired of what?"

"Me calling you on it. I don't know why you've stuck around as long as you have. There are other ranches. Why can't you go be an asshole somewhere else?"

"Maybe I like someone calling me on my shit." In fact, I loved it. My cock was throbbing with every bratty word that spewed from her perfectly fuckable mouth.

Lina groaned in exasperation, but I wanted to make her moan for other reasons. It didn't help being out here arguing in the dark. It only caused severe déjà vu. But at this point, I'd played that scene out so many times while fisting my cock in the shower, I should be used to it by now. Shutting my eyes, it all came rushing back.

Her chest rose and fell in anger while I held my breath to keep from saying the one thing that was on the tip of my tongue.

"You can't even apologize like a normal person without some ridiculous snide remark!" she yelled at me. "Why the hell do you care if I meet a guy at the bar anyway?"

I growled. I couldn't help it. My blood was boiling. "You don't fucking tell a girl to meet you at a bar for a date without expecting them to put out. That's all he wants from you, Lina."

"Again, why the hell do you care? And who's to say I don't want to put out. I don't think it's any of your goddamn business who I hook up with."

Frustrated, I pushed her against the fence post, biting my tongue until I tasted copper. There was so much I wanted to say, but all it did was make my blood boil.

She twisted my shirt in her grasp, tugging me closer to her. Her sneer melted, her lips parting with her heaving breaths. Fuck, I wanted to kiss her. Her eyes bounced to my mouth before returning to my eyes. If I didn't know better, her heated anger looked a whole lot like desire.

"Who's to say I don't want to put out?" she said again, her other hand wrapping around my forearm and tugging my hand away from where I pinned her shoulders against the post.

Her fingertips trailed down my arm, sending goose bumps down my flesh until she could take my hand and place it on her hip. My heart started to beat rapidly. My body went hot. And my breath was stolen right from my lungs. What the hell was she doing?

I hadn't touched her since that first night, and now with my hands on her, I didn't think I could ever let her go.

My grip on her tightened, my fingers digging into the denim at her hip when her own hands went to her pants, unfastening the button and lowering the zipper. "Do you not want me to go on this date?"

"No, I don't want you to go on this fucking date," I told her honestly. My chest heaved.

"You expect me to be a good girl and not hook up with guys in bars?" Fuck! Her eyebrows quirked in question, but her stare bore

into me intensely.

"I should've been the last fucking guy you picked up at a bar." I was getting too close to the truth, and my gut clenched.

"What if I wanted to get picked up? What should I do then?" she asked, taking my hand and bringing it to the bare skin between her shirt hem and waistband.

She was so soft.

I lowered my gaze, watching my rough, tan hands contrast against her soft, bronze skin. I didn't fight her. My mouth fell open on a deep exhale while she held my hand against her, pressing it down below the elastic of her panties until I could feel her wet slit.

"Fuck," I growled, lowering my forehead to hers.

Lina widened her stance, shoving my hand between her legs. "I want you to touch me."

My middle finger slid through her cunt. The tightness of her jeans pressed the heel of my palm against her clit, and she rolled her hips forward, letting it brush against her.

She whined, her nails digging into my shirt to hold me tighter against her.

"Do you need to come? Is that all this is?" I asked her. If she was just going on a date because she needed to get fucked, I would gladly give her what she wanted.

"If you don't want me to go on my date," she panted through clenched teeth, "you're going to have to make me come until I forget all about it."

I plunged my middle finger into her soaked pussy, stroking in and out. She moaned, her hips bumping into mine while she ground against my hand. My cock was painfully hard, and I could feel the precum leaking from the tip. She was going to make me come in my pants like a fucking teenager.

"Fuck my hand, baby. This pussy is only going to come for me."

"Oh my God," she moaned, dropping her head to my shoulder. I could tell she was close as she quickened her pace, her hips rocking, letting her clit rub against me while my finger fucked her. The night was quiet, except for the sounds of her drenched pussy and our heavy breaths.

"That's it. Take it. Take everything you need until you fall apart."

Her forehead rocked back and forth on my shoulder, as if she couldn't stand it. She smelled amazing, like vanilla and flowers. I wanted to bury my nose in her hair while I buried my fingers in her perfect little cunt.

"Two, cowboy. Two fingers," she ordered, breathless.

"You're not full enough?"

"I'm never full enough. Please."

I loved hearing her beg. I don't think Lina Larsen had begged for anything in her life. Except for this. Except for me. Or at least, I hoped so.

I thrust in a second finger, and she bit back a cry. She pushed her hips down against my hand, begging for it to go deeper. I could tell this would not be enough for her the way she was frantically grinding against me, chasing the orgasm she was desperate for. I drove the heel of my hand harder against her clit.

"I'm so close, Reed," she whispered. "Don't stop."

Her walls fluttered against my fingers, pulsing and squeezing. Just as soon as I thought she would let herself go, she froze. Then she pushed me away, her eyes staring past me. I turned, trying to make sense of the movement in the evening shadows.

"What the fuck?" she cursed in the darkness.

"Why are the horses out?" I asked, shocked and dazed.

"Fucking shit!" She frantically pushed against my shoulders. I took my hand away from her, feeling the shudder go through her body with the contact.

"Who let the horses out?"

The end of the memory snapped me back to reality, leaving me with just an echo of our raised voices. I looked around, scanning the fence line. It seemed quiet, but that night had seemed quiet, too.

Something didn't feel right.

"Let's ride down the line," I told Lina, turning my horse and heading down the slope to the fence line.

I heard her follow behind me, and before I even reached the fence, I knew what I was about to see.

"Shit!" The wire was cut and curled back against the post. "Someone was already out here tonight. How did we not see this?" Or it happened while I was distracted by Lina and the memory of her ...

I turned and surveyed our surroundings. The herd didn't look disturbed. It must have happened before we got out here tonight.

"Do you think any of them got loose?" Lina asked.

"I brought some extra wire in my pack. We'll patch it up

and have a look."

"You're letting me stay out with you then?"

I huffed a laugh. "Don't think I have a choice now, do I?"

She grinned, her pretty smile flashing in the dark, dazzling as bright as the stars. And it took my fucking breath away.

CHAPTER 5
Lina

Stepping into the Saddle Room at the Joseph Round-up a year later made my heart gallop. I was half expecting to see Reed leaning up against the bar, glowering into his whiskey glass, while the rowdy crowd mulled around him. But instead, it felt like his presence was haunting me while Kale, Christian, and I pushed our way up to the bar.

It was the last night of the rodeo. With all of our events behind us, we were ready to cut loose.

"The buckle bunnies are out in full force tonight." Kale grinned ear to ear, elbowing Christian's side.

Several women were hovering nearby, ready to grab some dick or shed their bras for a free T-shirt. *These women are absolutely feral.*

But I didn't blame them. I was right there with them a year ago. I just ended up learning my lesson the hard way.

"I don't fuck with that anymore," Christian reminded him.

"Yeah, yeah. I've heard."

"We've *all* heard that, Christian," I told him. "About a thousand times."

"I'm just waiting for you to change your mind," Kale

admitted as we sidled up to the bar, each of us slamming our tokens down.

"Whiskey?" the bartender suggested.

"On the rocks." I nodded curtly.

"Neat," the guys also chimed in.

The bartender set down three glasses, filling them with the amber liquid.

I picked mine up and swirled the ice cubes around before taking a sip.

"So is Sage … waiting for you to change your mind, I mean," I teased. He'd been obsessed with Kale's sister for almost two years now, and the poor guy didn't stand a chance.

"That's the point. I'll keep saying it until she believes me."

"You know you have my blessing," Kale, his roommate and one of his best friends aside from me said, clinking his glass with Christian's.

They both took long swigs.

Kale took another drink, momentarily doffing his cowboy hat so he could push his dark, wavy hair behind his ears. He was growing it out. "Well, if you're not fucking with them, I got the pretty brunette by the door." He straightened his hat on his head and peeled away from our little group, making a beeline for the woman standing with her friends, who kept looking our way.

"You don't have to stay with me." Christian sighed, glancing away from his friend to look at me. "Half the cowboys and roughies are checking you out."

I scanned the bar. I was used to eyes being on me whenever I walked into a room. My mom called it our "super power."

Our natural allure that drew people to us. Unfortunately, my powers ran out the minute I opened my mouth, very unlike my mother. The last guy I dated—a saddle bronc rider named Jones—said I was too "crude" for him and he preferred his girls "tamer." *Like, what the actual fuck?* The guy was nice, and he definitely knew how to eat pussy, but apparently, I was too wild for him. Screw him. Better yet, never again! I wasn't about to change who I was for some dude. And right now, this room seemed full of Joneses.

And no Reeds.

"Nah, I'm good." I just wanted to relax and celebrate my win. Maybe even rub it into Paige Gibson's *pretty, pretty princess* face. She was sitting at a table with her family. Her mom pinning her hair back beneath her cowboy hat. All of them looked rather serious while they drank their losses.

"Hey, Christian!" Kale shouted from across the room, waving him over.

"He wants me to play wingman," Christian grumbled.

"Better help your buddy out." I winked. "I promise I won't tell Sage." Holding my hat to my head while I almost doubled over, laughing.

He shot me a glare. "You okay sitting here, brat?" he asked, setting his now-empty glass down and getting a refill.

"Fine. I promise. Go on." I shooed him away.

A bar stool opened up. I downed the rest of my drink and leaned across the bartop. Pushing my tits up, I used that super power to my advantage to get the bartender's attention. I held back a giggle when it worked. He nearly fumbled rushing over.

"What will it be, miss?" he asked. He was cute, with sandy-blond hair and dimples.

I smiled at him, setting my second token into his hand, letting it linger a little bit longer so he could feel the brush of my fingertips. I wasn't feeling any of the cowboys, but perhaps the whiskey slinger.

"A double this time." I gave him a wink.

He closed his grip, brushing his knuckles across my palm, and gave me a cocky smirk. "Anything for our barrel racing champ."

"So you saw my run?"

"I might have caught it," he said, pouring my drink.

The gentleman beside me turned, his eyes blatantly traveling down my body. "I caught it. I watch you every year, and this was, by far, your best race," the man said.

I turned my head to look at him. His eyes were intense on my face, as if he could see through my skin, making it crawl. He looked to be close to my age, possibly a little older, with dark hair and whiskers that were in serious need of grooming. The man could have been handsome if he didn't give off creeper vibes. The hair on my arms stood on end despite the heat of the over-populated bar.

"Thank you," I said politely, turning to my drink.

He spun on his stool until his arm rested across the bartop, his hand inches away from where mine wrapped around my glass. His boots were kicked up on rungs of the stool, his knees splayed. Any closer and he would be bracketing me in.

"You know, someone handed me a Saddle Room tattoo when I came in," he said, lifting his palm. Lying there beneath his hand was a temporary tattoo with a bucking, saddled bronco, The Saddle Room labeled beneath. "Want another one?"

Another one? What the fuck did that mean? My heart began to thump wildly, as if alarm bells were going off in my chest. I raised my eyes to his. They were drilling into me as if he could see everything beneath the layer of denim and polyester.

"I don't think so," I told him, looking over at the bartender who was taking care of other patrons. *Come back over here, please.*

"Sure you do. I'll get you another drink, and we can have some fun tonight."

I picked up my drink, turning in my seat to look around for Christian and Kale. Both of them were busy chatting up the girls at the table.

"Thanks, but no thanks, buddy." I scooted off the stool, taking my drink with me to head over to the dance floor.

I sucked down the rest of the whiskey, dropping it off at a deserted table before joining the line dancers grapevining to "Boot Scootin' Boogie." Normally, I would be enjoying myself. Brooks & Dunn would get me every time. Right now, though, I was too busy trying to brush off the heavy feeling that was taking over all of my senses. A shiver of uncomfortable tingles shot up and down my back. I scooted along the floor, hoping that the click of my heels would ground me.

The uncomfortable feeling stuck with me and brought to mind a few other times I'd felt like I was being watched. I couldn't help but wonder if it was this creep.

Being part of the crowd made me feel better, but I could still feel his eyes on me as if they were burning into my skin. I felt like I was on fire, and not in a good way.

I didn't even need to look behind me. I could feel the air shift as a presence pressed against me. The heat of his body loomed over me like a dark cloud.

"I see what you're doing. I know, for a fact, you like to be chased." His breath was hot and moist against my ear, causing me to shudder.

Stopping mid-heel-toe, I pivoted, turning on him.

The dude was right in my space. I leaned back, attempting to put distance between us despite the crowded dance floor.

"Asshole, take the hint. I'm really not interested." I glared at him, making sure he could see my annoyance.

He frowned. I watched him dampen his chapped lips as his eyes wandered down to look at mine. "You sure seemed interested in all the other cowboys who've approached you. Pretty sure you love the attention." His breath was rancid from cheap beer as he leaned toward me.

"Dude, get out of my fucking face."

He stepped forward, blatantly ignoring me, but the dancers kept me locked in place so I couldn't retreat. His hand went to my hip. The audacity that men have these days. *Why am I fighting to be heard?*

"One spin around the dance floor?"

"Buddy, when a girl says no, she means fucking 'no.'" I pushed past him.

He wrapped his fingers around my bicep, ducking his head to whisper in my ear, "You sure were willing to put out for the last cowboy you met here."

I froze, cold sweat washing over me. *The last cowboy I met here?* Did he mean Reed? How long had he been there without me noticing?

"Get your fucking hands off me!" I snapped, my voice an octave higher than the music, hoping to draw people's attention to him. I wrenched my arm out of his snakelike grip. I could feel people turn to look at us. *Good.*

The dude was deranged because he smiled. He actually *smiled.* Like he enjoyed me telling him "no."

"Only if you ask nicely," he said as I barreled my way off the dance floor.

My eyes darted around the room, searching for Kale and Christian, but they were nowhere to be seen. Shit! My heart galloped as anxiety washed over me.

I bounded back over to the bar, cute bartender's eyes lifting to mine. *Thank you, whiskey gods.* Pushing out a long breath, I forced a smile and sidled up to the bartop in front of him.

"Was the double shot not enough?" He chuckled, flashing his dimples.

"Not nearly." I peeked over my shoulder to see if I was followed, but the spot on the dance floor was now empty. "I'm out of tokens, though."

He shrugged, picked up a highball glass, and set it in front of me. "It's on the house." He spun a bottle, flipping it to pour straight whiskey. "The name's Luke."

"Thanks, Luke."

His lips tipped. "Sure. It's Lina, right?"

"Yes, it is." I winked, taking a sip of my whiskey.

"Think you'll stick around till closing?" he asked.

I turned slightly to look around me again. Still no sign of

my friends. I wasn't about to leave alone now.

"I think I actually might." I tipped the glass to my lips, smiling over the rim.

Luke patted the bartop, beaming. "We'll continue celebrating your win."

I really wasn't in the mood to celebrate my win anymore, but leaving the bar alone was no longer an option. And hell, maybe Luke could help turn this night around after all.

CHAPTER 6
Lina

From the Augustus Stampede to the Molliville Showdown, I couldn't shake the eerie feeling that someone was following me … watching me. It threw me off my game, and for two rodeos straight, Paige beat my time by half a second. If I didn't shake it off soon, it was going to be a battle to retain my record. I was going to need to pull it together for the Bowman Desert Rodeo, or I could kiss my goal to win the Columbia River Finals goodbye.

"Doing okay?" Christian asked, genuine concern spreading across his smooth features as he pet Mushu's chest to calm him before our run.

Mushu seemed extra fidgety today. I knew he could sense my nerves, and I tried my best to calm my body so it wouldn't affect him, but I was getting nowhere. We were both antsy.

I shook my head at him and exhaled a long, shuddering breath in an attempt to shake it off. "I'm a fucking mess."

It didn't help that I was last in the draw, and it had been raining. The arena was dangerous—slick and muddy—which would make me have to work Mushu harder, digging deeper around the barrels for us to make a clean run.

His brows pinched beneath his cowboy hat. "You got this. Don't let it get to your head."

I knew he was right, but I could really use some comfort. I wished my dad was here.

Taking another deep breath, I looked around, and there, with his eyes fucking on me, was that creeper from the bar. His eyes bore into me like a laser. His mouth was set firm, and he wasn't smiling like he'd been at the Saddle Room.

I immediately felt sick.

"Whoa!" Christian held on to Mushu while he shifted beneath me. "What just happened? Your face went as white as a sheet."

I swallowed the bile in the back of my throat. I'd have to deal with that asshole as soon as this was over. I was done feeling like I was being watched. I couldn't continue going into each rodeo with eyes on my back. The dude seriously needed to fuck off.

I was going to have to take this into my own hands.

I shook my head at the same time Mushu tossed his, trying to shake off the nerves.

"Larsen, you're on deck!"

"I got this," I whispered, but Christian read my lips and nodded. His eyes were full of concern as he led us to the gate.

I don't think he believed me, and I certainly didn't believe myself.

As soon as Mushu was unsaddled and back in his borrowed stall for the night, I stormed right over to the creepy bastard leaning against the stands and gave him a quick knee in the balls.

"Stay the fuck away from me!"

He doubled over, grabbing his junk. "Bitch!" he hissed through his pain.

"When I told you to fuck off in Joseph, you should have listened."

"You fucking bitch," he spat, regaining his composure enough to quickly grasp my arm.

I squeaked, surprised by the fast and forceful movement as he spun me around. His arm looped around me like a boa constrictor, pinning my arms to my sides. He gripped the back of my neck with his other hand, pressing me up against the support rail.

I bucked against his grip, but his hand at my neck wrapped around my jaw, wrenching it to the side, putting a strain on my neck until he could press my cheek into the cold metal. His fingers dug into my skin as he squeezed. Squeezing so hard, I thought he might break my jaw. Air puffed out through my nose. My lungs heaved.

"Get the fuck off me," I tried to say, but it only came out like a desperate groan.

His body pressed against mine, and his sour breath reeked of beer and chew. It made me want to hurl.

"You think you're too good for me? All you needed to do was say 'yes' to a little dance, Lina. You should have let me show you a good time. I can *still* show you a good time." Hot air drifted across my face.

My heart raced, my chest heaved. I tried to buck my hips,

to squirm my arms loose, to push away from him, to get even an inch of separation, but he was stronger. The guy was getting off on this, the evidence of just how much was digging into my spine the more he hurt me. Bile crawled up my throat. I was going to vomit, but the way he was squeezing my jaw closed would mean I'd have to swallow it unless I wanted it coming out my nose.

"I know you like to play. Maybe you even like it rough." His thumb brushed the underside of my breast where his hand wrapped around me. I wanted to crawl out of my skin and pretend this was not happening right now.

There'd been more than one guy I encountered who got a little too aggressive or handsy, but I'd never had someone who couldn't take "no" for an answer. Fear washed over me like a bucket of ice water.

The sounds of my labored breathing and pounding heart almost drowned out the distant drunk laughter of the remaining rodeo-goers leaving the fairgrounds. They might be my only saving grace. Anyone could stumble upon us. I could feel him hesitate at my back.

"Next time, you're not saying 'no' to me." He pushed off me then, letting my cheek dig into the metal one last time before leaving me under the stands in the dark.

Tears stung my eyes, and I straightened my button-up shirt. My hands trembled as I brushed loose strands of hair away from my face, tucking a piece back into my braid. I was going to be sick. I opened my jaw, letting the joint pop. It already ached. Fuck. I clamped my eyes shut and tried to calm down, shaky breaths forcing their way through my lungs. Shit,

I was in trouble. I couldn't handle this alone. It was bad, *really* bad. The only question was, what was I going to do about it?

I turned around, peering out at the shadowed rodeo grounds illuminated by a few arena lights. Fortunately, I was heading home tomorrow. I needed to regroup. Maybe I could see if Dad would be able to come to the next rodeo with me? There was no way in hell I was going to continue traveling the circuit by myself when this guy made it perfectly clear he wasn't going to leave me alone.

Taking a steadying breath, I willed myself to move, to look forward and head straight to my truck. More than once, I'd slept in my vehicle while on the circuit. I'd get in, lock the door, and make sure my bear spray was within an arm's reach if anyone tried anything.

I turned the corner from the entrance, heading to the parking lot, when a hand whipped up, taking my arm.

I spun around, swinging my fist right into—

Christian's gut.

"Ugh!" He blew out a gust of air, grabbing his stomach. "Damn, slugger. What was that for?"

"Shit! I'm so sorry, Christian." My hands hovered over him, not wanting to touch him and not wanting him to touch me. I felt like my body was shaking, my skin vibrating with static.

"Did Jude teach you that?"

"Sorry," I said again, wincing. I knew I could pack a mean punch if I needed to.

"Is something up?" He rubbed his stomach, his face in a slight grimace. "You haven't been yourself the last couple weeks. You look as though something has you spooked … and, what's this?"

His hand reached for my right cheek, but I moved my head to the side before he could touch it. "Nothing."

"Did someone sock you in the face? Your jaw is swollen."

I raised a hand, my fingertips lightly touching the tender skin. Like a nervous doe, I scanned the parking lot around us. It still felt like I was being watched, and I fucking hated it. It made my skin crawl.

"Come with me to my truck."

"Lina, you're freaking me out a little bit."

I didn't say another word, my eyes darting back and forth as we walked to my truck.

"Get in," I said, unlocking the doors. I climbed in, waiting for Christian to get in the passenger seat and shut the door. I flicked the locks, the sound click echoing in the quiet cab.

"Lina, what's going on?"

I turned to my friend. His cool, green eyes were full of concern, and his mouth was turned down in a frown.

"Someone has been following me since—well, I don't know how long."

"Wait … what?" His brow furrowed.

"He hit on me in Joseph a couple weeks ago, and I turned him down. He didn't like that very much."

Christian's jaw ticked.

"He made it sound as though he'd been watching me for a while."

"Fuck, Lina. Who is this guy?" Christian's hands balled where they rested on his thighs.

I shook my head. "I—I don't know. He hasn't told me his

name, and I haven't asked."

"Was he here today? In the stands, I mean. Did you see him right before your run?"

"Yeah, he was there." I nodded.

"That's when you went all pale." Christian looked out the windshield, pondering, before turning back to me. "What happened tonight? Did he fucking touch you? Did he do more than what I can see right now?"

I shook my head furiously, gripping the steering wheel as tightly as I could, hoping it could keep my hands from shaking. "I thought I could tell him off, and I kneed him in the balls." I stared at my hands. *Don't shake. Don't fucking shake.* "He didn't like that. He—he grabbed me."

"So he did touch you!"

I whipped my head back to Christian. Even in the dark, I could see his skin go red with rage. Christian rarely got angry, but when he did, you could read it from a mile away.

"He made sure I knew he wasn't going to stop. That next time, he wasn't going to take 'no' for an answer." I breathed in through my nose and out through my mouth, attempting to quell the nausea.

"Lina, this isn't good. What the fuck?"

"No, shit, it's not good. I have a fucking stalker."

"Yeah, you do." Christian shook his head in disbelief. "You can't be on the circuit by yourself anymore."

"I'm not by my-fucking-self." I could feel my own anger rising now, but it wasn't at Christian. I was angry at myself for not handling this when he first approached me in Joseph. "I have you and Kale."

"Lina, I'm serious. You need to have someone with you all the time. Kale and I have our own events. We can't be by your side 24/7. Can your dad come with you for a while?"

I grimaced, knowing Dad would be wanting to kill this guy. "Maybe. He has a lot going on at the ranch right now, though."

"You have to tell him, or I fucking will. If that's what he did to your face in the middle of the fairgrounds, he can't catch you alone anymore."

Chapter 7
Reed

I rode in from moving the herd to the southern pasture. Lina was back, by the look of it, blocking my truck in the yard per usual. I shook my head, but I couldn't help the twitch of my lips. My heartbeat picked up the closer I got to the stables at the mere thought of seeing her. I could hear Chuck and Lina talking. A third voice jumped in, sounding low and irritated. *Jude.*

Something was going on because as soon as I dismounted and led Warrior in, they stopped speaking, and all three of them looked up from their huddle. Lina shifted on her feet, avoiding eye contact. The vice wrapped around my heart nearly broke it in two. Chuck rubbed his mustache like he was thinking, and Jude flipped his hat restlessly.

My brows lifted.

"Maybe we should talk to Reed about what's going on?" Chuck suggested, gesturing to me.

"Dad! What the actual fuck?" Lina threw out her arms in exasperation, shooting Chuck a look that would shrivel any man's dick, except her father's. And mine.

It was fucking hot.

Maybe that said something about me. I loved a strong, ferocious woman who didn't take shit. I loved it even more if I could get that fiercely independent woman to submit to me.

I crossed my arms and braced my feet while I held on to Warrior's reins, amused by whatever argument this was.

"I'm going to go with you," Jude demanded, his brow pinched.

"No, you're not." Lina spun her icy glare on her cousin. "You have a new baby and a wedding to plan."

My heart rate kicked up a notch, but for different reasons. Something was wrong. Lina was purposely avoiding my eyes, and I swear from here, her face looked darker.

"I'd go with you myself if it weren't for the vandalism and the missing cattle," Chuck explained.

"I thought you got the game cams up this week," she protested.

"We did." He heaved a big sigh. "But someone's tampering with them. We also have ranch hands running night shifts, and it's still happening. We lost a few head of cattle this week. I can't risk leaving right now with—"

"Put Reed in charge," she interrupted, gesturing to me, but she still hadn't acknowledged my presence.

He shook his head. "He's been running shifts with the others, but as I was saying, I also need to be here to go to Grandpa's appointments with him. His dementia is getting worse."

"What's this about?" I spoke up, tired of being ignored like I wasn't standing right in front of them.

Everyone's heads spun to me, but my eyes only went to

Lina's as they finally met mine. I thought I saw a flicker of anxiety before her lashes fluttered, and her gaze shifted to her feet.

Chuck's voice was firm and commanding. "Lina's had some trouble on the circuit. Some creep's been following her and harassing her."

"*Dad*," Lina warned through her teeth.

"We need to ask for help when we need it, darlin'. You know I'd go with you if I could. Maybe it's for the best that I don't. Otherwise, there might be a dead man who turns up on the circuit."

There may still end up being a dead man. I could feel my blood boiling. Warrior was shaking his head beside me, trying to jerk the reins from my fists, mirroring my agitation. But this was more than agitation. I was fucking on fire. I never felt this type of protective rage before, and I didn't even know the whole story yet.

Lina raised her head to look at her dad before risking a glance at me. My vision narrowed and my teeth clenched. I was going to fucking kill this guy. She glared at me as if warning me to chill the fuck out, but that was like asking an addict to flush their pills down the toilet. I wasn't going to fucking chill. Not when a man harasses a woman, and definitely not if that woman is Lina Larsen. The badass barrel racer who didn't take shit from nobody, who knew who she was even at the age of twenty-seven, who was unapologetically her, who told you like it was and you either accepted her for her or fucked off.

"We have a few more weeks to get the double-wide ready for you," Jude said. "You could go with Lina while we're finishing that up, and when you return, you and your daughter could move in."

"What needs to happen?" If my hands needed to get dirty, they'd get fucking dirty.

"I'll send you both with the fifth wheel," Chuck instructed. "No more sleeping in your truck."

"Dad." Lina shook her head.

"Lina, darlin', you are as stubborn as the days are long. This does not take away your independence. This will protect you so you can focus on your races."

She scoffed. "Like sending Reed is going to help me focus on my races."

I wasn't going to read too much into that, but my heart kicked up a notch thinking I rattled her as much as she did me.

"I could call Mom—" she started.

Chuck leveled her with a look that said, *Come on, let's get real.* "You think Vickie Morgan is going to leave the city to camp out for six weeks or longer? Do you think your mother could protect you if it came down to it?"

"Ugh!" Lina threw up her hands. "No. I know she wouldn't. I just don't want this asshat babysitting me, either. Besides, I can protect myself." She shot me a glare for good measure, and I couldn't stop my dick from twitching.

"Darlin', we all know you can protect yourself, but look at your face." He gestured to her cheek, and I noticed then the yellowing of an old bruise. "You still won't tell me how you got that. Consider this a little added protection. It's a good thing."

"So a bodyguard then?" She shook her head in disbelief.

"We haven't even asked him if this will work for him yet."

Jude crossed his arms. "Reed, we know you're dealing with the shit with your ex and trying to get full custody. This probably isn't the best time."

Lina's head whipped to me, her big, brown eyes curious and concerned for a split second before shifting away.

Yeah, this was shit timing. At least Elise agreed to give me every other week once I had us set up in the double-wide. But knowing her, she could go back on her word on a moment's notice. I spent my last paycheck on an hour with a family lawyer. I was basically told that unless she is determined negligent by Child Protective Services, mothers are almost always awarded primary custody in the state of Oregon. It would be a battle and a shitload of money I didn't have if I was going to drag her through mediation.

This would give me some time to figure it out, another way to earn a few bucks for a lawyer while also keeping an eye on Lina. I would do anything to protect my girls.

Maybe I paused too long because Lina said, "See, he can't do it."

The fuck I can't! I was more than capable of protecting her from some prick. "When do we leave?"

"In a couple days," Chuck replied.

"Fucking shit!" Lina shook her head. "So I get to hear his grumpy ass for weeks on end?"

"Or until this gets resolved," Chuck stated, throwing me a look that said, *You better resolve it if it comes down to it.*

Oh, I'd definitely make sure it gets handled. I nodded in understanding.

"Fine!" Lina turned on her heels, her ass looking amazing

in her jeans as she walked away. The shadows of the stables played on her curves as she headed out the back door toward the big house. "But I call the shots! You work for me, Reed!" she blurted over her shoulder.

Chuck grimaced and turned to me. "Sorry, man. I think you're in for it. I'll be sure to pay you double."

My eyes widened. "Double? Boss, you don't need to do that. I won't even be on the ranch."

"Believe me, it's going to be tougher than wrangling cattle. And the safety of my daughter is worth it."

I knew exactly what he meant. I'd do anything to keep Penn safe. I could use the money. Double pay would definitely go a long way with the lawyer.

"I understand. I'll make sure this guy doesn't even look her way." I meant that with every fiber of my being. No one was even going to glance her way with the intent to harm unless they wanted my fucking thumbs buried in their eye sockets.

Jude gripped my shoulder. "We'll have your place set up by the time you get back. Let me know if you need me to do anything while you're gone."

"Thanks, boss. I won't let you down."

"You're a good man, Reed," Chuck said. "I know you won't let me down."

I'd sure as hell let a lot of people down, my ex-wife and daughter included. But that was all about to change.

I wanted to see Penn before I left. I knew before I even put my truck in park that it was a bad idea to pull up to Elise's unannounced tonight. There was another truck here I didn't recognize, and I had a sinking feeling it was *his*. I instinctively reached beneath the driver's seat, my fingertips brushing the cold metal.

Of course Elise lied to me. She may have chosen this man to share her bed, but there was no way in hell I was letting him play house and parent my daughter. Fuck that! I couldn't leave town knowing Penn was around him. Lord only knows what she was being exposed to in that house.

Gripping the handle of my 9mm, I lifted the hem of my shirt, clipping it inside the front of my jeans. Sliding out of the truck, I closed the door with a soft click. If no one heard me pull up, I didn't want to alert anyone and have him run out the back. I adjusted the front of my shirt, making sure it concealed the fact that I was armed.

My body read cool and in control, but inside, I was seething. Being a person in recovery, there were too many times to count where I had a gun pulled on me. It was necessary for me to be packing. The last time someone shoved a gun in my face was the night Elise found out she was expecting Penn, and it was the wake-up call we both needed to get clean. While becoming a mom made her relapse, it made me more determined than ever to remain on the straight and narrow. The last thing I wanted was to revisit that time in our lives, but she was forcing my hand.

I knocked lightly on the front door and listened.

"Can you get that?" I heard Elise mumble from somewhere in the house.

Heavy boots sounded from the hallway, approaching the

door. The doorknob turned, and my hand disappeared at my waist, resting my palm on the grip, prepared to draw.

As soon as he opened it wide enough, I grabbed a handful of his shirt to pull him out onto the front porch, slamming him against the siding. With my hand twisted in his shirt and my forearm resting against his throat, I pressed the barrel against his temple.

A look of surprise flashed across his face, then was quickly replaced with the hard look of a man ready to fight. His light-gray eyes brightened when he registered who was staring him in the face. His lips curled in a sneer, ready to taunt me, yet he held up his arms in resignation.

"If you think you can be around my fucking daughter, you have another thing coming, Junior." I was so livid, my words were punctuated with spit.

Junior bared his teeth like a rabid dog. "Fuck you!"

"They should have kept you locked up."

"Good behavior. I got three years of parole." His grin turned vile. I fucking hated this guy.

"There is no way in hell I'm going to walk away from here without my daughter. You and Elise can wallow in whatever shit you're into for all I care. And if you ever come near Penn again,"—I dug the barrel into his temple—"this gun will be cocked."

I pushed off him, letting his head knock against the wood siding, before shoving the Glock back into my waistband and storming into the house.

Elise was lying on the couch, half asleep and probably high.

"Penn!" I called, walking past the living room of thrift

store furniture and down the hallway. "Penn!"

"Daddy?" Penelope came around the corner of her bedroom door.

"Hey, princess," I said as calmly and as smoothly as I could, not wanting to frighten her. But my heart was pounding out of my chest, and I felt as though I could barely breathe.

I knelt, letting her skip into my arms.

"Are we going to go see the horsies?"

"Yeah, we're going to go see the horsies. Let's get some stuff, and you can spend the night."

"Really?"

"Yes." I stood up, looking over my shoulder briefly to see Junior shaking Elise awake to tell her I was here for Penn. "Come on." I hurried us into her room, finding her Frozen backpack and quickly shoving clothes into it. "Grab your teddy and your blanket."

"I'm so excited! Can Mama come, too?"

My heart just about broke hearing her ask that. I shook my head. "No, sweet girl, it's just you and me tonight."

I swung the backpack over my shoulder and lifted her into my arms.

"You … you can't take her," Elise slurred as she sat up from the couch.

"The last thing I want to do is take her from her mother, but you're failing her, Lis. Things can't go on like this, and unless you want me to get social services involved, you're going to have to let me take her." I had no idea how calm I was sounding when I wanted to put my fist through the wall.

Junior hovered at her side, whispering something into her

ear, but I wasn't going to wait to hear what either of them had to say. I needed to leave before they both decided to put up a fight and this got ugly. I wasn't going to subject Penn to that shit. She deserved better than that. I knew all too well what it felt like growing up in this type of household.

I scooped up her boots at the door and marched out to the truck. Penn clung to my neck, looking back over my shoulder at her mother. My heart continued to break while my body vibrated with rage. I quickly buckled Penn in her booster and shut the door.

Junior stepped out onto the front porch right as I was about to get behind the wheel.

"Pull a gun on me again, and you can say goodbye to your little slut," he said from the front porch.

"What the fuck did you say?" I halted my boot on the running board. My hand gripped the door handle, keeping myself in place. Otherwise, I was about to march back over there and get in this dude's face. I was squeezing so hard, my knuckles cracked.

"You heard me. Pull a gun on me again, and Lina Larsen will see the end of mine."

"Get her name out of your fucking mouth," I gritted out between my teeth.

Junior's lips curled, knowing he struck a chord. Fuck him!

"It's about time. One less Larsen to deal with sounds good to me."

"Go anywhere near Lina, my daughter, or the ranch, and you'll wish you were dead."

I didn't want to hear any more of his shit. One more word

from him, and I'd make good on my promise. Climbing into the truck, I slammed the door. I didn't waste time turning over the engine and backing the hell out of there.

CHAPTER 8
Lina

"I wish you could go with me," I told Dad as we sat in front of the stone fireplace in the big house.

Grandpa built it with his own hands, and I could still see his initials, LL, and my late grandmother's ML with the date '64 carved into the wood mantel. The big house had replaced the original homestead, which was now the bunkhouse. One of my favorite things to do on a cool spring evening was to sit in front of the fire and bullshit with Dad while we sipped his favorite Scotch.

"I know, darlin'. I'll try to come out in a couple weeks, but Reed will keep you safe."

"Why do you trust him so much?" I shook my head before taking a drink. Letting the heat of the Scottish whisky hit the back of my tongue and then go down smooth.

"He's a good man. He's been through a lot. But he works hard, and he's proven to me, more than once, that he can handle the job."

"Handle me, you mean?"

Dad's mustache curved up with a grin, and he kicked his feet up on the leather ottoman. "It's no secret you don't like the guy, and you've done everything possible to run him off the ranch, yet he's still here."

"Un-fucking-fortunately."

He didn't know the half of it, and I wasn't about to tell Dad what went down with Reed and me. I slouched into the couch, wrapping my fingers around my glass, letting it rest on my belly. I already had a feeling this was going to end in a dumpster fire. We hated each other despite the overwhelming sexual tension. We would either end up fighting or fucking, and either option could end in disaster. My intuition was telling me he was going to *destroy* me. I may be strong, but I didn't think I could handle that—not after what he did. Not after I believed love at first sight was more than just a fairy tale. Not after my heart was shattered for the first time.

"Plus," Dad said, taking a swig of his drink. "Your old man has been around a long time, and the way he looks at you tells me I don't think there is anything you could do to get him to leave you … I mean, this ranch," he said, chuckling.

I flipped Dad off with a glare, but it only made him laugh harder.

"Some Dad you are. You're supposed to be on my side."

Dad may trust him, but I certainly didn't. Granted, I hadn't really given him a chance to prove himself, either.

He quickly sobered, his smile turning serious. "Darlin', I'm always on your side."

Boots stomped up the front steps, interrupting our conversation. We sat up, looking toward the door, before a fist knocked on the solid, hand-carved wood.

"What the fuck?" Dad's brow furrowed.

It was getting late, and it could only mean one thing.

I eyed the ranch walkie-talkie lying on the end table beside Dad's chair. "No one radioed you?"

He shook his head, heaving himself off his seat and heading to the door. "I wonder if they caught someone."

Answering it, I sat up straighter when I saw Reed darkening the doorway, his arms full with a sleeping child and a kid's backpack slung over his shoulder.

"Reed?" Dad asked, the surprise and concern in his voice evident.

"I had to get her out of there. She said he wouldn't be around her, but he was," Reed said in a quiet voice, not wanting to wake his daughter on his shoulder.

"Who?" I asked, setting down my drink and stepping up beside Dad.

"Here, come in." Reed stepped in, and Dad quietly closed the door behind him.

I could almost feel the anger vibrating off him. He was wired, his body tense and ready to spring. The flames from the fire flickered off the hard edges of his handsome face, shadows darkening in his eyes as they jumped from Dad to me.

"I just couldn't let her stay there anymore," he repeated.

"Okay." Dad nodded, his tone calm. "We'll make up a bed in the spare room. Stay here tonight, and we'll figure it out tomorrow."

My head spun to my dad and then back to Reed. "What happened? Who was there?"

Reed's eyes pleaded with Dad to remain quiet, and I didn't like that. I didn't like being left in the dark about what was happening on our ranch or with the ranch hands. Even if it was about Reed, I felt that I should know. A little voice in my head told me, *I needed to know, especially since it was Reed.*

When no one answered, I pressed, "Who the fuck was there?"

"*Lina,*" Dad scolded.

"She's asleep, Dad. She can't hear me."

"It's Reed's business, not ours."

"It's about to become my business since he's coming with me." I zeroed in on Reed, forcing myself to hold his eye contact. I didn't know it was possible, but his dark-brown eyes grew darker. It made my heart rate kick up a notch. "So you might as well tell me."

Reed swallowed, his jaw muscles twitching. "Junior," he said with a growl.

My eyes widened. "Wait … what? Junior's out of jail? Why was he at your wife's place?"

"Ex-wife," Reed corrected, his voice low and irritated.

I rolled my eyes.

"Junior got three years of parole," Dad informed me.

"Are you fucking kidding me?"

Dad shook his head, not bothering to get after me for my language. "Not kidding, unfortunately."

"He's engaged to Penn's mom," Reed whispered.

My mouth fell open in shock. "What?"

"Yeah." Reed pressed his lips together as if attempting to keep himself from raging, his large hand protectively encompassing his daughter's back. "They've been together for over a year," he said pointedly, his eyes drilling into mine in a silent explanation.

Realization dawned on me. They were together when I met him in Joseph.

I folded my arms over my chest, and I couldn't help glaring at him. "How come I'm just now hearing about this?"

"I didn't think it mattered to you," Reed accused, his eyes narrowing.

I humphed, shaking my head. "You don't think me knowing he was out of jail mattered to me? The man who terrorized Romy and endangered our horses? Of course it fucking matters. Not to mention, that asshole is now around your daughter. And who's to say he's not behind the fence cutting?"

"He just got out, Lina." Dad shook his head. "I don't think it's him. Coming near our land would be a violation of his parole."

"Like that's stopped him before," I snarked. "He had a restraining order, and he still held Romy at gunpoint."

Reed's brow furrowed, and he looked murderous at that reminder. He turned to my dad. "I can't take Penn with me on the circuit. I won't risk her. She needs stability and safety right now."

Dad nodded in agreement. "I know it's late, and you need to get that little girl into bed. We'll figure this all out in the morning. She has a place here. You both do. We'll talk to Jude and Romy, too. Come on, let's get you set up in the spare room."

Dad led them out of the living room and down the hall. I walked back to the sofa, picking up the whisky from the coffee table and draining it. Resting the cool glass on my heated cheek, I sighed. Reed and I were going to be sleeping under the same roof, and pretty soon, we'd be sleeping only feet from each other in a fifth-wheel trailer. I raised my eyes to heaven. I was fucked.

I pulled my cell out of my back pocket, tapping on my messages.

ME

I'll be home one more night. I think I'll take you up on that drink after all.

The sky was still dark when I tiptoed down the hall to the kitchen. The scent of fresh-brewed coffee calling my name. Most mornings, Dad was up well before dawn, cooking breakfast before he headed out to check on the herd. Mornings were my favorite—quiet and dark, slow and peaceful. It was only once the sun came up that I felt as though my brain were on speed and I was standing on a live wire.

Braiding my hair as I padded into the kitchen, I startled at the sight of the bare, broad back in front of me. Reed stood, unaware of my presence as he poured himself a cup of coffee. His shoulder muscles flexed as he lifted the cup to his lips, his back still turned to me. I stood frozen in the doorway as he slowly turned around, his eyes growing big as he spewed coffee from his mouth.

"Fucking hell!" I yelled, suddenly realizing I was only wearing panties and a tank top.

"Shit!" Reed said, brushing the scalding coffee off his shirtless chest.

A kitchen towel rested on the counter, and I moved over to grab it, covering myself.

Reed looked up then, his lips tipping when he saw I held the towel to my waist.

"*Please*, like I haven't seen you in less," he said with a teasing smirk.

I narrowed my eyes on him. "This"—I gestured with a flourish of my fingers over my curves—"isn't for *you* to see anymore."

His eyebrow quirked. "You sure about that?" He stepped toward me.

I took a step back, but my back hit the counter. *Shit. Shit. Shit.*

He took another step forward until he was mere inches from me. God, he smelled incredible. Like fresh linen and cedar, leather and cherry. His hair was still damp from his shower. My fingers itched to run through his dark locks. I pulled back, letting the cold tile cut into my back where my skin was exposed. Reed leaned forward, setting his coffee mug on the counter before bracing his palms on either side of me.

My breath caught. My heart pounded. He ducked his head, his lips brushing against my ear as he whispered. Each word dancing across my heated skin, scattering tingles down my spine. "You didn't leave much to the imagination when you came out to the fields in that tiny swimsuit wedged in that hot little ass of yours. Were you begging for my attention?"

I scoffed, but it came out weak. "You think that was for you?"

He pulled away slightly, his nose dragging across my cheek

until he could stare me in the eyes. I shivered. He was so close, all I could see was the dark depths of his eyes.

"It better not have fucking been for Marshall or Jace." His words came out deep and rumbling. I could almost feel them echo in my core.

"Jace is fucking hot," I confessed, but my words came out flimsy.

One side of his mouth tipped while his eyes smoldered. "You think that fucking idiot can handle you? Give you what you need?"

I shrugged. "He could try."

"Nah. He wouldn't even come close, killer."

"Killer?" My brows rose.

He bit his lip, dragging his eyes down my chest. Fuck. I wasn't wearing a bra, either, and my stiff nipples were visible through my white tank top.

He scraped his teeth across his full lip, making my breath hitch. "You're a cowboy killer, Lina Larsen."

I laughed softly at his ridiculousness. "Oh, and you think you're immune?" I nodded at him, my nose almost brushing his. I could feel heat rushing to my center, making my clit throb.

"No. I know you'd kill me—maybe even break me—if I let you in. But … maybe, just maybe, I could rope you and take that ass for a ride while the others are already six feet under. The difference is, killer, I don't want to tame you."

He reached for his coffee, his thumb gently tracing over my skin at my waist, as if he were branding it, burning it, where he touched me so faintly. He brought the mug to his mouth, and I couldn't help watching his lips mold around the rim as he sipped. He moaned as the hot liquid hit his tongue, his throat bobbing as he swallowed. My heart was pounding out of my chest. I may be a cowboy killer, but he may very well be the only one who could kill me. And I might just let him.

He pushed off the counter with a smirk as he took his coffee with him. I watched him leave, all hulking muscles and *man*. His jeans hung low, revealing the waistband of his boxer briefs. *Fuck me.*

Frozen, I let the towel fall to my feet. My knees wobbled, and I gripped the ceramic tile to keep myself from sliding to the floor. I released a long breath I hadn't realized I was holding in as goose bumps pimpled my flesh where the heat of his body had emanated from him.

I wished it wasn't five in the morning so I could pour something stronger than black coffee.

CHAPTER 9
Reed

"Keep brushing him while I go talk with Chuck and Jude," I told Penn, who stood on a stool beside Warrior. Her little tongue stuck out between her teeth in concentration as she brushed the dust from his coat.

Chuck and Jude were tacking up their horses for the day before heading out to check on the herd, then they'd lead trail rides with the tourists who came into town.

From the look of Jude, Chuck had already filled him in on the situation with Junior. His body was practically vibrating.

"So he's dating your ex-wife?" Jude asked, scratching his forehead beneath the brim of his hat.

It made me itch, too, and I couldn't help my own head scratch before adjusting my cowboy hat.

"They're engaged," I corrected. Although I wasn't sure their relationship truly mattered at this point.

"Well, fuck. Of course your daughter can't stay there." He leaned over to tighten the cinch. He wrenched it tighter, causing his horse to shift on its feet.

"I can't take her with me on the circuit, either," I told him.

"You have such a big house, Jude," Chuck chimed in.

"Would you and Romy be able to have her stay with you while Reed's with Lina?"

I knew Romy used to be a schoolteacher, so I had no doubt she was good with children. Watching her be a mother to their own baby the last couple months also made me feel better about leaving her with them.

"I have to talk with Romy, but it's a no-brainer that she should stay on the ranch while you're away," Jude agreed.

"I need to make sure she's safe and taken care of," I said, rubbing my chest, because it fucking hurt to leave her right now.

Chuck came around the horses to grip my shoulder. "We all have daughters, and I think we all know what we'd do to keep them safe. I'm trusting you, Reed. You have to trust us, too."

I glanced down at my boots to think. There was no other option, at this point, and this had to be the best thing for us both to move forward. Peering over at Penn in her little Carhartt overalls and boots, she looked like the little cowgirl she was going to grow up to be. I wanted her to have the life I didn't. I wanted her to be surrounded by people who loved and cared for her, on land that she would be able to call home. Whether it was here or somewhere else, I wanted that for her, for us. And if this was the first step in getting us there, I already knew the choice I had to make.

Looking at both Larsen men, I nodded. "I trust you."

"Go faster, Daddy," Penelope called from where she sat in front of me in the saddle.

I pressed my heels into Warrior's side, urging him to a canter as we approached Jude and Romy's place.

Romy invited us over for dinner so I could help Penn get settled before Lina and I left early in the morning. As we approached, I saw Chuck's UTV parked at the front door. Chuck said he was taking my night shift tonight, so I was surprised he was here. We slowed and sidled up to the hitching post.

"Whoa!" I pulled up on Warrior's reins, dismounted, and tied him up before helping Penn down.

"Can I wear it?" she asked, pointing at the Frozen backpack slung across my back.

"Sure, princess." I handed it to her, helping her put her little arms through the straps. She was a tiny five-year-old, and the backpack looked nearly as big as her. But she didn't seem to care. It held everything that was hers now. I needed to buy her more clothes once I got back.

"Hey, man," Jude called from the front door. "Just a heads-up. Sage and Lina are here, too. Romy invited them."

That explained the UTV. I heaved a breath, preparing myself to face Lina. After our run-in this morning in the kitchen, I had to jump in the shower again to take care of my throbbing cock that only Lina seemed to cause. I had a feeling I'd be rubbing one out every morning for the foreseeable future now that we were going to be sharing a space.

I shrugged as if it didn't matter to me, even though it 100 percent did.

Penn gripped my hand, her tiny fingers wrapping around

my wrist to hide behind my arm as I followed Jude inside. I'd spent many hours a day helping to finish their house, but this was my first time stepping inside and seeing it fully furnished.

We walked into the open concept first floor, where the living room flowed right into the open kitchen and dining room. Romy stirred a pot of red sauce, while Sage and Lina sat at the large island, sipping glasses of wine. They were laughing about something.

My eyes immediately went to Lina. God, she looked fucking beautiful. Her warm, brown waves draped over bare shoulders, and a tight, black tank top left nothing to the imagination about the curves underneath. Fuck, I wanted to run my hands along them. I don't think I'd ever understand what she did to me. It was as though she put a spell on me that night I brought her home from the bar in Joseph. And it never broke.

She was wearing makeup tonight, her lashes dark and her lips shining with gloss. Her brown eyes flicked my way and the laughter died, but her eyes still sparkled. A rush of hope filled my chest at the thought they sparkled for me.

"This must be Penelope," Romy said, coming over to us. I noticed then she had their baby girl wrapped up in an infant carrier on her chest.

"Is that a baby?" Penn asked.

My eyes flicked back to Lina. Sage was talking to her, but her eyes kept sliding back to me, her lips resting on the rim of her wine glass with a slight smile. Knowing that smile could be directed at Penn for any reason made me want to make Lina listen to reason and not hate me anymore. The thought of her caring for Penn had my mind fucking twisted.

"Yep." Romy crouched in front of my daughter. "Do you want to see her?"

Penn peered into the infant carrier. "Aw, she's so cute. What's her name?"

"Charli." Romy smiled at Penn.

"Is she one year old?" Penn asked.

Romy laughed. "No, she's only six weeks old."

Penn's eyes grew. "She's so tiny. Does she know how to play yet?"

Romy shook her head. "Not yet, but I bet I can help you hold her later."

"Do I get my own room?" Penn asked, changing the subject and looking down the hallway off the great room.

"I'll show you so you can drop off your stuff," Jude offered, leading us to the stairs.

❧

"I better get going," Lina said, excusing herself from the table.

"Oh yeah? Do you have a hot date or something?" Jude teased.

Lina flipped her hair over her shoulder. "Did you see the fucking shoes I walked in with? Do you really think I'm going to milk cows in these heels?"

"Okay, smart-ass, there are children present," Jude said, clearing plates.

"Dude, you just said smart-ass," she shot back, rolling her eyes.

Jude grimaced. "Touché! Sorry," he said to me.

I shrugged, dismissing his apology. "She's growing up around cowboys."

"See! He doesn't care," Lina said, her toe bumping mine under the table for what had to be the tenth time tonight. Was she doing it on purpose? She sure was doing everything possible to avoid eye contact while we ate our spaghetti.

"Daddy, what's a smart-ass? Is it someone who has a nice butt?" Penn asked beside me.

I chuckled, draping my arm over her chair to lean in to whisper conspiratorially, "It's Lina Larsen."

"Oh, I see." She nodded, studying Lina curiously from across the table. "My daddy thinks you have a nice butt."

The whole table busted up laughing, Lina included, though she was blushing, and it was fucking adorable to watch that shade of pink stain her cheeks.

"Oh, I like *you*," Lina said, leaning toward Penn from across the table. "You're fun."

"I like you, too," Penn replied with a little giggle.

I could feel my own face heat as everyone looked between Lina and me with hearts in their eyes.

Being too dumbstruck to deny I thought Lina had a nice butt, Sage said, "Oh boy," while wiping tears of laughter from her eyes. "I'd pay to be a fly on the wall in that camper."

Lina rolled her big, beautiful, brown eyes. "Shut up, Sage," she said good-naturedly. "We gotta go. My date is waiting, so are you coming with me or not?" She pushed herself up from the table.

At her mention of a date, I nearly bit my tongue clenching my jaw.

"I guess so, since you're my ride." Sage drained the last drop of wine from her glass. "I have to get back to Arlo anyway. If I stay too long, Christian will make himself *too* comfortable. When he offered to puppysit, I didn't think he'd try to move in."

"A live-in dog sitter like a live-in nanny?" Lina winked at her friend.

"One of my favorite romance tropes." Romy sighed dreamily. "Single dog mom with the puppy sitter? That could be hot."

Sage rolled her eyes. "Okay, bitches. I'm out of here."

Romy laughed, hugging Sage. "Thank you so much for coming."

"I'll see you in three weeks for the bachelorette party," Lina said, embracing Romy.

"The Rooster is providing all the booze," Sage confirmed, mentioning the bar she worked at as she shouldered her bag.

"And I won't get to drink any of it." Romy pouted, but her face was soft and loving as she gazed at the swaddled baby in the bassinet on the counter.

Lina hugged Jude. "Watch over your girls for me."

My gut twisted seeing Lina grow serious and Jude's jaw go tight. They shared a silent understanding as they looked at each other. I glanced back at Romy, but she didn't even seem to notice, picking up the rest of the dirty dishes and taking them to the sink. Jude must not have told her about Junior's release yet.

We finished our farewells, and I watched Lina's fine ass as she walked out in her heels on the way to her fucking date. Yet another date I had to watch her go on. At this point, after this morning's encounter, I was starting to think she was either in denial or doing it hoping to get a rise out of me.

Standing, I announced, "I'll get Penn to bed, but then I have to head out. I still need to get the fifth wheel packed and hooked up to my truck."

"Thank you for doing this, Reed." Jude gripped my shoulder, giving it a squeeze. "It's killing me not to be able to go with her."

"You and Chuck have a lot of other issues to deal with." I leaned down to wipe the sauce from Penn's mouth. "It's the least I can do to help. Especially now that you're also helping me out with Penn while I'm gone. So thank you."

"We'll have the double-wide ready for you when you get back."

"Thanks, boss."

Jude nodded. "Take care of my cousin, and we're square."

"Nothing's going to happen to her while I'm there."

I'd make fucking sure of it.

Jude patted my shoulder again, his face stoic and serious.

Romy had a big smile on her face. "I think you're just what Lina needs."

I sighed, picking up Penn. I wasn't sure about that, but she needed to stop dating these fucking douchebags.

"Come on, princess, let's get you to bed." Penn wrapped her arms around me and laid her head on my shoulder, releasing a big yawn.

After brushing her teeth and changing her into pajamas, I lay down with her in the bedroom that was to be hers while

I was away.

"Daddy?" she asked through a yawn, her voice quiet and sleepy.

"Yes, Penn?"

"Can I see the horsies tomorrow?"

I blew out an exhale. It was killing me to have to be away from her when she needed me the most.

"You can see them every day from now on," I told her, leaning down to kiss her forehead. I breathed in her sweet scent, trying to memorize it, imprint it on my soul until I could hold her again.

My chest squeezed, wishing none of this was our reality.

CHAPTER 10
Lina

Luke, the bartender from Joseph, pulled his SUV up to the big house, the headlights cutting across the driveway. As if he heard the sound of the motor, a figure stepped out from the fifth wheel that was now hooked up to his Dodge Ram. The lights illuminated him as he stood there like a hulking, domineering shadow. *Reed.*

Of course! I heaved a sigh before turning to Luke in my seat, plastering a smile on my face. "I had a great time tonight. Thank you for the drink."

Luke put his car in park. The guy was cute, I'll give him that. Tousled hair and only a shadow of scruff along his square jaw. He had dimples on either side of his mouth, and it turned out he had a witty sense of humor that had me in stitches all night as we sipped drinks at The Rooster.

"I'm glad I reached out when I got into town." He turned toward me and stretched to rest his hand on my headrest, his dimples deepening with a smile. He had a great smile.

My eyes flicked back to Reed, who stood in the dark, his arms across his chest, watching us like an overbearing father. Irritation skittered beneath my skin like a thousand little bugs.

Luke followed my gaze before looking back at me. "Seems like we have an audience. Brother?"

I shook my head against the seat. "Ignore him." I reached out, resting my hand on his cheek.

Luke's eyes heated, and his tongue flicked out across his lip in anticipation.

"Thanks for the date." I leaned forward, pressing my lips to his. They were plush and soft, which didn't surprise me because the guy applied ChapStick as if it were part of his personality.

He smiled into the kiss, but he didn't deepen it, pulling away. It was a nice kiss, but it didn't heat my veins.

"I'll tell my buddies about your suggestion to hike Thomas Rock," he told me.

I grabbed my purse, putting it over my shoulder before opening the door. "You won't regret it. The views are incredible when you get to the top."

"Not sure I'd regret much concerning you." He flashed a flirty smile. "Can I text you?"

I nodded. I wouldn't mind a second date. "I had fun. See ya, Luke."

"Bye, Lina," he said, getting ready to put his car in gear.

I hopped out, closing the door behind me. Stepping away from the SUV, I stood in the headlights to wave goodbye. My back was to Reed, and I could almost feel the heat of his eyes. I continued to wave as Luke backed out of the driveway and down the gravel road.

Reed huffed behind me. "Cowboy killer," he murmured softly.

I spun around to face him with a glare. His arms were

crossed, his face cast in shadows, but his eyes looked like two smoldering pieces of coal burning into me.

"Except he isn't a cowboy." I gave him my most evil smirk before turning away to walk toward the quiet house. My feet were killing me in these heels. "He's a bartender."

"Fucking worse."

I brushed past him. "At least he isn't just some fucking cowboy."

A growl released from Reed's throat at my taunting words. His hand whipped out like the mouth of a rattler, latching on to me and swinging me back to him. He stepped into me, sending me backward until he had my back pressed against the side of the camper.

"Aw, you found yourself a pretty boy. I bet he'll even thank you after you let him come. Newsflash, sweetheart. He can't—and won't—be able to give you what you need and want. He'll want it gentle, while you'll want it rough."

Perhaps that was true. I had yet to meet someone who could give me what I wanted, but I was always willing to try.

I raised my chin, stubbornly staring him in the eyes. Challenging him with a sly smile. "Oh, and you think you can give me what I want, cowboy?"

"Baby ..." His other hand went to my throat, squeezing lightly. His heavy gaze dragged down my face until it settled on my lips.

My eyes widened. He leaned in. My breath caught. He was going to kiss me.

Reed *fucking* Ownstead was going to kiss me.

Did I want it? Yes, right now, I fucking wanted it. I leaned into his grasp, my body betraying how much I wanted it.

"You need a man who is willing to let you explore every hidden desire." His voice went deep, quiet, and sultry.

Yes. I swallowed hard, feeling his hand only tighten.

"Who you can submit to."

Yes. I was tired of being the dominant one in bed. It meant my needs were never taken care of, and I was always left unsatisfied.

"And still make you feel like you are powerful and in control."

Fuck yes. I needed to feel worshipped, not just desired. I wanted to feel like I could completely let go while also feeling seen and empowered. No one had ever done that for me. I thought I'd felt that once with Reed, before it all went to shit.

My heart sped up, my lips parted, and I hoped he could read my face because I was pleading with him to do it.

"Who said I'd submit to you?" I dared.

He leaned even closer. My eyes shuddered closed as his lips brushed mine. I could feel the air leave his lungs in heavy puffs. His hands tightened even more at my neck and arm, the rest of his body pressing into me. His hips shifted slightly until I could feel his hard cock press into my belly. Desire pooled between my legs. Fuck, I was in trouble if this was how it was going to be on the road.

"Fuck," I breathed out loud, lifting my face even more until my mouth was perfectly lined up with his. Wishing he would just close the distance already.

"You can't lie to me, sweetheart. Your body is telling me everything you want, and it's this," he said as he slowly pushed his dick against me even more. I bit back a moan. "I bet I'd find you soaked between those pretty thighs of yours—and not because of the pretty boy who just drove away."

I inhaled heavily through my nose. He was right. My panties were growing damp, and I fucking ached for him. Luke hadn't even made my pussy flutter.

"Kiss me," I practically begged, my eyes still closed.

But he was quiet. I waited, but he still didn't close the distance. I frowned.

My eyes blinked open. My heart dropped when I saw him pull back, then felt him loosen his grip.

His eyes jumped between my lips and my eyes. "No, I don't think I will."

"W-w-what?" I stammered, confused, the rejection tightening my throat.

He let go of me then, taking a step back. "I'm not kissing you, though I think you need to be thoroughly kissed and by someone who knows how you like it. But there is no fucking way I'm kissing you, tasting some other man on your lips."

The feeling of rejection quickly turned to anger. "Oh, fuck you!"

"Only when you quit dating these fucking douchebags."

I spun on my heels, flipping him off over my shoulder as I stormed toward the house. "Fuck you if you think I'm ever going to let you fuck me again."

Reed's soft chuckle followed me in the front door. I was lying to myself—and to him—and I knew he could see right through it.

"We'll see about that," I heard him say in the dark.

I slammed the door behind me. Ugh! I hated him so much. This was going to be the longest circuit in the history of rodeo circuits.

Reed was officially my fucking shadow. By the end of our six-hour drive the next day, we pulled up to the campground at the Big Basin Buckeroo in Idaho. While I was unloading Mushu, Reed didn't waste any time setting up the temporary electric enclosure beside the trailer, filling his water bucket, or dishing him out a flake of hay. As soon as I left to check in, he hovered like a damn hawk, ready to dive, talons primed, if someone so much as looked at me wrong. Of course he was glowering and brooding the whole fucking time.

"You got the fancy shit." Kale whistled when he saw us walking through camp. "So does that mean we're partying at your strip?"

"Hell yeah," I said.

At the same time, Reed said, "No."

I gave him a glaring side-eye. "Back off, *daddy*."

His eyes only darkened at that. *Shit, that's hot.* It was like a warning, but I liked playing with fire.

"I see you brought a bodyguard with you. Shit. Christian told me what you're dealing with. I'm so sorry, Lina. We'll keep a lookout for this asshole."

"I got it handled," Reed said firmly behind me.

I rolled my eyes so only Kale could see. "Thanks, Kale. You're both welcome to come by and chill tonight."

Kale looked at me, then Reed, then back at me. Whatever

he read on Reed's face made him take a step back. I chanced a glance toward him. He was taking his job here a little too seriously. If he kept this up, I wasn't going to have any fun while I was out here. So much for letting off some steam with my friends.

"Uh … I'll text you later," Kale said before walking off.

I shook my head, storming back toward our fifth wheel camper, not even taking the time to see if Reed was following me. From the sound of the boots behind me, he was right on my tail.

Mushu glanced up from his feed as soon as we approached, his eyes curious.

I stopped at the side of his pen, spinning around to face Reed. Surprised, Reed skidded to a stop, his head lifting to stare at me beneath his cowboy hat.

"Look." I folded my arms across my chest, staring him square in the eye. "If you think you're going to run my social life while I'm here, I can promise you that we'll both end up miserable. If you're here to make sure that creeper doesn't get anywhere near me—which I appreciate—you're going to need to back the fuck off. I also have a job to do, and if all I have is you breathing down my neck every second of every day, you're going to stress me the fuck out. I need quiet and calm when I'm preparing for an event. And when I'm not, I need to be able to let loose and throw shit to the wind. You got it?"

Reed's jaw ticked, his brow furrowing. He didn't seem to like what I had to say very much. "Got it. Spoken loud and clear."

He walked around me, heading up the steps of the camper

to press the button to extend the window where his bed would be—in the convertible kitchenette. I shook my head. There was no way anyone was going to want to party at our RV strip with this party pooper glowering in the corner the whole time. I'd just have to go elsewhere to unwind, but how the fuck was I going to lose Reed? But even the thought of being out without his protection scared me a little.

Shit, this was so fucked up.

Chapter 11
Reed

Lina dropped her hands, giving Mushu his head as they sped through the alley into the arena. She sat atop the saddle like the fucking queen she was—long and lean, and stretched out low on his neck as they moved to the first barrel. Leaning back in her saddle, she looked over her shoulder at her next target. They were magnificent together as they moved as one, looping around and heading toward the second barrel at breakneck speed.

It was hard to drag my eyes away from her. My stomach twisted up in knots watching the timer tick up while scanning the crowd for threats. Not knowing what the fucking creep looked like had me on edge during the entire race. He could be anywhere. It made me want to rage that I couldn't keep him from watching her.

Lina and Mushu had already rounded the third barrel and were heading home when my eyes returned to her, so I readied myself at the gate to meet them.

She flew in, stopping the timer and locking in her time. She pulled up on the reins and let out a whoop as Mushu slowed to a near-skidding stop. The saddle creaked as she turned to check her time. I gripped Mushu's bridle, helping to steady him.

"I did it! I hit my old record, baby!" She was beaming, her face bright and her brown eyes dancing.

My breath hitched in my throat. Fuck, I wanted her to look at me that way, but she was leaning down to stroke Mushu's neck and whisper praises in his flicking ear. I never thought I'd be jealous of a horse, but here I was—for more than one fucking reason.

"You back on track?" one of her fellow contestants and friends asked while she and her horse waited in the hole.

Lina sat up straight in the saddle, her smile never faltering. "Back in the running, Viv. Good luck, Paige!" she called cheerily to the next rider at the gate.

But Paige, who was on deck, shot her a bitchy glare before turning her attention back to the arena while her trainer helped hold her horse steady. Lina only shrugged, turning her smile on me. I couldn't help my lips from tugging at the corners. God, she was beautiful. One brow raised in question, probably wondering why I was staring at her like a fool. She shook her head as if she didn't want to know, a soft laugh escaping her throat.

"How'd I do, cowboy?" Her mouth settled into a flirty smirk while her eyes turned playful.

"You burned the breeze," I told her.

"Oh." She laughed. "You're good." Then she shook her head again.

"What do you mean?" I asked, confused.

She continued to shake her head while she chuckled. "Don't start flirting with me now, cowboy. Not unless you intend to do something about it."

It was my turn to shake my head with laughter. She wasn't wrong. I wanted to fucking do something about it. It had taken everything in me not to kiss her the other night when she came back from her date. When she more than begged me to kiss her. I cleared my throat to keep the words from spewing out.

"Okay, sweetheart." I heaved a sigh. "Let's get you and Mushu—"

"You were incredible out there!" Kale yelled as he and Christian strode toward us. Their chaps flapped in the wind as they walked, their numbers pinned on their vests, ready for their event.

"Thanks!" Lina called back, dismounting. "Don't get bucked off!"

"Don't plan to," Christian said as they met up with us.

"Good because we're going to turn up tonight." Lina handed the reins over to me while she hugged her friends. "Break a leg, guys!"

They parted ways while they headed to the chutes, and we walked Mushu away from the arena.

"Where are we going to get drinks?" I asked, since the fairgrounds only had a beer garden that closed at ten.

Her head swiveled to look at me, her gaze narrowing. "What we're *not* going to do is manage my social calendar."

"I heard you, Lina, but I'm here to do a job."

Both of our smiles faltered, and I cringed inwardly at how harsh my words sounded. Fuck, I was an asshole. But how could I tell her I didn't want to just be here because I was being paid to protect her? She was the one who had to remind me that was the only reason I was here in the first place. There was no way in hell she actually wanted me here with her. She couldn't stand me.

"Jesus fucking Christ," she said under her breath as she stormed off, leaving Mushu and me to follow behind.

"Fuck you!" she said, grabbing her drink out of my hand.

Well, that didn't take long. I was just waiting for her to curse me out. Especially with the way the night was going. She was in rare form.

The dive bar in town was seedy and full of cigarette smoke. Christian and Kale were surrounded by women who flocked to them as soon as they walked in. The buckle bunnies all shot Lina scathing looks as she easily pulled the guys' attention away from them. I couldn't help my own spike of jealousy blazing through my chest while I watched her laugh and flirt with every man in her vicinity. Even the good ol' boys sipping their beer bottles at the bar turned on the charm for her.

Neon lights cut through the haze, making her look like a sexy demon, bathing her in a red glow. The stereo speakers were so loud, you could barely hear anyone talk. Everyone had to lean in to yell into each other's ears, and the way she was leaning toward every man who bought her a drink had me on fucking edge. Was I a jealous man? For Lina, I was all sorts of things. Jealousy was at the top of that list. If I had to watch one more jackass offer to buy her a drink, I was going to end up knocking someone on their ass.

"You're drunk," I told her.

"So fucking what," she shouted in my ear, her hot breath sending shivers down my spine. "Just do your *job* and leave me alone. My stalker isn't even here."

Oh, so that was what this was about. "I'm not leaving you alone, Lina."

"You can do your job from ten feet that way." She gestured to the entrance with her drink in her hand. The whiskey and soda sloshed over her fingers and dripped onto our boots.

I frowned. "Maybe we should call it a night."

She pulled away to shake her head, like an obstinate child. "Too late for you, old man?"

"Thirty-seven ain't old, killer."

Lina rolled her eyes. Fucking brat. "Oh, *okay*. Well, you can go if it's past your bedtime. Christian and Kale are here, and I can head back to camp when they're ready."

I wasn't about to leave her, especially when she was wasted. I crossed my arms over my chest and gave her the stern look that worked on Penn when she didn't want to pick up her toys. "I'm not going anywhere."

She didn't seem at all fazed by my tone. Instead, she seemed emboldened by it, ready to play with fire.

Her glossy lips circled around the straw in her drink, her eyes peeking at me from beneath her dark fringe of lashes. *Fuck.* That look while she sucked on her straw went straight to my cock.

"Fine. You're a stubborn asshole. Guess I'm not going to get any dick while I'm on circuit, am I?" She whined in a slightly lowered tone. "God, I'm so fucking horny right now."

I gulped. "Fuck, sweetheart. You can't say shit like that."

My cock throbbed painfully as her eyes coyly flitted up to mine.

"No? Why not?" She took a step forward, her toes bumping mine, her eyes challenging me.

I ducked my head down to talk in her ear, my cowboy hat shifting to allow her head to invade my space. God, she smelled amazing. Like vanilla and flowers. "You're right. You're not going to get some while I'm on circuit with you."

She turned her head, her lips brushing the shell of my ear. "Because you're a … Cock. Block?" She enunciated the last two words with a click of her tongue.

I nearly shuddered with how her breath caressed my skin, but I couldn't help chuckling at her question. "Guess I am. We both know there's only one cock you should be riding."

Lina pulled back slightly to look me in the eyes. "If you think you're talking about your own—"

"No more douchebags, remember?" I cut her off. "You deserve better than that."

"And you think that's you?"

My chest clenched. I didn't know if I was better for her, but I'd do everything in my fucking power to prove to her how sorry I was. "I can treat you better than any of these fucking pricks." I gestured to the bar where men had approached her and bought her drinks all night.

Fire burned in her eyes, and she looked even more like a succubus from hell with the neon reflecting off her. "You haven't so far, asshole."

"*Lina*, I've apologized. When are you going to forgive me?"

"When you stop killing my vibe and give me fucking space to breathe."

I wasn't about to argue with her when she was drunk. Her words were starting to slur.

"Ugh!" She threw up her hands in irritation when I didn't attempt to move. "Can you at least get yourself a drink, loosen up, and go sit somewhere else?"

"I don't drink, Lina. I've been sober for 386 days."

Narrowed with annoyance, her eyes appeared to soften as I watched her do the mental math … 386 days of sobriety … 386 days since I fucked up … 386 days since I met Lina Larsen. And 386 days of trying to convince myself that I wasn't such a horrible person, but rather, someone worthy of redemption.

I don't know what I was expecting from her, but silence wasn't it. I sucked air through my nose, disappointed. "Fine. Fuck it. I'll give you your space."

Her face fell, making my own heart go with it, while I walked away to post myself up at an empty high-top table by the door. She stood there for a moment, staring into her drink as if she didn't actually want me to give her more space. She had to realize I hadn't had a drink since Joseph—over a year ago now—when I fucked things up with her.

I had to clench my fists on my thighs to keep from going back over there and tugging her into my arms until she melted for me. Because that's what I fucking wanted more than anything.

I wanted to see her go soft for me, to run my fingers through her hair until I could pull her head back and line her mouth up with mine, kissing her until she went weak in the knees and gave in to me. I didn't know how much more of this I could take without touching her the way I really wanted to.

Chapter 12
Reed

Lina barely spoke to me as we packed up and moved out, heading to the St. John Rodeo in Washington. I wanted to explain to her the boundaries I'd set for myself after our night together. It had to count for something. It didn't excuse my behavior that night, but it had to lend weight to my apology now. But the fact that she hadn't responded to it only made me further disappointed. What was going on in her head?

By the day of her event, she wasn't even making eye contact with me. She had officially iced me out. It had only been a few days, and it was obvious she already needed a break. And maybe I needed one, too. It didn't help that I had to wake up every morning to her fumbling in the dark in nothing but a thong and thin sleepshirt while she made herself breakfast. Then being forced to give up my shitty bench bed so she could have her table back. Thank God she used up all the hot water by the time I got to the shower. Otherwise, my dick would be completely chafed by now. My nerves were officially fraying at the edges.

Whatever frustration and anger Lina held inside she

seemed to channel when it was her turn to run. She powered all her aggression into her heels, giving Mushu his head and winning yet another event. She was well on her way to being the top contender for the circuit finals in October. And if it meant being an asshole to get her there, I'd do my best to challenge her and piss her off every damn day. It definitely helped that she was sexy as hell when she was being pissy.

Mushu deserved all the praise and oats he could get for taking her to the top, and I'd gladly dish it out if it kept everyone happy. Giving him the rubdown he earned in his pen beside the trailer, I nearly missed the flash of tan skin and the stomp of heeled boots on the trailer steps. Lina was dressed in a tight black dress with a lace overlay that hit midthigh. It hugged her curves and gave me a delicious peek of her perky tits. I gripped the brush in my hand so hard, I didn't realize I was pressing it against Mushu's flank until he whipped his tail in my face.

"Where do you think you're going?" I called after her, her back now to me as my gaze traveled down her body. She looked sexy as hell in all black, and I wondered if her underwear matched. I couldn't help picturing my hands encompassing her bare waist while my pinky fingers dragged just beneath the waistband of those panties as she straddled me. My cock answered with a twitch.

Fuck. Yep, my nerves were fucking frayed.

She flipped her brown hair over her shoulder, her dark eyes slanting to mine. "Out. Christian and Kale offered to take me."

"They better be fucking going with you," I gritted out in near pain.

"My stalker isn't here. He hasn't been. Pretty sure he got the message when I kneed him in the balls weeks ago."

Perhaps she was right. There hadn't been any sign of the creep. I tried to ease the pain by exhaling a long breath. Fine. As much as I hated it, a break from being in her presence twenty-four seven would do my soul—and blue balls––some good.

"Do you have your phone?" I asked.

Her eyebrows shot up. "My phone? Yes …"

"Bring it here." I set down the brush and dusted my hands off on my jeans.

She walked over to where I was in the pen, pulling her cell out of her purse, unlocking it, and handing it to me.

"I'm putting in my number. You're going to call me when you're ready to come home." I clamped my teeth together at my last word. Home with her sounded way too good to my own ears. My head bowed over her screen as I punched in my number. I chanced a glance at her, but she didn't seem fazed by my insinuation. "Don't leave the bar until I get there."

"You're not going to demand to go with me?" She seemed as surprised as I was that I was letting her go without me.

"You told me you needed space to breathe. The last thing I'd want to do is make you feel confined, like you need to be tamed, like you aren't allowed to let loose sometimes." I handed back her phone, hoping my words sunk in. I was tired of her putting herself out there for dudes who didn't appreciate her wild side. Lina Larsen wasn't too much. To me, she was just right.

Lina's eyes went wide with surprise, her mouth falling

slightly open. "You're really letting me go by myself?"

"With Christian and Kale. You're not going to be by yourself, and you're going to call me when you're done so I can make sure you get back safely."

She placed her phone back in her purse, nodding. "All right. I'll call you when I'm ready to come home." Her smile grew, turning to leave. Hearing her refer to our little camper trailer as "home," just as I had, made my chest tighten.

"And if it's past midnight, then I'm fucking coming after you!" I called after her.

She grinned over her shoulder, her eyes twinkling, as she walked away. "I wouldn't expect anything less, cowboy."

My body was thrumming with anger and anticipation—anticipation of feeding the fire I was about to face as I stormed into the rodeo bar twenty minutes after midnight. The full bar was loud with country music blaring from the speakers, drunken laughter and hollering, and boots clacking on the wood floors as dancers two-stepped. She hadn't called or texted. I had warned her I'd come after her. My muscles tightened, preparing to mete out my anger and be verbally lashed by Lina's viperous tongue. If she would only fucking listen, I wouldn't have to worry.

I kept telling myself she was fine as I walked the six minutes from our cowboy camp to the bar on the rodeo grounds. Gripping my cell phone in my hand, I kept checking my screen, expecting a text as I charged into the bar, ready to fight her if I had to.

My eyes scanned the dark room, searching for that tight black dress, my ears straining to hear her sexy, throaty laughter over the din of the bar. I could feel the fear rising in my chest, needing to see her, needing to find her and make sure she was safe.

I couldn't see her. I couldn't hear her. Where the hell was she?

I pushed through the crowd toward the bar, trying to home in on her, hoping I could tap into my inner compass and it would point to her. I spun on my heels, my vision narrowing.

She wasn't here. I could feel it.

I spotted Christian and Kale, spinning girls on the dance floor, both of them oblivious to the fact that Lina wasn't right where she needed to be. With *them*.

Navigating around the dancers, I grabbed Christian's arm, halting him in his steps. Christian's eyes went wide, surprised to see me, while his dance partner smiled up at me expectantly, as if she thought I was cutting in.

"Where is she?" I demanded.

"She's … she's." Christian stumbled on his words, his own eyes taking in our surroundings, searching. "Shit, she was just over there at the bar."

"What's going on?" Kale asked, dancing with his date over to us.

"Where's Lina?" I growled. My heart was starting to pound.

"She's probably just in the bathroom," Kale suggested, doing his own assessment of the room, looking toward the hallway marked Restrooms.

"Help me find her."

Kale and Christian nodded, my own worry mirrored in their faces, before dismissing the girls as we picked our way through the crowd. I didn't care one fucking bit when I swung open the door to the women's restroom. Even when I got dirty looks and was told to "get the fuck out."

"Lina? Are you in here?"

There was no fucking answer.

Panic gripped my throat.

"She didn't leave with anyone?" I asked, running into Kale on the way out of the restroom.

"No. She'd tell us if she was leaving. We made her promise to let us know when you were coming to pick her up."

I pushed out a breath, my hands resting on my hips, staring at my boots.

"She's not here." Christian confirmed our worries as he approached us in the hallway.

"Fuck." She could be anywhere now.

I looked at my cell phone. Still nothing.

Christian and Kale pulled out their own phones, shooting texts to Lina before trying to call her. My heart pounded in my ears. I couldn't just stand here hoping they'd get ahold of her. I had to fucking move. I had to fucking find her. She could be anywhere. Every precious second we waited could be putting her closer to danger.

Christian had my number from working on the ranch. "Call me if you find her," I told him, moving around them and heading toward the door. "I'm going to go find her."

I didn't wait for their reply, bulldozing my way out of

the bar into the cool night air, the music fading behind me. I searched the parking lot, which was more like an open field of trucks and trailers. People still mingled, coming and going from the bar. The electric guitar and drumbeats of the late-night concert on the grounds, followed by the crowd's cheers, could be heard in the distance. Weaving between the cars, my head on a swivel, my eyes narrowed in on every little flash of brown hair and tanned skin in my periphery. Where the fuck was she?

I turned down another parking lane, heading back in the direction of camp. A man in a plaid shirt and jeans with an unkempt beard walked ahead of me, ducking between cars with his arm around someone. I picked up my pace, following him. Black boots stumbled and he stopped, hoisting her back up on her feet.

Long legs in black boots. I jogged over. My heart pounded. *Lina.* He pulled her toward him, his arm around her waist.

"Get the fuck away from her!" I yelled, coming up behind him, my fists balling at my sides.

His head whipped toward me. Seeing me coming, he spun on his heels, planting his feet firmly to face me.

"Mind your own fucking business." He pushed Lina behind him, as if he needed to protect her from me.

I was closing in on them, my long strides taking me to her.

"Get. The. Fuck. Away. From. Her!" I gritted each word out from between my teeth. My knuckles popped and cracked, I was clenching them so hard. Fear and murderous rage boiled up in my throat. I instinctively reached for the gun at my waist, but I'd left it in my bag.

"We're just going back to my trailer. Huh, baby?" He threw over his shoulder where I saw Lina's head loll slightly, but she didn't say a fucking word. Something was wrong. Something was terribly wrong about the way she was sluggish and not speaking. There was no way she would go silently with this guy.

I took my final steps to close the distance, my fingers flexing, readying to strike. My momentum carried me as I cocked my arm back and sent my fist right into his face. His nose crunched under my knuckles. He cried out, his hands going to his face. I didn't wait to see if he'd respond with his own hit. I wasn't about to let this guy leave.

"What the fuck—" He barely got the words out before I went in for an uppercut beneath his chin. He bumped into Lina as she sagged behind him and then stumbled back against a nearby truck.

I glanced at her, her glazed eyes going slightly wide, but her face was so slack. Yep, something was definitely wrong with her.

"Did you drug her, you fucking creep?" Blood was dripping from his nose and down his chin.

I gripped him by the shirt collar, sending my left fist into the side of his head and throwing him to the ground. "I'll ask you one more fucking time. Did you roofie her fucking drink?" I kicked him in his side as he crumpled up into the fetal position. He moaned and coughed.

"Reed?" I heard Lina ask, as if she just realized I was here.

I kicked him again before bending to land another punch into his bloody face. I grabbed his shirt, pulling him up to look me in the eyes. "Who the fuck are you?" I shook him, his head rolling loosely on his neck. "Who the fuck are you?" I spat out.

"Reed?" Lina asked again, her hand settling on my arm, stilling me. I looked over my shoulder at her, quickly assessing her up and down to make sure she wasn't injured. Maybe there were no physical marks on her, but she looked confused … like she wasn't sure if she was actually seeing me.

"Yeah, it's me," I told her, turning back to the asshole who was now a rag doll in my grip. "What the fuck did you do to her?" I seethed in his face. "What did you give her?" I shook him.

His brows pinched, his eyes rolling, attempting to focus. It looked disconcerting with his bloody grin, as if he thought this was fucking funny. "The slut wanted it."

I saw fucking *red*. Enraged, murderous red.

"That was the wrong fucking thing to say." I reeled my arm back, wanting to finish this guy, but by the looks of him, one more hit, and I was going to put him to sleep. I gripped his shirt harder, drawing him closer until we were nose to nose. "Stay the fuck away from her. If I see your ugly ass face again— or if you so much as approach her—my fist in your face will feel like child's play compared to what I will do to you."

And with a final punch and another crunch of his nose, I let his head fall back and dropped him to the dirt.

I didn't waste any time, stepping over his body and gathering Lina into my arms. I ducked my head into her hair, breathing in her sweet floral scent, assuring myself that she was safe.

She was trembling. Maybe out of fear, a chill, or the drugs coursing through her system. Just the thought of it made me want to turn back around and end the unconscious asshole on the ground for good, but it was time to take care of her. She needed me right now. Using the feeling of her pressed against me to center me, to cool my fury, I released a heavy breath.

"Come on. Let's get you back to the trailer," I said, picking her up. She may have been able to walk, but I wanted to get us out of here as quickly as possible. Not just because I didn't want us to be found beside a dude beaten to a pulp, but because I needed to make sure she was okay and as far away from him as possible.

I carried her to the bed in the front of the fifth wheel, laying her down on the mattress.

My fingers encircled her leg below her knee to pull off her boots. Her skin was like silk. I couldn't resist letting my fingers linger on her calf while I removed one boot, then the other, leaving her socks on.

She stretched out like a damn cat with her arms over her head, arching her back, pressing her tits in the air while her dress hiked up her legs until it was bunched at the apex of her thighs, giving me a peek at her panties.

Fuck me. *Black.* I was right.

Focus! Not the time for this.

"Stay right there," I told her, heading toward the kitchenette to pour her a glass of water.

"This feels––feels funny." She started giggling behind me until I was back by her side with the water.

"Here, drink this." I helped her sit up while she leaned on

her elbows, tipping the glass to her lips.

Her eyes fluttered up to mine, taking me in while she sipped. She plopped back on the pillow without warning, making the water slosh over the edge. Her teeth scraped across her full bottom lip, now wet from the glass.

She released a big sigh, as if exasperated. "You shouldn't come to the bar with me."

"We're not going to the bar, baby," I told her. "We're back at the camper."

Her brows pinched in confusion, and her mouth curved into a frown. "I'd never make you come with me if I knew, but I didn't know. You should have told me."

"What are you talking about, sweetheart?" She wasn't making much sense.

"You don't drink, and I forced you to be around *all* that alcohol." She waved her arms around to emphasize the amount of liquor being poured at the bars, and I had to bite my lip to keep from smiling.

"Don't worry about that." I shook my head. Her arms plopped back onto the bed. "It's a boundary I set for myself after my poor judgment hurt you. I'd follow you through hell, even if it meant fighting my demons to get to you."

Her face softened at my words.

"You came after me," she whispered, her thoughts seemingly skipping around. The moon cast light through the window, bathing her in the white glow, shining off her warm locks fanned out across the pillow.

"I told you I would."

The serene look on her face turned into a scowl. "Is that

why you followed me home?"

It was my turn to frown. "What do you mean?"

"Why you showed up at my ranch."

"I didn't know it was your ranch, but I'd hoped," I told her honestly.

"Fucking Reed." She said it like she was used to saying it to herself. Like it was a common curse coming out of her perfect, rosy mouth. She stretched again, licking her lips. "Why is everything spinning? Didn't you lay me down? I feel like Jell-O."

"I know, baby. He put something in your drink. You're not going to feel very good in a little bit."

I slipped my cell out of my pocket, shooting Christian a text that I found her and she was safe.

"Who did? What drink? I don't have a drink." Lina held out her hands, turning them in the air as if she was magically going to find a beverage in her grasp. She sat up and tried to swing her legs over the edge of the bed.

"Whoa there, sweetheart." I gripped her shoulders, steadying her. "Just one of the many douchebags I keep trying to tell you about."

"I have a fucking stalker, Reed," she whined, plopping back onto the mattress.

"Not for much longer." I'd make sure of it.

She sluggishly lifted her arm, resting her palm on my cheek. Her warm, brown eyes smiled at me. "You came after me, cowboy." She repeated herself.

"I'll always come after you."

Her hand felt so warm against my face. I wanted to lean

into it, brush my lips against her fingertips.

"Do you believe in love at first sight?" she whispered, as if talking to herself.

"I think I do." Because God, the pain in my chest right now seeing her like this, the pull I felt whenever she was near, like we were two fucking magnets, and the ache in my heart whenever she was gone, made me feel things I've never felt before. I thought I'd been in love with my ex-wife, but it never felt like this. The closest I think I ever really knew of true love was what I felt for my daughter, but this was different. This feeling of slowly dying not being able to touch her, to claim her as mine, hit me like a tidal wave the moment I saw her in the Saddle Room over a year ago. And I was still drowning.

"I thought I did, too." She frowned again, dropping her hand from my face. "The moment I saw you across that bar. I thought you were the one. I'd never felt so instantly attracted to someone before. It was like our souls were begging to dance while I watched you."

I sucked in a breath, the air freezing in my chest. "You did?" My words felt weak, shriveled, yet desperate with hope.

She nodded her head against the pillow. "I loved you, you fucking asshat." Her face crumpled as though she was about to cry.

"*Lina.*" I said her name on an exhale, slicing me right through the heart. "I'm so, so sorry. When I took you back to the house, it was to piss off my ex. But when I saw your face and how hurt you were, I knew I would do anything to make it up to you. From that moment on, you never left my thoughts. I didn't know how many times I would have to apologize, but if it meant every day for the rest of my life, I'd write it on my fucking tombstone."

"I think I'm going to be sick," she said, slapping a hand to her mouth. I grabbed the trash can, taking a seat beside her on the bed while I pulled her hair back and she puked it all out.

"That's it. Get it out," I soothed, rubbing a hand along her back while she continued to retch.

"Ugh," she moaned, wiping the back of her hand across her mouth. "This is terrible."

I helped her drink another sip of water, and she groaned in pain while she lay back down. "I know, baby, but I'll be right here the whole time." Helping her strip off her dress, pulling one of her T-shirts over her head, I shed my boots and jeans and crawled under the covers beside her, ready to help her if she needed it.

Even though she was safe, her warm body beside me, I knew this was going to be a long night. My whole body was on fire now being so close to her, but I wouldn't allow myself to touch her while she was in this state. There was an inferno of rage burning inside me, begging to be let out and unleash on that asshole, whom I left bloody and unconscious. A concussion and a broken nose was too good for that fucker. Between my throbbing cock and my body buzzing like a live wire, ready to protect her, there was no way in hell I was going to get any sleep tonight lying beside Lina Larsen.

Chapter 13
Lina

Was I dying?

I moaned, my hand rubbing my mouth. Spit had dried at the corner, and I wiped it away. God, my mouth tasted like ass. I smacked my lips. It was as dry as the Arizona desert. My bones hurt, too. Even my scalp fucking ached. What the hell happened last night?

I groaned, starting to stretch, but then froze, realizing something hard and warm was wedged between my legs, and a heavy arm. I lifted the sheet, and a very male arm with hair and veins lay across my stomach. Yep, that was his leg between mine, too. He shifted, his leg hitching up more until his knee was so close to rubbing right where I was starting to feel a pulse. His arm tightened around me. Then he pulled me to him, his thigh scraping against my sensitive skin, until my back was flush with his front.

Blinking to clear my vision, I reminded myself I was in our camper. That the person who was behind me had to be someone other than Reed … right?

Oh God! I turned to look over my shoulder.

"Shit," I whispered.

Reed lay behind me, spooning me, without a T-shirt. And based on the bare leg my pussy was now rubbing against, without fucking pants, either!

I turned slowly, silently praying he was wearing boxers. Silently praying I didn't do something stupid again.

Lifting the sheet, I looked down, hoping I wouldn't get an eyeful of Reed's dick because his morning wood was currently poking me in the ass. I breathed a sigh of relief. "Oh, thank God."

He thrust his hips, his hard-on pressing into me. "See something you like?"

I dropped the sheet at the sound of his voice. His rumbly, sexy, raspy morning voice that just vibrated through my entire body. My pussy clenched.

"No," I said, pushing him away from me. His hard pecs flexed under my hands. Christ! How does he make his muscles so … so … musclely? The man was carved out of fucking marble.

He removed his leg from between my knees, and I had to bite back a whine. Why wasn't he freaking out?

His mouth curved in a sleepy smirk, and he rubbed the scruff on his jaw. His dark eyes were soft, yet smoldered with an inner flame that made my skin feel as though it were on fire. Locks of dark hair fell across his forehead, begging me to run my fingers through it.

"Oh, God." I threw back the sheet, sitting up on the edge of the mattress. My head swam and I grasped it, just as a pounding headache set in. My legs were bare, too. I was practically naked, except for my sleepshirt and underwear.

"Fuck." I breathed into my hands.

"Do you feel like you're going to be sick?" he asked. The mattress dipped behind me as he moved, his hand going to the small of my back.

I stiffened.

"Yes," I groaned. I was two seconds from vomiting based on the way my stomach was now roiling.

"Here." He jumped out of bed, coming around to my side, bringing a trash can with a fresh bag close to my feet. "Or do you want me to help you to the bathroom?"

I looked at him then. Really, truly looked at him. His thick thighs dusted with hair as he crouched in front of me, his corded forearms resting on his knees, his abs flexing with each breath he took, his throat bobbing as he swallowed, his jaw ticking with concern, and his dark eyes with flecks of amber gazing at me with worry and something else I was entirely too afraid to name. My gut clenched and my heart sped up.

"Oh, God," I said again, pulling my attention away from him. I couldn't look at him anymore. I had to focus on anything *but* him. The window had a nice view of the camp—more like the side of the trailer beside us—but it was better than looking at him right now. "You and me. Did we …?"

"Lina." His voice sounded like he was smiling. "I don't think I've ever seen you at a loss for words."

Oh fuck the view! I shot a scathing look back at him, but he didn't even balk. "Did we fuck last night or not?"

Reed looked like he was having to bite the inside of his mouth to keep from smiling.

"Fuck you, Reed, if you think this is funny. I've never *once* gotten blackout drunk to the point of not remembering what happened the night before, and I feel like I should fucking remember if we—" Now I was the one biting the inside of my mouth. *Too close to the truth.* Because both times were still seared into my brain. "I don't even remember drinking that much."

Reed shook his head while his lips fought a smile. "We didn't. Believe me, I'd make sure you'd remember if we had."

"You're a dick." I huffed, relaxing my shoulders. Relief and regret settled in my chest.

Reed chuckled softly then. "Only for you, baby."

"Why do you have to be such an ass?"

"Do you have any other names you'd like to call me, or are you done?"

"Ugh!" I sprang to my feet, pushing past him, hoping he'd fall on his ass, but he only rocked on his heels while I made my way to the bathroom. "Maybe go back to just grunting all your words because the ones you say now are fucking annoying."

"Damn, sweetheart. You wound me."

"Oh, fuck off!" I slammed the door of the bathroom to the sound of his booming laughter.

Needing to wash it all off, I took a quick shower and brushed my teeth. By the time I was stepping out with a towel wrapped around me, I could smell fresh coffee and bacon on the stove. I peeked past the door to see Reed fully dressed in jeans and a T-shirt, tongs in his hand while he flipped the strips of bacon. Tiptoeing to grab my own jeans and shirt, I took my clothes back to the bathroom to dress.

"Do you want toast?" Reed called, not even turning around

to see me walk out. He didn't wait for my answer, putting two slices in the toaster on the counter.

"Are you seriously making me breakfast right now?" I asked.

"Already checked on Mushu and gave him breakfast, too."

My heart fluttered seeing this man with bare feet in the kitchenette, cooking over the stove for me. No one other than Dad ever made me breakfast. Not even my own mother.

Reed plucked the bacon from the pan, laying it out on a plate with a paper towel to soak up the grease.

"Here." He turned with a mug of coffee in his outstretched hand. I reached for it, our fingertips brushing while his eyes tracked over my body, leaving a trail of heat in their wake.

"Thank you." I swallowed the lump forming in my throat, wondering if I was going to throw up after all.

Reed gave a single nod. "Two sugars and a splash of milk, right?"

He knew how I made my coffee. I shuddered a breath. Why was getting my coffee order right making my chest tight? "Right."

"Let's sit and eat, and then I need to talk to you about what happened last night." The muscle in his jaw twitched and he averted his gaze, turning back to the toast that popped up.

"That doesn't sound good." Anxiety twisted my gut. I had a sickening feeling that what happened last night was bad, and the reason I couldn't remember anything had nothing to do with how much I drank. "What happened last night?"

I immediately started replaying everything I remembered. The last thing I recalled was heading to the bar ... or was it dancing with someone on the dance floor? And then making a beeline for the bar to get another drink. I think … it was only my second drink of the night, or was it my first? My heart rate sped up, my breath leaving my chest in little gasps. Why couldn't I fucking remember?

"I only had two drinks, I think." I'd heard of girls getting roofied in college, and maybe it happened on the circuit, too, but I was always so careful who I got drinks from. "I bought that last drink myself." How could someone have gotten something in my drink? I squeezed my eyes shut, trying to force my mind to recall the night. Did I turn away from my drink at any point while I was at the bar? Maybe? "I can't fucking remember anything." I was starting to get frustrated with myself that I didn't know what happened. I was on the edge of panicking.

"Let's sit down," Reed suggested, plating our food and setting it down on the table.

I slid onto the bench, and Reed sat down across from me. I set my coffee down, suddenly not wanting it or the food in front of me. A wave of nausea was threatening to overpower me.

"Please, just spit it out." I was growing impatient.

Reed's eyes were hard, as if he was remembering what I couldn't. He rested his elbows on either side of his plate and laced his fingers together, his gaze intent on me. "When you hadn't texted me by midnight, I came looking for you."

"Just like you said you would." The lump in my throat stung.

Reed nodded. "You weren't at the bar anymore. Christian and Kale didn't know where you'd gone, so we went looking for you."

"Did he—did *he* have me?" I swallowed the vomit. I hated throwing up. I'd much rather swallow it. I wrapped my hands around the warm mug, letting it settle me.

"He had you," he said matter-of-factly, knowing I just needed to hear the truth. One thing about Reed was that he was a straight shooter, and I was so appreciative of that. I needed someone who was willing to just rip off the Band-Aid and tell me like it was. "But I caught up to him and stopped him before he could take you."

My nose stung, and my mind immediately jumped to the worst case. "Oh, my fuck! He could have raped me." I had to say it out loud. I had to speak my thoughts into existence, or I'd spiral.

Reed shook his head. "No, he wouldn't have. There is no scenario here where I'd ever let that happen."

"Reed, he drugged me and took me away from the bar."

"He put something in your drink, you're right, but there is no way in hell he would've ever walked away with you. I was coming after you no matter the cost."

"Fuck." I dropped my forehead into my palm, propping it up to keep myself from passing out. "You could've been too late."

He reached over to me, his hand resting over the one still clutching my coffee. "Look at me," he said softly. I lifted my head, my gaze finding his for a moment. "I will always come after you." I could almost hear him swallow down the lump in his own throat.

Pain was etched all over his face. He was beating himself

up about this. *He was almost too late.* That's what that look told me.

"You stopped him?"

"We won't be seeing him again."

I gulped. "You didn't—" I couldn't say the word.

"No, I didn't. But he may wish I had. If he's smart, he'll stay far the fuck away from the circuit from now on."

"How can you be so sure?"

Reed's face fell, staring into his own mug of coffee. "I'm not."

He'd been right. He couldn't leave my side. Not anymore. Not when it was so easy for my stalker to slip something in my drink and drag me away without anyone noticing.

My head shot up, almost too quickly, the room spinning with it. I grimaced. "You didn't happen to get his name, did you?"

Reed's mouth turned down at the corners. "No, we still don't know who he is."

I nodded in understanding. We could go to the police about this, but all I had was a description, and from the sound of it, Reed delivered a message that we didn't need the cops knowing about.

"I don't think I—" I forced down the vomit as the acidic taste flooded my mouth. I popped to my feet, ready to dash to the bathroom. "I don't think you need to give me space to breathe anymore," I forced out before covering my mouth, desperately needing the toilet.

"Are you going to be sick?" Reed's brows rose in concern as he hopped up, ready to help.

I only nodded before rushing to the bathroom.

I was shook.

I needed my dad. One more rodeo, and he'd be out here with us.

I totally tanked my time at the Salmon Ridge Rodeo. Mushu felt my shot nerves, and of course, he struggled making those turns when I was on edge. I felt like I was being watched, and no matter what Reed did to stay in my line of sight, I couldn't shake the feeling—like insects were crawling all over my skin. I was in a damn pissy mood, and Reed, of course, got the brunt of it. I hated that I needed him now more than ever, but not being next to him gave me anxiety like I'd never experienced before.

CHAPTER 14
Lina

"**D**ad!" I squealed, running into his arms as soon as he climbed out of his truck.

"Darlin'." He chuckled, taking me into his embrace, giving me the biggest squeeze we both could muster.

"I've missed you so much." I gripped his shirt, not wanting to let go, letting his firm, warm arms wrap around me, and his familiar scent of fresh soap and spicy aftershave comfort me. My heart finally felt as though it could return to its natural rhythm instead of the heightened rate it had been at since St. John.

He rubbed my back. "I've missed you, too. So glad I was able to come out. We gotta get you that win today, baby girl."

I gave him a final squeeze before pulling back. He looked good, his salt-and-pepper mustache trimmed and ... "Are you growing a soul patch?"

He stroked the new hair on his chin. "Do you like it?"

"You're giving me Riley Green vibes, but if he were forty-seven," I told him.

Dad snorted a laugh. "Is that good?"

"Dad, you're a zaddy. Watch out. You may have some

buckle bunnies buzzing around you tonight."

"I don't know about all that, Lina." He huffed another laugh. "I think your ol' man may be done dating. I left those days on the circuit long ago."

"Nah. You can still get some tail."

"*Lina*," Dad chastised. "I don't think daughters are supposed to talk to their dads about getting laid."

I shrugged. "Well, you look happy."

"I'm here with my baby girl. Of course I'm happy."

I gave him another hug before feeling the blistering heat at my back when Reed officially caught up with us. I'd lost him when I took off running at the sight of my dad's truck.

"Taking care of my girl?" Dad asked Reed over my shoulder.

I could almost feel Reed's brief nod. "We should talk." It was the only thing he said. It was icy cold and serious. I knew what this talk was going to be about, and I had already prepared myself to tell Dad what happened. This was not going to be a fun talk. Thankfully, Reed was prepared to fill in the gaps, especially since I still couldn't remember any of it.

Dad sensed the seriousness, pulling away from me. He gave me a once-over before giving a nod at Reed. "Let's take it to the trailer." Dad's voice had gone 30 below, and I nearly shivered despite the 80-degree day.

Dad's face was like glass, his jaw clenched tight. I was worried he'd break a tooth with the way he was gritting them.

"Say something, Dad."

Reed had just finished apprising Dad of all the details

of the night—that I was drugged and almost abducted and assaulted. I clenched my hands in my lap while we sat in the fifth wheel. Dad and Reed sat across from each other at the table while I sat cross-legged on the couch.

Dad rubbed his new whiskers, before turning to look at me. His eyes were hard and angry, but I could tell he was trying to hold it together.

"You're not to leave Reed's side," he finally said.

"Dad, I know. I just didn't think—"

"I know, darlin'. None of us would've thought any of this would've happened. You're going to need to accept that you can't handle this all on your own now. I know you. You're strong and independent. You don't take shit. I raised you to speak your mind and hold your own, but this feels like more than someone who's just obsessed with you. He's downright dangerous."

I picked at my nails. "I know. I understand the seriousness."

"Thank God we're all going home after this rodeo. I'm ready to have you back on the ranch."

"Me, too, Dad." I was so ready to go home. We had Romy's bachelorette party and then the Willows Rodeo. I was tired and emotionally drained, eager to be recharged by Oregon's high desert. I needed Thornbrush more than Thornbrush needed me.

Dad pushed himself to his feet. "That's all we're going to say about this today. We have a race to win, and that's our focus." Spoken like a true rodeo dad.

I smiled at him, my eyes flitting to Reed, who was cracking his own slight smile as he looked at me. My heart did a silly little gallop, and I had to clear my throat before speaking.

"Let's go make Prineville Rodeo my bitch." I'd fake it if I had to.

CHAPTER 15
Lina

"Sage!" I cried, skipping and running into the arms of one of my best friends. "What are you doing here?"

"Kale told me what happened." She held my shoulders, pushing me away from her to look at me. She was a sight for sore eyes, dressed in cutoff shorts that showed off her long, brown legs and a crop top that gave a peek of her belly button piercing. Her thick, curly, dark hair was piled into a messy bun, as usual. But her amber eyes were sad, and her signature red lips were turned down in a frown as she took me in from head to toe, making sure I was all in one piece. "Are you okay?"

"I'm fine. We're good," I told her, but I don't think I was convincing anyone, at this point. I was only trying to convince myself. "Come on, we need to celebrate my win." Better just to brush it off, enjoy my friends and family, and get a nice little buzz to take the edge off.

I pulled her with me across the sticky wood floors of The Watering Hole, the dirtiest little rodeo bar this side of the Rockies, in Prineville, Oregon. It was as old as the earliest pioneers who'd settled here. Pretty sure the floor still held the dirt of the first cowboys who stomped through. There was even an antique cash register the size of a barrel atop the worn bartop that still clanged when you pulled the lever, just as it had a hundred years ago. The night was still young and the crowd had yet to fill the tiny space, allowing the ancient stereo system to rattle the walls with classic country.

Looking over my shoulder, I checked to see if Dad and Reed still trailed behind me. I was concerned that maybe it wasn't okay for Reed to come into the bar with us, but he was a big boy and could make his own decisions on that. Right? He had so far. He was just doing a job, right?

Christian and Kale were already at the bar, and we stepped up to join them.

"Did you see how I jumped off that fucker?" Christian asked Sage when we reached them, his eyes shining hopefully at her like a child seeking praise.

Sage barely glanced at him. "Yeah, you're lucky you didn't get a horn in your ass." She turned to the approaching bartender. "Pilsner, please."

"Make that six," Kale jumped in, ordering for us.

"Oh, bottle, please," I added quickly. We could never be too safe. Especially now. I glanced back over at Reed, who settled at a table with Dad, remembering what he told me about how many days he'd been sober. Was that accurate? My chest tightened at the thought, and I cleared my throat in an attempt to stuff the feeling way down deep. "Actually, make that five. He'll have a Coke." I shot a thumb over my shoulder.

The bartender nodded, heading to the cooler.

"This fine ass?" Christian continued, examining his own

butt. "Nah. It's impenetrable. Rock hard, baby. Wanna feel it?" He turned around, showing off his ass to Sage. It really was a nice one. The chaps always helped.

"Ew. Gross. No, thank you." Sage inched away from Christian, holding out her hands for the drinks being passed over the bar by the bartender before Christian practically pushed his rear end in her face.

I took a bottle from Sage, sipping it. The wheaty, refreshing taste hitting the back of my tongue. "You're saying you haven't even been tempted to touch it?" I teased my friend. "Not even a little bit? He does have a nice ass. You'd be lying if you didn't think so."

"Thank you, Lina." Christian nodded at me appreciatively.

"Any time, buddy. Besides, I thought for sure the ice would have broken after a few months of watching Arlo."

"You know our Sage. She'd hate to admit she wants me, but I'm growing on her." Christian winked her way.

"I'm not *yours*, and there's no part of me that wants you." But her eyes shifted away like she was trying to cover up the lie.

I attempted to hide a smile behind my drink. There was nothing I'd want more than to see my two friends finally hook up. I knew Sage. She was the yin to my yang, complete opposites. She needed time to think and feel safe, and *then* she needed even more time. But in the last few years that I've known her, I've never once seen her date or heard her mention anyone she was interested in. Sage spent the majority of her time either in her art studio she hoped to one day turn into a gallery, or working her ass off at The Rooster. I was thankful she now had Arlo. It got her out more, and she seemed less lonely than she had been.

"We'll see about that. Listen up!" Christian hollered at the near-empty room, his arms outstretched, the full beer sloshing foam over the edge. About a dozen patrons turned to stare.

"Oh, God." Sage ducked her head, her hand covering her face. Her freckled, bronze cheeks pinkened.

I wasn't hiding my smile anymore. I loved this!

Like one of those sports announcers calling Jude's fight, Christian belted, "I vow that by this time next year, not only will this woman"—he pointed at Sage, who was now trying to hide behind me—"touch my ass, but she'll *like* it. And not only will she like it, but she'll beg to do it again."

"Oh, my fucking God," Sage whispered, shrinking even more behind me.

"You sure you don't want to fuck that?" I asked over my shoulder, stifling a laugh.

"No," she groaned.

"Oh, this is pure gold." Kale had his arms crossed over his chest, a smug look on his face.

"Fuck off, Kale!" Sage stepped away from me, glaring at her brother. "And you," she said, thrusting a finger in Christian's face. "Embarrass me again, and your dog-sitting duties are over."

Christian dropped his arms, hiding his own grin behind his beer as he took a gulp. "Aw, we can't do that to our baby. He'd miss ol' paw too much."

"Ugh! He's *my* dog, and I'm pretty sure *you* would be the one who would miss him. So don't act like this is some joint-custody arrangement." Sage spun on her heels, grabbing the rest of the drinks like she was working a shift to take them over to my dad and Reed.

"You know how to get under her skin," I told Christian.

He bit his knuckle like it was slowly killing him as he watched Sage walk away. "It's just our foreplay."

Kale patted his buddy on the shoulder. "My sister's a hard nut to crack, so the fact that you can get any reaction out of her is a stroke of genius." He chuckled. "Keep it up, and I bet you'll eventually break down her defenses. She might even like you one day."

Christian sighed like a lovesick puppy. "I'm never giving up."

"You know I got your back." I winked at him, leaving the boys to head over to where Dad and Reed were hunched over the table, looking deep in conversation now that Sage left them to peruse the jukebox.

Dad's back was to me and Reed's eyes flitted up, noticing me, then shot Dad a warning glance.

"… drought."

I halted right behind Dad at the dreaded D word every rancher feared. *Oh, he was in trouble now.* My eyes bore into Dad's back.

"She's right behind me, huh?" he asked Reed, knowing full well that I was looming with my hand on my hip behind his chair.

Reed only nodded before taking a sip of his soda.

"Come on, Dad, what the fuck? When were you going to tell me?" I blurted out.

Dad slowly turned in his seat, like he was scared to look at me. I was pissed. I hated when he kept things from me because he didn't want me to worry, and he *knew* better.

"I even asked you on the phone the other day for an update on the ranch, and you very conveniently left out that little tidbit."

He gave me a sheepish look. "The last thing you need to be worried about is what's going on at the ranch. You have to focus on the circuit. And now, knowing what this asshole is willing to pull … you need to just worry about keeping your guard up."

Reed bowed his head, hiding his face from me beneath his cowboy hat. That only confirmed what I already suspected from him. Of course Dad, and probably Jude, too, were keeping him apprised as to what was going on at the ranch––and with his daughter, Penn.

I shook my head. "You keeping things from me, too, Reed? About *my* family ranch?"

"Now that's not fair, Lina," Dad chided, fully turning around in his seat to face me. "Don't put this on him."

"You're right. I shouldn't put this on him. He's too damned chickenshit to say anything he really means." Reed's head shot up, his brown eyes nearly black. In the dimly lit bar, they felt as though they were burning right into me. I didn't really mean it. Reed was a man of few words, but he never once gaslit me or sugarcoated the truth. More than once, I could tell he stopped himself from saying what he really wanted to say, though, and I liked challenging him. I tapped my toe to keep the rest of my body from fidgeting. "Let alone, tell me something that *you* were keeping from me. At least he's smart. He knew it should be coming from you, not him."

"Lina––" Reed tried to interrupt.

I flipped him off to silence him.

"I'm not some delicate flower, Dad. You know that. Don't think all of a sudden that you need to protect me from the truth. You and the ranch are far more important to me than winning the finals. If I need to drop out––"

"Don't you dare finish that statement." Dad gave me a stern look, like I was about to be sent to my room. "For one, you've committed to this, so you're going to finish it. Larsens don't bow out. And second, I'm your father and I love you, but sometimes you don't need to know everything. I'm a grown-ass man who raised you and Jude to be great adults, so don't question my decisions."

"Fine. Then don't fucking keep things from me."

Dad's throat bobbed as if he were swallowing down more secrets. I narrowed my eyes on him.

"If I come home and find out you're keeping more shit from me, I swear to God, Dad, I'm going to flip the fuck out."

With that, I chugged a few gulps of my beer, hoping to cool my insides, and turned away from their table, heading to the jukebox. Looping my arm through Sage's, I charged to the other side of the bar. As far away from Dad and Reed as I could get.

"What was that all about?" Sage asked, once we settled into our seats at a two-topper.

"Nothing," I glowered, watching Christian join Dad while Reed headed to the bar for another drink.

Sage and I chatted and nursed our beers. After last weekend, I wasn't quite ready to load myself up with liquor while the bar started to fill up for the night, getting louder and more rambunctious. Brooks and Dunn reverberated through the terrible stereo system.

Dad and Christian were now in some sort of heated debate across the room. I could tell it was heated because Christian was using his hands a lot, and Dad was pinching the bridge of his nose like he was getting a headache. Knowing both of them, it probably had to do with the rodeo or training. In the last year, Christian had taken on training all the rookie bull riders, while Dad continued to train the junior broncs who came to Thornbrush for lessons.

I was still angry with Dad, and I didn't think all the beer in the room could cool my insides right now. My blood was nearing its boiling point. I didn't typically get this mad at him, but I was feeling so raw after the last few days. Everything felt like it was just too much.

Plus, I couldn't help my eyes continually being drawn to Reed.

An attractive woman sidled up to the bar, squeezing between him and another patron. She touched his arm and gave him a bright, flirtatious smile. Reed gave a small smile in return and shook her hand. It shouldn't bother me that a woman was hanging on his arm right now where he leaned against the bar, but it did.

She had copper hair, and I wondered if he had a thing for redheads. From what I remembered, his ex-wife had red hair. Each time he said something to her, she leaned closer to him, her hand still resting on his muscular forearm. My eyes narrowed. Pretty sure her full tits were brushing against his biceps, too.

A sharp pain shot through me like a lightning bolt.

"Want a different drink?" Sage asked.

I turned to her and cleared my throat, hoping that would also clear the spike that felt lodged in my chest.

Her head was tilted, as if considering something.

Shit. Did she see me staring at Reed? Had she been talking to me while I was in my head?

I noticed then that her bottle was empty and mine was half full. My fingertips stilled, midpick. Apparently, I was also sexually frustrated from the way I was peeling off the label. I downed the rest, hoping it would dislodge this feeling of … jealousy?

"Another beer would be fine."

Sage nodded, weaving her way through the crowded bar.

Why would I be jealous of another woman? I didn't get jealous. Like *ever*. I may have been raised surrounded by cowboys, but I could be a girl's girl. While some women were catty and territorial, I never felt that I had to be. I was trying to rack my brain, but I don't think I ever once felt as though I had to compete with another woman for a guy's attention. Maybe it was because I never had to work for it or really didn't care to try. I was always 100 percent myself, and that typically attracted plenty of men to choose from.

With Reed, though, all that went out the window. Seeing a woman on Reed's arm … it made me feel things I wasn't used to. Hell, it even pissed me off more. I mean, she had great tits, and I don't think I would have faulted her one bit for showing them off. Fuck, I'd do the same thing. There was no reason for me to hate her, other than the fact that she was *touching* Reed. And he was *letting* her.

I felt as if I were about ready to blow a gasket. All these feelings needed to go somewhere, and I was never one to keep them bottled inside. I was ready to fling open the gates and release the hounds, so to speak.

Reed ducked his head to whisper something in her ear, and I felt like I was so close to losing it.

My hand clutched around the now-empty bottle, and I wanted it to crack and splinter until it shattered in my grip. I wanted to feel the sting of it cutting into my flesh and the blood oozing down my arm, if only it meant to distract me from this fucking *feeling*. Or … chuck it at his head. That would work, too.

"Grab my ass again, and you're going to get a knee in the fuckin' balls." Sage's voice cut through my thoughts as she returned with our beers. My gaze swung to where she stood off to the right of our table.

"Come on, baby." Some cowboy was nearly rubbing himself against her like a feral cat.

Her hands full of beer, she elbowed him in the ribs to push him away.

The hell if I was going to let my friend get groped by this jackass who didn't take no for an answer. I shot to my feet and hurried to help, taking my drink to free up one of her hands.

She stepped to the side, allowing us both to face this prick head-on. He wasn't a bad looking guy, but he had a porn 'stache that told me he thought he was God's gift to women. My nose wrinkled at the pungent smell of his cologne, like he fucking bathed in it.

"You heard her, douchebag. Step the fuck off," I told him.

"This has nothing to do with you, sugar," he said snidely, glaring at me.

"Don't call me sugar, asshole. Touch my friend again. I *dare* you." I took a step closer, putting myself between him and Sage, my boots nearly bumping his. He was several inches taller and maybe had fifty pounds on me, but I could still inflict some damage if I had to.

"Lina, he's not worth our time. Let's go." Sage put a hand on my elbow, but I brushed her off.

I was wanting a fight. I *needed* to fight. To let out this anger bubbling inside me and prove to myself that I wasn't some damsel in distress. I could rescue myself—and my friend while I was at it—if the situation called for it.

The dude stepped closer, and like a knee-jerk reaction, I tossed my full drink in his face and watched his eyes flash red as the beer dripped down his now-hardened expression, the bottle shattering at his feet.

"What the fuck, bitch!"

I raised my arms, about to push him, when a strong arm wrapped around my middle, lifting me off my feet, pulling me back against his hard chest. I immediately started flailing, my legs kicking and arms swinging. I wanted to hit this asshole in his ugly mug. I wanted to kick and punch whoever was brave enough to hold me back.

No one should ever fucking hold me back.

Chapter 16
Reed

Lina thrashed in my arms as I pulled her away from the asshole I was now shooting daggers at. He had planted his feet and clenched his fists at his sides, like he was prepared to swing.

"You fucking going to fight a woman?" I barked.

Christian, Kale, and Chuck were already rushing over. Christian went straight to Sage, while Kale and Chuck bracketed either side of this dumbass, ready to drag him away if need be.

"Get this guy out of here," Chuck ordered one of the bartenders who was ramming through the commotion of the bar to reach us.

"Let go of me!" Lina cried, pushing on my arm to loosen my hold.

"Neither one of these bitches are worth it," the motherfucker said, shrugging off the bartender's grip and turning to head out of the bar.

"Stop fighting me," I growled in her ear.

"Then get your fucking hands off me." Lina pushed at my arm again, her feet no longer kicking.

I set her down.

Wrong fucking move.

The girl took off, plowing through the crowd and following him on his heels.

"Fucking hell," I muttered. My heart lurched, seeing her take off after this dude who looked as though he wouldn't hesitate to hit a girl.

"Shit," Chuck cursed beside me. "Get her back to the camper."

He didn't need to tell me twice. I was already going after her, bulldozing my way through the crowd that gathered to watch.

"What did he say to get her so pissed?" I heard Christian ask Sage as I walked away. I could hear Chuck's boots stomping behind me.

Lina was charging through the door of the bar as I hurried to catch up with her. An evening breeze brushed across my face as I stepped outside, but it might as well have been a heat wave the way I was sweating.

Lina bounded after the guy, who was now crossing the dirt parking lot.

"Lina!" Chuck scolded behind me as we closed in on her.

She ignored him, not stopping in her pursuit.

"You're going to need to get her," Chuck instructed. "She's still pissed at me. I'll follow close behind just in case there's trouble."

Chuck and I exchanged knowing glances before we both surveyed our surroundings for more than one threat. Thankfully, I didn't see any sign of her stalker as Chuck fell behind and I closed in on her heels.

She was moving quickly, but in three long strides, I was on her. I went to grab her around the waist, but it was like she sensed me closing in. She twisted, and her arm extended to backfist me right in the fucking throat before I could even touch her.

"Kuh-huh!" It felt as if her bony knuckles lodged themselves right into my windpipe, causing me to cough. I think she meant for it to connect with my jaw, but with our height difference, she fell short of her target. "Fuck, sweetheart," I said between clenched teeth.

Her arm reeled back like she was going to go again, but I caught it in midair, my fingers wrapping around her wrist.

"Don't try to stop me, Reed."

"Don't hit me again."

She wrenched her arm out of my grasp, breaking my hold.

"We're not fucking doing this," I told her, quickly gripping her waist and swinging her over my shoulder with effortless ease.

She released a surprised scream at the change in altitude. "Put me down, asshole!" Her nails dug into my back.

I adjusted my grip and held her around the back of the thighs to steady her.

Lina thrashed, trying to wriggle her way off my shoulder.

"Stop fighting me!" I swatted her ass. She let out a muffled cry as if she was biting it back. As if she didn't want me to hear that it hurt. I hoped it fucking stung. At least enough to quit her squirming so I could get us out of here.

"You're a fucking asshole!" Her nails dug deeper, and I

hissed a breath.

"Yep, I'm a fucking asshole," I confirmed, staring down the guy who was standing there, watching us. I hope he thought I was an asshole, too, and saw it as a warning. His mouth hung open now, but when our eyes connected, his teeth clicked closed. "*You*," I directed at him, "better go before I change my mind and let her loose. She won't just be swinging at me."

He tipped his chin in a jerky nod of understanding before turning on his heels and disappearing between the parked cars. At least he wasn't a complete moron.

"He grabbed Sage's ass without her fucking permission!" Lina cried. "He needs to get the message, or he's going to put his hands on another girl without her consent."

In my periphery, I could see Chuck approaching to my right. We exchanged quick glances and he gave me a nod, silently letting me know he'd handle it before turning in the direction of the ass-grabber.

Gripping her against me, I quickly charged through the rodeo grounds, heading to our trailer. The sensation of her body wiggling against me, and my palm gripping her ass, was putting me on fucking edge. I felt like I was on fire, and my dick was painfully hard against my zipper. This girl was fucking trouble, and all I could think to do was push her to her knees while I fucked her smart-ass mouth.

"Put me down. I can fucking walk," she said again, her hips shifting against my shoulder.

"Not a fucking chance."

"Just let me go, then you can go back to your pretty redhead."

"What are you talking about?"

"You were all over each other back there. Reds are your favorite, right? Aren't you tired of babysitting? You could be getting your dick wet right now instead of this."

Her words were pissing me off, making me hurry my steps so I could close us in the trailer. It was like one step forward, five steps back with Lina every fucking time.

"Just let me go. Lock me in the trailer for all I care. But just let me fucking go!"

"Will you quit!" I slapped her ass again and she gave another muffled cry, making my dick grow even harder.

The fifth wheel was in my sights. I was more than ready to lock her in that trailer. Lock us *both* in the trailer.

"Fuck you, Reed! Leave me alone, and go fuck your redhead."

"Shut the fuck up, Lina," I growled. I was so sick of her running her mouth. "I have no interest in that woman back at the bar."

"What? You didn't think she had great tits? She looked like she could get you off just by sticking your dick between them."

"Jesus Christ, Lina." I stomped up the steps of the fifth wheel, pushing open the door. I ducked inside and kicked the door closed behind us.

"What? Don't you want someone to fuck your cock with their tits?"

I lowered her down then, letting her body drag down mine. I could feel every inch of us connecting while I ran my hands up the backs of her thighs, over her ass, and the curve of her waist until they rested just beneath her breasts.

She stuck her chin up defiantly. "Someone to let you glide your dick back and forth between them until you bust a nut and make a sticky mess all over them?"

We were so close, I could feel Lina's breath catch in her chest. My thumbs brushed beneath her full tits. My own chest heaved—out of frustration, anger, irritation, and desire.

Her big, brown eyes found mine, and they were fucking heated, matching in anger and arousal.

Her tongue darted out across her rosy lips, and it was like a tether snapped.

I couldn't hold back anymore. I wanted Lina Larsen. I wanted all of her.

Slamming my mouth to hers, letting our teeth clash, I walked her backward until her legs hit the table behind her. She moaned into my mouth when I nipped her full bottom lip, her hands going to my shirt, gripping it, pulling me against her.

But I thrust her away from me to spin her around, my hand running up her spine to push her down against the table.

"I want you just like this, sweetheart. Your perfect ass in the air, ready for me."

I wanted to claim her. To punish her. To fuck her until she was writhing, losing all semblance of power and control. I wanted her to surrender to me.

"What, you're not going to gag me so I shut up?" Lina challenged, her cheek now pressed against the laminate tabletop.

"Is that what you want, sweetheart?" I gripped her hip while I ground against her, letting her feel how hard she made me. "You want me to fucking gag you while I fuck your pussy?"

"Do your worst, cowboy," she challenged. "Make me shut the fuck up."

I growled. "Not this time. I want to hear you scream. I want to hear every fucking sound you make while I fuck you against this table."

"You think you're going to make me scream?"

I ran a hand up her spine, my fingers threading through her long, brown hair until I could gather it in my fist. I thrust my cock against her ass again, gripping her hair so her head rose off the table, her eyes fluttering up to look at me. "Just so you know, I prefer brunettes." Her eyes narrowed on me, burning with such intensity that I could feel my control slipping.

That's what Lina wanted, though. She wanted me to lose control, and she wanted to *be* controlled.

"You're going to fucking scream. You're not going to hold anything back. Do you understand?" I gritted through my teeth as I gripped a little tighter.

I tugged on her hair, forcing her head farther back while I leaned down to capture her mouth. This time, our lips molded together, gentle at first, then urgent, possessive. The heat of our breath mingling. Her lips were so fucking soft, yet firm and strong, ready to take everything I had to give.

She bit my lip. Hard.

"Fuck." The taste of copper bloomed in my mouth.

"I fucking hate you," she spat against my lips. "Are you sure you don't want me to hold back? You think you can handle that? No man ever wants to hear the truth. Bet you can't make me come, either. Don't worry, I'll fake it so your ego leaves intact. *Oh, Reed, Reed. Just like that, baby.*" She faked moaning as if she was on the verge of an orgasm.

I clicked my tongue in disappointment, wrapping her hair even tighter around my fist. "That fucking mouth. You don't hate me, sweetheart, and I think I know exactly what you need to get you there." I returned her bite with my own, and she responded with a heady moan, her lashes fluttering as her eyes closed in pleasure. "You like a bit of pain, don't you, baby?" I whispered against the shell of her ear.

A shudder ran through her, echoing through me while I pressed my chest against her back. "No," she said.

"You fucking liar." I licked up the curve of her neck to her pulse point, feeling her heart thrum against my tongue. "I'm going to ask you again." I ran my hand down her side, finding the waistband of her pants. "If you lie to me again, this stops right here and now."

"You're an asshole."

I chuckled, dragging a fingertip along her waist, the whisper-soft touch making her squirm.

"Now tell me. Do you like a bit of pain while you get fucked?"

"Yes," she whispered so softly I barely heard her. But it was enough.

I reached beneath her, unbuttoning and unzipping her pants.

"Has no one ever asked you what you want?"

She shook her head. Panting.

"Don't go all quiet on me now, sweetheart." I ran my fingers beneath the waistband of her panties, teasing her. Her stomach sucked in with her heavy breaths. "Fucking fools."

"What?" she asked, her voice breathy.

"Those boys you've been with. Selfish pricks who didn't take the time to ask you what you want. Who only cared about getting themselves off." I continued to draw my fingertips along her heated skin beneath her panties, inching closer and closer to her clit. "You think I can't fucking handle you? Give it to me. Give it all to me. Tell me what you want, and I won't come until I have you losing control. Is that what you want, Lina?"

She rolled her hips, her ass rubbing against my dick, tempting me. Fuck.

"Brat." I pushed against her spine, putting space between us while I continued to stroke her skin inches away from her clit. "You're going to make *me* a fucking liar if you keep rubbing your ass against me like that."

"*Reed*," she whined, her hand pushing mine closer to where she wanted it.

I pulled on her hair again, and she hissed between her teeth. "Use your words. Tell me what you want."

"I want you. I want you to fucking make me come. I want you to rub my clit while you fuck me from behind. I want to let go and stop thinking. You ruined the first time. Give me the do-over I fucking deserve."

"That's right. You do deserve that. I fucked up, but I'm not going to fuck up this time," I confirmed, rewarding her with a swipe of my finger over her sensitive clit.

She moaned, her hips rocking against my hand while her hands went to push down her pants.

"Hands on the fucking table, Lina."

She hesitated for a moment, and a shadow of a smile flitted across her lips. I halted the circles I was starting to make.

"I'll keep you on edge until you do as you're told."

"Yes, *daddy*."

I growled, but she complied, gripping the edge of the table on either side of her. I hooked my fingers into the belt loops of her jeans, slowly, torturously bringing them over her hips and down her thighs.

"Fuck, sweetheart." My hands ran up her thighs, kneading her ass that was covered in black lace, cut high on either side of her hips. "Were you hoping someone fucked you tonight when you put these on?"

"You can never be too prepared," she panted, her sultry voice dripping with arousal.

I slapped an ass cheek, watching it jiggle and then turn a delicious pink at the edge of her panties. "Next time you wear these, I want to watch you fucking crawl to me."

"Oh God," Lina whimpered, arching her back and pushing her ass toward me.

I kicked her feet farther apart and pressed against her spine to force her chest against the table. "Do you want me to fuck you from behind? Do you want me to fuck you with my fingers while I rub your clit or eat your ass while I kneel behind you? What do you want, Lina? Tell me what you need to come, and I'll give it to you."

Lina moaned in desperation, her hips still rocking, needy for it. "Please, Reed. Please eat my ass while you fuck me with your fingers."

I released a heavy breath. "Fuck, baby. I'll give you anything you need."

I ran my hands over her curves, dragging her panties down as I kneeled behind her. They were fucking soaked. I couldn't help myself. My tongue darted out, eager to taste her.

This woman was driving me to my fucking knees.

CHAPTER 17
Lina

His tongue ran up my slit, swirling my tight hole, before a single digit dove inside my pussy. I pushed against him, moaning as my fingers dug into the table. I wanted him to drive into me, to punish me with his thrusts and his tongue.

"Fuck, Reed. Fuck me with two fingers," I commanded him, needing more. One was not enough.

"You need to be full, baby?" His lips brushed against my ass when he asked it. His hot breath danced across my skin while his beard burned, sending shivers up my spine.

"Please, Reed. One isn't enough."

He was right. The guys I dated were always looking to get themselves off. They rarely took the time to find out what I needed. It was why I was never truly satisfied. Probably why I was always dating, searching for my thirst to be quenched, but never finding it.

He slid two fingers inside me.

"Yes," I whimpered, grinding against his hand, his tongue diving between my ass cheeks, circling. "Press your thumb against my clit."

"There we go, baby. Tell me exactly what you need." His

thumb brushed against the sensitive bud, but he didn't press down. "Set the pace. Make a mess of my hand, and I'll gladly lap it up."

I rocked my hips, using the table as leverage. His tongue never stopped. I'd never had anyone eat my ass before, and I was realizing how sensitive it was with each flick of his tongue. It felt fucking amazing.

"Fuck, Reed."

"You're fucking drenched. Are you able to come like this, sweetheart?"

I was chasing the climax, seeking the friction and pressure. His fingers inside me flexed, twisted, and stroked. But it wasn't enough. Not nearly enough. I couldn't help thinking about how large he was. How full I'd felt that one night together. How deep he went, hitting every sensitive spot along the way. The slight stretch of pain. The intensity at the fullness. I wanted that. I fucking *needed* that.

I shook my head against the table, trying to dislodge the memory.

He stood, pressing his chest against my back, letting me feel the weight of him, while he kissed up my neck, then bit down. I cried out, surprised and fucking needy. Wanting him to mark every part of me. His teeth scraped against the sensitive skin beneath my ear before he soothed it with his lips.

Squirming, I pushed my hips against him, feeling just how thick and hard he was in his pants as he thrust it against my bare ass.

"Can you come like this?" he asked again, punctuating it

with a curl of his fingers while his thumb rubbed against my clit.

"No," I whimpered. I wanted to come so badly, but I needed the foreplay. I needed it to drag out until I was desperate. Until I was right on the edge and the only thing that would push me over the precipice was him diving in deep. "I need you to fill me with your cock. I need you to fuck me."

"Fuck, Lina," he groaned, his fingers slowing while his dick pressed against my ass, his jeans rubbing against me.

"Condom. I have condoms in the bathroom," I managed to say.

"Where?" Reed asked, but his voice turned hard.

I gulped, feeling him pull away from me.

"In my makeup bag on the counter," I said hurriedly. I started to push away, but Reed shoved me back down.

"Don't move."

I heard him walk away, and I turned my head to watch him leave, biting my lip to keep myself from saying "fuck it" and asking him to fuck me raw. I was so close to begging for it. I wanted him to fuck me. To fuck me until I could no longer remember why I ever hated him.

He returned, whipping his belt from his belt loops. He stepped behind me, the leather snapping in his hands. Then he slapped it against my ass, causing an unbidden squeak to rip from my throat. The sting rippled through me, sending a zing right to my clit. My pussy clenched, greedy for more, and I found myself pushing my ass toward him. "Do it again."

Reed chuckled, setting the belt down on the table at my side. "Oh, you liked that, huh? You like being spanked?"

I bit my lip, humming an affirmative yes. "Only by you, daddy." I twisted slightly to get a better view as he unbuttoned his pants and slid them and his boxers down his thighs.

"Fucking shit," I breathed when his dick sprung free, thick, long, and hard. "Was it that big before?" My breath now froze in my chest. "Are you pierced? I fucking know that wasn't there before. I'd remember that!"

A smile kicked up the sides of his mouth, warming his dark eyes, and my breath caught.

Even in the dimly lit camper, I could see him in all his glory.

Reed stroked a hand up and down his cock. "Do you like what you see?"

"When did you get those?"

He ripped the condom package with his teeth and slid it on. "After our first time, I wanted to punish myself for what I did to you. I wanted to make sure that when I got another chance––if I got another chance––it would be a first for both of us. I want my dick to be the thing that brings you pleasure, and Jacob's ladder is all for you."

"Reed …" My pussy clenched at the same time my chest squeezed, kick-starting my rapid heart rate.

He did that just for me? I couldn't fathom anyone willing to endure something like that for me. Did that mean he hadn't been with anyone since? Just like he'd confided he'd been sober since we'd met …

I licked my lips. "Next time, I want to taste you. I want to run my tongue over that metal and make you feel good." The words came out sounding whiny and needy. Desperate for him.

I don't think I've ever felt so greedy.

A hand went to my ass, rubbing it, kneading it, while I felt him stroke the tip of his cock up and down my slit, coating himself with me. I could feel the barbells through the latex. "Oh, so there's a next time?" he teased.

Ugh! He caught my slip. "Asshole."

Reed huffed a laugh, notching his dick at my entrance. He slid an inch in, and I shifted my hips, desperate.

"Just fuck me already." I pushed against the table, arching my back as he gripped my hips, but he froze, shoving me back against the table.

"You told me what you wanted, but I'm not rushing this." His words were hard and stern. "You fucking rush this, Lina, and I'll go grab Mushu's lead and tie you to this table so I can drive you to the edge, over and over, until you can't take any more."

"Shit. You'd do that?" I asked, my already-heated skin shooting up ten more degrees. I was burning, and I could feel my pussy flutter around the tip of his cock.

Reed picked up the belt and gave my ass another slap, the hot sting making me whimper.

"Don't fucking tempt me. I think you'd like that a little too much, and I'm not about to reveal all my tricks tonight. I want you coming back for more. Coming back to *me*, Lina. Only me."

He slid another inch in and I groaned, my legs shaking as I tried to hold myself still. I didn't think I could stand this slow fuck anymore.

"You hear me, sweetheart? You're only coming to *me*

when you want to get off. No more fucking around with these immature jackasses. You want to fucking come? You come to me."

Yet another inch, and I was about ready to combust.

"Why is it that as soon as you have your cock in me, you're all of a sudden the fucking chatty one?" I asked.

Then he slammed all the way into me with a frustrated shout. I cried out as he hit bottom. He didn't take time for me to adjust to him, the burning pain only heightening my arousal.

"YES!" I yelled.

"Fucking say it, Lina," he gritted out as he pulled back before thrusting all the way back in, pummeling the deepest parts of me. The ridges of his piercings thrashed every point of pleasure along my walls.

I panted, my legs trembling, the pressure already building. "Make me come, cowboy."

Moving in more frantic thrusts, he pounded into me. Again and again and again. "Only me, you hear me? Only I will make you come."

"What if I want to make myself come?" I challenged, raising an eyebrow playfully.

"Lina," he growled. "Not even you. This is my pussy. You want to touch yourself? You ask for permission. Now say it. Who's going to make you come?"

He withdrew until only the tip was buried inside. I could feel his own resolve wavering, the hands at my hips trembling as he forced himself to stay there.

"Say it," he said through gritted teeth. He was teetering on the edge of pleasure, and I was right there with him. "Or

I'll keep you from coming. I'll get you close, then draw out my cock before slamming back in. I'll bring you to the edge over and over until you're fucking begging for it."

"Reed, please. I want to come." I *was* begging for it, my pussy pulsing and fluttering, urging him to go deeper.

"Then fucking say it. Who does this pussy belong to?"

"You, Reed." I nearly came at the way those words rolled off my tongue.

"That's right, baby," he groaned. "It's fucking mine. Your pussy knows it, too. I can feel it sucking me in. This pussy is fucking *mine*."

I was having an out-of-body experience. It felt so euphoric, I couldn't even respond to him.

And with that, he pounded into me with one single, hard thrust. All I could feel was him.

I screamed. I'm not even sure I said words. If I did, they were unintelligible.

"That's right, baby. No one ever shuts my girl up."

Hearing him call me "his girl" made my chest warm and my stomach quiver. The thought that I might actually belong to him made any of the ice coating my heart––protecting me against him––slowly start to melt.

"No one ever tries to rein you in. You understand?" His voice came out a growl, like he was angry for every man who ever made me feel like I was less than, who made me feel like I was too much for them. "You want it? You'll fucking take it. I'll give it all to you. Anything you want. You want a rough fuck? I'll give it to you. Now fucking take it."

I lost my ability to speak, his thrusts pounding me against

the table, my body absorbing every hit to my nerve endings. The pleasure was building with each stroke of his cock deep inside. His fingertips dug into my hips—I'd have bruises there in the morning—while his other hand wrapped around my breast, drawing me back against him, slamming into me.

"Fuck, I'm close," I managed to say through trembling lips. I've never felt this close to orgasm before—not solely from penetration anyway. He was able to reach, and touch, every sensitive spot.

"Come with me," he begged as he pulled me against him, thrusting erratically, the slapping of our flesh echoing through the fifth wheel.

Pressure was building, heat beginning to pool in my center, my pulse thumping as his thick cock continued to plunge deep inside, drawing out every moan and spike of pleasure from me.

"That's it, baby. Squeeze my cock."

"Fuck. Fuck. Fuck." My eyes rolled to the back of my head as a heady rush overcame me. My body tensed. My heartbeat thudded like a drum in my ears as I came. I felt as though I were crashing through the atmosphere, trying to catch my breath.

Reed stilled behind me, grunting, while his cock throbbed and pulsed inside me, sending aftershocks through me. "Damn, baby," he said between gasps of air. This moment, with his hands still on me, holding me to him, was one I wanted to live in forever.

But then he froze.

His fingers flexed where they were wrapped around me.

"That was … that was …" My lips tingled with the effect of

my orgasm. I blew out a steadying breath.

Reed pushed me back down on the table.

"Oh my God, you want to go again?" I asked, the heat already building. He wouldn't have to persuade me.

"Shh!" Reed shushed. "Stay here."

He withdrew so quickly, I cried out in near pain feeling him pull out. It felt like he was being ripped away from me.

"What the hell, Reed?"

He let go of me and stepped away. I pushed myself up off the table, my body already feeling stiff from being bent over while he fucked me senseless.

"Stay here, Lina," he repeated, this time more harshly as he took off his condom and tossed it in the trash under the sink before pulling up his briefs and jeans.

"What? What is it?" I started to panic. My brows pinched together as I watched him pick up his discarded hat off the counter and place it on his head. I didn't remember him taking it off.

"Shh," he snapped, going to his bag beside the bench seat and pulling out a revolver.

My mouth fell open. "Reed?" I could feel my heart plummet as I began pulling up my own pants. "Why do you need that?"

He held out a hand to stop me. "Stay here. Lock the door behind me. Don't open it until I say."

"What's going on?"

"Someone was watching us," he said shortly.

My heart never settled from the intense orgasm, and now it kicked up again, my eyes going wide to scan the windows, but all I saw was darkness. Reed buttoned his pants, shoved his gun in his waistband, and headed out into the night.

CHAPTER 18
Reed

I quickly covered the perimeter of the camp. The .38 was heavy at my waistband. I wish I had my Glock from the truck for this situation, but my revolver was what was within reach. My fingers twitched at the ready.

I hadn't gotten a good look, but I saw enough to assume it was Lina's stalker. *The piece of shit.* The figure wore black clothing, the whites of his eyes flashing in the dark above a thick beard. I hadn't known how long he was standing there, but he'd seen enough to make me want to gouge his fucking eyeballs out of his skull. My body was wound up tight, the hair on the back of my neck raised, and I felt this overwhelming protective need to wipe out every memory and vision that man now possessed of Lina.

She wasn't his to look at.

I wanted to end him for what he saw, for any familiarity he thought he had in the feel of her body now that I knew exactly how it felt to lose myself in hers.

With no sign of him, I returned to the trailer, desperate to get back to her. God, that woman had me by the throat. The sounds she made when I spanked her with my belt, the feel of her walls constricting around my cock, the rock of her hips responding to my thrusts, greedily chasing her release. I didn't want her to hold back. I wanted her to take everything she needed.

And I wanted to give it all to her. Not just the pleasure, but my heart, too. She said she was in love with me the moment she saw me in the Saddle Room all those months ago. That was well before she knew I had a daughter. She still didn't really know about my past, other than the baggage with my ex-wife. For better or for worse, it was all a part of me. Penn and I were a package deal. Would she want to be a part of our lives? Would she want *me* after she knew what I was?

I wouldn't be satisfied just fucking her. Not anymore.

I wanted more from her. Did she want that, too?

I tried the handle to the trailer door. She locked it just as I told her to. Good. At least for once, she decided to listen.

"Lina, it's me," I said softly, trying not to freak her out more than she probably already was. I lightly rapped on the door with my knuckles.

The lock clicked before Lina opened it wide enough to let me through. The trailer was brightly lit. She'd closed the blinds and turned on every light, as if she hoped it would scare away the shadows. My heart clenched, knowing I'd left her alone while I went after him. Her beautiful face was pale, her eyes wide with fear. Fuck, I wanted to go back out there and hunt the bastard down just for making my fearless girl scared.

She was *mine*. I was hell-bent on making her mine as soon as my mouth marked her beneath the temporary tattoo that first night in Joseph, 414 days ago.

"Was he out there?" She looked worried, wringing her hands while she stood in the light now in her panties and sleep shirt.

I closed the door behind me and stepped into her, wrapping my fingers around hers, steadying them. As soon as I touched her, desire and need for her surged back with the pulse of my blood. She stilled, her big, honey-brown eyes, turning up to me. Her lips pursed as she was considering saying something more. Her throat bobbed on a swallow, and I couldn't resist putting both my hands on her, tracing the column of her neck.

"He's gone," I told her, attempting to reassure her while I let my hands roam so that my thumb could brush along her pulse. It kicked up a notch. My eyes traveled up her throat to her lips, still swollen from our kisses.

Whatever she saw in my eyes caused her to suck in a breath, her cute little nose pinching briefly before flaring.

My cock twitched. My chest tightened.

"Reed." Her voice sounded desperate as her eyes searched mine, the light reflecting specks of amber in her gaze like a brewing fire.

I licked my lips, taking a step closer until our chests bumped. I could feel how stiff her nipples were through her shirt.

I'd gladly let her fire burn me. Over and over again.

I was desperate for her.

I made my decision then. I wanted us—just *us*. I set my cowboy hat on the table, running a hand through my hair. "I'm not done with you yet, sweetheart."

Not waiting for a response, I toed off my boots and ripped

off my shirt, hoisting her up into my arms. Her breath hitched, and she let out a little squeal when I pulled her to me, her arms locked behind my head while her legs wrapped around my waist. My palms encompassed her ass, holding her to me while I walked us to the bed in the front. I felt her hips roll, seeking friction.

Her lips were inches from mine, her breath coasting across my mouth. I could almost taste her in the air between us.

"Fuck, Lina," I breathed.

I couldn't wait to cross the distance to the bed and pushed her up against the wall. My lips ghosted across hers, lightly teasing the bow of her lip. My tongue darted out, tracing the seam of her mouth, urging her to open for me.

"Reed," she said again, this time pleadingly. It was just enough for me to deepen our kiss, my tongue stroking the length of hers until I could run it across the roof of her mouth.

"God, you can kiss. That fucking tongue." She moaned, my own following hers.

She rocked her hips again as I pressed her harder against the wall. My hands tightly gripped her ass, wanting to leave my mark all over her while I helped her rub against me.

"Fuck, baby." My cock throbbed painfully. I was so fucking hard, I'd be surprised if I didn't come in my pants with the friction she was building.

"Thank you," she murmured softly against my mouth.

"For what?"

"Those piercings. They're the best apology you could've ever given me."

I couldn't help but smile, holding back a chuckle as I kissed her, relief coursing through me.

"Are you going to be a good little slut for this cock?" I asked, my voice thick with want.

Lina groaned, her head tipping back to hit the wall. "I feel so fucking empty. I need you to fill me."

Fuck. I could already feel myself leaking with another brush of her pussy against me.

"Please," she whined.

"Baby, you don't need to beg. Not with me." My hands traveled up her sides, burying into her locks, bringing her head back up so I could kiss her again.

I peeled us off the wall and walked to the bed, letting us fall onto the mattress.

Staring down at her, she looked so gorgeous beneath me. Her hair splayed on the pillow, her eyes glistening with a twinkle, and I wondered what she was thinking. She was so quiet. Unnervingly quiet.

"What is it?" I prompted. "Do you need something, sweetheart?" I asked her, suddenly feeling concerned and a little self-conscious. "Is this too much?"

She shook her head, her teeth dragging across her full bottom lip, momentarily distracting me before she spoke. "It's not enough. I want to feel you, Reed. All of you. When I said I need you to fill me, I meant I want you to fucking *fill* me."

My eyes shot to hers at that, my heartbeat kicking up a notch at what I thought she insinuated. "You want me to fuck you bare?"

"I want to feel you slick on my thighs, even long after you leave me. I want you to fuck me sore so tomorrow I can feel the echo of your cock inside me."

Jesus Christ, this woman was going to be my undoing. "Oh, fuck, baby." I was in pain hearing her words. My chest heaved. My muscles tightened, attempting to hold myself back, because she stirred this primal urge deep within me, something that I'd never experienced before.

"Please, I want you to leave marks all over me so when I look in the mirror, it's a map of where you've been."

I exhaled an exaggerated sigh, my arms now starting to shake while I held myself above her to keep from crushing her. She ran her palms over my shoulders, down my chest, my ribs, my abs. Her fingers brushed strokes down the ridges of every muscle before landing on my jeans. She didn't waste time unbuttoning and unzipping my pants, her hand diving into my boxer briefs, finding me already swollen and ready for her.

Her thumb slid against the tip, spreading my precum and making me shudder.

"Are you sure?" I asked calmly, though internally, I was raging and ready to get my hands all over her soft, silky skin.

"Please, Reed," she urged. "I'm clean. I get checked regularly. I'm on birth control—"

I cut her off. "I said you didn't need to beg. I'll give you anything you want, baby. Anything you ask for. I haven't been with anyone else since we met, and I'm clean, too." I wanted to feel all of her. Every flutter and stroke while my cock pulled in and out of her.

"Good, then fuck me."

I growled like a fucking beast, something primal awakening deep within me at her request. Not wasting time, I peeled off her shirt, leaving her in her sexy, black lace. I traced the curves and swells of her breasts, my fingertips dancing lightly over her stomach, tenderly caressing the soft skin inside her thighs. She was mesmerizing, responding to every stroke. Her body arched and writhed. The sweetest sounds of pleasure slipped from her throat, and truthfully, it made my blood run hot, my cock throb, and my own groans rumble deep in my chest.

"This gorgeous body deserves to be worshipped. It deserves to be given everything it craves."

"I'm fucking parched," she whimpered.

"Then let's fix that, baby. Should I let my cum fill that smart-ass mouth?"

She moaned. "Please, Reed. I want to gag on your cock."

My cock twitched on cue, painfully restrained by my boxer briefs. I needed to get these fucking pants off. I pushed off the bed and dragged her to the edge of the mattress.

Quickly stepping out of my pants and boxers, I let my cock spring free. The cool air sent tingles over my heated skin.

Lina's eyes flared at the sight of me, her tongue darting out to lick her lips. She didn't need instructions, her hand reaching out to wrap around the base, her fingers tightening. I let out a strangled noise. Blood pulsed at the root with the feel of her warm palm against my skin while she stroked up and down.

"Do they feel good when I touch them?" She turned her head toward me where she lay on the side of the bed, her tongue swirling the tip, lapping up the bead of precum and tracing the barbells.

"Yes, everything with you feels good, Lina." She ran her tongue down the underside of my dick, her lips brushing my heated skin and cool piercings while her hand tightened and stroked behind it. "You're driving me fucking crazy." I gripped her hair, urging her to take me. "Tilt your head to the side and open for me."

It was the only instruction she needed, her mouth drawing me in, her lips wrapping around me, her tongue running over my length.

My head fell back for a moment, almost unable to contain myself. I wanted to fuck the back of her throat. "Fuck," I groaned, my hand tightening on her hair. My gaze returned to her, her beautiful eyes staring up at me through her thick lashes. "Fuck, you look gorgeous taking my cock in that smart mouth." She hollowed out her cheeks, pulling me in deep as she sucked.

My balls tightened. "Where did you learn to suck cock like this?" Her eyes flicked up to mine, a mischievous, teasing glint in them. The corner of her lips tipped. I gritted out, "Don't. Answer. That."

She released a little giggle in her throat, the vibration sending a jolt of pleasure through me, wiping any thought of jealousy from my mind.

"You're fucking mine now. These lips. This fucking mouth." I thrust to the back of her throat, punctuating my possession of it. She was spread out for me on the bed. *Mine* to touch and adore.

My fingertips ran up the inside of her thighs and her knees parted farther, her hips needy and rocking, begging for me to touch her. I pushed her panties to the side to trace her sweet pussy with a single finger, spreading her wetness, circling her clit so lightly, she couldn't help but groan against my cock in desperation. Then I cupped her between her thighs and let my middle finger slip inside.

"This fucking cunt. Mine. Got it? Are you going to be a good girl? Always ready for me?"

I tried to pull out to let her reply, but she only sucked me deeper, her mouth like a vise around my cock.

"God." I heaved a laugh. "You're such a brat."

She hummed in confirmation while she smiled around my cock. My chest squeezed, a feeling of pride spreading warmth through me. I was so proud of her for taking exactly what she wanted.

She tightened her grip. Saliva pooled at the corners of her mouth, making her mouth and fingers glide effortlessly over my skin. Her tongue continued to stroke and swirl while she sucked, taking me as deeply as she could. My balls tightened and contracted. Pressure built deep in my lower back as I was about to come.

"Fuck, Lina, I'm going to come. Swallow every drop." I came in a rush, my cum coating the back of her throat, my hand buried in her hair, holding her there while I watched her throat bob. "That's it, baby. Every last drop."

She continued to suck me dry while I fingered her. My hand was soaked.

"Now, tell me," I said, her swollen lips finally releasing me. I was still semi-hard. I stroked myself, spreading the wetness from her mouth and her pussy along my dick. I groaned. "Does this mouth"—I leaned down to brush my lips across hers—"belong to me now?"

"Reed."

Fuck, my name sounded like heaven on her lips. She breathed against my mouth as I climbed back onto the bed, shifting her with me to the center of the mattress.

I hooked my fingers in the waistband of her panties, slowly dragging them down her long, sexy legs and tossing them on the floor. Then I unclasped her bra, throwing it over my shoulder. God, she was beautiful!

Hovering back over her, I wrapped her in my arms while I parted her with my knees to settle between her thighs. I gave a light thrust, letting her feel the heaviness of my cock, the thickness of my tip brushing against her center.

"Tell me, sweetheart. Is this all for me? I'm not going to be satisfied with just tonight. You need to tell me."

"You want to keep me, cowboy?" she asked, her words breathy and raspy. Fucking sexy. Her smoky eyes were heavy with desire. Her hips responding to me touching her, her pussy already trying to draw me in.

"Fuck, yes, I want to keep you," I said, inching forward. I'd never been so sure of anything in my life. She was so wet, so warm, so ready for me. I was about to black out from how good she felt wrapped around my cock.

"God," she said on a moan.

"No, baby. I'm your god," I whispered into her mouth while I pressed in a little more and she groaned over the stretch. "No other name will leave these lips while I make you come."

Her hips rocked, her back arching to urge me on.

"You want me buried deep? You want to be full of my cock? Then you need to say it, Lina." My arms shook while

I held myself steady above her. Her breaths heaved. Her hard nipples brushed against my chest, sending jolts of electricity straight to my balls. I wanted to wrap my mouth around those perfect tips, but first, she needed to say it. "Quit being stubborn and just submit to me," I told her.

Her eyes found mine, boring into me while little pants escaped her lips. She stilled her hips even though the walls of her pussy were already fluttering around my tip. I wasn't even fully inside, and we were both on edge, desperate to have each other. I could read it all over her face.

"I surrender to you, Reed. My mouth"––she arched up, nipping my bottom lip––"belongs to you. This pussy"––she rolled her hips, causing me to push deeper inside––"belongs to you."

I sucked in a breath through my nose, my entire body aching for her, impatient with need. I wanted to ask her if her heart also belonged to me because mine sure fucking belonged to her, but I wasn't ready to broach that subject. Not yet, anyway.

This would have to do for now. I wrapped an arm around her shoulders, dropping a soft kiss to her lips before resting my forehead on hers, our eyes fluttering closed just for a moment as if we were both relieved to surrender to each other.

Then I pulled back slightly because I wanted to watch her beautiful face while she took me.

With one heavy thrust, her mouth fell open on a pant and her brows pinched. My dick stretched her walls that were already pulsing and gripping me with such ferocity, the intensity nearly took my breath away.

"Fuck, baby. You feel so fucking good. This pussy was made for me."

I continued to rock and thrust against her, my cock sliding in and out of her.

"Reed!" she cried. "Fuck."

She started to grind against my cock.

"You want to rub that little clit against me while I fuck you bare?"

"Yes." She rocked her hips forward.

It was so easy for me to read her body. I knew exactly what she needed. "Here." I grabbed a pillow, pushing it under her hips while I was still deep inside her. Repositioning myself so I was higher above her, her mouth brushed the pulse at my throat. The angle changed so I could still be deep inside while the base of my cock rubbed against her clit. Her legs wrapped around me, bringing me closer to her, her hands pressing into my lower back to keep me there. She knew exactly what to do, my sweet little vixen.

"Move, Reed. Please."

"Don't worry, baby. I got you."

I started rocking against her, my cock sliding in and out of her tight little cunt while it brushed her clit. Her fingernails dug into my lower back while she panted against my neck, her teeth grazing my skin, sending shivers all along my spine. She was the one marking me instead. I wanted her to leave her brand on me. I'd gladly bleed for this woman.

Fuck, she'd already made me bleed tonight. I'd let her do it again.

"Fuck, Reed! I'm so close!"

"Me, too." Pressure started to build again, and my balls began to tighten. I could feel her walls clench around me. "Come with me, baby."

"Fuck! Fuck!" she screamed, her legs still wrapped around me.

"Fuck!" I yelled, thrusting deep, my cock pulsing in time with her pussy while my orgasm rocked through me, my cum painting her walls.

Unable to hold myself up any longer, I collapsed on top of her, pushing her into the mattress, her legs and arms still around me while we caught our breath. The feel of her body beneath me, hot and sweaty, my cock still throbbing inside her, made me feel as though we didn't just belong to each other—she was made for me.

I rolled off her, pulling out. She groaned as I left her, peeling us apart for just a moment before I tucked her into my side. She nestled into my shoulder, her leg draping over mine.

"That was incredible," she said, out of breath.

I planted a kiss into her hair, inhaling deeply and memorizing her vanilla floral scent, breathing it in. Wanting nothing more than to go to sleep with her wrapped around me.

"You're stuck with me now, sweetheart. You know that, right?"

She looked up at me, her hand resting on my pec, a soft smile flitting across her lips. "Even when I'm a brat?" She crooked an eyebrow.

"Especially when you're a brat. You get my fucking blood boiling, and all I want to do is tie you up and fuck the sass out of you."

"I can get down with that," she said, now climbing on top of me.

I held her thighs still, gazing up at her as she ran her fingers through her hair and stuck out her tits. They were still begging for me. I sat up, capturing one tight bud between my teeth. "I think I still need to mark you as mine," I said against her heated skin. "What do you say, baby?"

"Yes."

Chapter 19
Lina

It had been a long time since my brain was quiet. Ever since I was a kid, I felt like my mind was going ninety miles per hour. My body was barely able to catch up, always running the risk of being overstimulated and burning out. Riding helped that. It centered me and gave me a focus. As a teenager, I was wild, unruly even. Testing all my limits, pushing to see how far I could go before Dad yelled at me or he let me get bucked off. He'd pull me to the side and just ask in a level tone, "Now what can we learn from that?"

I was always too much for Mom. When I told her I wanted to live with Dad permanently, she seemed almost relieved. I understood her response, even if it stung that my mom didn't want me staying with her. I was too much for most people. But fuck them. I never once tried to rein myself in to make myself more palatable for them. If they didn't like me for me, they weren't worth my time anyway.

It was probably why I never had a steady boyfriend. I had plenty of friends growing up. I was the fun one. The one who was always organizing the parties and shenanigans. But the boys came and went. They were mostly there for the sex. I didn't blame them. I was there for the sex, too. Fun one, remember? As soon as it turned into a relationship, though, I was suddenly too much for them.

I never felt as though someone could accept all of me. That I could be secure in the fact that I belonged to someone. That I was just enough for someone.

Until now.

Standing in the middle of the arena back at Thornbrush, leading Mushu in a circle while Reed's daughter, Penn, sat on top, made me feel as if I could have it all. Watching her grip the reins, a huge smile on her little face beneath her helmet, made my chest tighten.

My brain was quiet, too. Just enjoying this moment of peace, smelling the sawdust and hay, hearing the clomp of Mushu's hooves and Penn's giggle made me feel as though my boots were pulling energy from the earth. The warmth of being home spread through my bones and rejuvenated me. I hadn't realized how much being on the circuit had drained me.

As soon as we got back home, the double-wide was ready for Reed and Penn, and Jude and Reed were busy moving everything in. Seeing Penn fly down the steps of Jude and Romy's house into her dad's outstretched arms after we drove up made my ovaries hurt. What the fuck was that? Since when did my baby-making clock start ticking? I hadn't even thought about kids. I think in my mind it was just something far off in the distance. Something I'd eventually do when I got older, but I was twenty-seven. Maybe this was just something that happened to most people around this age? Or maybe it was just something people thought of when they found a compatible partner?

"Shit," I said under my breath. So much for my thoughts not spiraling. I had no idea what I was doing, but Penn sure was fucking cute in her little Carhartt overalls and cowboy boots, her wispy, dark-blonde hair tied back in a low ponytail.

"Oh, Mushu." Penn giggled, petting his mane.

I turned in a circle, holding his lead while Mushu walked.

"Do you think my dad is done setting up my room?" she asked.

"Just about. One more turn, and then you can help me unsaddle Mushu before we head over there."

"I can't wait to see it," she practically squealed. Mushu bobbed his head as if he were as excited as she was.

After another turn around the arena, I walked Penn and Mushu back to the stables. It was a warm July evening, the sun still high in the sky, promising another hot day tomorrow. Dad wasn't kidding when he said we were entering a drought. It hadn't rained in over fourteen days. Willows Rodeo had already canceled their world-famous fireworks show, pivoting instead to a small drone show. It wasn't going to be the same, but I was thankful they were taking precautions. We were entering wildfire season, and there was already a report of a four-thousand-acre fire in southern Oregon, prompting evacuations of ranches and communities as it continued to grow.

Mushu nuzzled Penn's cheek as we doled out his hay. "Aw! He loves me," she declared, a sweet smile breaking across her face.

I smiled, taking her little hand as we closed his stall. "I think he might."

"Bye, Mushu!" she said, giving him a quick wave as we left. Mushu picked up his head briefly from his dinner to flick his ears toward her voice.

My chest warmed seeing her interact with my favorite guy.

"Do you think he's going to win?" she asked. "My daddy said you're the fastest barrel racer he's ever seen."

I swallowed, feeling my cheeks heat. "Yeah? Your daddy said that?"

She nodded, her little feet skipping as we walked away from the stables and I loaded her into the UTV parked outside.

"Can I drive?" she asked. She was definitely not shy. I loved a girl up for anything.

"Fuck yes, you can drive," I told her.

"Fucking yes!" she exclaimed, climbing onto my lap in front of the steering wheel.

"My kind of girl." I chuckled. "Don't get me in trouble with your dad, though."

I revved the engine to life, pushing on the pedals and helping her steer our way through the property to the other side of the ranch where the double-wide sat.

All the lights were on. Jude had treated it to a fresh coat of white paint. Fern baskets hung from the awning over the front porch. The door opened, and my heart did a silly little flip seeing Reed step out onto the porch. My pussy clenched in response to him in a tight, white T-shirt showing off his muscles and Wranglers that hugged those tree-trunk thighs. He rubbed the scruff of his beard and narrowed his eyes when he saw Penn driving us to a stop.

Now that we were home, I already missed having him in my bed. One night, where I had him three times before we fell asleep in each other's arms, and then again in the morning before we even got out of bed, only had me wanting more. Seeing the bruises on my throat and breasts every morning since then gave me a nice reminder of where his mouth had been. I was desperate to have him again, to ease the ache between my thighs.

"Daddy!" Penn yelled. "Look at me! Lina let me drive!"

"She did, did she?" His dark eyes pinned me down.

I gave him a big grin. "She's a pro at it. She'll be racing down the trails in no time." I winked, tossing my hair over my shoulder.

Reed crossed his arms, watching us cut the engine and step off the UTV. "I'm going to be in a heap of trouble with you two. How was riding Mushu?"

"The fucking best!" Penn cried out, running toward her dad on the porch.

Reed shot me a look over his shoulder as he scooped her up, his lips pinching together to keep from laughing.

I shrugged, not holding back my own laughter. "Yep, you're in for it, *Daddy*." I gave him a sexy wink.

His jaw flexed and his throat bobbed at my words, his eyes giving me a heated warning. God, I loved testing him. Seeing how far I could push him before he snapped. And this time, it may result in him bending me over the porch railing or tying me to a bedpost. I was here for all of it.

"Can I see my room now?" Penn pleaded, putting her palms on either side of his face, turning his attention back to her.

"Yep, it's all done now."

"Is it a princess room?" she asked, bouncing up and down in her dad's arms.

"You'll just have to wait and see for yourself."

She wriggled from his arms, running into the house. Reed and I exchanged glances before following her inside.

"It is! It's a princess room!" she yelled from down the hall.

"Jude did a great job getting it ready for you," I commented from the entryway, taking in the updates. He'd traded out his leather couch for a gray, microfiber one for durability. A shelving unit was set up by the TV with baskets for toys and books.

"I'm beyond grateful for your family's help in getting us set up here," Reed said, his fingers brushing mine at my side as we followed Penn's excited cries down the hallway.

I smiled up at him, his dark eyes warm as he looked at me. My chest clenched. "I'm glad we're able to help you and Penn."

Penn met us at her door. "Come on, Lina, you have to see this!" She grabbed my hand, yanking me into the room that was once an office and was now a kid's room, complete with twin bed, dresser, and toy bins.

She started naming off everything, pulling out all her toys to show me, and the whole time, Reed's eyes were glued on me, caressing me like the softest, warmest touch. It was something I could get used to. And as much as it should … it didn't scare me.

Sage and I stocked the last of the makeshift bar beneath the raised beams of Jude and Romy's new barn. The DJ I hired—because go big or go home—was already testing out his setup with a Brooks and Dunn tune. I couldn't help shimmying my hips while I unpacked the bottles Sage brought over from The Rooster.

"This is a little overkill for just the three of us." Romy wasn't one to have a plethora of friends … only a few close ones whom she knew and trusted. But I didn't think that was a reason to not still throw her a party. "I'm glad you decided to let the guys come, too," Romy said, stepping over the wall frame to join us. She looked amazing in a cream-colored maxi dress with a slit up her leg, a turquoise belt cinched at her waist. It didn't even look like she just had a baby.

"Lina didn't take my 'no' for an answer," Sage grumbled at my side.

I rolled my eyes. "You know Christian would've made some excuse to drop by anyway, just like he does when we have our movie nights. He's always crashing girls' night. The guy is obsessed with you."

"Ugh!" Sage complained. "I'm popping this bottle so I can get drunk before he gets here. He's more tolerable when I've got my buzz on."

Romy and I exchanged glances. The girl was always trying to convince us that she didn't have any feelings for the guy.

"Might as well pour one for me, too," I told her, pushing a champagne flute closer to her. "What about you, Romy?"

"Fine. Just a small one."

I set another flute in front of Sage while she uncorked the bottle and poured the bubbly. The bubbles tickled my nose when I brought it to my mouth.

There weren't any barn walls yet, just the frame, giving us a clear view of the ranch, the expanse of sagebrush and wild grass disappearing into the ponderosa pines. The day had been a scorcher, and I could still feel the sweat dripping down my spine, making my black crop top stick to my back. An evening breeze was beginning to kick up, cooling my heated flesh and ruffling the fringe of my mini skirt. I twisted my hips to the music, letting the fringe brush across my thighs. I sighed in relief with a cool drink in my hand and the air wafting across my skin.

"This is better than strippers," Romy remarked behind me.

I spun around, looking past her to see Jude, Reed, Christian, and Kale strutting toward us in full cowboy getup, complete with chaps, hats, and boots. Baby Charli was tucked inside an infant carrier on Jude's chest. Seeing him completely embrace fatherhood made me so happy. He was already such a great dad. Watching Penn tug on Reed's hand was making me experience a completely different feeling. Something I hadn't felt before. A feeling that made my heart feel warm and full all at the same time.

They'd all been out working the ranch earlier, but now they were all cleaned up with fresh jeans and button-ups. As they approached, I could smell the cologne drifting toward me. I licked my lips when my eyes connected with Reed's, his own mouth tipped for a moment before disappearing into his usual scowl.

"Who's idea was this?" Sage asked, gesturing to their outfits before shooting back her champagne and pouring herself another one.

My eyebrow rose in question. "Seeing Christian in chaps making you hot and bothered?" I asked her.

She shot me a death glare over her champagne glass. I snorted a laugh.

"Jude roped us into this one," Christian remarked as they all ducked their heads beneath a low two-by-four.

Romy went to Jude's side, beaming up at her fiancé while he lowered a kiss to her lips. "Anything for my honey. Do you want me to keep these chaps on for later?" he asked her with a lopsided smirk, brushing her lips with another kiss.

"Why is it even a question?" she asked, a glint of mischief in her eyes.

"So it's obviously foreplay for the soon-to-be newlyweds, but how did you manage to convince this one?" I probed, gesturing to Reed with my glass.

His eyes were so intense on me, raking down my body, that I couldn't help the flush that crept across my skin while I waited for his reply.

"I owed him," Reed answered simply in his deep voice, his gaze still not leaving me as it traveled down my bare legs to where they disappeared into my boots.

"We'll hang out for a little bit, but then we're on kid duty for the rest of the night while you ladies have fun," Jude explained.

I squeezed my thighs together, my eyes still watching Reed, and the movement did not get past him. His lips tipped as his eyes found mine once again.

"We may have another surprise, too." I heard my dad's voice come from my right. I turned to welcome him to the party and froze when I saw who stepped into the barn with him.

Romy let out a sob before she muffled her cries with her hand.

CHAPTER 20
Lina

Hazel Miller stepped into the unfinished barn as if she'd never left Thornbrush. Her blonde hair, a little darker than Romy's, was braided. Dark circles shadowed her eyes, and smile lines bracketed the corner of her mouth. She looked older and tired after the ordeal she'd gone through, but she was tan and fit, as though she'd been working hard outside for the past few months. And perhaps she had. Last I'd heard, she was released on bail to Sanctuary Ridge, a rehab facility for rescued horses and battered women, while she awaited trial.

"Hazel!" I squealed. I bounced on my heels, impatiently waiting for Romy to release her sister so I could get my arms around her.

I'd missed her so much. She was my barrel racing buddy and trainer—one of my favorite people growing up—and I desperately wanted to tell her how much I wished I'd seen the signs.

"I hear I have a niece now," Hazel was saying through tearful laughter.

Jude started bringing Charli over, but I swooped her up out of her carrier.

"Hey!" Jude exclaimed.

"She's my baby now." I rushed over to Hazel with Charli in my arms.

Her eyes met mine as she pulled away from Romy, warming with affection.

"Finally locked her down, huh, Jude?" Hazel asked, her eyes flicking to him momentarily, her usual easy smile breaking through the tears as she took Charli from my arms.

"She's never getting rid of me now," he commented, wrapping an arm around Romy to comfort her. She ducked her head into his chest in an attempt to let the tears subside.

"She looks so much like a Larsen." Hazel peered down at Charli, a big-bow headband with horses covering her dark hair. "What's her name?"

"Charli after Dad," I beamed, sneaking in a side hug with Hazel and the baby. I was so proud to claim Charli as one of us.

Hazel's eyes looked past me to Dad, a flicker of something passing momentarily, before returning her gaze to the bundle in my arms. "It's a perfect name for this little sweet pea. Mom would've been so proud, Rom. May I?" She held out her hands.

"Of course, auntie," Romy said, giving permission for me to pass the baby to Hazel.

Charli started to fuss slightly and Hazel didn't skip a beat, rocking her as if she was a natural with infants. But that was Hazel. She was a natural at everything and had that nurturing instinct I felt I lacked.

"Does this mean you're going to be here for the wedding?" Romy asked from where she was tucked into Jude's side.

Hazel, still swaying, said, "That's the hope. I'll find out

more when I meet with my lawyer tomorrow. The court has been dragging out the process for so long. I'm ready for this just to be done and behind me."

"We all are." I brushed loose hair behind Hazel's ear since her hands were full. "I wish I'd seen the signs," I told her, lowering my voice. Her gaze drifted to mine, soft and understanding.

"I know. I should have asked for help before it got as bad as it did, but I didn't know how. Not at the time, anyway. I think I started believing I deserved it. That is, until I was at my breaking point. I just couldn't let it happen anymore, you know."

I nodded, even though I didn't truly know. I could only imagine. I'd like to think that if I were in the same position, I'd fight tooth and nail to get out. I would probably even do the only option I thought I had left to free myself.

"I hear you're on the circuit to win the finals," Hazel said, breaking the somber mood, her big, beaming grin coming quicker now.

I couldn't help returning her smile, but it was because she was home, not because of the topic change. "You'll have to critique my run before this weekend."

"I'll be happy to give you some pointers, but I have a feeling you're faster than I ever was on Bronte. Mushu is a runnin' son of a gun."

"We can race across the pasture tomorrow and settle it once and for all."

Her smile widened, brightening her hazel eyes. "You're on."

She gave me a glimpse of the old Hazel, making me feel hopeful that the therapy she received while she was away was exactly what she needed. But I knew she'd never truly be the same.

"Can I introduce you to our two other new additions to the ranch?" I asked her, my attention drifting to Reed and Penn.

Hazel's face softened when she saw whatever played across my own.

"Reed Ownstead," he said in his deep, gravelly voice, stepping up to shake her hand, ever the gentleman with his country manners. "And this is my daughter, Penn."

Hazel beamed, her gaze turning on me. "Well, Reed, if I know anything about the Larsens, once they claim you as one of their own, you're practically family."

Romy and Hazel sat around the firepit while the rest of us stood around the bar, their heads together, whispering and wiping tears from each other's cheeks.

"To get it down from twenty-five years to three years is better than we'd hoped," Dad was saying.

My eyes drifted down to Hazel's ankle, where she wore a monitor. Since Thornbrush was her previous residency, and she was due to appear in court soon to receive her sentence, the judge decided she needed to return. Thanks to Oregon's "stand your ground" laws regarding the act of self-defense, the lawyer was fighting for the sentence to be reduced even further to cover just the unlawful carry and use of a firearm and evading arrest, hoping the homicide charges would be dropped. While the verdict was still out, Hazel was under house arrest at the big house.

As a rodeo queen and barrel racing champ, I idolized her growing up. Seeing her go through all that shit last year, and now knowing the abuse she had endured at the hands of Jesse Matheus, my heart hurt for her.

"I'm glad she's here, Dad. She's been through enough shit. The least we can do is be the family she needs right now," I said.

Dad's eyes flicked to Romy and Hazel huddled together before returning his gaze to me. "I'm glad too, darlin'."

"Can't say Frank is much of a parent for her," Jude commented, bringing his beer bottle to his lips.

Romy discovered her dad, Frank, was doing more than drinking when she found him and Junior in the stables last summer. Frank was getting painkillers from Junior, and apparently, he owed him. No one had spoken to him since. Last I heard, he wasn't invited to the wedding.

"No, unfortunately he's not. If I could go back and change things, I would." Dad's knuckles turned white around his bottle, and I reached out to soothe his grip.

"You can't keep beating yourself up about this," I told him. Dad had been making little comments like that since it happened, and it stung to know he was dealing with regret. There were very few signs Jesse was beating on her. I hadn't seen it, either. I just thought it was a toxic relationship that would play out, and eventually, Hazel would dump him. I liked him just fine. He was always respectful to Dad and I, plus he was a hard worker. Maybe that was all a cover-up for what was really going on. If I'd known, I would have done something to stop it, too. But hindsight is twenty-twenty.

Alarm beeps started going off.

"What's that?" Sage asked, her glass halfway to her lips.

We all stopped in our conversation to listen, but Dad and Jude wasted no time pulling out their phones from their pockets.

"What the fuck?" Jude said, opening his notifications.

"The game cams," Dad announced.

"Shit! The game cams! Is someone fucking with the fence?" I asked, peering over Dad's shoulder to look at his phone as he opened the app.

There, in night vision, was the herd running straight through a broken-down fence.

"Goddammit!" Dad stuffed his cell back in his pocket, turning to leave. "We gotta go!"

Jude was still staring at his screen. "There's a group of riders driving them off!"

"Can you see who it is?" Reed asked, his eyes wide.

"They're all in black clothing," Jude said, returning his cell to his pocket and beginning to unstrap the carrier.

"I'll take her," Sage offered, removing Charli from his arms.

"What's going on?" Romy asked, as she and Hazel returned to our group.

"Someone's fucking with the herd," I explained.

Romy took the infant carrier from Jude.

"Are there bad guys?" Penn asked, poking her head up from where she was playing with rocks, lining them up across a pile of salvaged wood.

"Sorry, ladies. I guess we're going to have to cut this party short," Dad called over his shoulder, heading to where his truck was parked by the house.

The men were already moving into action, Jude kissing Romy, and Kale and Christian jogging to their own respective vehicles.

"Guess we're on kid duty." I shrugged.

"Fuck that," Hazel said under her breath, setting down her beer. "I'm coming with you, Chuck!" she called after him.

"The hell you are!" he hollered back, reaching his truck.

"Do you mind taking Penn back to the house?" Reed asked me. I looked up at him. His face had grown dark, but his eyes were pleading.

I nodded. "Just go." I pushed him away, sending him toward the trucks. "We got her. You're wasting time now."

His jaw ticked, and he gave me a jerky nod before turning on his heels.

Hazel was already racing over to Dad's truck to hop in the passenger seat.

"Well, this has been eventful." Sage sighed, swallowing the last of her champagne.

"No kidding."

"You better be safe out there, Jude 'The Bull' Larsen!" Romy shouted to her fiancé, who was adjusting his hat while he hopped into his truck.

"I'll settle up with the DJ if y'all want to take the rest of the party into the house while we wait," I suggested.

My toes tingled in my boots, itching to run after them and join the hunt. This was my ranch, too, and I'd gladly fight anyone who was fucking with our fence and cattle. Reed gave me one last glance before he hoisted himself into his truck. The look gave me the acknowledgment I needed. As if he could read my thoughts from here, it was a look that said, *You should be with us, but there is no one else I'd trust with my daughter.*

Air froze in my chest.

If he trusted me with his daughter, then I knew I could trust him with my ranch.

A tiny hand wrapped around my fingers. I looked down to see Penn gazing up at me. "Do you know how to do Anna braids?"

My mouth curved in a smile. "Yeah, I do, princess. Do you want to see my Disney movie collection while we wait for your dad to get back?"

Her sweet little smile nearly took over her round cherub face.

CHAPTER 21
Reed

We were too late.

We'd missed them by the time we had reached the north pasture. As soon as we got saddled and rode out, all that was left was broken ground where they'd rustled up the cattle and drove them off. About a hundred yards of fence line was pulled down or trampled on. It was going to be a shit ton of work to fix the fence and locate the cattle.

"Ready to call the livestock commission now?" Jude asked Chuck.

"The most they can do is help us track down the missing herd. They can't do shit about the vandals or the theft," Chuck replied.

"You could turn the game footage in to the authorities. Maybe they can identify them," Christian offered.

Hazel scoffed beside Chuck where she sat on top of her horse. "Hate to break it to you, Christian, but no one's going to help us out here." Her tone was bitter.

I didn't know Hazel at all. This was my first time meeting her, but I'd heard stories from Chuck about Willows' golden girl. I pictured a smiley, bubbly girl who was ready to make everyone her best friend. She definitely was not that. In fact, she reminded me a lot of Romy. Maybe a little bit more outspoken, and her blonde hair was a shade darker, but there was an edge to her that only trauma could carve. She had sharp, hazel eyes that studied our surroundings as if she were looking for something. Her mouth was set in a firm line as though biting back her thoughts.

"What is it?" Chuck asked, his gaze locked on her.

"How many riders did you see on the cam?" she probed.

"It looked like three."

"Huh." Hazel clicked her tongue, urging her horse toward the broken fence line.

We remained in our circle, sitting on top of our mounts, watching her.

"What do you think she sees?" Jace asked.

With the new game cams installed, everyone had been much more relaxed about shift changes. Jace was supposed to relieve Marshall, but at some point, Marshall had already started heading back when the alarms went off. By the time Marshall had turned back around, the herd and the riders were already gone.

I eyed them both. How would someone know to come out here in between shifts?

Both of them watched Hazel, like everyone else. But I was watching them. Something wasn't sitting right with me.

She turned her horse around, trotting back toward us.

"Looks like they headed toward the river," Hazel hollered as she approached. "I'm not sure these riders knew how to drive them out. May have just wanted to spook them enough to make our lives harder, not steal cattle. They just wanted to cause a stampede. They'll be heading downhill."

Chuck nodded, considering what she said. "Running to a water source," he added, finishing her thought.

Hazel bobbed her head. "Precisely."

"All right, then. Let's see if we can track them before they get too far. From now on, no break in the patrol, and everyone is carrying. Jace and Marshall, you're both going to need to take double shifts while we're at the rodeo this weekend," Chuck instructed.

"Sure, boss," Marshall said.

"Done," Jace agreed.

My gaze narrowed on them. I wasn't sure they were the best ones to take double patrols while we were all away from the ranch, but I wasn't sure it was my place to say it, either.

"I'll take a shift with them," I volunteered.

Chuck turned in his saddle. "You're needed with Lina."

"You don't think there might be a connection here?" I blurted out.

Everyone swung to look at me then.

"What do you mean?" Hazel asked, her face like a stoic mask, like she was hiding her own thoughts and suspicions.

My brows pinched. I wondered if she and I were drawing the same conclusions. She seemed like a smart cookie.

"It just seems like a coincidence to me that while Lina is dealing with a stalker, the ranch is dealing with vandalism and maybe a cattle thief." I rested my arms against the saddle horn, waiting for them to pick up what I was putting down.

Hazel seemed to jump on my train of thought. "Lina has

a stalker?"

"She does. He's gotten pretty bold, too," I told her.

"When did this all start?" Even in the moonlight, her face had gone pale.

"Beginning of May," Chuck and I answered together.

She exhaled a deep breath as if trying to keep the fury from rising. At least, that's how I was feeling. "There are very few people who are familiar with the ranch at night, and his brother would have shared it *all* with him," she said.

I could almost hear Chuck's molars grind. "Junior?"

I sucked in my own deep breath at his name.

"I don't think I was able to stop him in time," Hazel said, her words like a ghost in the warm night breeze.

Despite the temp, a chill ran down my spine.

Whether she was talking about Jesse or Junior, I wasn't certain, but Chuck seemed to know. His fingers gripped the reins, causing his horse, Gus, to toss his head in annoyance.

"Is there something we should know?" Jude asked, looking between Hazel and Chuck.

Chuck seemed to shake off his anger, returning to his typical, laid-back persona. "Let's find the herd, but then we should talk."

"Lina will want to be included," I told him, remembering how pissed she was when her dad didn't tell her about the drought.

He nodded. "Before the rodeo, then."

The sky was already growing light as I walked up the steps

of my new home. My body was tired and sore after riding all night through rugged terrain. We'd found the majority of the herd grazing along the riverbank, but a few of them were still missing. Chuck reported the missing cattle to the livestock commission so they could start searching for the branded cows.

We all moved the herd to the eastern pasture, and Chuck and Hazel decided to stay out there to give Jace and Marshall a rest. All I wanted to do was check in on Penn, drink a big glass of water, and go to bed. But sleep would have to wait. I was supposed to let Lina know that Chuck called a meeting at the big house directly after breakfast.

The double-wide was dark, the only glow coming from the nightlight through the cracked door of Penn's room down the hall. I toed off my boots and tossed my gloves onto the entry table at the door before padding down the hallway to peer into Penn's room.

My chest tightened and my heart skipped a beat at the sight of Lina curled up on Penn's twin bed beside her. Both of them were sound asleep. Penn had her arms raised above her head like she always did when she slept, her legs sprawled beneath the covers. She was wearing her favorite Frozen jammies, and her hair was in two braids. Lina slept with an arm folded beneath her head, her lips pursed in quiet, even breaths. At some point, she had changed into a pair of my sweats and a tee, her hair piled on top of her head. Her face was clean of any makeup.

She looked absolutely perfect there, sleeping beside my daughter—as if she belonged at her side. I wanted to encapsulate this moment, engrain it in my brain, and tattoo it on my heart.

She said that she thought it was love at first sight, and maybe it was. I felt something then, too. I just didn't know what to call it at the time.

I stood there for a few more minutes, watching them both sleep, their steady breaths causing their chests to rise and fall while they snuggled together. This felt like a significant moment that was about to change everything. And even though I was dead on my feet, I couldn't pull myself away from the doorway.

Taking my phone from my vest pocket, I snapped a photo so I could save this memory forever.

CHAPTER 22

Lina

The sound of voices—one sweet and lilting and the other deep and rumbly—pulled me from the haze of sleep. The smell of bacon and coffee made my stomach growl as I stretched out in Penn's bed. My eyes sprang open. I hadn't meant to fall asleep in her bed, but when she started missing her dad, I had lain down beside her and we'd both fallen asleep.

I was alone in her twin-size princess bed now and I sat up, adjusting my hair in its messy bun before tiptoeing out to the kitchen where I heard Penn and Reed. I stopped at the couch. They hadn't noticed me yet. Reed's back was to me, holding Penn on his hip. He flipped bacon in the pan while Penn was talking his ear off about the movie collection I showed her in our basement. Her eyes had grown into the biggest saucers when I'd turned on the lights and she saw the floor-to-ceiling shelves of DVDs and old VHS tapes.

My heart did a little flip, and my ovaries made that funny little twinge again watching them together. To see a man as gruff and grumpy as Reed go completely soft for his daughter was absolutely panty-melting and heartwarming all at the same time.

"Hi," I said, approaching the kitchen island. Reed turned, his eyes growing wide for a moment before softening and traveling over my frame.

"Hi," he said back, his gaze returning to mine. Even with that one simple word, I could feel it reverberate through me and scatter goose bumps all over my skin.

My cheeks warmed.

"Lina!" Penn wriggled out of her dad's hold to rush to me. I bent down for a hug, which allowed me to hide my blush.

"Hey, Princess Penn." I grinned brightly.

She smiled wide. "You remembered!"

She insisted I call her Princess Penn last night after we finished watching *Beauty and the Beast*. One of my favorite princess movies.

"Of course, milady." I exaggerated a curtsy, causing Penn to giggle and jump up and down in her kitty slippers.

Over Penn's head, Reed was frozen, tongs in hand. He bit his bottom lip as if attempting to keep himself from saying something. His dark eyes glinted in the early morning light, a sheen I hadn't noticed before, and it made my breath hitch.

"Can we ride horsies after breakfast?" Penn asked, grabbing my hand and dragging me into the kitchen to stand beside her dad.

I had trouble pulling my eyes away from him. It was as if our gazes were locked—connected in a way I couldn't explain. The air seemed to thicken now that I was this close to him, making it hard to breathe. His Adam's apple bobbed on a swallow, and the muscle in his jaw ticked. I wanted to ask him if he, too, felt as though he couldn't breathe.

Reed cleared his throat, forcing himself to break free from our stare. He seemed to recover quicker than me, noticing now that Penn had a hold of both of our hands. I gulped, seeing our hands gripped in her little dimpled ones.

Nerves flipped my stomach. What was this? What could this be? Could I take on a relationship with a man who was a dad?

"We can't today, princess," Reed was saying. "We're going to the big house after we eat."

"Is this about last night?" I asked, my stomach going from flirty flutters to shooting right into my throat. I needed something to drink. To shake all these crazy, fucking feelings. To push it down until my nerves could settle. Instead, I spotted the coffeepot, dropping Penn's hand to open the cabinet above to grab a mug and pour myself a cup.

"Milk's in the fridge," he said casually. "Your dad wants us all over there. He said we should talk. I'm assuming it's about what's happening on the ranch."

"At least he's roping me in on it this time," I said. It was meant to be a sassy little comment, but instead, it sounded bitter. I needed to get some coffee and then get the fuck out of here before I said or did something stupid. "Let me just have some coffee, and then I'll take off. I can meet you over there."

Reed was already fixing three plates with bacon and toast. "Sit, Lina." He jerked his chin to the stools at the counter.

"Oh, you don't have to feed me. I can get something back at home."

Reed glowered at me, two plates in his hands, while Penn skipped over to climb up on one of the stools. "Sit by me, Lina!"

Penn was patting the stool beside her, her face eager and excited.

"Just sit and eat, then we can go over there together." Reed set the plates down in front of the stools.

Both of them were looking at me expectantly, but Reed gave me a more pointed look … like this was not a request and it was better that I listen. A thrill ran through me. I hated to admit it, but seeing him in bossy dad mode was making my libido go haywire.

"Fine." As soon as I was sitting down at the counter, I crossed my legs, hoping it would keep my pussy from clenching.

It didn't help when he slid into the stool beside me, his knee pressing into mine like he knew exactly what he was doing to me.

It felt weird walking into the house I'd grown up in with Reed and Penn in tow, as if we were a unit and they belonged to me. It was still my house, but something had shifted, and now it felt like a transition was happening that I wasn't quite prepared for but didn't entirely hate.

Dad seemed totally unfazed that I hadn't slept at home, walking into the living room with Reed and Penn. In fact, he had an annoying smirk on his face.

"Shut up," I told him.

"I didn't say anything." The knowing smile still on his face. He was liking this a little bit too much.

"It's the look." I dropped into my usual, leather-bound chair.

Dad was still sipping his coffee, settling into his own recliner and turning down the walkie that was on the side table.

Reed sat down on the couch, pulling Penn onto his lap.

"What's this all about, Dad?"

"Let's wait for Jude and Romy to get here."

Hazel shuffled in then, pulling her hair back into a ponytail. She had jeans on, covering her ankle monitor, and a Willows Rodeo T-shirt. She shifted a glance at Dad for a split second—she either knew something or something was up. I didn't take the time to question it, ready to get on with my day.

"They better hurry up. I have a rodeo to prepare for," I said impatiently.

"Want to do a warm-up after this?" Hazel asked, her brows raised, eyeing Reed's sweats—I had to roll the waistband up three times to keep them on—and my beat-up tennis shoes.

"That would be great. As soon as this is done, I'll get dressed and meet you out at the arena," I told her, tapping my fingertips on the armrests. The rodeo-day energy was already buzzing through me, making it nearly impossible to stay still. Not to mention, I was dying to know what Dad wanted to share with all of us.

"Get any sleep this morning?" she asked, sitting down beside Reed as if they were old friends now. That was Hazel, though. She could turn anyone into a friend, even her own worst enemy.

For the first time ever, I felt annoyed by Hazel. A feeling of possessiveness washing over me. Or was it jealousy? I really needed to figure out my shit.

"A couple hours. Before this one decided to wake up." He

bounced Penn on his knee, causing a little giggle to escape her.

"Can I go down and look at the movies again?" she asked.

"Great idea!" Hazel exclaimed, her eyes lighting up. "I can take her downstairs, if you don't mind."

"Aren't you going to miss what Dad needs to tell us?" I questioned.

Hazel was already getting up, taking Penn's hand. Her smile never faltering, she said, "Chuck already apprised me of the situation. Y'all stay. I got her."

"Thanks, Hazel," Reed said, letting her take Penn.

Just then, Jude and Romy walked in, baby Charli asleep in the carrier on Romy's chest.

"It's already getting hot out there," Jude commented as he took the seat Hazel had just vacated.

"Have a seat, darlin'," Dad said, offering up his own for Romy.

"I better not. She has some sort of sixth sense. As soon as I sit down, she screams." Romy stood behind the couch, patting Charli's bottom while she rocked back and forth.

"Do you want me to take her, honey?" Jude offered.

She shook her head, resting her other hand on his shoulder. "I'm good. Let's hear what your uncle has to say."

Dad leaned forward, relaxing his elbows on his knees and lacing his fingers in front of him. "When all of this started happening, I went to talk to your grandpa," he began, exchanging glances with Jude and I.

Grandpa Lloyd had been in assisted living for about a year now. His dementia was getting worse. Guilt shot through me, knowing I needed to be better about visiting him.

"I needed to speak with him before he couldn't remember anything." Dad cleared his throat, a solemn look on his face. "The Matheuses used to ranch some of this land nearly eighty years ago. When I was a kid, with the success of the Willows Rodeo, your grandpa was looking to grow Thornbrush. Old Ernest Matheus passed and the family needed to pay off debt, so they held an auction for the land. Some of the land was claimed by the state, but the rest was bought up by Dad."

"The Matheus family—like Junior and Jesse—are from here?" I asked, surprised. I hadn't heard of them until Jesse came to work on the ranch.

Dad gave a brief nod. "Your grandpa agreed they could remain on the land and work for him … until, that is, about thirty years ago when they lost everything in a fire."

"Where was that?" Jude's jaw clenched, as if he already knew the answer.

"Where the burn pile used to be," Dad said quietly, his eyes bouncing between Jude and Romy.

Jude flipped his hat around, his knee starting to bounce with nerves. Romy rubbed his shoulder to help ease his tension.

"The construction company that laid the foundation for our house excavated some old pipe," he commented. "Pipe that ran to an old well."

Dad continued, "I should have said something." A furrow was deepening between Dad's brows. He was not enjoying this conversation. "His only surviving son, Jack Matheus, perished in the fire. Jack's wife and kids moved away after that happened. I didn't think I'd ever see any of them again."

"Did you know who Jesse was when you hired him?" Jude

asked.

I looked toward the hallway where Hazel had disappeared with Penn. No wonder she was willing to step out. I'm glad Dad told her privately before telling us.

"I did." A look of guilt washed over his face, his mustache turning down in a frown. "I knew there were some hard feelings between our families, but I was willing to set it aside, thinking time healed all, and this was a good way to repair old wounds. I didn't realize Jesse knew the family history, but I suppose he would have been old enough to remember the fire. He was a hard worker and took great care of the herd. When I was moving Dad into assisted living, I told him, and he warned me, but I didn't listen. I should have listened. He warned me that the Matheuses felt as though they still had a claim to the land."

"Did Hazel know this at the time?" I asked, because I certainly didn't. But I wasn't the one dating Jesse.

"I let her know. She did tell me that he'd make comments every once in a while that he was mad that we let the old Matheus homestead become a burn pile, that we let the sagebrush grow over what remained and never rebuilt it. But when Jack was killed and the family left, I thought they were gone for good. There was no reason to rebuild."

"Then Jesse was killed, Junior was harassing Romy—assaulted her—and let the horses out." Jude's face was growing red, his hands balling into fists on his thighs.

Romy stalled in her massage of Jude's shoulder, her own body going rigid. The whole room went tense.

"Fuck," I said under my breath, putting all the pieces together. My heart beat wildly. "Junior's behind this."

"We don't know that for sure," Reed said.

I shot him a look. "We don't bullshit here." I could tell he'd already put the pieces together even though he was still new to Thornbrush. Anyone who was here long enough could see there was more going on.

"He seems to like digging his claws in," Reed commented, glancing at Jude.

He jerked his head toward Romy behind him. "I told her," he confirmed. "She knows about your ex-wife and Junior."

I watched Reed's face turn hard, and I could feel my own fury building for him, Penn, and my own family. "This is so fucked up!" I cursed.

"Yeah, it is," Romy agreed, her voice carrying an edge to it. "Junior should've been charged with obstruction of justice, not just breaking a restraining order."

"For real." We were on the same page.

"Is there more?" Jude asked, leveling Dad with a look that was so reminiscent of 'The Bull,' his cage fighting persona.

"All of that being said, I think Junior may be behind the vandalism. He has the motive."

A thought dawned on me. "Do you think he's using your ex-wife?" I asked Reed. "Maybe he thinks he has some sort of in to get what he wants since he knows you're working here."

Reed's eyes grew darker than usual. "It crossed my mind, but he was with her before I ever came here. It could just be an added bonus for him."

"God, he's a fucking asshole." I slumped in my seat, my mind reeling. My legs felt antsy, like if I didn't move or do something, I'd lose my fucking mind.

"We need to be extra vigilant," Dad was saying, giving instructions to Jude and Reed, telling them they were going to need to start carrying and patrolling the fence lines until the perpetrators are caught.

I stood from my chair, wiping my sweaty palms on my pants. I could feel the spiral starting. As much as I wanted to know about the whole sordid family history, I really didn't want to talk about Reed's ex-wife. Because if Junior was using her, would he leave her as soon as he was done with her? Would she come to her senses and run back to Reed for help? Would he drop me and take her back so they could be a family? My chest tightened.

"Thanks, Dad, for filling us in. I'll take a patrol while I'm home, but I need to get ready." I needed to leave before I started pacing the room like a caged lion.

"Lina——" Dad started.

"Better just say 'okay,'" Reed suggested.

I gave him a small, appreciative smile. He saw me, and I was feeling that warmth spread through my chest again, calming me. It was exactly what I needed before an event.

Dad exchanged a look with Reed and Jude.

"Reed's right," Jude said.

"Ha! I never thought I'd hear you say that," Romy teased, jiggling baby Charli as she started to fuss.

Jude gave her a lopsided smirk over his shoulder. "Reed here is all right. And look,"—he gestured to Reed at his side—"Lina hasn't killed him yet, so he must be growing on her, too. Right, cuz?" He gave me a wink.

"Growing on me like a damn fungus," I teased, but I

couldn't help the smile that threatened the corner of my lips.

Reed's own mouth twitched at the corners.

"All right, but we're all patrolling in pairs," Dad cautioned. "No one goes out alone, especially now that we know there are multiple people involved. And no gaps in patrol. You wait until the others come to relieve you."

"Agreed," we all concurred.

Dad slapped his hands on his thighs, pushing himself up to his feet. "We have America's birthday to celebrate and a rodeo to get to. My baby girl is going to win her second Willows Rodeo in a row today."

I pulled my cell phone from the pocket of Reed's sweatpants to peek at the time. It was almost 9 a.m. "Shit, I gotta get going." I immediately started ticking off the mental list I usually kept before an event. I still had warm-ups to do. I needed to load up Mushu and the tack before eleven o'clock if I wanted to get to the rodeo grounds when the gates opened. "Love you, Daddy! Thank you for sharing the family secrets! Yeehaw!" I hollered, flashing a grin and Reed a wink before rushing out of the living room.

Reed's gaze followed me like a damn caress. I wanted him tonight. I'd take him however he was willing to give himself to me, too.

"I don't know why I don't have more gray hairs," Dad commented.

"I heard that!" I called back.

"Good!" Dad hollered.

CHAPTER 23
Reed

Penn was pulling me, her little legs pumping as quickly as she could go, trying to get into the gates of the rodeo as fast as humanly possible. I don't think I'd ever seen her so excited. Her face was going to be hurting by the end of the night with how big she was grinning. Zac Brown's "Chicken Fried" was playing over the stadium speakers, while the announcer's voice boomed over the cheering crowd, making her little boots skip. I chuckled. Her joy was contagious, and it warmed my heart to see her so happy. I wanted nothing more than to give her the happiest childhood I could afford.

Her mother hadn't called asking to see her or speak to her. She hadn't tried to come get her, either. It hurt my heart knowing that this was Penn's reality.

The summer heat was stifling, causing me to remove my hat and wipe the sweat from my brow. Good thing I found some sunscreen. Otherwise, Penn would be fried to a crisp, just like all the rodeo food that saturated the air.

"Reed!" Jude and Romy were standing at the entrance, noise-canceling headphones covering the ears of the baby in the carrier Jude was wearing.

The crowd milled around them.

"We're at a rodeo!" Penn squealed, slipping from my hold, making her way around the maze of people to Jude and Romy.

She held her cowboy hat to her head.

"Look at you!" Romy preened. "You look ready for the Fourth of July."

Penn was wearing jean shorts and a tank top with red and blue stars, American flag bows at the ends of her braids she had begged Lina to do before she left. Lina, already dressed in her rodeo gear, took the time to sit on the grass beside the horse trailer with my daughter. Penn didn't even hesitate to plop into her lap, as if it were the most natural thing in the world, and my heart *clenched*. My chest felt so tight, watching her gently do Penn's hair while they talked softly together.

"I am! I'm ready to cheer on Lina and Mushu!" She couldn't stop moving, bouncing on her brown cowboy boots.

"What's up, man?" Jude asked, bumping my fist.

We exchanged greetings, then followed them to the seats Chuck and Sage saved for us. The crowd was deafening while a saddle bronc rider held on during his ride in the arena.

"Where's Hazel?" I asked, Penn and I taking a seat on the metal stadium rafters.

Romy's eyes went sad, and I immediately felt like an ass for asking. I liked the woman, though. I was hoping to get to know her better and see the former rodeo queen in her element.

"She wasn't ready to be out here," Chuck replied.

I nodded with a grimace. "I understand. Sorry I asked. I should've figured as much."

"It's all right." Romy shrugged.

Chuck stood, giving me a firm pat on my shoulder as he shuffled out of the seat. "I gotta be ready to lead Lina in, now that y'all are here."

I couldn't help scanning the stadium for her mysterious stalker—or Junior. Everything that was happening at once didn't sit right with me. None of this felt like a coincidence. While I surveyed the audience, my gaze was drawn to my daughter, who was in complete awe of her surroundings.

Penn sat riveted, her eyes large, whooping and hollering at the top of her lungs while we watched the saddle broncs.

"You may be in trouble with that one," Sage teased. "You got a cowgirl on your hands."

"Don't I know it." Penn shared a smile with me. Pretty sure she knew it, too.

The barrel racers were up next, followed by the bull doggers and bull riders.

"When's it Lina and Mushu's turn?" Penn asked after every participant entered the arena.

"Soon," I repeated each time.

Jude and I walked with Penn to the concessions to grab hot dogs for everyone. Lina had just finished her run and was probably already untacking Mushu. She'd won the race, beating her last Willows Rodeo time. I was dying to see her, but Penn was whining that she was starving.

"I'll grab the beer," Jude offered, passing the rodeo bar.

"Mama!" Penn yelled, catching us both off guard.

Just as she'd done when we entered the rodeo to greet

Romy and Jude, she pulled from my grasp. And before I could stop her, she was rushing over to where Elise and Junior were exiting the bar.

"Oh, my baby!" Elise cried, dropping to her knees in front of Penn and taking her into her arms. Penn was so forceful in her hug, she almost knocked her over.

My gut knotted up seeing both of them now within reach of Penn. Jude and I hurried over.

"Come here, princess," I called, wanting her to come back to me, out of their grasp. "Let's let your mom and Junior get back to their drinks." I attempted to make my voice gentle for Penn, but it sounded too harsh to my ears. A flash of fear washed over me when Elise glared at me over Penn's shoulder.

My whole body tensed, and I could almost feel Jude vibrating beside me. I could hear his knuckles crack, as if he were preparing for a fight.

"You need to let her see her daughter." Junior's voice was threatening. *Asshole.*

I barely gave him a glance, but I hoped he saw the warning in them. "Penn, come on. Let's go get hot dogs, and then we can go see Lina."

"Better go check on your slut before someone else does." Junior's words were like acid on my brain, burning and fueling my rising fury.

"What the fuck did you just say?" Jude fired at him.

At the same time, I said, "Shut your fucking mouth."

"You heard me," he pressed, his gaze turning to Jude.

"You have something to do with Lina being stalked?" Jude hissed through his gritted teeth.

I needed to get Penn out of here before this turned ugly. She didn't need to see either one of us losing it in front of her. But hearing what Junior said—and then Jude's question—made the alarm bells go off. How the fuck would he know Lina was being stalked unless he had something to do with it?

"Penn. Now," I ordered sternly.

"Can Mama come sit with us?" she asked.

My heart fucking broke hearing her ask that. Of course she was missing her mom, but Elise had put in zero effort to show up for our daughter. As much as I hated the thought of her growing up without her, I needed to protect Penn from the really poor decisions Elise was making right now. She didn't know or understand that.

"No, princess, you need to come with me now." My hyper-vigilant dad radar was on high alert, bouncing between where Elise had her arms wrapped around our daughter and where Jude was mean-mugging Junior.

"The way she puts out, I'm not surprised she has unwanted attention. She probably gets off on it."

My head swung to Junior. I couldn't take this any longer. I took one big step, getting into his face. I was larger than him, and standing toe-to-toe, I forced him to look up at me.

"What? No gun this time?" he jeered, a snide grin spreading across his face.

"Who said I'm not packing?" I stared him down, right into his beady eyes, waiting for him to back down. He didn't. Junior was a fucking idiot.

Junior scoffed. "Nothing's going to happen in front of Penn."

"Don't you dare say my daughter's name. I will fucking tear that tongue straight out of your mouth if I hear you speak her name again. You might be Elise's fiancé, but you have no say in what I will or will not do in front of my daughter. *Ever.*"

I could feel Jude step up beside me, backing me up. Junior's eyes flicked briefly to the side, seeing him. Jude had knocked him out with one punch before and could easily do it again with those prized hands of his. Junior's bravery faltered before returning his narrowed gaze on me.

"Take your girl and leave—*now!*" Jude growled. "I don't have a contract to worry about this time, and I'm pretty sure after what you tried to pull last summer, law enforcement will be on my side if you go whining that I knocked your sorry ass out again."

"You fucking Larsens are all the same."

"Same with you Matheuses, it would seem."

"Fuck you, Jude. You don't own this town."

"Pretty close to it. I'm sure those two uniforms coming this way will appreciate knowing what you two have been consuming today. Not to mention what you two were into while a child was under your care."

I turned my attention to Elise, whose face grew pale. She looked like she was about ready to throw up. "Come on, Penn," I said calmly, even though I felt anything but.

"Please, Reed. Can I please see her?" Elise slurred her 'pleases,' tears choking her words. She was two seconds from causing a scene.

"Penn, give your mama one last hug. We need to go see Lina before she loads up Mushu."

"Bye, Mama," Penn said, giving her mom one last squeeze. She looked hesitantly between her mom, Jude and Junior, and me. She was a perceptive child, so I wasn't surprised she was reading the room. If I could shield her from all of this, I would. But this was the best I could do right now, and if it meant keeping her away from her mother until she got the help she needed and dumped Junior's ass, I had to do it.

"Reed, please." Elise was crying now.

"Get your girl," Jude said to Junior again. "You're about to get more attention than you want." Jude nodded at the two police officers who were meandering our way. They hadn't noticed yet, but they were about to.

Junior backed away, gripping Elise by the arm and pulling her to her feet. "Let's go, baby."

She released Penn when she stood and I swooped her up, holding her tight, as if she could be ripped from me at any moment. My heart was pounding. Blood rushed in my ears like a siren, warning me of the threats to my daughter.

"Reed, please." Elise was still pleading through her inebriated tears.

"I'll have my lawyer contact you," I said simply, taking hurried strides away from them and wishing there was a whole continent between Elise, Junior, and me.

I was exhausted after only having had two hours of sleep in the last thirty-six hours, and that was compounded by the surge of adrenaline caused by the encounter with Elise and Junior. Now that Penn and I were back on Thornbrush——now that we were *home*—I felt that we were safe.

I've never felt like I had a home before. Not like this anyway. My parents moved around a lot because my dad could never keep a steady job. I was the only child of two adults who had no business being parents—too busy and self-absorbed—who half the time didn't even seem as though they liked each other ... or me, for that matter. We didn't do love. I'm not sure I really knew what it meant to love or be loved until Penn was born. My love for my daughter was all-consuming. I would do anything to keep her safe and protected, to ensure she grew up healthy, happy, and loved.

My mind drifted back to Lina. I picked up my phone at my bedside, opened the photo app, and pulled up the picture I took of Lina curled up beside Penn in her bed this morning. They both looked so peaceful. My heart skipped a beat. A similar, all-consuming feeling sat in my chest—a desire to keep Lina safe and protected ... a drive to treat her as though my world revolved around her. I wanted to be the reason she was happy. I wanted to make her feel loved and cherished.

A lump formed in my throat, and I couldn't seem to swallow it down. If I hadn't already let it cross my mind, it was now. I couldn't escape it. I was falling in love with Lina Larsen.

I sucked in a deep breath through my nose, hoping to steady my emotions and relieve the tightness in my chest.

A key jiggled in the front door, followed by it creaking open. I held my breath, silently setting down my phone. As quietly and slowly as possible, I threw the covers off and started to head to the dresser to pull out my revolver.

"Reed?" came a soft whisper from the hallway.

I turned to the door but halted because Lina was already there.

Even in the dark, she was a goddamn smokeshow. Her lips were parted, panting, as if she'd run here. Her fingers wrapped around the doorframe like she was holding herself back. Her hair lay in loose waves around her shoulders. My pulse sped up as my gaze traveled down her body. She was wearing that fucking fringed jacket she'd worn the one day she decided to cool off in the stock tank.

"Dammit, sweetheart. What are you wearing?"

She leaned into the doorway, her hands still gripping the frame. The jacket parted, revealing a bare strip of skin between her breasts, clear down to those fucking black lace panties. Did she really just run across the ranch in nothing but her underwear? *My wild girl.*

"Just a jacket." Her voice was smoky and sultry.

"I can fucking see that." The air was trapped in my lungs.

She dropped her hands, stepping toward me until her breasts were brushing my bare chest.

"You told me if I needed to come, I should come to you."

"Are you drunk?" I asked, trying to sniff liquor on her breath, but all I could smell was her sweet, floral scent like she'd showered before coming here.

She shook her head. "Why would I need to drink when you give me a better buzz?"

"Is that right?"

She ran her hands down my pecs, over the ridges of muscles, sending shivers across my skin despite the flood of heat rushing to my dick. Her fingertips hooked into the waistband of my sweats. Lina barely had to tug to bring me flush against her.

"That's right, cowboy." She bit her plush, bottom lip. It was utterly distracting, and I was jealous of those teeth digging into her mouth. I wanted to fucking suck on it, too. Her eyes jumped between mine as if she were thinking, considering her next words.

"Lina?" I asked, concerned at the switch in her demeanor.

"How many days has it been?"

My brows raised at her question, "What do you mean?"

Her brown irises sparkled in the moonlight as she captured my gaze. "How many days have you been sober now?"

I wasn't quite ready to have this conversation with her, but she needed to know. I knew it was clear she didn't remember our conversation from when she was drugged, after time had lapsed and she still hadn't brought it up. "It's been 428 days. Since the day after we met."

She repeated, "It's been 428 days …" Her voice waned, as if she wanted to say more, but she stopped herself. Then she said, "I'm sorry I dragged you to all those bars with me."

I needed to touch her, to comfort her as much as her presence soothed me. I cupped her cheek. "I should be the one still apologizing, atoning for hurting you. It's a boundary I set for myself, but that doesn't mean I'm tempted every time I walk into a bar. If anything, being with you is my motivation to stay on the straight and narrow."

She pressed up on her tiptoes, brushing a soft kiss to my mouth. The press of her lips felt like gratitude and forgiveness, like tenderness and affection.

"We don't need to go drinking. I'm happy just to get wasted

on you." Her breath danced across my skin with her words.

I could feel the heat brewing between us, the yearning growing with every shared inhale and exhale.

I dropped my forehead to hers, my hands going to her waist to bring her closer. She'd walked all this way across the ranch in only two articles of clothing. To come to me.

She was irresistible. A temptation. One from which I was not going to deny myself.

"So tell me then, sweetheart, what can I do for you?"

Our chests were both heaving, as if we were trying to suck in mountain air but it was too thin and our lungs were too tight.

She leaned away from me slightly until I could see her blown-out pupils. "I want you. I want you to eat me out until I come, and then I want to ride you until we're both careening over the edge."

"Fuck, baby," I whispered, before wrapping my arm around her to pull her closer and crush my mouth to hers.

Chapter 24
Lina

Reed hoisted me up, letting me wrap my legs around his waist while he carried me to his bed. We both fell into the plush mattress, the duvet already thrown back from when he got up to meet me at his bedroom door. Our lips didn't leave each other. He was an amazing fucking kisser. I could probably orgasm just from his kisses alone. As the weight of his hard body covered me, I parted my knees wider, my hips pressing toward him to feel his growing cock between my thighs.

While my tongue tangled with his, I shrugged off my jacket. A groan emitted from his throat when he felt my stiff nipples brush his chest.

"Lina," he whispered into my mouth.

His lips started to leave mine, but I wasn't ready to stop kissing him.

"Show me how you're going to suck my clit." I traced my tongue over his mouth.

"Fuck." He captured the tip of my tongue lightly between his teeth and then sucked it into his mouth.

It was my turn to moan, my eyes fluttering closed, feeling

the pull of his mouth all the way down into my clit like a fucking tether. My pussy pulsed, and my hips bucked in response. I was desperate to feel his mouth everywhere. His kisses were like the craziest aphrodisiac.

His hands caressed my curves, one palm pausing at my breast to drag his thumb across the tightened bud.

"Now move that mouth to my tits," I whispered against his lips.

"You're doing so well, baby, telling me exactly what you want."

My lips twitched with his praise. "I'm a quick learner."

"Yeah, you are, and you're going to get everything you asked for."

"Reed," I whined, my hips grinding against his now as if I were a cat in heat.

He chuckled into my skin, his mouth coasting down my throat, across my collarbone, and down my chest. His tongue flicked out, drawing circles on my breast as he inched closer to my nipple. The tip of his tongue swirled around the stiffened peak until he drew it into his mouth.

I moaned, arching into him, wanting him to suck me dry. His teeth scraped the sensitive tip.

"Is the other one getting jealous?" His lips brushed against my heated skin as he said each word, teasing me.

My hands traveled up his arms, over his shoulders and neck, until I could bury my fingers into his thick, dark hair, holding him there. "Yes, please, Reed. Suck on my tits."

He pushed himself up on his elbows, peering up at me between my breasts, and I whined in impatience. Even in the dark, his eyes appeared like midnight pools, reflecting the moonlight. His mouth was set firm, and he was looking at me with such intensity, I felt as though I were melting into a cloud.

"These are perfect," he said, his palms encompassing my breasts. His thumbs swiped across the tips, making my pussy clench.

"I know." I smirked down at him.

"No, I don't think you do."

I gulped. "What are you talking about? Of course I know my tits are perfect."

"Lina." The way he said my name was always halfway between a scolding and a prayer, and it made my heart skip a beat. "Don't bullshit me. I don't want any other man getting off on these tits. They're mine. You're perfect for me, just the way you are."

Shit! How did he see through me like that? I always thought they were too small and my ass was too big. Why couldn't they just be more proportionate? Of course it had bothered me when that redhead with the big tits was all over him, and he was giving her attention.

"You hear me, sweetheart?"

I nodded against the pillow, suddenly unable to speak. He was pulling at all kinds of heart strings tonight. Was this a mistake coming to him?

"I'm going to worship them because they are my altar. You feel so good in my hands." His thumbs continued to drag across the tips, driving me wild. "I want to show you how perfect you are." He trailed kisses down my chest. "Can I eat now, baby?"

"Yes." I barely found my voice to say one word, yet it still sounded small and distant to my ears.

Thank God he heard it and took it as my consent because if he continued to talk to me like that while he played with my breasts, I was going to cry, and my panties were not going to be the only thing drenched.

Reed wasted no time now, returning his attention to my other nipple, swiping his tongue over it until he could draw it between his teeth and suck it into his mouth. I nearly shot off the bed when, at the same time, his fingers found my clit beneath the black lace, pressing down while he sucked and flicked his tongue over the stiff tip.

"*Fuck*," I breathed out. "You're going to make me come just playing with my tits."

"Not yet, baby. You're going to soak my face first."

My fingers didn't leave his locks, tugging on them harder, but he didn't seem to be bothered by it. Instead, it seemed to encourage him to keep going. His hands traced my curves. The man did not lie. It felt like he was worshipping me.

He brought two fingers to my mouth, painting my arousal on my lips. He barely broke away from my breast to say, "Suck. See how amazing you taste."

I opened my mouth for him, my tongue dragging across his digits, hollowing out my cheeks and sucking them in, picturing it was his cock in my mouth.

"Fuck, baby." He sighed. "Get those fingers good and wet, so I can use them on your clit."

I sucked, sliding my tongue between each finger, letting the saliva pool in my mouth, my tongue and teeth dragging across while he moaned against me. My hips bucked, begging for him to touch me or to feel his thick cock and those damn piercings I loved. He was still on his knees between my legs. Too far away, in my opinion. I wrapped my legs around his middle, using my heels to pull him closer.

"Impatient, sweetheart?"

I bit his finger then. Not hard, but enough for him to hiss between his teeth and answer his question.

He released a throaty laugh, letting it rumble through me, adding to the sensations that were driving me wild.

Peeking up, his beard tickling my skin, he watched with rapt attention while he withdrew his fingers from my mouth. His own mouth hung open, his eyes heavy with desire, while his fingertips dragged across my bottom lip.

"Your mouth feels so fucking decadent. These fucking lips, Lina." The pads of his fingers traced them. "I don't know how anyone has not died at the look and feel of these perfect, full lips."

I wanted his mouth back on me. "Don't stop." I raised my hips. "I want your face between my thighs."

He started running his palms over the curves of my breasts, circling the peaks, before letting them travel down my belly to hook at my waistband. "I'm starving for you, baby. I'm going to fuck you with my fingers while I suck your clit, and when you're about ready to come, I'm going to fuck you with my tongue so you can soak my face and I can lap you all up."

"Reed," I whined again. I was already on edge. "I want that so badly."

"Whose pussy is this, baby?"

"Yours. All yours. Make me come. *Please.*"

He dragged the edge of my panties down. I raised my hips to help him get them over my ass, but I was also desperate to close the distance. Tossing the underwear to the side, I was completely bare for him, my pussy now at his eye level, and I wanted nothing more than for him to latch on to me like a fucking leech.

"You're driving me fucking crazy, cowboy."

With a featherlight touch, Reed danced his calloused fingertips up the insides of my thighs until they were at the edge of my pussy. He traced the seam at my hips, over the sensitive lips, tugging lightly to see how much I glistened, but he didn't plunge his fingers in or touch my clit. It was like when the sun touched your skin on a hot day, it wasn't physical but you could feel it just the same. The most sensual touch, and it was driving me fucking wild. It was a tease and a promise, and I could already feel myself unraveling. I couldn't help writhing beneath him.

"If you keep doing that, you're going to miss me coming on your face."

Reed gave me a lazy, sweet smile that made my breath catch. "You think you can orgasm just by me skimming my fingertips along your skin?"

"With those hands, absolutely. But your mouth would make it ten times better."

With a smile on his lips, he pressed a kiss right above my clit. And it fucking throbbed when his beard barely brushed across it. "I'm so fucking ready for you."

He dragged a finger down my slit. "Yeah, you are. You're fucking soaked." He didn't waste time, sliding in one finger, then two. I groaned, bucking against them. "Does that feel good, baby?"

"Fuck yes."

"How about this?" He lowered his mouth then, covering my clit and letting his tongue flick across it while he twisted his hand so he could curl his fingers. The fullness of his thick fingers and the massage of them along my G-spot was enough to undo me.

"Yes," I moaned, now involuntarily grinding against them. I buried my fingers into his hair, tugging at the roots, keeping him there while he sucked, the pressure already building.

His fingers continued their come-hither motion while his mouth suctioned on my clit and his tongue flicked.

"I'm going to come," I said through heavy breaths.

He pulled his fingers out, causing me to whine in protest. "Now be a good girl and grind this pretty pussy all over my face. Soak me like we both know you want to."

The tip of his nose dragged along the inside of my thigh as his tongue traced the outside of my slit until he could thrust it inside me. I was right on the edge, his fingers drenched with me, sliding across that sensitive bud while his tongue speared into me. I hooked my ankles behind him, my grip on his hair becoming desperate while I ground my pussy against his mouth.

"Fuck, Reed." I wanted to scream but held back, not wanting to wake up Penn. But he was driving me fucking insane. "That's it. Don't stop. I'm so close."

His fingers continued to circle and glide over my swollen clit, while the walls of my pussy throbbed and pulsed against his tongue, his lips and beard brushing against me, adding to the sensations. Just when I was about to fall over the edge, he pressed on my clit while his other hand dug into my hip to hold me there, letting me grind against his face and hand until the pressure broke, allowing me to flood his mouth.

I bit back a cry, my eyes fluttering closed while I held him there, and he let me ride it out. Even when I thought I was done, and I started to relax and come down from the high, he darted his tongue out one last time, his fingers dancing over my sensitive lips, causing aftershocks to ripple through my body.

It was so intense, I started to giggle. It was involuntary. I couldn't help it. But it was either that or cry, and I didn't fucking cry.

When my eyes finally opened to peer down at him, he was watching me with such wonder and awe, my breath hitched. God, this man was beautiful. I couldn't get enough of him.

"Come here," I said, pulling him by the arms. "I want to kiss you."

His mouth glistened with me, but the last thing I wanted was to lose the connection right now because it felt so fucking good.

Reed lightly pressed his lips against mine, our tongues caressing, letting me taste myself on him.

"Don't you taste like heaven?" he asked.

"I want to taste you," I whispered into his mouth.

"First, I want you to come on my cock like the good girl you are for me. Then you can clean up your mess so you can taste us together."

"Yes," I nodded. He had me so compliant right now. He

could say anything, and I would fold.

"I want to bury myself in this perfect pussy."

"Reed," I moaned into his mouth. "I want you so badly."

"I got you, baby. I have everything you need."

"Please. I want you inside me."

"You want me to come inside you or on your tits?" he asked, shedding his sweatpants and briefs, letting his hard, thick length bob out in front of him. My hips twitched, needing him to be inside me.

"I want us to come together. I want you inside me as we both lose control. I want to feel you leaking out of me." The words tumbled out, sounding needy and desperate. And maybe I was. I wanted so badly for him to fill me. To never lose this connection. My heart was beating out of my chest. I felt like I was burning with desire for this man.

"God, sweetheart." His hands brushed the hair out of my face, his thumbs swiping my flushed cheeks, while his eyes studied me, looking for answers we were probably both hiding.

Because maybe the truth was I never truly hated him. Maybe the truth was I'd been in love with him this whole time, and I just needed him to show me he was the man I remembered and thought him to be.

"Make love to me." *Shit!* That was an inside thought. There was no stopping the word vomit now, it would seem. I bit my lip in my attempt to clamp it down.

But it didn't seem to shock him or make him withdraw, unlike any of the boys I dated who blanched at the moment I conveyed any sort of feeling. No. Reed grinned the biggest fucking grin I'd ever seen on his grumpy ass, and it only made my heart rate accelerate. Because the man was drop-dead gorgeous with all of his rough edges and big dick energy. I wanted him inside me, and I wanted him *now*.

"Lina——" he started to say, but I cut him off.

"Don't make this a big deal. Please." *Coward!* I scolded myself.

He nodded as if he could read me and knew exactly what I was feeling and what I needed. He leaned down, resting his forehead against mine. I closed my eyes, focusing on the weight of him, my breath slowing, but my heart didn't seem to settle. *Fucking Reed* had my heart, whether I liked it or not.

Then he started pressing tender kisses along my jaw and throat, whispering in my ear the words I had stopped him from saying earlier. "There is nothing in this world I want more than to make love to you."

I was still so tight from my orgasm that I wasn't sure I was ready for him, but he was patient. Rubbing his tip through my slit while his lips brushed the curve of my neck, making me melt beneath him. I followed his lead, letting my hips slowly rock with the movement, reveling in his kisses, his teeth nipping at the sensitive spot beneath my ear before he soothed it with his tongue. My center pulsed as he notched himself at my entrance.

"Breathe, sweetheart. I got you." He said it over and over again while I slowly opened for him.

I didn't know if my heart could take this glowing, bursting feeling. He buried himself deep, his lips never leaving my skin, as if I were a treasure he wanted to keep.

"Reed," I moaned, adjusting to him.

"You got this, baby. You're doing so good."

I felt like I may combust. "Move," I whined, my hips rocking.

He pulled back slightly to look me in the eyes. I felt captured by that dark gaze, completely mesmerized, as though he were seeing my very soul, and he was loving it better than I ever did.

"Your heart is beating out of your chest," he said.

It was then that I felt his, too, our bodies pressed together. "I feel yours, too."

"Is this too much?" he asked, his brow furrowing.

I shook my head. "No, I think our hearts are finally in sync."

His face nearly crumpled in pain. "God, Lina, I feel as though I've waited my whole life for you."

I knew what he meant … like our souls were made for each other. "I'm so glad I found you, even if it meant getting through the asshole phase first."

He huffed a laugh, a smile tipping his lips. "I knew I'd wear you down eventually."

I mirrored his grin. "I'm glad I didn't succeed in running you off the ranch after all."

"Yeah? You actually thought you'd ever be able to do that? As soon as I saw you yelling out your truck window when you pulled up, I knew I wasn't going anywhere."

"Thank God you're a stubborn ass." I pressed a kiss to his jaw.

"*Determined* to get what I want is more like it."

"Reed?"

"Yeah, sweetheart?"

My cheeks hurt from grinning so big. "Can you move now?"

He chuckled, leaning in to capture my mouth while he pulled out slowly and thrust back in. He gripped my hips, holding me open for him to drive deep, and the whole time his eyes never left mine. Watching us come together, over and over again, until we were both falling over the edge, all we could do was hold each other as we tumbled.

CHAPTER 25
Reed

Wrapped around Lina the next morning, I woke still exhausted, but I could sleep when I was dead. There was ranch work to do, and we needed to get ready to drive out later. It was getting harder to leave Penn, but I knew she was in good hands with Jude and Romy.

As if my passing thought was a damn broadcast to the world, my bedroom door creaked open to a sleepy little face. Lina yawned beside me, and I pulled her closer to me.

"Daddy?" came a quiet voice.

Lina's eyes sprang open. "Shit," she said, diving under the covers.

I chuckled, my arms still around her while she hid under the blankets.

"Maybe if I stay absolutely still, she won't see me." Lina's stifled whisper sounded like there was an edge of panic.

"She's not a bear," I told her. "Good morning, princess. Did you sleep well?"

"Yes," she said, pushing the door open wider and stepping in. "Hi, Lina."

"Hi," Lina squeaked from beneath the blankets.

"Why are you under the covers?" Penn asked, walking over to the bed.

"Just making a cave," came her muffled reply. A smile spread across my face.

"Can I come in?"

"No," Lina said at the same time I said, "Yes."

"Yay!" Penn jumped onto the bed.

"Reed. *No.*" Lina sent a quick elbow into my gut.

"Oof! God, your elbow's fucking pointy."

"I'm naked," she hissed quietly.

Penn climbed over our legs, oblivious to our state of undress, wedging between us on top of the covers—thank God. It was obvious Lina wasn't ready to explain this, even if I was.

"Can I come into your cave, Lina?" Penn asked, pulling on the edge of the duvet to try to sneak a peek beneath.

Lina popped her head out, keeping herself covered. Her hair was wild, and I fucking loved it. She looked good and thoroughly fucked, and it was the most beautiful sight in the world.

"Phew!" Lina blew out. "It was getting hot in that cave."

"Is that why you don't have your jammies on?" Penn asked innocently.

I had to hold back a laugh watching Lina squirm.

"Uh … um, yeah. You know," she said, stumbling on her words. "It was already so hot yesterday, I just couldn't sleep, so I took them off."

Penn's light brow pinched as if considering Lina's words, but then she nodded. "That makes sense." And that was all there was to it before she switched gears. "I'm hungry. Can I have pancakes?"

"It may have to be a cereal morning. I have to get to work," I told her.

Penn's bottom lip protruded. "Please, Daddy."

"I can make pancakes," Lina offered. "Do you have blueberries?"

"Really?" Penn lit up. "Daddy, do we have blueberries?"

"Yes, we have blueberries."

"Yes!" She pumped her little fist in victory.

Lina laughed that husky laugh of hers, and I couldn't help the twitch of my dick. I adjusted myself beneath the covers. "Princess, why don't you pull out the blueberries from the fridge? Lina will be right there."

"Okay!" Penn flew off the bed, skipping across the floor and out the door.

"That girl doesn't go anywhere slowly."

Lina ran a hand down her face. "I don't have any clothes, just my jacket and panties, and I have no idea where those ended up. I seem to have a habit of losing those around you."

"Don't worry, I know where they are," I told her.

"You do?"

"Uh-huh. And I don't mind you walking around in just that jacket."

She slapped my chest with a scoff. "I'm not going out there to make your daughter breakfast naked."

"If it wasn't for Penn, I wouldn't mind …"

"Asshole," she said with a smile in her voice.

I scooted off the bed, then went to the dresser to remove

one of my T-shirts, a pair of drawstring sweatpants, and a lace pair of underwear I had buried beneath everything. I set them beside her on the bed before pulling on my own underwear and sweats.

"I'm not wearing some chick's lingerie," she said, crossing her arms over her breasts. She looked so indignant, her brow furrowing. It was so fucking cute.

"It's not some chick's lingerie, sweetheart."

"Then whose is it?"

I gave her a pointed look. "You said so yourself. You seem to make a habit of losing them around me."

"What?" I watched it slowly dawn on her. "You mean …" She picked up the panties from the bed, holding them up. "Fucking shit. Are these the panties I lost that first night? You've had them this whole time?"

I nodded. "I kept them this whole time."

"Why?" she asked, shaking her head in disbelief.

I shrugged. "Because they were yours. And because I knew I'd see you again."

"*Reed.*" There she went again, saying my name the way she did. Making my heartbeat trip up and my dick throb.

"I washed them, so they're clean," I told her, gesturing for her to put them on.

She laughed. "So you aren't some perv who kept them just so you could sniff them?" she teased.

My lips twitched. "I'm a man, Lina. I never said I didn't do that first before I threw them into the wash."

She shook her head, still huffing her throaty laugh while she pulled them on.

Her golden skin on full display again, her perky breasts begging for me to touch them. Fuck! Why did I have to go to work right now? I could spend all day worshipping that body. "Fuck, baby." She pulled my shirt on, her nipples cutting through the fabric. My balls already felt too heavy. "I can't wait to have you all to myself again."

She gave me a little, seductive tip of her lips, and I couldn't help it. Seeing her in my clothes did something to me. She was kneeling on the bed now, rolling up the waistband of the sweats so they stayed on, and I couldn't resist. I planted my hands on either side of her, leaning into her, letting my nose drag along the side of her cheek, breathing in her sweet, vanilla scent, until I could capture her mouth with mine.

Lina tipped her chin up, letting me deepen the kiss. We didn't touch each other, but the way our lips seemed to nestle right between the other was like fitting together two perfect puzzle pieces.

"I can't get enough of you," she whispered against my mouth.

"Same, baby, same."

"Found the blueberries!" Penn declared proudly, skipping back into the room.

Lina started to pull back, but I stopped her by grabbing the back of her neck. Giving her one last solid kiss. I didn't care if my kid saw it. I was ready to shout to the world that this woman was mine.

"A promise for later," I whispered, before straightening and turning to my daughter. "Okay, princess, let's get breakfast started."

CHAPTER 26
Reed

The Big Buckin' Showdown was one of the rowdiest rodeos on the circuit. I'd heard tales of cops having to swarm in to break up fights or dangerous bulls breaking loose into the stands. It didn't help that it was hotter than the devil's armpit. That meant more drinking and more fucking assholes. It also meant that I was on high alert, sizing up every guy who seemed to strut around like they were here to either fuck or fight. I wasn't about to let anyone ruin this for my girl. She was well on the road to winning the finals.

It didn't seem to faze Lina in the least. Mushu still inhaled those fucking barrels like he was made for it, and all Lina had to do was sit, look, and let him run.

I was there waiting for her when she ran him home, pulling up on the reins to slow him down, not even looking back to check her time. Her teeth sparkled in the high-noon sun that seemed to scorch everything but Lina. She looked windswept, hair coming loose from her braid, her tan perfect beneath her hat. Sweat poured down at her temples, and Mushu's coat glistened with it.

"Woo-hoo!" Lina hollered, seeing her eighteen-second-flat

time. "Beat that, Paige!" she bragged to the snooty barrel girl in the hole.

"Shut up, Lina," she grumbled back, saying more under her breath.

"What was that, bitch?" Lina asked, getting ready to swing down from her saddle.

"*Lina*," I warned. I didn't catch what Paige said, but whatever it was, it was enough to piss her off. However, this was not the place to start shit.

She gave me a side-eye before glaring at her opponent. "You know what? Fine. Say what you want to say. Just say it to my fucking face next time. But if I were you, I wouldn't wish bad things on others. The universe has a real good sense of humor when it comes to that shit."

"Whatever," Paige scoffed, returning her gaze to the arena.

"Come on," I said, clipping Mushu's lead rope to his bridle and pulling him away from there. "This heat is getting to both of you. I think you and Mushu could use a good rinse off."

Lina sighed. Her grin didn't return, but I was treated to a little tip of her lips. "I think I could use a cool shower and a drink tonight"—she faltered—"if that's okay."

I nodded. "Anything you need, baby."

Her smile grew, reaching her eyes, as if I was giving her a gift. I seemed to be rewarded with a lot of those looks lately, and I loved how it made me feel. Like I was the only one who got this soft, sweet side of Lina. The Lina who had a big heart for the people in her life, and I desperately wanted to be one of them for as long as she was willing to have me.

"Your turn, cowboy," Lina announced when I walked into the trailer after hosing down Mushu and giving him his dinner.

Lina was perched on the counter in cutoff shorts and a crop top, showing off more of her beautiful, golden skin. I had to resist the temptation to run my palms over every inch of her any chance I got.

She was sipping on a big glass of chilled white wine. Her wet hair was combed out and drying in natural waves. She never wore very much makeup, but a pretty, pink gloss painted her lips, and it looked like she might have put on some mascara. I wanted to see that gloss painted all over my dick by the end of the night. I wanted those lashes fluttering up at me while she gagged on me.

I moved to her, my arms outstretched and ready to encompass her waist with my hands, but she raised a bare foot to my chest, stopping me from reaching her.

"You need a shower, and then you can touch me." I didn't blame her. My shirt was sticking to me. Even my balls were sweating.

But I couldn't resist, and she didn't stop me when I wrapped my fingers around her calf, my thumb brushing lazy strokes across her skin. Her only response was her toes curling into my shirt.

Setting her glass down, she picked up a chilled Coke bottle she'd set on the counter and placed the top to the edge of the counter. Then with a quick hit, the heel of her hand came down on the top, popping it off.

My brows rose, impressed. "You know that's a twist-off?"

She shrugged. "One of my party tricks," she admitted with a wink. "Don't take the fun out of it."

I shook my head with a smirk. "You're something else."

"I know," she said, tipping the bottle to her own smiling lips. I watched her obsessively while her mouth wrapped around the top, her throat bobbing while she took a swig.

"Fuck, sweetheart. You're making it hard not to touch you."

The woman knew exactly what she was doing, the little tease. Her mouth released the bottle with a little pop before she handed it to me.

"Your shower soda, sir."

It was cool in my heated grasp, and I needed my thirst quenched in more ways than one tonight. I looked at it. Some of her lip gloss was left behind. Putting my own mouth where hers had been felt more than sensual. It felt downright intimate. My eyes studied her while I drank it. The cold, refreshing taste of cola cooling my insides while I gulped. Her eyes quickly became heavy with desire.

Winking back at her, I turned to head toward the shower.

"No jerking off in there," she called after me. "I want you fucking desperate for me."

I groaned. "I already am, sweetheart."

This fucking rodeo was trouble.

But so was Lina Larsen.

I wanted to take her on a date. A real date. With limited options out on the road, and knowing my girl needed to unwind, I didn't mind taking her out to the rodeo bar. It was full by the time we got inside, and people were already getting kicked out. They were probably trashed before they even walked in, drinking half their body weight in beer during the rodeo.

"Fucking amateurs," I grumbled, my hand resting on the small of Lina's back as we headed to the bar.

On a compact platform by the dance floor was a stereo system. A DJ was busy running the tracks, spinning classic country music. I scanned the room, immediately looking for any threats, taking in the dudes who sat at the bar alone, registering the ones who appeared as though they worked out and were spoiling for a fight—or eyeing the drunk girls who might be willing to go home with them.

I pressed through the crowd, keeping close to Lina, feeling as though I needed to advertise to this whole fucking shithole that she was *mine*.

I didn't even ask what she wanted, already knowing her order. "Whiskey sour and a Coke," I told the bartender as soon as they were ready for our order.

Lina raised her brows at me. "You've been paying attention."

"I'm always paying attention when it comes to you," I told her honestly, wrapping my arm around her to bring her closer.

It was already suffocatingly hot in here with all the bodies. By the looks of the bouncer at the door, though, he was ready to show some of them out. There was some blonde crying and arguing with her girlfriend by the restroom hallway, and I could tell the bouncer was waiting to give her the boot.

"Keeping an eye out for trouble?" Lina pushed up on her tiptoes to ask in my ear.

"Always looking for threats."

It felt like it was ingrained in me at this point—part of my wiring. Something that only intensified when I became a dad. Now whenever I was out with Lina, I was on high alert all the fucking time.

Once we had our drinks and found a high table by the dance floor, I pulled her chair toward me so her knees were bracketed by mine. I wanted her as close as possible tonight. I didn't want any prick thinking they had a chance with her.

Feeling possessive, I put a hand on her knee while I sipped from my glass, letting my thumb draw circles on her skin.

"We don't need to make it a late night," I told her, already impatient. I wanted to take her back to the trailer. My dick was already hard against my zipper, and my balls were fucking black and blue at this point.

She gave me a flirtatious tip of her lips above her cocktail, as if she could read my thoughts. "We just got here. I think you can last a while longer."

I leaned into her until my lips were brushing the shell of her ear. "Baby, we'll stay as long as you'd like, but I can't promise that I won't drag you to an empty stall and fuck you against the bathroom wall."

Her breath caught in her throat, and I loved hearing the throaty sounds she made. She was so damn sexy.

"What's stopping you from doing it right now?" she challenged, pulling away to peer into my eyes.

She wasn't teasing. Her eyes were heated, her lashes batting, taunting me. She took another sip of her drink, a drop catching on her bottom lip.

I reached out to wipe it, my thumb dragging across her pouty lip before pushing it into her mouth to let her tongue swirl over the pad.

She released it from her mouth with a pop. "Finish your drink, cowboy." Her voice was husky with arousal, and it made my cock throb. My jeans were too fucking tight. I wanted to bury myself in her.

To my surprise, she threw her glass back, chugging down her cocktail. She didn't stop until it was nothing but ice, slamming it down against the tabletop.

Seeing my face, she started to giggle. "You look as if you've never seen someone chug a drink before."

I shook my head in wonder. "You're one of a kind, Lina. I don't know why I should be surprised by you."

"I know how to do a keg stand, too," she said with a wink.

"Of course you do." I sucked down my own drink then, letting the carbonation cool my insides.

I set the glass down beside hers and grabbed her hand.

"Come on, sweetheart."

She looked at me with a giddy grin. "We're really doing this?"

I pulled her down from her stool. "I can't wait any longer."

I walked past the drunk girls crying in the hallway until I reached the women's restroom. I wasn't about to take her to the disgusting men's room. I pushed open the door where there were more drunk women, but no one seemed to notice or care that I was walking in. I nudged Lina inside the first stall, quickly locking the door behind us.

As soon as it was closed, I pounced on her, my lips finding

hers, my hands unbuttoning and unzipping her shorts. Her own hands fumbled with my belt and jeans, until she had me in her grip. It felt so fucking good having her warm fingers wrapped around my throbbing cock. I pressed into her palm, desperate for friction. I pushed my hand beneath the waistband of her panties until I could swipe my fingers through her center.

"Fuck, baby, you're already soaked and dripping wet for me."

"I've been wet for you since you walked into the trailer all sweaty," she whispered into my mouth.

I spun her around, shoving her up against the tile.

"Hands on the wall, sweetheart."

Lina bit her lip while she looked at me over her shoulder—her sign that she liked the sound of that.

"Fuck me, cowboy."

She splayed her palms on the wall, wiggling her ass enticingly.

"Fuck," I breathed, shimmying her shorts down her thighs. God, her ass was something magnificent—round, juicy, and perfect. I ran my hands over her curves before pushing my pants and briefs down. With my dick in my hand, I gave it a couple pumps before notching it at her center.

She was ready for me. I thrust forward, her pussy sucking me in. She felt so fucking good, so fucking tight, I couldn't see straight. Her walls were already pulsing and fluttering, squeezing me.

"Fuck, baby." I leaned forward until my chest was pressed to her back.

I thrust again, wrapping my hand around the front of her

neck, while my other hand was gripping her hip for dear life.

"Reed," she moaned.

No one seemed to notice our heavy breathing and moans that filled the air. Drunk girls came and went with their friends. Their loud, inebriated chatter, mixed with the din of flushing and water running, covered up the sound of my balls slapping against her ass as I fucked Lina against the wall.

"Fuck, Lina, you take me so good," I whispered into her ear.

"You feel so good. I'm already close."

"I am, too, baby. I was ready as soon as I saw you chug that drink."

"Yeah?" she asked through heaving breaths as I continued to pump in and out of her.

The pressure built in my spine, my balls tightening, blood rushing to my cock as I took one last thrust.

"Fuck," she groaned, arching, her head falling back against my chest. "I'm … I'm coming."

My cock pulsed and throbbed, pumping hot ropes of cum into her. Her walls tightened around me with her orgasm, only adding to the intensity of mine.

"Fuck. You're perfect."

Our chests heaved, her pussy continuing to flutter while my dick twitched inside her, milking me dry.

"Reed." She said my name almost reverently, her arm reaching back to wrap her hand around the back of my neck, holding me to her.

I leaned down, burying my nose into her hair, pressing my lips to her crown. I wanted to say it. It was on the tip of my tongue to tell her exactly how I felt, but instead I asked, "Will you dance with me?"

Her body rumbled with her laugh, causing my cock to twitch again at the sensation. "You want to dance with me?"

"I do." I dropped another kiss into her hair.

"Do you even know how to dance?" she quipped.

"Why don't you say 'yes' and find out."

I gradually withdrew, both of us sucking in a breath with the last bits of pleasure. I grabbed some toilet paper to clean us both up before pulling up our pants and straightening ourselves out.

"Okay, cowboy, I'll dance with you." She smiled as brilliantly as she had earlier after her race, and I felt my heart burst.

Fuck. I was in love with this woman.

We exited the stall without a word, sharing soft, knowing smiles while we went to wash our hands. The women around the sinks stopped their drunken chatter, their eyes going wide.

"Did y'all just fuck in there?" one of them asked overly loudly. It was the blonde one who was out in the hallway earlier.

I ignored her while I washed up and dried my hands.

"Yes, yes we did." Lina didn't even look at her, checking her makeup and hair in the mirror.

They all stood in stunned silence.

Lina ran a finger over the corner of her mouth, fixing the lip gloss that smeared. She grabbed my hand and pulled me out of the restroom.

Before the door shut behind us, I heard the excited screams and giggles from the girls.

"Did you see that cowboy's ass in those Wrangler's? I'd *so* tap that!" was the last thing I heard before the door closed.

Lina peeked at me over her shoulder, her eyes lit up with mirth. "They'll be talking about us all night."

I slowed my steps, turning her to look at me. The noise of the bar seemed to fade, the lights appeared to dim, and all I saw was *Lina*. The glow of the neon like a halo around her, the flush on her cheeks from her orgasm, and her hair tousled and sexy. She took my fucking breath away.

The music changed to the slow, bluesy beat of "Tennessee Whiskey." I leaned into her, ducking my head so my lips could brush her ear, and said, "Let's give them more to talk about."

She nodded against my mouth, and when I pulled away, her demeanor had changed. Her smile faded, replaced with a look I couldn't yet identify. She looked serious, but her eyes grew soft and affectionate.

I led her onto the full dance floor, pulling her into me until her chest was pressed to mine. With her hand in mine, I placed her other hand on my chest. I gripped her hip, just letting us sway to the music.

As the music picked up, I took a step forward, leading her into a slow two-step, and I watched her eyes grow big in surprise. I spun her out and then pulled her back in, dipping her.

"Holy fuck," she breathed. "You can dance."

I winked. "I have party tricks, too."

She beamed then as she came up from the dip. I held her to me, grinding my hips with hers before I repeated the steps.

The whole time, we couldn't take our eyes off each other.

Nothing seemed to matter at that moment. All the bullshit with Penn's mom, with Junior, the trouble on the ranch. None of it mattered with her in my arms. With Lina—this fierce, independent woman who was full of sass but had the biggest heart—I just knew we'd be able to conquer anything.

Chapter 27
Lina

This quiet, sometimes brooding man was full of surprises tonight. First, whisking me away to fuck me in the bathroom, and now he was spinning me around on the dance floor as if his shoes were made of glass. Who was this man? Where had he been hiding? He actually knew how to have some fun.

My cheeks were hurting because I couldn't stop smiling. I hadn't had this much fun since … well, maybe since I met him.

He led me in one two-step after another, some of the music quicker than others, but he didn't miss a beat.

"Where did you learn to dance like this?"

"My mother. My parents went out a lot." A brief shadow crossed his face with whatever memory that provoked. "Usually, we would be waiting for my dad to come home from work, she'd put on some music, and she'd have me practice with her until they left for the night."

"They left you at night?" It made me sad to think of Reed as a little boy being left home alone.

He shrugged before spinning me out and bringing me back to him. My hand landed on his chest, feeling his heartbeat quicken beneath my palm. "Sometimes the neighbor would sit with me until I went to bed. They weren't the best parents. Neither one of them were very involved."

My smile broke. "I couldn't imagine not wanting to be involved in my child's life, but I understand. My mom has never been interested in what I was doing. She kind of has her own life and family. I didn't exactly fit in with it."

"She doesn't come to any of your events?"

"She used to … early on. I mean, that was her life before I was born—when she met my dad. You know he was a bronc rider?"

Reed nodded. "I've made the mistake of asking about it."

I laughed. "Yeah, Dad likes to talk about it."

"It almost always turns into bragging about you, though."

"That man." I shook my head with a grin. "I don't have to question whether he's proud of me. Apparently, he was wild when he was younger. He always had all the buckle bunnies following him to his trailer. That's how he met Mom."

"Then they had you?"

"Yeah, but they were never together. I think it was more of a fuck–buddy type situation. She never wanted to move out to Willows and live on the ranch."

"Did you just live with your dad then?"

"Nah. Probably for the first fourteen years of my life, I went back and forth between my mom's place in Portland and the ranch. Once I got more involved with barrel racing, I told Mom I wanted to live with Dad. She seemed to think that was a great idea." I laughed, but there was little humor in it.

"I'm sorry." Reed frowned.

"Don't apologize. Mom and I are like oil and water. We chat, but it's hard to carry on a conversation with her for very long. We're nothing alike. She's my mother, but the woman is a little vapid. Everything is surface level with her, ya know? So I let her live her life with my half brothers and stepdad in the city, and she lets me live mine with Dad on the ranch while I race. Do you have any siblings?"

Reed shook his head, dipping me before helping me back up. "One and done for my folks. Being parents wasn't really part of their lifestyle."

"Were you lonely?"

"Sometimes, but I knew how to entertain myself, and there was a ranch nearby. The rancher used to pay me in beef for helping, so our freezer was always full. Taught myself how to cook, too."

"Shit, Reed. No wonder you're such a great dad."

"I don't know about that. I'm not sure I've always made the best decisions for her. But when I found out I was going to be a dad, I promised myself I'd be better than my parents ever were. I wanted to be better for Penelope as soon as I held her in my arms. If I do anything right in my life, it'll be to make sure that little girl knows how loved she is every single day."

Fuck. He was making me melt. "Penn's lucky to have you."

Reed grunted under the praise, obviously a little uncomfortable with it.

"So is Elise," I said before I could even stop it. *Inside thought*, I scolded myself. I meant she was lucky to have him care for their daughter the way he did when she obviously couldn't right now.

The music slowly came to an end, Reed coming to a stop. His jaw ticked at the mention of his ex-wife, and his eyes darkened.

"Sorry. I shouldn't have brought her up." I stepped out of his arms, ready to go find another drink.

But he reached out an arm, stopping me. He shook his head. "It's fine. Let's go get you another drink."

"You're reading my mind." If Elise was going to be an off-limits topic, I'd take his lead on that one. At least for now. I knew that if we were going to try a real relationship, we'd eventually have to talk about it, even if it was uncomfortable. Even if I didn't want to hear it, either.

As we stepped off the dance floor, heading to the bar, we came face-to-face with Kale, Christian, and my barrel racing friend Vivian, sitting at a table with their drinks. They were staring at us with the most moonstruck expressions on their faces. Christian even had his head resting in his fists, as if to keep his jaw from hitting the floor.

"Aw, you two are so cute!" Vivian nearly squealed.

"I fucking knew it! Pay up." Christian held his palm open in front of Kale.

"Ugh!" Kale grumbled, cursing under his breath while he pulled his wallet from his back pocket.

My whole body flushed having been officially caught with the enemy.

"Was it you two in the girl's restroom tonight?" Viv asked, a cheeky smile on her face while she wagged her brows.

I huffed, shaking my head at my friends, but I suddenly felt very aware of Reed beside me. The heat of his body, his firm, calloused hand holding mine like it was the most natural thing in the world while advertising to the whole fucking bar that we belonged to each other.

"Y'all know I'm not shy, but I don't kiss and tell," I told them. But it was near impossible not to crack a grin.

Viv squealed again. "That means they fucking did!"

"Does this mean you two are together?" Christian asked, pointing at our hand-holding, a smirk on his lips.

Reed and I exchanged glances.

He looked at me apprehensively, his eyes questioning.

I slowly nodded my head. "I think we're figuring some things out, but also, no one better fucking touch him." The last words were laced with laughter, but I was also dead serious.

His lips tipped up at the corners.

He grabbed the belt loop of my shorts, pulling me back to him until we were chest to chest. Was he going to kiss me in front of my friends? In front of the whole bar?

I tipped my chin up. "Might as well do it," I told him. "You already fucked me in the bathroom and had me on the dance floor."

Reed captured my chin between his thumb and forefinger, angling my mouth in just the right way. He leaned down, taking his hat off as his plush lips pressed against mine, fitting perfectly between my pout. My heart rate accelerated with the whoops and hollers of my friends, the entire bar erupting with catcalls and whistles.

"It's official, Lina Larsen," Reed whispered against my lips. My eyes fluttered back open, not realizing I'd closed them, to peer up at him. His dark gaze was now sparkling like a midnight sky. My breath caught. He placed his hat on my head. "Every cowboy here now knows you're mine."

"Reed …" I didn't know what to say.

"What do you want to do, sweetheart?"

"Forget the drink. Let's go home."

His lips broke into that big grin, and I was probably looking at him like a lovesick puppy, but I didn't care. We had a lot of good night left, and I didn't want to spend it with him in a rowdy bar. I wanted him all to myself.

One of my dad's, and my, favorite movies growing up was *Sleepless in Seattle*. There's a part at the end when they finally meet at the top of the Empire State Building. In that scene, I wasn't sure at first if they'd leave together, but Sam holds out his hand and says, "Shall we?" She takes his hand, and as they walk away together, his little boy leads them as they get into the elevator. The whole time, they're staring at each other like they can't take their eyes off one another. Like if they looked away for even one second, the other would cease to exist.

That's what it felt like walking hand in hand through the dark camp to our trailer. If not for watching where I was stepping, my eyes were glued on Reed. It was as though something had shifted. Everything in my life had lined up for this one pivotal moment, and if I looked away for any reason, I'd miss something important.

"Do you believe in love at first sight?" I asked him. I wasn't scared to hear his answer. I was genuinely curious. I wanted to know.

He led us around a corner as we headed down the lane to our campsite.

His eyes barely strayed from mine, some knowing look flitting across them while a soft smile played at the corners of his mouth.

Heat washed over me, wondering if I shouldn't have asked. Was this another moment where my filter wasn't working? "What's that look for?"

"You asked me that once before."

"Shit! I did? When?" I gulped, suddenly feeling self-conscious, my mind racing to remember when I'd said it. The muscles at his jaw ticked, and that was enough to give me the answer. "It was … it was that night you found me being dragged away from the bar." I still hated to think of that night, let alone talk about it. Anything could have happened if Reed hadn't found me.

"Hey, baby." He stopped us, shifting to look at me. "It's okay. It was always going to be okay."

"He stole that moment from me. I don't even remember saying that." Tears welled in my eyes, but his warm, solid hand squeezed mine affectionately.

Reed shook his head, gritting his teeth while his brown eyes reassured me. "He has no place here in this moment because I can tell you now that I never thought I believed in love at first sight—until I met you."

A lump formed in my throat, and I felt a sting behind my nose at his declaration. I cleared my throat. "You felt it, too? When we first saw each other?" A surge of hope washed over me. The lump grew despite my attempt to swallow.

"Lina, it was as if my whole world tilted on its axis the moment I saw you. I haven't been the same since."

My vision blurred, but I trusted him to make sure I didn't stumble as he continued to lead us to our campsite. We reached our fifth wheel, pausing in front of the parked trucks and horse trailer, when the first tears broke free, slipping silently down my cheeks. I tipped my head back to peer up at the stars. My watery vision was like a kaleidoscope of light, while I attempted to hold them back. But there was no use. They were already falling.

Reed stepped into me, reaching up to wipe the tears from my cheeks. "It was you. It's always been you." His own voice broke. "It's you for a reason."

"God, Reed." I shook my head, my chest tightening hearing him say those words.

"Look at me, sweetheart."

I lowered my chin, catching his own glassy gaze. Fresh tears sprang to my eyes seeing the emotion in his. My face scrunched, two seconds away from an ugly cry.

Cradling my face, his thumbs continued to swipe across my cheeks. I couldn't help leaning into those big hands, wanting to feel the heat and roughness, to ground me and comfort me.

"I honestly believe you were put into my life for a reason." His brow furrowed as if he, too, were holding back the tears. "Put into my life ... and Penn's."

"I thought you broke my heart, but here you've been piecing it back together this whole time." My voice broke on a sob.

"Oh, baby, if I could go back ..." He sniffed. "I'd do anything to protect you. Even if it meant protecting you from me. I should've never hurt you the way I did. I was a mess when you found me. But you were the one thing I needed most. And I screwed up. If I have to make it up to you every day for the rest of my life, I will. I'll do anything I have to do, Lina, if it means I get to love you."

"Goddamn you! You have me ugly crying now," I wailed.

A deep laugh rumbled quietly in his chest. "I know. I'm an asshole."

I gave him a watery huff. "Well, I've been no walk in the park, either, cowboy." There was no stopping the tears as they streamed down my face, soaking his hands where they still held me. "I'm in love with you, Reed." I shrugged, unable to help how I felt. "I've been in love with you from the start."

Tears welled up in his eyes, and I sobbed. I couldn't bear seeing him cry. It broke me.

"Lina, I've been falling for you for 435 days now. I'm so in love with you. There's no life without you in it."

His lips tenderly pressed to mine, our tongues softly stroking, the salt of my tears mingling. I closed my eyes, absorbing the feeling. The warm summer night, the crickets chirping, his kisses, and his hands taking care of me. His fingers brushed the hair behind my ears, trailing down my neck, my shoulders, my arms. A caress so light, it felt like a breeze on my heated skin.

"I love you, Reed Ownstead," I whispered against his lips.

"I love you." I felt the words rumble through his chest, penetrating me, embedding in my very being. I never believed anything more in my whole life.

Reed pulled away to peer down at me, to examine my tear-soaked face. He wiped the tears away again as I tried to catch my breath. "Come on, sweetheart, let's take care of you."

I gave him a watery smile, nodding.

"Come on." He kissed my forehead before taking my hand and leading me to the trailer.

Just as we passed the truck, my eyes drifting to my boots to watch where I stepped in the dark, Reed stopped abruptly.

His body went rigid, startling me.

"What?" I demanded.

I glanced up at him. His face was like stone, and he was looking straight ahead at our fifth wheel. I followed his gaze.

The door was left open.

Chapter 28
Reed

My entire body went on alert, the hairs on my arms even standing at attention.

"Lina, stay behind me," I hissed, stepping in front of her and pulling her flush against my back.

"Did someone break in?" she whispered. She was so close, I could feel her breath against my neck.

"Stay close."

I instinctively reached for the .38 at my waist before realizing it was in my bag in the trailer.

Hopefully, it was still in my bag …

"Shit," I cursed under my breath. "Let me go in first and make sure it's safe."

She gripped the back of my shirt, her nails digging into my skin. "Fuck that. You're not leaving me out here. I'm coming with you."

I gave a nod, scanning the campsite around the fifth wheel. She was right. The threat could be out here, waiting for us. Waiting for *her*.

"We're going in slowly, then. Stay with me."

Lina didn't reply, her hand only becoming a viselike grip on my shirt.

I held my breath, walking as lightly as I could on my boots as we inched closer to the open door. We took the three steps quietly, peeking inside.

The trailer was cast in the shadows. Everything appeared undisturbed. My ears pricked up, straining to listen for movement, but all I heard was silence.

We entered together. My duffel bag was still zipped up beside the booth seats. In two strides, I was in front of it, pulling out my revolver and cocking it.

I led with the gun, steadying my arm as we walked through the dark, stepping wide into the doorway of the bathroom and then around to Lina's bed. We both froze. The wardrobes on either side of the bed hung open, Lina's clothes and gear strewn across the bed as if someone was searching for something. Fury boiled in my gut. To see her things touched, searched, and discarded … I ground my teeth. My fingers gripped the handle.

I warned him.

"What the fuck?" Lina asked, now releasing her grip and stepping out from behind me.

We both scanned the area, searching for something we were missing in the dark. Lina flipped the switch, bathing the room in yellow light.

"What was he looking for?" Her voice was no longer teary from earlier, but hard.

"He must've heard us and left in a hurry," I gritted out, uncocking and stuffing my gun in my waistband. "Stay here and lock the door behind me. Look to see if you're missing anything."

"Reed—" she began, reaching out to stop me, but I was already walking back out into the dark.

The campground was silent, except for some distant crackling of fire and laughter and crickets. I scanned our camp again, peering into the shadows to see if anyone lingered in the trees.

Then I saw him, ducking under a branch. He was quick, but I was quicker. I ran after him, drawing my revolver. I reached out for anything I could grip, grabbing his arm and using his momentum to carry him into the side of my truck. His cowboy hat flew off his head, revealing dark, sweat-matted hair and a crooked nose above his chew-streaked beard.

I leaned the weight of my forearm into his throat while I gripped his shirt collar and pressed the barrel against the underside of his jaw, forcing his head back to look me in the eyes. His brow furrowed, and he bared his teeth like he was the fucking predator in this scenario.

"What the hell do you think you're doing breaking into a woman's trailer at night? Sicko!" I slammed my weight harder against him. He gave a choking noise. For a moment, his eyes flashed with surprise before returning to their original glare. "Why the fuck are you going through her things? Did you find what you wanted, asshole?"

He was silent for a beat, then he leaned into my arm, straining his neck, his voice raspy with the chokehold. "I took nothing."

"Empty your pockets," I gritted out. He didn't move, his eyes bravely drilling into mine. "Now!"

He didn't even flinch. Heaving a sigh, the revolver still

trained on him, I fumbled through his jean pockets, tossing his wallet and cell phone into the bed of my truck. Producing a switchblade from his back pocket, I growled, returning the full weight of my elbow into his jugular.

"Were you planning to fucking use this on her? Were you hoping you could force her at knifepoint?" I was fucking fuming now, the potential fear and threat to Lina making me see red. I had a million questions. "Who the fuck are you? I swear to God, you need to tell me now, or I will not hesitate to use this on you."

"Bullshit," he hissed through his teeth.

It was my turn to bare my teeth at him. "No bullshit here. We're in a region where if someone comes onto my property whom I deem to be a threat, I have every right to shoot first and ask questions later. The law will be on my side here." I watched as blood drained from his face as it dawned on him. "Name. Now."

He cleared his throat to eke out, "John Wayne."

I scoffed, but none of this was fucking funny. "You do realize I'm now in possession of your wallet. Might as well make this easy on yourself. Who are you? And why are you stalking Lina?"

An evil, tobacco-stained grin spread across his face. "Check my fucking ID. It's Wayne Urban, and my interest in Lina Larsen has nothing to fucking do with you."

"The fuck it doesn't. Do *not* say her fucking name. Do you know Junior Matheus? Do you know Elise?" His expression did not crack once at the mention of their names. This man was a fucking psycho. "Do you know who the Larsens are?"

"Everyone knows who the Larsens are," he seethed.

"Do you know anything about the vandalism on Thornbrush Ranch?" I know I wasn't giving him any time to think, but I needed to know what the fuck he wanted.

"Feeling a little territorial? Is she your little plaything, too?" he asked, his chin nodding toward the trailer. "Need to piss on her so the rest of the dogs stop sniffing around the porch?"

I fucking growled liked a deranged beast. "You're pushing your luck. Answer my fucking questions." I cocked the gun this time.

"She likes it from behind, doesn't she?"

"Fuck you, asshole. Do you have a death wish?"

He gurgled a laugh. "Yeah, I know Junior. He may've learned about my little obsession with Lina."

"Don't. Say. Her. Fucking. Name," I warned again, more sternly this time. I could feel my control slipping. The murderous rage rattling my bones. My mind begged me to pull the trigger, but something was holding me back. Penn and Lina flashed across my vision. Them snuggled in bed together. My future. "What did Junior tell you?"

"Just that I should keep doing what I'm doing ... that eventually, she'll put out."

My mind was reeling, trying to process this. Trying to think what his angle was. But my brain was foggy with the anger pumping through me. I needed to reel it in so I could make some sense of this.

"Why the fuck would he tell you that?" Other than the fact he hated the Larsens.

Wayne shrugged, no longer fighting against me. "Said it could be a good distraction. Whatever the fuck that means."

What the fuck is Junior up to?

"I'll tell you what. You find out what the fuck he meant by that, and I'll let you walk away from here."

I pocketed his switchblade before reaching over into the truck bed to get his wallet and cell phone. Uncocking the revolver, I stuffed it back into my waistband before flipping open his wallet. Sure enough, he'd given me his real name. I pulled my own cell phone from my back pocket, opening the camera to snap a photo of his ID.

"But now that I know where you live, *John Wayne Urban* from Livingston," I said, shoving his phone and wallet into his chest, "the next time I see you—let's say in two weeks—you better fucking have answers for me, or my face will be the last thing you see. I promise, you won't want me to come looking for you."

Wayne gulped, the natural human emotion of fear finally registering, before he offered, "I'll make it easy on you."

"Appreciate that." I said the words calmly, but I was anything but calm. Next to the boiling rage in my gut was a sense of panic. I needed to get back to Lina. "Now let me see you walk away from here, and don't fucking look back."

Wayne nodded, backing away before turning on his heels and doing exactly what I told him to do. Once he had disappeared into camp, I hurried back to the trailer. Lina let me in as soon as I knocked and called out to her. Just like she had last time, all the lights were flipped on and her hair was frazzled, like she'd been running her fingers through it while waiting for me.

"You found him." She nodded, stating it like a fact.

"Did you hear us?"

I watched her throat bob on a swallow. Her face was pale. "He knows Junior."

I grimaced at his name. "Yeah, but he's going to find us some answers."

She shook her head now, a look of panic mirroring my own. "We need to go home to Thornbrush."

CHAPTER 29
Lina

Romy met me in the stables as soon as we pulled in. She had Penn with her, who ran full speed at her dad when she saw him. It warmed my heart to see them reunited. I could tell he missed her. Reed practically lit up, swooping her up into his arms.

"Hey, Rom," I greeted her, going in for a hug. It was the first time I saw her without baby Charli, and she appeared absolutely frazzled. "You look like you're stressed out. Getting some wedding jitters?"

Romy suffered a laugh while helping me unload Mushu's tack. "You arrived just in time, it seems. We moved the wedding up to this weekend."

"Wait … what? Why?" I blinked rapidly, trying to clear my tired brain, then leveling her with a look. "You already got knocked up, so there's no need to rush it. We all know you're not a virgin."

She smiled at my joke, but I could tell that whatever was bothering her was causing her to withdraw. "You're not having second thoughts, are you?"

I followed her into the tack room, both of our hands full.

Mine with the saddle, hers with the bridle, reins, and lead ropes. As we put everything away, she said, "Hazel's being sentenced next week. Her lawyer told her it's looking like she is going to be serving three years. It's the minimum, which I guess is good, but that means she'll miss the wedding. We want her to be part of our day while she still can."

"Oh, Romy." I positioned the saddle on the rack before taking her in my arms. "Of course you need your sister on your big day. I know Dad would've loved to walk you down the aisle, but there is no one better to do it than Hazel. She'll probably steal the show," I teased.

That received a watery laugh from Romy. She pulled away to wipe a stray tear from her eye. "Ever since I became a mom, I'm all waterworks," she complained.

"But you look gorgeous doing it. I'm sure Jude would've married you a year ago if you'd let him."

Her cheeks flushed, and her eyes shone at my mention of Jude. "Being in Vegas last summer, I'm surprised he didn't drag me into one of those chapels after his fight."

"Kicking and screaming, probably."

She giggled at that. "Don't worry, I'm not running this time. Jude has me talking with a therapist. There won't be a runaway bride at this wedding."

"Oh, God, I hope not. Otherwise, we may need to hog-tie you."

"You'd probably like that too much," she teased back.

"Look at you with your smart mouth. I must be rubbing off on you. But yes, you're probably right. I would like that too much." I winked.

Reed entered the stable, Penn skipping at his side while he led Mushu to his stall. I couldn't help it. I had to stop and look at him. The man was pure sin. Even after the roadside car sex earlier today, I was ready to go again.

"Looks like *someone's* rubbing off on you, too," Romy quipped, her eyes flitting to Reed.

I shot her a look to try to warn her off, but I couldn't help my lips twitching.

Her eyes and mouth grew big. "No fucking way. I knew it!"

"Oh my God!" I threw up my hands. Reed and Penn glanced our way at our commotion. "Does everyone know?"

She nodded her head slowly, as if to punctuate the affirmative yes. "We were just waiting for you to catch up. So," she whispered, "is the sex phenomenal?"

I could feel myself blushing, and I never blush, even when talking about sex. Ever. "Romy, let me tell you, it is the best fucking sex I've ever had. The way that man knows how to play with my body. And,"—I lowered my voice even further, leaning in conspiratorially—"he's fucking pierced."

She slapped a hand over her mouth to keep from yelling.

I pressed my lips together to keep myself from squealing, nodding in agreement.

"No," she said in near disbelief. "What does it feel like?"

"Oh, baby, it just rubs in all the right places." I hummed thinking of that deliciousness.

Romy and I both looked at Mushu's stall, watching Reed with his daughter.

"I'll never look at him the same way again," she said wistfully beside me.

I grinned, crossing my arms to watch the best fucking sight in the world. The horse I loved. The little girl I was falling for. And the man who was my everything. "Same."

Progress had been made building the barn beside Jude and Romy's place. The floors were laid, horse stalls were framed out, and the roof was in place, but the walls weren't up. The sunset would be the backdrop as soon as Romy and Jude said "I do."

The flower arrangements Sage and Hazel helped assemble decorated the space. Blue, purple, and yellow wildflowers lined the center, creating a makeshift aisleway. A few folding chairs were on either side, where Christian and Kale sat. Christian held a boombox—he was on music duty—and Kale was ready to shoot video on his cell phone. After moving the date up, they couldn't get a DJ and photographer in time. But this was Romy's style anyway, and Jude didn't care as long as she was his for life.

A centerpiece sat on top of a small, round table at one end, where they would exchange their vows. Dad stood there now, rocking on his heels, while he read over the script he'd printed out. He quickly got ordained online to be able to officiate.

"Are you ready, Dad?" I asked.

"There's one thing I don't care for, and that's public speaking," he grumbled.

"You'll do great."

"I just hope you don't ask me to do this for your wedding. I'll probably already be a mess."

I blanched at the mention of my wedding, my stomach doing a somersault. My wedding? I gulped. I'd never thought that far ahead. I'd never been one of those girls who had their colors picked out and a dress circled in a magazine by the time she was fourteen. Horses and rodeo consumed any plans I'd made. But now, with Reed … I suppose I had to start thinking that far ahead.

I wasn't sure I was ready to get married. Or to become an instant mom. All of this was rushing that reality to the forefront, and it scared the shit out of me. There seemed to be a lot we still needed to discuss. I was so in love with him, and I now knew how he felt. But would he even want to get married again after being divorced? Did I want to get married?

Never seeing a happy marriage—well, maybe my mom's if you considered being happy meant getting a Porsche and a limitless credit card—I didn't really know if it was for me. Would it hurt Reed to know that? I'm sure he was not going to bring a woman into his and Penn's life without the potential to create stability for his daughter. Marriage meant commitment and permanence, and I just didn't know if I was there yet. Would that be a deal breaker for him? My heart seemed to crack just thinking about it.

Jude walked out, interrupting my spiraling thoughts. I whistled. Dressed in a suit, Jude looked every bit "The Bull" this evening. "Cuz, you look like you just stepped off a *GQ* photoshoot."

"I've done one of those, and I'd much rather scoop horseshit," he complained.

I scoffed. "Of course you would. Are you disappointed

Alex couldn't make it?" His old coach was planning on flying out from Vegas, but with the abrupt change in plans, he wasn't able to make it.

"It's all right. I would've married Romy anytime she wanted. It could've just been me, her, and Charli, and I'd be a happy man. Why were you able to get back early?"

I shrugged, not wanting to dampen his day. "Just had a feeling I needed to get home. And I'm glad I did. I wouldn't miss this for the world." I wrapped him up in an embrace, giving him a big kiss on the cheek. "Proud of you."

He wiped his cheek, checking his hand to see if my lipstick came off.

"Rude!" I hit him in the arm before rubbing his cheek. "Just rub it in."

"Is it off?" he asked.

"You're good. It's waterproof anyway, asshole."

Hands wrapped around my waist, drawing me back to a solid, warm chest. I squeaked in surprise before peeking over my shoulder, but I already knew it was Reed.

"Hey, sweetheart, you're a smokeshow in this dress," he whispered in my ear. He leaned down to press his lips to my bare shoulder, goose bumps scattering beneath the tight, strapless, black lace maxi dress. I loved this dress, mostly because of the slit that went straight up my thigh so I could show off my black cowboy boots, and it gave plenty of room to move.

I lifted my gaze then. Jude and Dad's eyes were burning right into me. Heat washed over me, replacing the goose bumps.

I held my breath. My cheeks flamed. Thank God for the

two pounds of blush and bronzer I was wearing. "Well, I guess this is as good a time as any to let y'all know Reed and I are together." I reached back to grip Reed's neck, arching into him, claiming him in front of my family.

I didn't know what I expected from either of them, but it wasn't the smug look on either of their faces. Christian and Kale already knew, and I could hear them snickering behind me. Without even turning around, I flipped them off.

"I don't think you could have chosen a better man," Dad said, reaching out to shake Reed's hand. I released a breath in relief. "I'm just glad you eventually saw what I saw."

"*Dad.*" He was going to make me choke up. What was it about love that turned me into a fucking pile of mush?

Jude leaned back on his heels, his arms crossed, a lopsided smirk on his face and humor in his voice. "Good luck to you, man. I think you might need it with this one."

"Hey!" I scolded.

But he winked, teasing, before his face went stony, staring Reed down. "But if you break her heart, I *will* break your fucking legs."

"Okay, Bull," I huffed, giving his chest a solid thump. "Go back to your corner."

Jude relaxed a bit, dropping his arms, his eyes then growing wide and his face softening as he looked past us. Dad's attention shifted, too, his smile growing.

We turned to see Hazel dressed in a yellow sundress holding Charli and a bouquet, with Romy at her side. Romy looked absolutely gorgeous. Her blonde hair in big, shining waves, pinned up on one side, a cream-colored, mermaid-style, lace wedding dress with a plunging neckline, and a bouquet of wildflowers in her hand made her look like the picture-perfect bride. Sage helped fluff out the short train, letting us get a peek of her white cowboy boots beneath. Penn hopped up and down in her blue princess dress and boots, a basket in her hands. She was so thrilled when Romy asked her to be her flower girl.

Tears shone in both sisters' eyes as they looked at each other, exchanging a few words. I couldn't help the lump growing in my throat as we all took our positions. Reed and I took our seats on the bride's side, while Sage posted up by the aisle to take photos. Christian hit play on the boombox, a slowed-down piano version of "Bless the Broken Road" streaming through.

Shit! I made the mistake of glancing at Jude and Dad. Their eyes glistened, and Jude was biting his lip as if holding back tears. I should have brought tissues. I sniffed, but Reed seemed to read me, his arm draped over the back of my chair, his thumb dragging comfortingly across my shoulder. I wish I could say it was helping, but it was making me even more emotional, thinking this could be us one day.

I cleared my throat, turning back to watch Penn walk down the aisle, tossing flower petals until she could hop on the seat beside her dad. Then Romy and Hazel started to walk, their eyes set on the two men in front of them at the altar. Jude's leg bounced, impatiently waiting to get his hands on his bride, while Dad stood handsome in his suit and cowboy hat, his eyes shadowed but flickering with a light I'd never seen before.

My head tipped curiously, looking back and forth between him and Hazel. Their mouths trembled at the corners with soft smiles. Silent communication passed between them, making me wonder. But then Hazel and Romy reached the end of the aisle, their gazes shifting to the bride and groom.

Romy leaned in to hug her sister, whispering "thank yous" and "I love yous" before dropping a soft kiss on Charli's head. Then turning to Jude, she accepted his outstretched hand, and they both took deep breaths. It was as if the moment they touched each other, the whole world was set right again. I knew what that felt like now.

Hazel joined us, handing me the bouquets so she could sit down with Charli. I glanced at Penn, who was leaning into her dad's side now, although she fidgeted in her chair.

Just then, Reed's phone rang. "Sorry." He grimaced, quickly pulling it out of his pocket to silence it before returning it.

His cell kept vibrating, and as he removed it from his pocket, I saw Elise's name displayed on the screen. I sucked in a breath, and Reed's body went as tight as a bowstring. The arm that was draped over my shoulder retreated as he rested his cell phone face down on his thigh.

I'm sure my own body language might have given my anxiety away as I readjusted in my seat, crossing my leg away from Reed. I tried not to be distracted, to enjoy the ceremony. My cousin and one of my best friends were getting married.

Each time his cell buzzed, Reed peeked at his phone screen. His face hardened, and his jaw muscles ticked. By the time Dad pronounced Jude and Romy husband and wife, Reed was like a statue beside me, his knuckles white where they gripped his phone.

Reed leaned in to whisper in my ear, "I'll be right back." He turned, stroking a hand over Penn's head. "Be right back, princess," he said, before standing and walking out of the barn.

I watched him as he picked up his phone and headed toward the house.

I stood, too, announcing I'd go get the champagne that was chilling in Romy and Jude's fridge, while everyone congratulated the couple and Sage took pictures.

As I stepped out of the barn, I saw Reed standing by the side of the house on the other side of the full driveway.

His voice was deep as he tried to remain quiet, but I could tell it was strained with unease. "Calm down. Can you start from the beginning again? What's going on?"

My heart pounded, my gut wrenched. I had to fight the urge to march over to him, making a beeline instead into the house to get the bottles of champagne.

When I stepped back out of the house, he was hanging up the phone. Shoving it back into his pocket, he lifted his head.

In just a couple long strides, he stepped in front of me, halting me in my path.

He scratched his brow beneath the brim of his cowboy hat, then adjusted it. He looked upset.

"Everything all right?" I asked, knowing it probably wasn't.

"I'm going to have to go," he said.

My brows raised at that. "Right now? We're about to make a toast."

His eyes wouldn't connect with mine. "I need to take care of something really quick, and then I'll be back."

"Anything you need help with?" I wanted him to talk to me, to include me in whatever he was dealing with, but this was all so new. I didn't know how much he wanted me to be involved when it came to Penn or his ex-wife.

"It's all right." He wrapped an arm around me, giving me a peck on the cheek. "Can you watch Penn for me?"

I didn't know how I felt about being asked to watch his daughter when he was going off to deal with his ex, but it definitely did not feel good.

"Yeah, I'll keep an eye on her," I told him, breaking the hug.

"Thank you. Hopefully, I won't be long."

I nodded, watching him hustle off to his truck.

Sucking in a deep, calming breath through my nose, I adjusted the weight of the champagne bottles in my arms, steeling myself against the questions from my family and friends and whatever imminent talk was on the horizon for Reed and I.

One thing I did know for certain was that a big fucking glass of champagne was calling my name.

Chapter 30
Lina

The reception was already in full swing by the time I returned. Christian turned up the boombox, a slow country song playing. Jude and Romy, with Charli in their arms, were sharing their moment. Dad was dancing with Hazel, then spun her out, trading partners with Jude so he could dance with Romy and his namesake. Kale was a good sport, twirling Penn in her princess dress. Sage continued to snap photos, oblivious to the fact that Christian couldn't take his eyes off her in her green sheath dress and wide-brimmed hat.

I took the champagne bottles to one of the tables that was set up with flutes and cupcakes Hazel had baked for the occasion. I popped a bottle, giving a celebratory *whoop* like I usually did, but it was lackluster.

"Okay, what's wrong?" Sage asked, setting the camera down so she could give me her full attention. "Where did Reed go?"

I poured myself a glass before setting down the bottle. "His ex called him needing help or some shit," I grumbled, taking a sip of the champagne, letting the bubbles swirl in my mouth.

Her brows rose to her hat. "He left?"

I took another drink, hoping that it would cool my insides, but the fizz felt exactly how my blood felt, and I didn't mean effervescent—I meant *boiling*. Ready to bubble over. I was pissed because here I was, feeling fucking embarrassed, just like I had after that first time we'd met.

"It's bullshit, really," I told her. "Here I was, ready to have a relationship with the guy, have him at my side at a family wedding, and what does he do? He leaves to go to his fucking ex-wife." Of course I leave out the part that I'm desperately in love with him.

I couldn't bear to look Sage in the eye. "Did he say what's going on?"

"Nope." I popped the P. "Just said he needed to take care of something real quick and that he'd be right back. So ... he asked me to watch Penn." I was also worried. Whatever it was had to be bad enough to make him leave and ask me to watch his daughter. Was this about the stalker? Was this about Junior?

"That's shitty. I'm sorry, Lina." Sage poured herself some champagne. "We could happily drown our woes in the corner if you need a drinking buddy."

"You don't want to dance?" I asked her. The music changed, and Christian stood from his chair, about to head over to us.

"Not really."

"Because it looks like someone wants to dance with *you*."

Christian was already striding over, his smile deepening his dimples.

"Oh, God." Sage threw back her champagne flute. "He

doesn't know when to throw in the towel, does he?"

"I really don't think 'I give up' is in his vocabulary."

"And that's the fucking problem," Sage said, almost distantly, as if remembering something. "He needs to."

"What's the problem?" Christian asked.

"Just that you won't give up on her," I told him, giving her a smirk.

"Bitch." She shook her head and rolled her eyes, but there was a flicker of a smile on her lips. "No, the real problem is that Reed left without an explanation."

"Oh, shit." Christian grimaced. "He's a dead man, isn't he?"

"More than likely," I confirmed.

"Do *we* need to have a talk with him?" he asked, gesturing between him and Sage.

"Fuck." She sighed at his emphasis, throwing up her hands. "I don't know why I even try anymore."

"You can stop fighting it and just dance with me?" Christian held out his hand.

"It's just us, Sage." I bumped my shoulder with hers. "Whatever happens at the bonfire, stays at the bonfire," I said, referring to the place we all stood, even if there wasn't a burn pile anymore. "You know, we never talked about Jude and Romy getting it on in his truck last summer."

"What the fuck?" Romy asked, her and Hazel joining us.

"Oh, come on." I rolled my eyes. "It's no secret. We all saw you then, adjusting your clothes when we returned to the stables."

"Shit." Her cheeks flushed pink.

"See, Sage?" I poured Romy a glass, handing it to her. "Go dance with Christian. We won't say anything for at least … well, not until next year." I laughed at my own joke.

"Fucking fine," Sage relented, slamming her champagne flute down.

"Shit, don't break the glass," I scolded, holding the unlevel table steady as the rest of the glasses rattled.

"Really?" Christian asked. His eyes went wide, and he was beaming like a fucking idiot. "Is this a dream? Quick, Sage, pinch me!"

He held out his arm to her, but she slapped it away, grabbing his hand instead. "Don't press your fucking luck. I'll give you one dance."

His grin was so wide, I thought it might break his jaw. "One dance it is, baby. I can live on the memory for the rest of my life and die a happy man."

Sage rolled her eyes, but there was a smile begging to break free.

"So what's going on with you and Reed?" Hazel asked, as we watched Christian take Sage in his arms.

I poured myself another glass. "We apparently still have some things to work out."

"Where did he take off to?" Romy asked.

"To his ex-wife." I pressed my lips together, starting to get pissed all over again. Sage and Christian had only been a momentary distraction.

"Yikes. Wrong move, buddy," Hazel commented.

I shook my head. "He didn't even tell me what was going on, just that he'd be right back."

"At least he's not just grunting anymore. But it does sound like he needs to work on his communication skills," Romy said. I nearly laughed, remembering her communication skills with Jude early on. At least there'd been growth since then.

"Oh, don't you worry. I'm going to force that man to fucking communicate with me as soon as he gets back."

"What's this I'm hearing?" Jude questioned, joining us with Charli held to his chest. "Do I need to go break some fucking legs?"

"I think she's got this one handled." Romy patted his arm.

"Do you want to dance with us, Mama?" he asked, bouncing a sleepy baby Charli.

Romy's eyes lit up, her face going soft and happy. "Always," she said, taking his arm and heading back to the dance floor. God, I wanted that. As I glanced out at the dance floor, watching Sage enjoying her dance more than she'd ever admit, and seeing Jude's little family join them, I knew I wanted all of this with Reed. But everything that came with it honestly scared the shit out of me.

So much for "being right back." I don't know what provoked me, but once I got Penn to bed, I grabbed the six-pack of beer I'd swiped from Jude's house and headed out to the backyard. There was no way in hell I was going to sit in the quiet house while she slept and I waited for Reed to come home. I needed to blow off some steam, and the champagne had fallen flat, not even taking the edge off. My mind was spiraling and my body had to fucking move. Otherwise, I was going to scream.

A roping dummy sat in the yard, and rope hung from the nearby hitching post. I cracked open a can, sipped down the foam, and set it on the picnic table. One of the upgrades Jude made to the double-wide property was putting in grass and a play area for Penn. There was even a paddock, ready for Penn's riding lessons. I was already making plans to teach her to circle barrels.

Gathering a rope in my hands, I ran it out until I had the lasso in my grip. Swinging it above my head, I threw it at the dummy horns. The loop landed and I pulled tight, lassoing the bull just like my daddy taught me. I loosened the rope, yanking it back into my grasp. Resting my hand on my hip, I picked up my beer to take another sip before lassoing again.

The back screen door swung open behind me, the hinges creaking in the summer night. I chanced a glance over my shoulder, knowing it would be him. I picked up the can, chugging a few gulps. I wiped my mouth with the back of my hand, watching the lipstick smear across it.

"Shit, so much for waterproof makeup," I grumbled to myself.

I felt the air shift as Reed stepped up beside me. In my periphery, his head was bowed beneath his cowboy hat, and his hands were stuffed into his pockets.

I went again, lassoing the dummy horns like it was second nature.

"You were gone awhile," I said matter-of-factly. I tried to hold it back, wanting to hear him out, but I couldn't help the venom dripping in every syllable.

"I know, I'm sorry. Did Penn go down okay?" he asked

sheepishly.

We still hadn't looked at each other.

"She went down fine. I had to lie down with her for a little bit while she was falling asleep. She misses her mom and dad." I knew my words stung, but he needed to hear them.

Reed grimaced. "I know. I hope this won't be forever. We're just going through a transition right now."

I spun on him. "So this is just a transition? For how long? Until Elise gets dumped by Junior? Until you decide you want your family back?"

Reed's eyes were smoldering beneath his hat brim. "That's not what I meant. I meant, transitioning into being a single parent, transitioning Penn into this new arrangement. Trying to figure out this shit with her mom."

I nodded, running my tongue over my teeth. "Sounds like you need some time to figure out your shit, and all I've been is a distraction. You should be focusing your energy on Penn and your transition into single fatherhood, not on me. She needs her dad right now."

Taking another swig of beer, I set down my empty can and walked over to put the rope back on the hitching post.

I turned to see Reed still standing there, his dark eyes boring into me, his jaw tight and his chest heaving. I froze. He looked like a bull ready to charge. He took long strides across the yard, heading toward me. My heart began to pound. One more step and he was stepping into me, his hand wrapping around my neck and pushing me back against the hitching post.

"Sweetheart, you're the one thing I don't need to fucking

figure out."

His mouth crashed down on mine, his teeth nipping on my bottom lip, begging me to open for him. I savored his taste for only a second before pushing as hard as I could on his chest to get him off me.

"Then why the fuck did you go to her? Why did you fucking go to her and leave me during a family wedding? Do you know how embarrassed I was? Or should I say how embarrassed I am … *again*? It's bullshit!"

His brow furrowed. "I know. I'm so sorry, Lina. Fuck, that's the last thing I wanted. I didn't mean to embarrass you, to leave in the middle of Jude and Romy's wedding. Should I expect a visit from Jude soon?" His words were serious, his last question edged with sarcasm in his attempt to break the tension.

"No, I think you showed everyone tonight that they aren't worth your time." I knew full well no one thought that, but I was hurt—and hurt people hurt people.

He stepped back as if I'd just slapped him. "That's not fair. I had to deal—"

"What? What did you have to deal with that was so important that it had to happen right at that moment? Is this going to happen every time your wife––"

"Ex."

I rolled my eyes. "*Ex*-wife calls and needs help with something? Is this what I should expect? You'll drop everything to run to her? Because if that's what I should expect, then I don't know if I can fucking do this, Reed. I deserve more than this. And so does Penn." My nose stung, and tears sprang to my eyes. I don't know if I was ready to hear what he had to say, either. Maybe I was preventing the inevitable heartbreak now, but I needed to know, and he needed to know exactly where I stood.

"You absolutely deserve more than this." Reed's voice lowered an octave. He devoured the distance between us, again wrapping his hand around my neck, his fingers putting slight pressure on my throat, walking us backward again until my back hit the hitching post. "You deserve everything you could possibly wish for—and more."

His palms then trailed down my neck, over my collarbone and shoulders, down my arms, my skin prickling under his touch.

"What do you think I wish for?" I jutted out my chin, my voice breathy, yet demanding.

"I know you, Lina. I see all those emotions swirling behind those big, brown eyes. You need release, an outlet to surrender them all to. I can give you that, if that's what you need right now."

CHAPTER 31
Lina

I gulped. My blood heated. A flush traveled over my skin until my pussy was pulsing. "You think I trust you enough for that?"

"I think you want to. Do you trust me not to push you past any boundary you're not willing to cross?" His fingers intertwined with mine, raising them at our sides until he could spread my arms across the hitching post. He stepped between my legs, letting his thigh press against my center. I involuntarily rocked forward, the slit of my dress inching up just enough for him to see the thong underneath.

"Fuck, Lina. I want to touch you so badly."

"Fuck you, Reed. I'm pissed at you." My eyes pierced into his. And I hoped it was the death glare I imagined it to be.

"I know, sweetheart. I'm a fucking asshole."

"Yeah, you are."

"I need you to hear me. You have to see what you do to me. I can't stay away from you, sweetheart. You can be pissed off at me as much as you want, but I need you."

"You fucked up."

"Yeah, I did. It will never happen again."

"I don't believe you."

"I will never lie to you, Lina. I promise. Please, let me touch you. Let me show you. And if you need to fuck me like you hate me, I'll give you that, too."

My hands involuntarily balled with his. Fuck, I wanted him so badly. The tension was like an inferno inside me, ready to explode, and I needed the release. But I loved him so much, my heart was aching. I could easily hate-fuck him right now, but there was no way for me to protect my heart in this.

"Fuck me," I said through gritted teeth. "I can't stand here and not let you touch me, Reed. This is just too much. Too much anger. Too much hurt. Too much love. It needs to go somewhere."

"Then let me help you, sweetheart."

I raised my chin in near defiance, tipping it slightly in a brief nod.

"Thank fuck. Keep your arms there, baby, so I can feel you." I did as he said, arching off the beam of the hitching post toward every place his hands traveled. "All of you." Over my breasts, the curve of my stomach, my hips, until he reached my panties beneath my dress. His fingertips dragged along the edge, dipping ever so slightly beneath.

"Reed." I whispered his name as if he were my god.

"Getting mad at me makes you wet, doesn't it? Is it the fact that I'll have to make it up to you? Or is it the thought of me taking control?" His voice was husky in my ear, each word like a caress over my clit.

"Yes. Yes to fucking all of that."

"How am I going to keep you from touching me? How am

I going to keep you from falling when I fuck you?" His large hands continued their perusal over my body, reaching back up to my arms.

He spotted the rope hanging on the end of the post, a slow smirk breaking across his face. His eyes caught mine, black in the night, yet bright as if a fire brewed behind them. "I'm going to ask you again. Do you trust me, sweetheart? You need to tell me now because I don't think I can stop otherwise. I want you too fucking bad."

My breath hitched as he gathered the rope up in his hands. "What do you want to do to me?"

"Oh, sweetheart, too many things. But first, I want to fucking spread you out across this hitching post like you're being served to me on a fucking platter. Strip you of those panties that drive me fucking mad. Then wrap this rope around those perfect little ankles, spreading you wide for me so I can see that pretty little cunt."

"Reed," I moaned. His words alone were driving me to the edge.

"You'll be crying it's too much as I drive you to the edge over and over again with my cock buried deep. But you won't be able to pull back or slow it down. You'll just have to take it until you're shattering on my cock."

"Fuck, cowboy."

"That's exactly what I'm about to do. So what's it going to be, sweetheart?"

I was still upset with him, and we still needed to have a serious talk. However, that would have to wait until we were both not turned on and our heads were clear of this lusty haze.

Neither one of us was thinking straight—not right now. All I wanted was for him to take control, dominate my body, let me release the coil of emotion that cranked my muscles tight enough to snap.

"Yes, I trust you with my body, but I'm going to need more from you."

"I'll give you anything you ask for. Do we need a safe word?"

"I need a safe word?" I nearly squeaked.

"Turn around." I did as he commanded, keeping my hands on the hitching post. He started with my wrists on the post, first wrapping and then tying a square knot with the rope. "Now what's it going to be?"

I said the first thing that came to my mind. "Jackpot."

I watched him over my shoulder as he gave me a cute smirk that was borderline dangerous. "Jackpot it is."

Giving the knot a good tug, he ensured it would not come undone but was not so tight that it would cut off my circulation.

He gathered two more ropes. Leaning over me, he wrapped his fingers around my jaw, tipping my head back to give me a kiss. And not just any kiss. His mouth covered mine, his tongue forcing its entrance, making me moan while it stroked against mine. He started to pull away and I leaned back to try to follow him, but the rope did its job keeping me in place.

I whined in frustration.

"Hold on, sweetheart. I'm in charge, so you just relax."

He crouched down behind me, his palms coasting over my calves and up my legs, pushing the fabric of my dress up, revealing my ass. His hands never left me as he kissed every piece of flesh he could touch.

"Fuck, baby. Seeing those perfect ass cheeks split down the middle with a string of fabric. I just want to tug on it and watch it spread you open for me."

"Reed." My breaths were coming heavier now. I squirmed, my skin itching to be free. "Get them fucking off me."

Stopping immediately, he stepped back.

"No, I'm going to need you to be a good girl and ask me again."

"Please, Reed. I want your dick so bad."

He chuckled, a deep, throaty laugh, while he hooked his fingers into the sides of my thong, dragging it down over my ass and down my legs. I could feel the warm breeze flutter across my soaked center like a tease.

"Step out." He helped me step out of the thong.

Whether it ended up in the grass or in his pocket, I didn't give a fuck. At this point, I just wanted him to fuck me.

"Spread your legs, baby."

I widened my stance, but he nudged my feet even wider until they were right where he wanted them. Wrapping and tying my ankles the same way he did my wrists, he tied them on both ends of the hitching post, making me spread out for him.

"Lean on the post and stick out your ass. I want to see you on full display for me."

He gathered the fabric from my dress around my waist, baring me to him. I didn't know how much more I could take of this delicious torture. I squirmed. "I want you so badly, Reed. Please."

"Look at you being so good and asking nicely." He strummed two fingers down between my cheeks, pressing lightly on my tight hole before dipping into my pussy. I was so wet, they slid right in.

I ground against his hand, rolling my hips as his fingers dipped, then glided, out and over my ass. Pulses of pleasure throbbed through me with every slide of his fingertips.

"Fuck, Reed. You're driving me crazy!"

"You need to use that safe word already, baby?"

"You're going to have to do more than that for a jackpot, cowboy."

"Goddamn, sweetheart. All you need to do is ask."

"Please, Reed. Please fuck me with your big dick. I want you going hard and deep. Make me come, cowboy."

Reed growled at that, obviously losing some of his control. I heard his belt jingle as he undid his pants. He brushed a light kiss over my ass while he took down his pants, and then I felt him. Thick and hard. Sliding through my slit. Gliding over my clit, spreading my wetness.

"Beg for it. Tell me what you want."

I moaned, almost unable to bear the feel of his cock slipping through me, continually passing right where I wanted it.

"Touch me. Anything, Reed. Please." I wiggled my ass, trying to position him closer to where I wanted him, but I couldn't move. The restraints held me in place. The rope rasped against my wrists as I strained against them, but they didn't rub uncomfortably. They only added to my arousal. I was dripping for him, and he was coating himself in me. "Please," I begged again.

"Good girl." He positioned my hips so my ass was sticking out farther for him, my head now resting against the post. He wrapped a hand around the back of my neck, the other pressing the small of my back to arch for him. "Never question my intentions again, and I'll give you what you want and need. Tell me you're my little slut for this cock."

He notched his head at my entrance.

My breath was coming quicker now with the anticipation of him right there. I was so greedy for him. "I'm always a slut for your cock, daddy."

"That's right, baby." He inched in torturously slow, even though I was sucking him in. His fingertips dug in at my hip, keeping me from bucking against him, making it so I felt each and every piercing hit my walls. He was so thick, I had to breathe to release the pressure as he spread me wide open for him. "God, your pussy's heaven. You feel so good."

He started to move then, his movement deliberate and rhythmic as he thrust in and out. His hand gripped my neck to keep me steady, his other putting pressure on my lower back to create the angle he needed to hit that sensitive spot deep inside.

Our breaths came heavy now, punctuating the summer night, a featherlight breeze brushing across our heated skin. The distant lowing of cattle, the chirps of crickets, and the rush of the Deschutes River were our soundscape while Reed fucked me.

I could feel the coil deep inside winding tight. The pressure building, ready to burst free. "I'm going to come," I whimpered.

"Not yet, baby." He slowed down, gradually pulling out, making me shudder. "I'm going to keep you on edge, prolong your pleasure, until it's so intense, you're yelling jackpot."

He swiped a finger through my soaked pussy before swirling it around my little rosebud.

"Breathe in through your nose." I did as he said, his thumb massaging and circling the sensitive hole. "Now out through your mouth." Just as I released a breath, he slid his thumb in.

CHAPTER 32
Reed

To see Lina Larsen tied up on my hitching post, spread out for me, willing to trust me even when I fucked up tonight––I was such an asshole, and I'm glad she fucking called me on it––made me love her all the more. I wasn't planning on letting her go, but if this was the last time … if that's what she wanted after tonight … I'd give it all to her.

We were both on edge. Seeing her completely submit to me was the biggest turn-on. It was sexy as hell, and I wanted to make this last forever.

I thrust back in. Her walls were already fluttering around me. "Fuck, baby, you're so fucking tight." With my thumb and cock now inside her, she was barely holding on.

"Fuck," she moaned. "I can't take it." She was straining against the rope, her body quivering.

"You're doing so good, sweetheart. You can take it. I know you can. My badass barrel racer. You're burning it up with a horse between your legs every week. I know you can handle me."

I didn't know if *I* could fucking take it. My spine tingled and my balls tightened. I wasn't about to end this for either of us, though. Her pussy felt too damn good. I wanted her wrapped around me and to stay buried deep forever. I could live there. I had to slow down the pace, though. Otherwise, it would end sooner than I wanted, and I intended to draw this out. Make this last, intensified for both of us.

I ran my free hand up her ass, over her back, up her shoulder, and down her arm. Her hands were twisting and turning in their binds.

"So fucking full," she breathed. Thrusting at this angle, while she was unable to move her legs and spread them as she wanted, added friction for both of us.

"You're so gorgeous, baby. How did I get so lucky? To have you totally submit to me like this. You like this, huh? A little slut for me?"

"Yes," she moaned out. "You feel so good, cowboy."

"You like being at my mercy? Letting me play with your body however I like?" I laced my fingers with hers. My heart thumped in my chest seeing my hand intertwined with hers, holding her steady, while I was deep inside her.

She moaned again, pulling at her ropes. "However you want, cowboy." Her voice was breathy and raspy, dripping with sex and desire.

"Fuck." I withdrew my thumb, bringing my hand around to rub her clit. She groaned, her hips rocking to now grind against my hand while I thrust slowly in and out.

"Yes, like that. Don't stop. I'm going to come."

"No," I growled.

I quickly pulled out and removed my hand, taking a step back.

"Reed," she whined.

"I told you I was going to edge you, baby."

She circled her hips, seeking some form of relief.

"Let me just take you in for a moment. You look so perfect trussed up there for me, sweetheart." The moonlight was beaming down on her, making her dark hair gleam. Her hands gripping the post where she was tied. She was a fucking sight. I stroked my cock, feeling her wetness between my fingers. I wanted to memorize this if this was going to be the last time.

"Reed, please."

"What do you need, sweetheart?"

"I need you to make me come."

"What if I just want to watch you for a while, all tied up for me while you thrash and writhe, desperate for my cock? Watch you dripping for me, those pretty thighs glistening, begging for me?"

"You're an asshole," she growled through her teeth.

"I'll be whatever you want, sweetheart. Do you want me to be the asshole tonight? Because I can be that. Do you want me to be your cowboy, and you can go for a ride? Because I'd gladly do that, too. Or do you want me to be your daddy tonight and do exactly as you're told?"

She groaned again, her ass still squirming, searching for me. "Fuck, daddy, tell me what to do."

"Daddy's good girl is going to stay just like this for a little bit longer while I get on my knees for you and lick up that mess you're making. But you're going to tell me when you're about to come."

"Thank fuck." She sighed.

I tucked myself in and walked around the hitching post, taking her in. Her eyes were heavy with desire, peeking from above the post, begging for me to relieve the tension.

I chuckled as I knelt before her in the dirt, gathering her dress up so I could be face-to-face with her beautiful pussy. I looked up at her as she peered down at me. "I didn't say I was going to make you come … yet."

"Asshole," she gritted out.

I gave her clit a little slap. She moaned, her knees nearly buckling. God, those legs were strong. I marveled at her calves, dragging my palms over them and up between her thighs until I could part her.

"No, I'm your daddy tonight. If you want to come, you'll tell me when you're close. Say, yes, daddy." My stubborn girl glared down at me. I wet my lips, wanting so badly to taste her. "Don't be a brat, Lina. I want to taste you."

"Yes, daddy," she said through clenched teeth.

"That's my good girl. Now don't take your eyes off me while I eat you."

I kept my eyes on her while I flattened my tongue. I held her open with my thumbs as I ran my tongue through her wetness from pussy to clit. She tasted so fucking good, like fucking cake. She could be my dessert every night for the rest of my life.

She pushed her hips toward me, greedy for it, rocking, as my tongue fucked her and then circled and sucked her clit. I did it over and over again while her hips rolled. Glancing up, she was doing so well listening, not taking her eyes off me, watching what I was doing to her, my face buried in her pussy while I devoured her.

"Reed," she breathed. "I'm close."

I gave her clit one last suck before pulling back to see her face tight, so close to orgasm. "You're doing so good, baby. Listening just like I want you to, sweetheart. I think you earned that orgasm. Ready to come down from there?"

"Mmm," was the only response I got from her, her forehead rolling against the post. She was so close to letting go completely for me.

Walking back behind her, I began undoing the knots around her ankles, removing the ropes. I rubbed her skin where it left a little burn. Wrapping an arm around her middle, I loosened the rope at her wrists until she could slip through. She nearly collapsed in my arms, leaning back into me.

"Come here, sweetheart. I got you." She was already weak for me. I swooped her up into my arms.

"Please, let me come," she murmured, gripping my shirt in desperation.

I walked us over to the picnic table, laying her out for me. She squirmed up on the table as if trying to get away from me.

"Nuh-uh. No, you don't. You're going to stay right on the edge here. Bend those knees, baby. Let me see that pretty pussy."

I dragged her back down the picnic table until she was on the edge in front of me. She bent her knees for me, and I parted them wider. She was soaked and swollen. I swiped a single digit through her slit so I could taste it one last time, sucking my finger. God, she was my addiction.

"Reed, please," she begged again.

"I know, sweetheart. You need it so bad. And you've been such a good girl for me. I'll give you exactly what you want." I pulled down my pants, letting my throbbing cock bob between us. Precum was already leaking at the tip. It wasn't going to take much more from me, either. "Now give me those beautiful, brown eyes and watch how perfectly we fit together."

I gave myself a stroke before positioning at her entrance.

"Reed, I love you. Please don't break me," she whined.

My gut clenched, my eyes jumping from where I was sliding into her to her face. She was still watching me as I disappeared inside her. She was so goddamn heartbreakingly beautiful. I gulped, my heart cracking, thinking this may be the last time I ever heard those words from her once she knew about my past.

As I bottomed out, I stilled, tipping her chin back to look at me as I laid her head back on the table. "I'll always love you, Lina Larsen."

Her brows pinched as if she were in pain, and I wondered if she could read my thoughts. I leaned down to brush a kiss across her lips, letting her taste us, as I started to move inside her. She wrapped her arms around my neck, holding me to her, pressing her mouth to mine. Her knees tightened at my hips while I thrust inside her. Her nails dug into my shoulders as it intensified.

I pulled back, then, to look at her, needing to see what she looked like beneath me. Wanting to sear this moment into my brain. Her eyes were closed, her mouth falling open, panting.

She looked like she was in complete rapture. On another plane. I wanted to be on that ride with her.

"Come for me, baby?" I asked, but she only responded with a throaty groan. "Fuck, baby. I can't hold back anymore. I need to fuck you." I wrapped my hand around her throat, squeezing not too tight but just tight enough, feeling her thumping pulse beneath my fingers. I gripped her as I fucked her, pounding her pussy as it tightened around me like a vise grip, milking me.

She cried out, her nails digging deeper, puncturing my skin beneath my shirt. I hoped those fucking marks were still there in the morning. Her body stiffened beneath me.

"You're mine!" I yelled, not caring who heard.

The pressure in my spine burst through my balls, my dick twitching as I spilled into her, filling her to the brim. Her pussy fluttered and pulsed around me while I shot rope after rope of cum into her.

Her body settled beneath me. I held her, not wanting to lose this connection. Our chests heaved as we caught our breath, hearts pounding in sync. I continued to twitch inside her while I felt her pulse, riding aftershock after aftershock. Her warm breaths were like wind gusts against my neck as she caught her breath.

I kissed her temple, trailing my lips down her cheek and along her jaw, down the curve of her neck. She arched against me, though her limbs were loose, her body spent. I ran a hand down her chest, my lips never leaving her as I slowly pulled out. I was leaking from her. I couldn't help myself and had to shove it back in. Her body twitched at the sudden invasion of my touch as I pushed my cum back inside her with my finger.

I lowered her dress, helping her sit up. Gathering her in my arms, I whispered in her ear, "Come on, sweetheart, let's get you inside and cleaned up. There's something I need to tell you."

CHAPTER 33
Reed

My heart was pounding out of my chest, and I felt like I was going to be sick. This was not going to be a fun conversation, and I've never been so nervous in my life. I could feel my body tightening like a bowstring, like a cocked gun ready to fire. But I needed to take care of Lina first.

I wet a washcloth and cleaned her up in the bathroom. I dropped tentative, healing kisses to her wrists and ankles before rubbing lotion into the slight rope burns that were left behind. Her eyes were heavy with fatigue, her body soft and pliable. She didn't resist me when I took her dress off, replacing it with one of my T-shirts, then scooping her up and taking her to sit on the couch with me.

"Do you want something to drink?" I asked her, needing to break our silence. It was unnerving for her to be so quiet, and it put me on a different kind of edge than earlier.

"Water, please." She stretched out, pulling a blanket off the back of the couch to wrap around her.

"Don't fall asleep," I warned her, heading to the kitchen.

"You won't get off that easily, cowboy," she fired back.

There she was. It brought a small smile to my lips and broke some of the tension.

I poured us both some water and returned. Her eyes were closed, but they fluttered back open when I sat down. She sat up when I handed her the water glass. We both took sips, setting the glasses on the coffee table.

I inhaled deeply, releasing my breath slowly. It was not very often that I shared this with people. The last person was Chuck. I had to tell him before he agreed to hire me. He was understanding and empathetic. I could only hope his daughter would be the same.

"There are things about my past that I'm not proud of. Things that are still a part of me, that will always be a part of me."

"Okay …" She was staring at me intently, her brows pinched, her mouth set firm. I wanted to make this easy for her, not for me.

I took her hand from her lap, letting me feel her strong yet delicate bones. Hands that were comforting yet used to working hard and taking control. I lifted it, pressing my lips to her palm, before setting it back in her lap.

"Because of this, there are some things that make having a relationship with me complicated. Things that you may need to consider before you decide to be with me. Things I should have told you before we ever invested our feelings, and I'm sorry I made that mistake."

"You're scaring me, Reed." Her mouth turned down.

I glanced up at the ceiling for a moment, gathering my emotions, before returning my gaze to her. "I should have just let you keep hating me. Things would've been so much easier that way."

"Are you going to break my heart?" Her voice cracked.

A lump formed in my throat. "That would be the last thing I'd ever want to do."

"Just tell me."

I swallowed hard, but the lump wouldn't budge. I'd have to just talk through the emotions and hope my voice didn't break with my heart.

Taking another steadying breath, I tried again. "I don't just avoid alcohol anymore. I'm also a recovering addict, Lina. Elise and I met because we both partied with the same people and we had the same fix. Pills. Painkillers, mostly. Sometimes something harder. It got risky, at times, and we had some dangerous friends. Well, they weren't really friends but people who wanted to get high, too, or were dealers."

Lina was silent, her brow smoothed out now. She didn't look tired anymore, but alert and listening. It looked like wheels were spinning behind her eyes.

"When Elise found out she was pregnant with Penn, we were both still using, but trying to quit. We were over at our dealer's place, and someone who was looking to collect their debt pushed their way in, holding all of us at gunpoint until he gave him the money. That was my moment of clarity. Sitting there, knowing our baby was in her belly, and having a gun in our faces. I couldn't jeopardize Elise or our baby. They were both too precious to me.

"I thought that was enough of a wake-up call for Elise, too, but she had her own shit. That was the day I vowed to get clean. Then, when I finally held Penelope in my arms, I'd never seen a more perfect little girl. She was my everything. I wanted to give her the things I never had, and that meant staying clean. From that day forward, I haven't touched a single pill. Not even over the counter pain medicine. I can't. It would be too much of a risk for me."

Lina nodded slowly, taking it all in.

"My addiction will always be a part of me, Lina. I have to find other ways to cope, to relieve pain. Or I just deal with it. Whoever is going to be my partner is also going to have to be in this with me. I may have weak moments where I consider giving in, but I haven't for five years, and I don't plan on starting now.

"But being with an addict isn't an easy thing. I would know, having stayed with Elise for almost three years after Penn was born. I thought I could help her, but there were complications and she needed surgery, so the pills were available to her again. Her depression and anxiety were so bad after Penn was born. It was a breaking point for her. I tried so hard to help her." My voice hardened with the memories.

"The fights we would get into almost always ended with her throwing things and crying, shutting us both out, so Penn and I had to sleep together on the couch. I wanted to help her because I loved our family, and I wanted to give Penn the love and family I never had. But then she cheated on me and left me for the man who could feed her addiction. I thought I could fight for us and have enough determination for it to work for the two of us, but then it came down to Penn's safety and happiness. I wasn't going to put her through that anymore."

"I'm so sorry you went through all that," Lina said. I believed she genuinely meant that, but she seemed distant, like she was pulling away, and I hated it. An ache shot through my chest, and I rubbed it, hoping it would ease.

"Thank you. I will always put Penn first, no matter what. It will be a battle with her mom to get full custody, but I think I can win it. She's not fit, but I will not completely put her out of our lives. She's Penn's mother, after all."

Lina nodded again, looking down at her hands as they twisted in her lap. I hated this quiet version of her.

"When she called today, she was freaking out. She and a friend were hanging out, and her friend had a bad reaction. She couldn't get ahold of Junior, so she called me. I still feel obligated to her since she's Penn's mom, but I also feel some guilt that I couldn't help her when she needed it most."

"So you'll always go to her when she needs help?" Lina asked, her voice now with an edge to it. She wasn't looking at me, though.

I shook my head. "I shouldn't have gone over there. I shouldn't have helped her. She didn't want me to take her friend to the hospital because she was scared it would look bad for her case, which it does. But I did it anyway. That's what took so long. I drove her friend to the ER, dropped her off, then made a call to my lawyer. I'm documenting everything in hopes it will strengthen my case so I can get full custody of Penn.

"Penn comes first, Lina, and I'm going to do everything in my power to keep her safe." I took her hands in mine again. "And I promise you, I will not be going over to help her again, at least not until she's clean. I told her as much. But she will be in our lives, and I need you to understand that, for Penn's sake."

Lina glanced up at me then, tears brimming her eyes. "I understand," she said, but her words were flat.

"I can understand if this is too much for you. It's your choice, Lina. I told you I don't need to figure anything out with us. I want you. I love you. I want you in Penn's life. But I can't do this … not unless it's for the long haul. I can't put Penn through that. I can't put *myself* through that. You have to want this just as much as me and accept all that comes with it. I'm not perfect. I'm far from it. You have to decide if this is what you want."

She nodded, biting her lip, looking away, her face so near to crumbling.

"I'm so sorry, sweetheart. I should have told you sooner. It hurts me knowing that I hurt you. I would be devastated if you told me right now you can't do this, but I would understand."

"It's a lot," she mumbled, a tear now slipping down her cheek.

"Shit, baby." I wiped the tear away. "I know it is."

"I think I need to go home." Her words were choked with emotion.

I could feel my heart being wrenched from my chest. "Are you sure? It's late. You can stay here tonight."

She shook her head. "No," she replied as she stood, gathering her dress and boots in between wiping tears from her face. "I need some time to think. I need space."

I sucked in a breath, nodding.

Lina averted her eyes as I stood and followed her to the door. She stuffed her feet back into her boots. Her dress was slung over her arm. I wanted to pull her into my embrace, bury my nose into her hair, especially if this was going to be the last time, but I gave her what she asked for—space.

"Good night," she said, pushing up on her tiptoes to press her lips to my cheek.

I opened the door for her, watching her walk away in my T-shirt, wanting nothing more than to drag her back and make her stay. But sometimes when you love someone so much, you have to let them go.

CHAPTER 34
Lina

I sat on the steps of the back deck watching the sunset the next day, staring out over the brown grasses and pine trees. It was so hot and dry, and I worried if we had enough for the cattle to graze. Dad, Jude, Reed, and the other ranch hands had spent the day moving the herd, hauling stock tanks, and repositioning the lateral sprinklers to irrigate the pastures and hayfields. Unfortunately, because of the drought, they could only be run early each morning.

I spent the day leading a trail ride, mucking stalls, and bathing the horses. It kept my hands busy, but now that it was quiet, I couldn't help but dwell on everything Reed told me. I really didn't care if he was a recovering addict. That didn't bother me in the least. I felt that was something I could handle, and if he needed me to be strong for us both in times of weakness, I would do that in a heartbeat.

It was the shit with Penn's mom that I wasn't sure I could deal with. Penn came first, as she absolutely should, but was I ready to make all my decisions solely based on the needs of his daughter just like he had to? Could I do that? Did it mean that he wanted us to get married? To be a family to create stability for her?

Watching Jude and Romy get married yesterday, seeing them with their little family and being so in love, made me realize I did want that … eventually.

But could I do that with Reed? If it came down to choosing Reed and everything that came along with him or losing him forever, could I make that choice? Shouldn't this be an easy decision?

We were supposed to be heading back out on the road in a couple days up to Washington for the Lakeview Round-Up next weekend. I wasn't sure yet if I was ready to return to the close proximity of the fifth wheel with Reed. I wouldn't be able to think straight around him, and this was something I had to have a clear head for. I didn't just need to make the right decision for myself, but also for a little girl and her dad, too.

Was *I* the right decision for them? Could I be a parent to Penn? Could they be my family? I never saw myself as marriage material, but maybe I was … for the right person … for Reed.

The screen door behind me creaked on its hinges. I turned to see Hazel walking out of the big house, barefoot, her monitor on her ankle, in shorts and her Willows Rodeo tee. She had two ice-cold drinks in her hands with lemon wedges.

"What do you have there?" I asked, forcing a smile for her.

"Thought you might need one of my famous lemonades," she announced, taking a seat beside me on the step and handing me a glass.

The glass was chilled. I took a sip, nearly spitting it out, when I discovered there was almost half a glass of Crown Royal Apple Whisky in there. "Holy shit! I don't remember them being so strong."

She gave me a wink. "You looked as though you needed a double pour tonight."

I groaned, rolling the glass against my forehead, letting the condensation cool my heated skin. "Thanks."

Hazel took a sip of her own, puckering and humming with appreciation. "I make a damn good drink."

"A *dangerous* drink," I corrected her. "They're so good, you'll have to roll me into bed tonight."

"Not going to stay over at Reed's again?" Her brows raised in question. "I noticed you snuck back in late last night."

"You did? I'm sorry. I tried not to wake anyone."

She shrugged. "I was heading to the bathroom and noticed your light was on."

"Yeah …" I trailed off, taking another drink to keep the words from spilling out.

"Did he explain why he had to leave the wedding?" she asked.

I sucked in a deep breath before exhaling. "He did."

"Anything you want to share?"

"It's complicated. Something I need to process on my own."

Hazel nodded but didn't press further. We both took a drink before she said, "I have to say, you two look good together. I think your dad is happy that you're happy and that you found a man who will take good care of you. Whatever it is he told you, Reed does seem like he's good people."

"He is good people." I sighed. "I don't know. My dad would be lonely if I left him alone in the big house all by himself."

Hazel shrugged, taking another sip of her drink before setting it down on the deck beside her. She leaned back on her hands, crossed her legs, and stared out across the ranch. "I think your dad would be just fine. He just wants to see the people he loves happy. And if Reed is what makes you happy, I think you should go for it."

I cleared my throat and took a big gulp, letting the liquor hit. I'd already cried enough tears into my pillow last night. I didn't need to cry any more.

"What makes you happy?" I asked her, hoping to steer the conversation away from Reed.

She sat there quietly for a moment, her head tipped to the side as she peered out into the distance, thinking. After a moment she said, "It's taken me some time to find it again, but … taking care of the people I care about, my horse, and chocolate. I *love* chocolate."

I giggled at that, wrapping my arm around her and pulling her in close. I laid my head on her shoulder. It felt so familiar. I'd done this exact thing with her too many times growing up. She almost always found me in a similar mood, as if she had a radar for this shit. She knew I needed someone to take care of me, and here she was, plying me with her very strong lemonade to ease the pain.

"I can get down with some chocolate," I told her in agreement.

"What makes *you* happy?" she shot back.

"Of course you have to fucking turn my own question on me." I rolled my eyes at her.

She laughed, her teeth flashing and her eyes sparkling. She looked like the Hazel I remembered. The Hazel who was our rodeo queen. Even though I knew she wasn't that person anymore. Not after all the shit she went through—and was still going through.

I breathed in a big, steadying breath. "Barrel racing and riding fast with Mushu. But you know what? I think what makes me truly happy is just being with my people. Being with them at home on the ranch, around a bonfire, at a rodeo, or a bar. Wherever. I just want to be with my people where I'm understood and loved. When I don't have to mask or try hard, and I get to be me—Lina—not just a girl trying to win a buckle or fight to be loved."

It was true. Every time I was with those I loved, I was happy. Reed and Penn made me happy. They had become my people. I'd do anything for them. I'd do anything to protect that happiness.

Hazel nodded in acknowledgment. We sat in companionable silence for a while, sipping our lemonades, letting the alcohol dull the aches and taking in the sunset over the bluffs that led down to the river.

She released a heavy sigh beside me. "And this place. This makes me happy."

I mirrored her sigh. "I couldn't agree more. It's my peace."

After a beat she said, almost distantly, "You know, I haven't been able to go near the bunkhouse. The stables are as close as I can get. I can't even look that way when I walk by."

"I get that. I don't think I'd be able to, either."

"Do you think it will eventually get easier?"

I rubbed her shoulder. "Time. At least that's what I've heard. Time heals all wounds. We just need to give ourselves the space to do it."

Now she was the one to put her head on my shoulder. "I'm going to miss you, Lina."

"I'm going to miss you too, Haz."

"Fuck," Hazel said with a watery laugh, sitting straight.

We both looked at each other with tears in our eyes. "We're quite the pair tonight, aren't we?" I laughed through my tears.

"Do you want another one?" She shot to her feet, straightening her shorts and picking up our drinks.

"Are you trying to take advantage of me, Miss Miller?" I teased.

"Maybe. You know I love you Larsens," she teased back, winking. "I won't make the next one as strong."

I watched her walk back into the house. Seeing her here seemed like the most natural thing in the world. I wished she didn't have to go. I wished she would've had an even lighter sentence. This was going to change her in ways I couldn't even fathom. Why did life have to be so shitty sometimes?

I couldn't do this. There was no way in hell. I was bent over, my hands resting on my knees while I tried to catch my breath.

How was I going to get through a whole rodeo weekend with Reed as my shadow?

He did exactly as I had asked, giving me time and space. But now that we were back on the circuit, and he was my babysitter or bodyguard or whatever the fuck he was again, I felt like I couldn't fucking breathe.

I could feel him stopping with Mushu on the lead behind me. I was supposed to race today. How the hell was I supposed to race when I felt like shit?

"Are you okay, Lina?" he asked.

Just hearing his concerned voice made me want to curl up in the fetal position and cry my fucking eyes out.

I sucked a breath through my nose, blowing out a gust of air before straightening.

"Fine," I told him, squaring my shoulders and resuming my walk to the gate.

It didn't help that I was bottom of the fucking draw today. I hated being bottom of the draw, and Paige looked rather pleased about it as she peered back at me from her position on her horse, currently in the hole.

"Bitch," I cursed under my breath.

Ready to mount, I put my foot in the stirrup and swung up into the saddle, taking the reins, Reed still holding the lead. Mushu was already antsy to run. I could always feel his energy shift the closer we got to the ring.

"Be thinking," the rodeo staff shouted at me.

My chest felt so fucking tight, making it difficult to take deep breaths. Mushu's ears flicked to the side. I gave him a pat, hoping that would assure him I was okay. I watched as rider after rider beat each other's time. It was getting late in the season, so it didn't surprise me that regular circuit riders would all have close times. Once again, Paige's time would be the one I'd have to beat. She was my biggest competition with her leading barrel racing horse.

"We're going to have to drag ass around the barrels, buddy," I told Mushu, giving him another pat once we were on deck.

Reed unclasped the lead as he helped hold Mushu steady.

His closeness as he checked to make sure the cinch was tight caused his forearm to brush against my leg and send electric shocks through me. My body went rigid. I attempted to shake it off, refocusing on Mushu. He was raring to go. I held high up on the reins, preparing myself.

"Up!"

It was my turn. Reed and I exchanged glances, his dark-brown eyes beneath his cowboy hat capturing mine one last time.

"Burn the breeze, sweetheart," he said before letting go.

CHAPTER 35
Reed

She was barely speaking to me. The tension was so thick, I didn't think there was anything sharp enough to cut it. It felt like it did last summer. The few words that I did get out of her were quick and cutting. She was hurt, and knowing Lina, she knew exactly how to ice me out.

"Do you want me to get dinner?" I asked her as she came out of the shower.

Her hair was still wet. Fuck! This was torture.

She was wearing Daisy Dukes and a crop top, showing off more skin than I needed her to right now. My cock twitched against my zipper.

"Do whatever you want," she said, not even looking at me while she shoved her feet into her boots.

"Going somewhere?" I grabbed one of my boots, preparing to go with her.

"Out," she said simply.

Seeing me shoving my feet into boots, she straightened up, looking me in the eyes. My breath caught. There was so much pain and sadness there.

"Please, don't come with me," she pleaded.

"Lina—"

"Please." Her *please* broke my heart. "Christian and Kale are meeting me. I'll be fine. I won't leave my drink unattended for one second. I promise."

It was the most she'd said to me in several days. I didn't want to dampen her spirit and tell her no. I wanted to give her everything she needed. And if she needed this right now to help her blow off some steam, I had to let her go … even if it killed me … even if it felt like every muscle was being torn from my body to let her go without me.

I gave her a nod. "Text me if you need me to come get you."

She gave me a small, sad smile, and it was the biggest punch in the gut. "Thank you," she said before leaving me behind in the trailer.

I tried not to worry, stretched out on the shitty kitchenette booth bed. I lay there, my hands behind my head, staring at the ceiling and listening to every sound around our camp. Every voice sounded familiar. Every crack of wood sounded like someone sneaking around in the dark. Every horse whinny sounded like an alarm that someone wasn't where they were supposed to be. I had my bag right beside me, just in case I needed to retrieve my .38 if we had an unwanted guest.

My ears strained to hear Lina's boots running up the stairs. She didn't go anywhere slowly. She went mach speed, just like Mushu. I didn't want to be the one who slowed her down. She was young and vivacious. Anyone who locked her down would be lucky, but it didn't need to be now. It didn't need to be me.

Not unless she wanted it—*truly* wanted it. I wasn't about to push her into anything she didn't want to do. I would love her but leave her wild. She would always be my wild girl.

But goddammit, I was losing patience. My heart was bleeding in my chest, and I needed to stanch it. Otherwise, I was going to bleed out.

I needed her to put me out of my misery.

I was so on edge. Jude called me tonight after Lina left, telling me that they were going to go after some lost cattle and didn't know how long they'd be gone. Marshall and Jace were moving the herd to rented pasture and would remain on watch duty. He assured me Penn was with Romy, but they were going to be the only ones on the ranch for a little bit. Hazel had turned herself over yesterday to serve her sentence, and now it was just Romy with two kids. I didn't like the sound of that.

I needed to talk to Lina about leaving first thing in the morning.

Junior was up to something. I felt it.

Unable to lay there, I threw the blanket off, shoved my legs into pants, and shrugged on a shirt. I pulled on my boots and picked up my wallet, keys, and cell phone.

I checked my phone and sent Lina a text.

ME

Your time's up, sweetheart.

I wanted to give her all the time in the world to process and make a decision about us, but time didn't feel like it was on our side anymore. Not when I could feel something ominous was brewing, like a shift in the wind. I needed to find out Junior's whereabouts, and unfortunately, there was only one person who could tell me.

ME

Did Junior ever show back up after I was there the other night? Is your friend OK?

ELISE

Friend's fine. You checking up on me now, husband?

Okay, bad idea to text her. She must be on one.

ME

Nevermind. Forget I asked.

ELISE

Don't be an ass. Sure he has. Going to let me see Penn soon?

ME

I'll have my lawyer call you again.

ELISE

I don't want to go through your lawyer, Reed.

ME

It's your only option now.

ELISE

She's my daughter! It's not my only option.

Fuck! This was going south quickly. Without a text back from Lina, I headed out the door. Going to my truck to get my Glock from under the seat instead of my .38 because it concealed better, I clipped it beneath my waistband, covering it with my shirt.

My cell buzzed in my pocket and I pulled it out, reading it as I walked back toward the rodeo grounds.

LINA

> Please, Reed. I still need time. You need to fucking give it to me.

Yep, she was still upset and probably drunk. Perfect combination for Lina.

ME

> Something's up at Thornbrush. We don't have time for this anymore.

LINA

> What's going on?

ME

> I don't know, but Jude called and said they needed to go find some missing cattle. Penn's with Romy, but they're the only ones on the ranch right now. This doesn't feel right to me.

At the same time, Lina's text came through.

LINA

> Fuck! Just tried calling Dad. His phone went straight to voicemail. They must be out of range wherever they are.

Me

Where are you? I'm going
to come get you.

LINA

I'm leaving now. I just told
Christian.

ME

Don't leave by yourself. Stay
there. I'm coming to get you.

"Fuck," I cursed, quickening my pace, not wanting her to leave the bar by herself.

LINA

Already left. Walking back now.

I was running now, needing to get to her before someone else did. My heart pounded out of my chest. I couldn't let anything happen to her.

Then I saw her silhouette speed-walking toward me.

"Reed!"

She picked up her pace, and I ate up the distance with my long strides until I could grip her arms, steadying her. She tipped her chin up to look at me. Her face was stricken, her eyes wide. She smelled like bourbon and shampoo, and her hair was now dry in wild waves.

"God, you're beautiful." I couldn't help myself. She looked wilder now than I'd ever seen her, and with the thought that I couldn't reach her in time if something happened to her … I don't think I'd ever be able to live with myself. "I need you, Lina. This has been torture. I'm in fucking pain."

"Like I'm not in pain? I know. It's torture for me, too, but this hurt feels different," she said, shaking her head. "What's going on at Thornbrush?"

"Some of the herd is missing, and they're all heading out to search. Romy is alone on the ranch."

"Shit! That's not good. You think it's Junior?"

"We need to find out for sure. Have you seen your stalker looming around at all tonight?" I asked, looking around us as if he was going to pop out from behind a tree at any moment.

"No, I haven't seen any sign of him. I was glued to Christian and Kale's side the whole night, even though Kale was getting fucking annoyed with me shooing off the buckle bunnies." She huffed a laugh, but there wasn't any humor in her voice. She sounded as frantic as I felt. "What should we do, Reed?"

"Well, you can't drive tonight if you've been drinking. I could drive us and take Mushu's trailer, but that would mean leaving the fifth wheel and your truck here. I think it's best we wait a little bit and leave first thing in the morning."

"How am I going to sleep after this?"

"I know. I'm not going to be able to sleep, either. Come on." I slipped my hand to her lower back not wanting to push my luck, leading us back to the trailer, the whole time scanning our surroundings. "He didn't fucking come like I told him."

"What do you mean?"

"Wayne Urban. He was supposed to come with answers. It's been two weeks. I warned him," I growled, my fist clenching at my side. I felt the weight of the Glock at my waist.

As soon as we were in the trailer, Lina went to pull away, but I swung her back to me, needing to hold her.

"Reed, I—"

"I know, sweetheart. You don't need to tell me anything. Not tonight. I just need you."

I could feel her breath freeze in her chest. Her heart was pounding against mine. I tipped her chin up to gaze into her smoky, brown eyes. Eyes that had captured me from the beginning when I saw her across the Saddle Room bar. So full of desire and mischief, big and beautiful just like her heart. Eyes that made me fall in love with her from the moment I saw her.

"Reed ..." She hesitated. I hated that she hesitated. "I—I can give you that."

"That's all I ask." I leaned down, pressing my lips to hers. Feeling her immediately melt against me as I deepened the kiss, stroking down the middle of her tongue with mine.

She moaned into my mouth.

Her hands gripped my shirt as she started to walk backward, her mouth never leaving mine. We stopped momentarily to pull off our boots, coming back together while we unbuttoned and shucked our pants. I set down the Glock on the counter and helped her out of her shirt and bra, letting my palms run over her hardened nipples until she gathered the fabric of my shirt to help me out of it.

We left a trail of clothes on our way to the bedroom. The back of her legs hit the bed, and I hoisted her up onto the mattress, my hands never leaving her, wanting to feel every curve and dip. I ran my fingers up the inside of her thighs, parting them so I could fit between them.

Lina scooted up the bed until her head rested on the pillow.

Her hair spread out like a halo around her.

"You're so beautiful. I can't get over how gorgeous you are. Every time I look at you, it's like the air is sucked right out of my lungs."

"*Reed*." Her brow furrowed like she was in agony. I couldn't stand hurting her.

"I know. You're my fire. Sucking the oxygen right out of me. If this is the last time I have you, that I can feel you, I want to make this last."

She arched up, capturing my lips, nipping and sucking. "No talking. Please."

I wanted to make love to her, let her feel everything I felt in every touch, in every kiss, in every whisper against her skin. I was going to worship her first, and then once both of us were desperate, needing more, I was going to bury my cock inside her, leaving my mark. Claiming her because no matter what happened after today, she would always have my heart whether she'd accept it or not.

"You have me, sweetheart."

I didn't need her to reply. She just needed to let me love her.

I trailed kisses along her jaw, pressing my lips down her throat, sucking on that sensitive spot beneath her ear. Her fingers threaded through my hair, holding me to her. My hands cupped her tits, dragging my thumbs over her stiffened peaks. She hummed. Her hips rolling beneath mine, seeking that friction I knew she was already desperate for.

"Reed," she whined. "I need you inside me."

"Not yet, baby. I need to taste you first."

I continued my journey, my mouth coasting over her chest until I could pinch her nipple between my teeth. I gave a little bite before capturing it into my mouth, letting my tongue swirl over it. Her hips bucked in response, nearly coming off the mattress, my dick brushing her clit.

"Do that again," she pleaded.

"Can't have the other one jealous." I pressed kisses to her sternum as I traveled to her other breast, taking it between my teeth until I could suck on it, flicking it with my tongue just like I knew she wanted me to do to her clit.

"Oh, Reed." Her back arched.

I lowered myself, letting her feel my weight above her, letting her rub against my piercings while I paid special attention to her tits. I could feel myself leaking onto her pussy. I was already desperate for her.

"Sweetheart, if you keep that up, I'm going to come all over you before you can even feel my cock inside you, and I still need to suck that pretty little clit."

Her hips stilled. "Can't have that."

She pushed on my shoulders then, and I couldn't help chuckling. "Feeling a little greedy, are we?"

"I need your mouth on me, cowboy."

I inched down her body, pressing my lips to her belly, along her hip bones, and right above her clit. Her hips rolled in response.

She nearly flew off the bed when I wrapped my mouth around her clit, swirling my tongue just as I'd done to her tits. Her breaths came fast and heavy. Her hands gripped my hair with intensity.

"That feels so good." She moaned.

"You taste like heaven," I whispered into her core, my lips brushing against her while she writhed. "The best fucking dessert."

"I need your tongue," she demanded.

I speared my tongue inside her, as deep as I could go, while I drew circles around her clit with my fingertip.

Her hands gripped me harder, but I could tell she needed more.

"Baby." I got up, repositioning us so I was on my back and she was on top. "Sit on my face. Take what you need."

I scooted down until she was directly above me and pulled on her hips.

"Sit, sweetheart."

CHAPTER 36
Lina

I put my hands against the wall above the bed, lowering myself onto his face. I wanted to take everything he was willing to give me. Desperate, buzzed, and heartbroken, I needed this. Even if this was it for us, I needed something to live on.

Did I want this to be the end of our story?

My brain was like mush with my pussy grinding against his face, his tongue fucking me, his teeth nipping at my lips and my clit before sucking on them.

"Fuck, Reed. That feels so damn good."

"That's it, sweetheart." He hummed against me, the hum causing my body to tighten my core.

I moaned, already feeling the pressure building in my belly. "I'm going to come."

"Smother me. Soak my face."

I ground against him, riding his tongue as if he was deep inside me. "God, I want your cock."

But he didn't let up until I was shattering and quivering against him. He purred, the vibration adding to the intensity.

"Reed!" My pussy clenched and pulsed against his mouth,

and he lapped me up as I made a mess of him.

Limp from my orgasm, he gripped my hips, spinning us around until I was on my back again and he was above me.

His face glistened with me. "Taste how good we are together."

I opened for him, letting his tongue enter my mouth. I tasted it. Musky and sweet. I sucked his tongue into my mouth, wanting to savor it. His hand was on his cock as he dragged it up and down my slit, letting it hit my now sensitive and swollen clit while he kissed me.

He pulled away. "Look at me, Lina. I want to watch your face while you take everything I have to give."

Gripping my wrists, he raised my arms, holding them there above my head with one hand, while his other hand notched the head of his cock at my entrance. Slowly, he pressed forward.

My mouth fell open on an exhale, adjusting to the feeling of fullness he always gave me. I don't think I'd ever feel full again.

"That's it. Look at you. You always take my cock so well."

His other hand joined the one wrapped around my wrists, holding my arms above me while he thrusted. His eyes never left mine as his hips rolled. Those midnight pools shining with love that made my heart fracture and shatter.

"You're doing so good, sweetheart."

"You feel so good," I breathed.

Releasing my wrists, he skimmed his palms down my arms and over my breasts until he could grip my ass, propping my hips up to allow my clit to press against him while he continued to pump in and out.

"Grind against me while I fuck you."

I pressed my hands against his lower back, pushing him more firmly to me while my clit rubbed against him. His fingers dug into my ass, holding me there.

"I'm so close," I whined, the pressure building again. "Don't stop."

"Never, baby." His brows pinched, and his jaw ticked as he clenched it. "Come with me."

It was all I needed to let it all go. Just as I came, I couldn't help the tears pricking my eyes.

"Reed," I croaked. "I … I … I'll always love you."

We awoke early, our bodies still intertwined, our cum dried between my thighs. The weight of his arm was around my middle. While his hand cupped my breast, his thick thigh nestled between mine, and his chest was firm and warm against my back. I wanted to live in this moment forever, but we needed to get home to Romy and the girls, and I needed space to think, to find clarity, while my heart was aching.

Thankfully, we had a long drive ahead of us. He would be in his truck pulling the fifth wheel, while I was in mine hauling the horse trailer. It gave me some time to breathe and think, as long as I didn't spiral. And knowing me, I'd be all fucking twisted by the time we got home.

After cleaning up and getting dressed, we drank a quick cup of coffee and ate some toast before packing up the trailers and loading Mushu. We were on the road in record time, only stopping for gas. By midday, we were pulling into Willows.

"Go check on Penn," I told him as soon as we parked and got out of our trucks. "I'll take care of Mushu. We'll unload the fifth wheel later."

He gave me a jerky nod. I could tell he was worried, his face taut as he unhitched the camper so he could take off with the truck to Jude and Romy's place.

It was weird how quiet the ranch was. All the horses, except the ones the guys took, were in their stalls, so there were no lessons or trail rides happening today. The ranch hands must all be out with the herd or with Dad and Jude.

I took my time with Mushu, unloading and organizing the tack, brushing him, making sure he had fresh shavings and hay in his stall while I tried to settle my thoughts. Being home helped, but I still couldn't make sense of my feelings. I loved him. I loved Penn. I'd do anything for them. Marriage and kids seemed so far in my future.

Now knowing what it all entailed with Reed, I still wasn't sure if I was ready for it—even if it was something I wanted with him. Maybe if there was no Elise to factor into all of this, it would be different, but she was Penn's mama, and I would never try to take that from them. And it broke my fucking heart. It wouldn't be fair to him or Penn if I wasn't all in. I wanted to be there so badly for both of them. I just didn't know if I could.

After making sure Mushu and the rest of the horses had food and water, I unhitched my truck and headed over to Romy's house.

Reed's truck was already gone, so he must have taken Penn and headed back to the double-wide. Hopefully, everything was okay or someone had heard from Dad or Jude.

When I walked into their house, Romy's face looked pale while she stared into space, leaning on the counter. Her head shot up when she heard me come in.

"Oh, thank God." She breathed a sigh of relief.

Baby Charli was in her high chair with what looked like peas on her face, and Penn was sitting on a stool, eating crackers. Why was Penn still here?

"Lina!" she shouted, jumping off her stool to run to me.

I leaned down, wrapping her up in my arms. "Hey, princess." I held her to me for a moment, just needing her comfort.

My brows pinched. "Where's Reed? I thought he was heading over here."

Romy looked confused. "He was here for a minute. After he saw that we were all okay, and there still wasn't any news from the guys, he said he was going to go unpack. I figured he was going to head back to the stables to help you."

I shook my head. "I didn't see him. I would have passed him on my way here."

"Huh. I wonder where he could have gone. Do you think he went to the double-wide?" she asked.

"Maybe." I pulled my cell phone out of my pocket, tapping Reed's name. Putting it to my ear, all I heard was ringing. Was it the phone or my ears? I felt like my consciousness was outside my body, staring down at me.

"You've reached Reed Ownstead. Please leave your name and a brief message at the beep."

I tried again. It went to voicemail. *Shit.*

"He's not picking up. When was the last time you heard

from Jude or Dad?"

"Last night. Right before they headed out."

My heart rate kicked up, and a sickening feeling soured my gut.

"Shit … is it just me, or does it feel like something is wrong to you, too?"

"I've felt it since this morning. I can't stay here just waiting to make sure everyone is okay." Her voice cracked on her last word, and I could see it now, her knee bouncing behind the counter. She was going against her very instincts right now when I knew all she wanted to do was fight or fly.

"I need you to stay here, Romy. Lock the doors and stay inside with Charli. If you hear from Dad, Jude, or Reed, call me right away, okay? I'll do the same."

She nodded. "Are you sure that you and Penn should head to the double-wide?"

"I want to go see my daddy," Penn whined at my side.

"I know, princess. We're going to go see your dad," I said, stroking her hair before turning back to Romy. "I should take her home anyway. Hopefully, that's where Reed is, too. I'll text you as soon as I get there so you'll know we're safe."

I rounded the counter, taking her into my arms and whispering in her ear so Penn didn't hear me. Knowing this was the old Matheus homestead, I couldn't help but feel this was a target. "If you see Junior, I'm going to need you to get one of Jude's rifles and call the police."

Romy flinched, pulling back to look at me. Her silver eyes were flaming. "You think it's him?"

I nodded, taking Penn's hand. "I'll text you as soon as I'm

there."

She nodded back, sucking in a couple deep breaths. "Okay. Okay. We got this."

"Yes, we do."

But it didn't feel like we had it at all.

Chapter 37
Lina

"Please be there. Please be there. Please be there," I prayed as we drove down the dirt road to the double-wide on the other side of the ranch. Reed had to be there. I tried calling him again, but he still didn't pick up. "Shit!" I hit the steering wheel.

"What's wrong?" Penn asked from where she sat in the front seat.

"Oh, nothing. Just don't tell your daddy that you got to ride in the front without your booster."

Penn giggled into her hand. "I can keep a secret."

"Can you? Because I need you to keep this one. Hopefully, he doesn't see us pull up just like he did when you were driving the UTV. Otherwise, I'm in big trouble."

"Do you need me to hide?" She started to duck beneath the window.

But when we pulled in, Reed's truck wasn't there. "No …" My voice waned, biting my tongue to keep from cursing again in front of Penn.

I parked and cut the engine. "Let's just go inside, and I'll try calling him again. He may be on his way over here, so let's just stay here while we wait. We'll go inside and see if we can find a movie to watch. Come on."

I jumped out of the truck and hurried to the passenger side to help her down.

"Can we watch *Frozen*?" she asked as I picked her up and set her feet on the ground.

"Absolutely." Holding her hand, I fumbled for my key ring with all the ranch keys. I inserted the key into the lock but found the front door already unlocked. "Does he usually keep the front door unlocked?"

Penn shrugged. We got inside, and I helped her take off her boots.

"Can I go get my Elsa doll to watch the movie with us?"

"Sure, princess." I toed off my boots, trying to find some semblance of calm so as not to worry Penn. "I'll get the movie started, and then we can find some snacks."

She skipped away down the hall to her bedroom while I went to the living room to turn on the TV. It took me a few minutes to figure out how to stream the movie, but once I had it cued up, I turned to head to the kitchen. Blowing out a big breath, I told myself everything was fine. There was no need to worry. Reed probably just went back to the stables and would be back soon.

"Penn!" I called. "What would you like for a snack?"

Opening the pantry beside the fridge, I looked inside, searching through the different cereals and crackers.

Boots sounded in the hallway, and for a moment, I thought it must be Reed. But that didn't quite make sense to me.

"Penn?"

I closed the pantry and walked out of the kitchen, stalling in my tracks. My heart lurched in my chest, my entire body going rigid.

"Hi, Lina."

Reed

"You can't keep running from me!" I yelled into the pines, starting to get frustrated.

He was still a few yards in front of me, fallen branches cracking under his boots. I was leading with my 9mm as I navigated through the trees. Wayne Urban was a sneaky bastard. I had to give him that. Probably why he was so good at stalking Lina.

I had to be on his heels now. My ears strained to listen to his movements, to follow which direction he was going, but my heartbeat was so loud in my ears, it was nearly drowning out his footfalls. It didn't help that we were starting to go deeper into the wooded area, away from the ranch, where dried pine needles created a carpet on the forest floor, muffling the sound.

"We had an agreement!" I called out to him. "And I made you a promise if you didn't follow through on your end!"

I stopped to stand still, hoping to quiet my pulse enough to hear what direction he was going. Even breathing sounded like the roar of jet engines to my heightened hearing.

"Fuck," I cursed to myself.

When I was on my way to Romy and Jude's house, I spotted

him creeping along one of the fence lines. I intended to go to his house soon, but fortunately, he'd come to me. After quickly checking on Penn, I hopped back in the truck, speeding down the dirt road to where I saw him last. Swinging the steering wheel to the right, I hit the gas and off-roaded across the field. I'd barely cut the engine before I grabbed my Glock from beneath the seat and hopped the fence after him.

The crunch of what must be a pine cone sounded behind me. I spun on my heels, leveling the barrel in that direction.

Movement shifted behind a tree. Our eyes connected. His going wide, mine narrowing, before he pivoted and started running again.

I growled, clipping the gun at my waist to bolt after him. This time, with him in my sight, I wasn't about to let him go. I used every bit of power I had to propel myself forward, gaining on him as he stumbled and fought for his footing on the uneven ground. He may have fear fueling his flight right now, but I had rage and a family to defend, and that was far more powerful. I needed to know what Junior was up to before it was too late. Before he got near Lina. Before the whole ranch was at risk.

Hissing breaths through gritted teeth, I threw myself at him, tackling him to the ground.

He grunted, the air leaving him momentarily, giving me a chance to wrap my hand around his neck and dig my knee into his back. Kicking his legs, he squirmed, trying to get out from under me.

"Going somewhere, Wayne?" I pulled my gun, pressing it to the back of his head.

He froze beneath me, his hands raising to his sides to show he was unarmed.

"You're an idiot if you think you can trespass on private property and not get shot. The least you could do is come armed."

"Who said I was unarmed?" he grumbled against the ground.

"What? Do you have another knife somewhere ready to slice me?" I asked, letting go of his neck to check his pockets and coming up empty.

He tried to shift, to loosen my hold, but I dug my knee harder into his back and pushed his head into the dirt.

"I warned you what would happen. You didn't want me to come after you, Wayne. That was the wrong move."

I put as much of my weight as I could against him. "Get off me," he muttered against the ground.

"You think this is what Lina felt when you cornered her?" I moved my hand from the back of his head to his jaw, digging my knuckles in, pressing his face as hard as I could without breaking it. "Do you think this is what she felt when you put your hands on her? Doesn't feel very good, does it?"

He groaned a sound that sounded a little bit like a "no."

"Now you're going to tell me what you know."

Lina

"Get away from her," I said firmly. I was surprised my voice sounded so calm compared to how my entire body was vibrating with panic.

Junior's hand rested on Penn's shoulder. Her little eyes were big, bouncing between Junior and me as she hugged her Elsa doll.

"I don't think you have a say in any of this," he said, stroking his dirty-blond scruff that shadowed his face.

"The fuck I don't," I ground out between my teeth. My hands balled at my side as I searched the kitchen for anything I could use as a weapon within reach. "Come here, Penn."

Penn took a step toward me, but Junior's hand gripped her firmly, making her stall in her tracks and look up at him. "Don't you want to go see your mama? She's been missing you."

She stared at him, not saying a word. She looked so scared, and I was barely holding my shit together, not wanting to freak her out more, but this was so fucked up.

"Reed's going to be back any minute," I warned him.

He cocked his head, looking at me like I was the stupid one. "No, I don't think he will be. He's a little preoccupied at the moment."

I could feel my face fall and my stomach twist. "If you did anything to him, I'll make sure you don't walk off my ranch in one piece this time."

He clicked his tongue in disappointment, shaking his head. "See, that's where you Larsens keep fucking up. This isn't just *your* ranch."

"Fuck you," I seethed.

His lips tipped up. "I don't think there is anything I need to worry about here."

He leaned down, picking up Penn. I gulped, fear washing

over me like acid. "Don't." I took a few steps toward them, my muscles locking up when I noticed the grip of a gun sticking out from his waistband.

"It's all right, Penn," he said, stroking her hair.

I felt like I was going to be sick.

"We're going to go see Mommy now."

My mind reeled, trying to make sense of what was happening, trying to figure out what I should do as he turned his back to me and walked out the door with Penn in his arms.

CHAPTER 38
Lina

It only took a moment for me to put myself in gear. I shoved my boots back on and made sure I had my cell phone just in case Reed called.

Tapping his contact on my way out the door, I pleaded silently for him to answer as I heard ring after ring. He still wasn't picking up. What Junior had said about him being preoccupied had me terrified. Was he with Elise? Did she call him again asking for help, knowing he'd come? Was that part of their plan? Keep him busy so they could abduct Penn?

"Shit," I cursed, racing down the porch steps.

The sun was setting, and the evening breeze was starting to pick up. It was a warm night, and the breeze did little to cool me. I walked down the driveway, thinking Junior's truck was just parked on the road. Instead, he was walking away into the nearby pasture, his long strides eating up distance with Penn in his arms.

I couldn't let them get away. Jogging after them, I held my phone to my ear, trying once again to get ahold of Reed. This time, I was leaving a voicemail.

"Reed, you need to get back here. I don't know what's

going on, but Junior has Penn."

I ended the call and shoved the device into my back pocket, needing to pick up speed.

Junior was running, too, now, cutting across the southeastern pasture, leading toward the fence bordering the ranch. A trail rutted by truck tracks ran along the other side of the fence, separating the property from the woods. A truck, which I assumed was Junior's, was parked on the trail.

Penn's dark-blonde head bobbed at his shoulder as she held on with her arms wrapped around his neck. She was watching me coming after her, and I hoped she believed I would do everything in my power to reach her before he took her.

"Junior!" I screamed after them.

He slowed only momentarily to look over his shoulder, seeing me gaining on him. I couldn't let him reach that truck. I couldn't let him take her.

As he approached the fence line, Junior set Penn on the other side. He still had to climb over the wire himself, and I hoped it fucking cut him up.

"Run, Penn!" I hollered at her. She turned to look at me, her face painted with fear, mirroring my own. "Run!" I screamed at the top of my lungs.

She hesitated, seeing Junior pick up plywood from the ground and walk to a point in the fence where it sagged. The fucker must have already used it to bypass the barbed wire.

"Shit. Run, Penn!" I yelled again across the pasture.

This time, she didn't hesitate, spinning on her heels to take off down the trail.

I didn't let up, not even for one second, pumping my legs,

hoping I was fast enough to reach her before Junior could. My chest ached from the exertion and the fear, my side pinching as I pushed myself.

Junior was already climbing over the plywood. He wasn't going for Penn as she continued to run, not looking back. I was proud of her. She was so brave.

Instead, I watched in pure horror as he went to the back of the truck, pulling out a red gas tank. I skidded to a stop.

"No, no!" I shook my head in disbelief. I was not fucking watching this right now.

He was pouring gasoline along the fence line, scattering it.

"Run!" I screamed at Penn. "Run!"

His eyes flicked over to where Penn was still running. Emptying the tank, he threw it in the back of the truck bed. Junior pulled out a lighter from his pocket, flipping the lid.

It was like slow motion.

Like I was underwater, and I couldn't move fast enough.

Everything was magnified, yet the air sparked and flexed with heat waves, blurring my vision.

He tossed the lighter to the ground and took off after Penn.

CHAPTER 39
Reed

Wayne huffed frustrated breaths against the ground, kicking up little puffs of dust. It was so fucking dry, I thought I could smell smoke.

"Tell me!" I yelled into his ear, pushing him harder into the dirt, wishing I could push and push until the earth swallowed him whole, burying him beneath.

He gurgled a word beneath the force of my hand against his jaw. I racked the slide, chambering the round, punctuating just how serious I was this time.

His lips moved, trying to form words. I eased up enough for him to get some sound out. "Your daughter," he managed to say.

My stomach dropped, and cold, clammy fear washed over me. "What about my daughter?"

The scent of smoke permeated the air, and I thought I could hear the crack and popping of wood as it was consumed with fire. I sniffed, lifting my head, looking around me. A tree about a hundred yards from me was burning, smoke building and billowing behind it.

From the direction of the ranch!

"Fuck!"

I sprang to my feet.

Wayne sputtered and coughed, rolling onto his back. The side of his face was all scraped up from the rocks and dirt. "It smells like you're too late," Wayne said, chuckling through his coughs.

The fire was building and growing, inching closer as if a clock were ticking down.

I glared at Wayne, aiming the gun at him. "Where's my daughter?"

His dirt and tobacco-stained teeth flashed at me in a snarling grin. "Where do you think?"

My hand gripped the Glock, my finger squeezing the trigger as I aimed for his thigh. The gun was heavy in my grasp as I steadied my hand, then fired.

It took him a moment, but then he gripped his leg in shock. "You shot me!"

"Where's Penn and Lina?" I repeated, clearing the chamber.

Wayne's eyes narrowed on me in defiance.

I knelt down beside him, and he looked at me suspiciously. Digging the barrel of the gun into his now bleeding leg, he flinched, then cried out when I dug harder. "Fucking tell me!" I roared.

He cocked his head toward the fire that was quickly consuming the forest around us. I looked toward the flames, but all I saw was smoke. I could feel the blistering heat now.

I stood, turning my back on Wayne where he lay, still holding his thigh.

"Let's see how you get out of this one," I said, racking

another round and aiming for his foot. The shot rang off the bluffs, and he howled in pain. "I hope you fucking burn." I turned away from him.

And ran toward the fire.

I held my shirt collar over my nose and mouth, my eyes burning from the thickening smoke all around me. I was determined to reach them. The fire seemed to intensify the deeper I went, the heat feeling like a fucking sunburn against my skin.

But I was nearing the southeast property line of Thornbrush. I knew if I walked nearly a mile away from the fire, I'd reach a trail that separated the dense pines from the ranch. The trail ran along the fence line. I could get around it, then, and hopefully reach Penn and Lina. We'd have to start evacuating the horses.

Fear and love fueled me. My muscles were straining and my lungs burned, but I didn't fucking care. I needed to reach them before it was too late.

Lina

"Penn!" The fire was spreading, catching every dry blade of grass, cutting off my path. Junior was already scooping her up. Panic was rushing through my veins. "I'm coming!" I yelled, rushing over to the stock tank and turning on the spigot. The well-line thumped and sputtered with air before a gush of water rushed out to fill the bone-dry trough.

The hum of an ATV sounded in the distance, and I spun around to see Romy with Charli on her back in a carrier behind the wheel.

"What the fuck are you doing?"

The last thing I wanted was to risk Romy and Charli. Jude would never forgive me.

She didn't even respond, her chin set stubbornly as she jumped off the vehicle and ran to unstrap the buckets she had on the back.

"I saw the fire from the house," she explained, rushing over to me. Charli bounced at her back, oblivious to everything as she sucked her fist. "I already called the fire department."

We did not have any time to wait. Who knew how long it'd take for firetrucks to reach us out here.

"Thank fuck." I sighed, taking a bucket from her.

We both rushed over to the stock tank, scooping up water and running to extinguish the flames.

Junior wrestled to get Penn in the truck. But I was so proud of our girl. She was thrashing, kicking, and biting. Doing everything possible to make it challenging for him to keep hold of her as he dragged her back to his truck. The flames separated us, only giving me glimpses as the fire moved like waves in the ocean.

The fire was spreading fast—*too fast*. It had already jumped to the other side of the trail, lighting the forest on fire.

I paused in shock, taking in the blaze around us. Dried grass and sagebrush was starting to light, spreading toward us, scorching the earth black.

"Romy!" I cried. "Our ranch is on fire!"

I couldn't believe it. My family's land. My home. How were we going to stop this?

We were driven by fear and panic, filling bucket after bucket of water, dousing out what flames we could as it licked across the pasture.

"Penn!" I heard a terrified cry.

I spun toward his voice and froze, seeing Reed sprinting toward Penn and Junior.

"Daddy!" she yelled back, still fighting against Junior's hold.

"Get your fucking hands off my daughter!"

Desperate now, I grabbed another bucketful. "We need to find a break in the line," I told Romy. "Reed is over there. We need to get them out of there!"

My heart pounded with my feet. I didn't stop. Frantically moving my way down the fence line with each bucketful.

"Junior!" Reed roared.

He was pointing his pistol at Junior, who now stood frozen at his driver's side door, Penn still thrashing against his grip.

"You're not going to shoot me, Reed." Junior's voice was unnervingly calm. "Not when I have your daughter."

"Let her go." Reed leveled his eyes on Junior, aiming well above Penn.

I wanted to cry out to him, but I was too scared that any distraction meant taking his eyes off Penn for a single second. A single, precious second Junior could use to throw Penn in his truck, creating an even greater barrier to reach her.

"Shouldn't you be over there helping your slut save *her* ranch?" Junior sneered. "See, you fucked up, Reed. All I had to do was give you Lina's little stalker, and I knew Penn would be reachable."

Reed's eyes flicked to me for just a moment, a flash of fear as he spotted me on the other side of the fire. But it didn't cause Reed to lose focus. The determined, strong man that he was only turned his hard gaze back on Junior.

"Are you really going to let the land you believe to be yours burn over a woman and her child?" Reed threw back at him. "Because I can tell you right now, if you don't let my daughter go, I will put a bullet through your head and this land will *never* be yours. Any claim you think you have will die with you, right here and now."

"Reed." I sobbed, hearing his words. He had to see the gun at Junior's waist. He had to know he could pull it just as easily as he could. My heart pounded, the smoke stinging my eyes and throat. "Reed, please," I breathed, knowing I was too quiet for him to hear me against the roaring flames … knowing I could barely get the words out as I watched him take a step toward them, the barrel trained on Junior.

"Let her go, Junior. You're burning your land down."

Junior appeared to be contemplating something. His jaw moved as if he were chewing his thoughts as his wheels turned.

Without a word, his hold barely loosened, and Penn was out of his grasp.

Running toward her dad. "Daddy!"

I choked a sob. Tears were streaming down my face, the heat drying them as soon as they fell.

Junior hopped into his truck. The engine roared to life. He put it into reverse, hitting the gas pedal. Hard. The truck barreled backward down the trail. Backing up right toward them, gaining on Penn as she tried her hardest to outrun the tires.

"Penn! The truck!" I screamed, my voice cracking against the choking smoke. I couldn't watch this. I couldn't see this terror play out.

Reed took off running toward her. My heart was in my throat, watching him as he swooped her up into his arms and took one giant step off the trail just as Junior's truck rushed past them, nearly clipping them.

I clapped a hand to my mouth, sobbing.

"Give me that bucket." Romy grabbed the bucket from my hand.

I stumbled toward the fire, watching them on the other side. I was completely helpless. My body was trembling. I couldn't reach them. The fire was spreading, growing, covering them. What wasn't ablaze was as black as tar.

"Reed," I cried.

He looked at me through the flames, his eyes tortured as he gripped his daughter to him.

"It's okay, sweetheart," he told me.

"No," I shook my head. "No."

"Go, Lina," Romy pleaded. "Go get Mushu and Warrior. Tell Reed to get to the river. You're going to need to ride fast now. I'll keep shoveling buckets until the fire department gets here."

I turned to look at her. I couldn't leave her and Charli to deal with this.

But her mouth was set in determination, her eyes bright

with urgency. "Go!" she repeated.

I gave a single nod, staring at Reed and Penn for the last time.

"Get to the river!" I shouted over the blaze. "I'm coming to get you."

Chapter 40

Lina

I hit the throttle on the truck as soon as I reached the double-wide. I'd never driven so fast in my life. Dust and gravel spit from the wheels like shrapnel as I sped down the road to the stable and bunkhouse. I barely put it into park when I arrived there.

Twilight was setting in, quickening my steps. I had to reach them before night came. I had no idea how I'd find them or how they'd find the river in the dark.

My hands trembled as I grabbed Mushu's bridle. I tied his lead to the outside of his stall. His eyes were bright and big, his ears flicking, reading me like he always did. Sensing the panic in the air. He nuzzled his nose against me, as if to check if I was okay. I nearly collapsed, leaning my forehead against his neck, breathing in his familiar horse scent.

"We're going to need to go the fastest we've ever gone," I whispered to him, my words breaking. "We need to find them."

I stroked my palm over his shoulder, feeling his strength and power, knowing he'd ride aggressively for me. I just hoped Warrior would be able to keep up.

The smoke was permeating the air now.

As soon as I finished with Mushu's tack, I took a quick glance around the stable, mentally cataloging the horses in the other stalls, praying we could get back to evacuate them before the fire spread.

I rushed to Warrior's stall, hooking the lead rope to his halter and bringing him out beside Mushu. Grabbing a handful of mane and his withers, I hopped myself up onto Mushu's bare back, gripping the reins with one hand while I held Warrior's lead in the other.

"Come on, boys. We don't have any time to lose," I told them, turning us out of the stable and into the yard.

I could already tell Mushu was raring to go, only holding back until we were on open ground.

The gray light was darkening by the time I turned us into the pasture. Dark smoke billowed in the sky. Whatever light was left on the horizon was turning orange, reflecting the flames.

I clicked my tongue while I squeezed my heels into Mushu's sides and gave him his head. Racing toward the bluffs. Toward the river. Toward Penn and Reed. To where my heart was hopefully waiting for me.

I was racing against the night. Not a clock. Not against other racers. Not for a buckle. I was racing for the love of my life— the *loves* of my life.

I could feel the fire at my back like a threatening weight, looming down on us. My heart was pounding in sync with the horses' hooves. I didn't know how much time we had. I didn't know how in the hell I was going to find them.

But if it meant staying out here all night, tracing up and down the river, letting the fire consume my ranch, I'd do it. I'd do it in a heartbeat. Over and over again until I found them.

When we finally reached the river, the wakes flickered red and orange with the fire now towering over the tree canopy. I peered up into the sky. Any stars that could light my way were quickly being choked out by the smoke.

As soon as we reached the trail along the river, I started calling out to them, "Reed! Penn!" My heart cracked each time my cries were met with silence. The rushing waters and the crackling flames carrying their names away from me, smothering them out.

Anxiety and fear gripped me. "Come on, Reed. Where are you? I don't know what I'd do without you." I sobbed into the night. Tears streamed down my face, blurring my vision.

Mushu and Warrior looped down the trail. I was no longer guiding them, letting them feel their way.

The smoke was starting to choke me, stinging my eyes and throat. "Reed. Penn." My voice was weakening the farther we went.

The darkness seemed to consume us. The fiery glow flickered off the water—our only light on the trail.

"I don't know how I'm going to do this." I sobbed, slouching against Mushu's neck.

The adrenaline was starting to dissipate. I didn't want to voice it, but my mind was starting to spiral, to think the worst. That I might never find them. That they were going to be lost to the fire.

We started to slow. The horses were spent, too. We'd ridden hard to get to this point. I rested my head against Mushu.

"Mushu, please find them, take me to them. How will I live without them?" I croaked.

Mushu shifted his weight beneath me, as if to rock me, to soothe me. I gripped his mane.

Then I thought I heard someone in the distance. I sucked in a breath, listening intently for sounds of them.

I heard it again.

I sat up, alert, listening, squinting to see through the smoky, orange haze.

"Li-na!" It was far off, but I'd recognize his voice anywhere.

"Reed!" I rasped, trying to yell back, but it was like a knife in my throat.

I kicked my heels into Mushu's side, urging him forward, pulling Warrior along with us, heading toward him.

"Reed," I tried to call back again, listening for a reply.

We kept moving forward, the smoke we were wading through thick as soup.

"Lina!" he bellowed again.

This time it sounded closer, yet pained and hoarse.

Then I saw them.

He was barely staying on his feet. Stumbling through the smoke and undergrowth, Penn still in his arms. His face was streaked with soot and sweat.

I swung down from Mushu's back.

"Reed!" I sobbed, racing toward them.

I threw myself into his arms, wrapping them both up in mine. I gripped his face in my hands, pulling his mouth down to mine, kissing him. Penn wrapped her little arm around my shoulders.

"Lina." She coughed.

"Oh, princess, I'm so sorry I couldn't get to you. I didn't think I'd be able to find you. I didn't think I could reach you. We rode so fast."

He leaned his forehead against mine. A blanket of peace washed over me, telling me this was exactly where I needed to be. Except we needed to get out of this inferno.

"I would have fought through a war to reach you." Reed's voice cracked and strained with the words. "There was no version in which I didn't come back to you."

"I wouldn't have stopped. Not until I found you and Penn."

"I know, sweetheart. That's why I had to keep going."

I held them both to me.

The heat of the fire grew and sparked, and the horses blew their noses behind us, reminding me that we were standing on the edge of a growing wildfire. We still had to get out of there.

"We gotta go," Reed announced, grabbing my hand and pulling us over to the horses.

Reed helped me back up onto Mushu and handed Penn to me. I gripped her tight as coughs racked her little body, pinching my gut with worry.

"Hold on, princess," I told her as we grasped the reins.

Pulling himself up onto Warrior's back and gripping the halter, Reed looked back at me, his brows furrowing. "Ready?"

I nodded. "Get us outta here." I patted Mushu's neck. "I

trust you to get us home, boy."

We turned around on the trail, pointing our compasses home. Sensing the urgency, it didn't take much for the horses to take off, leading us out of the fire.

Chapter 41
Lina

We reached the double-wide before we could reach the stables. I followed Reed into the yard where the hitching post and paddock were. I immediately thought of Romy and baby Charli, my eyes searching for where we left her fighting the flames. I breathed a sigh of relief when I saw her sitting on the ATV with Charli in her arms. She looked spent, but they were safe, even if the land wasn't.

As soon as we pulled up to the hitching post, Reed swung down from Warrior, tying the horses to the post before he drew Penn into his arms. I nearly slid off Mushu needing to get to him. Needing to feel both of them. Needing to know they were okay.

"Reed," I croaked, rushing into his arms.

His hand went to my face, his eyes full of concern. "Are you all right?"

"I'm okay. Are you hurt?" I asked.

"No." He shook his head.

I looked at Penn, wiping the soot off her brow. She covered her mouth as she coughed.

"Fuck, Reed, I'm so sorry."

"For what, sweetheart?" His brow cinched in confusion.

"For wasting time. I wasted so much of our time."

"Oh, baby, no. You didn't."

"Yes, and I almost lost you—both of you."

"*Lina*." He pulled me against him, and I buried my face into his shoulder, letting my tears fall.

"It was my heart, Reed." I cried, tipping my face up to look at him. "My heart has been yours since the very first moment I saw you. You've been mine all this time, and I wasted that time being hurt and angry, instead of just letting you love me."

"Oh, Lina."

Tears were now escaping the corners of his eyes. He cupped my cheek. I leaned into it, wanting to feel the roughness and strength of him. To live a life never to feel those hands again … I didn't even want to imagine it.

"I've never felt love like you've shown me," he confided, "wild and free, formidable and powerful. From the moment I laid eyes on you, I knew you were it for me, sweetheart."

I choked a sob. "*Reed*. I don't know how you were able to wait so patiently for me. You knew, didn't you?"

"That you were mine?"

I nodded into his palm, barely trusting my voice to ask, "When? When did you know?"

"When you walked in with those Daisy Dukes in the Saddle Room. It was like my whole world went still. And then I knew." The fire flickered in his midnight eyes, and I felt as though I was getting lost in them all over again, just like I had all those months ago. "I didn't know how broken I was until you stood in front of me, offering yourself to me. I didn't know love could hurt and heal all at the same time."

"Reed." I cried. "I know. I was so hurt because I was in love with you from the very start." Penn nuzzled against my neck, a little yawn escaping her mouth. "I fell in love with you *both*. I love you so much, Reed. Even if it meant I had to fall and break all over again, I'd do it in a heartbeat."

"I'm not perfect."

"Neither am I."

"I'm going to mess up sometimes."

"And you know I'll call you on it."

He huffed a laugh that turned into a hacking cough. "I've never had someone believe in me so much. Someone willing to stick by my side and love me, even when it hurts."

I wiped a tear from his eye, smearing the soot. "Loving you is worth it to me. All the hurts and pains."

"I wouldn't have blamed you if you'd decided it was too much."

I sucked in a breath. It felt like a dozen tiny splinters in my throat. "You and Penn are worth it to me. A love like *this* is worth it."

I pushed up on my tiptoes, pressing a kiss to his mouth.

"I love you, Lina Larsen," he whispered against my lips.

"I love you, cowboy."

I laid my head on his shoulder, staring up at him and Penn. They filled my vision, glowing in the firelight. I reached up to her, brushing the soot away from her eyes. "My cowboy and my princess."

Sirens sounded in the distance, getting closer. Lights flickered against the orange smoke.

"Look, Daddy and Lina! Fire trucks!" Penn perked up, pointing at the fire engines that were pulling up.

Dad and Jude came leading the trucks up the drive on horseback. They both looked windswept and exhausted, their eyes full of terror.

Jude swung off his horse the fastest. "Where's Romy?" His eyes were wide with panic.

"We saw the fire and went to the house first, but they weren't there," Dad explained.

"Romy." I sniffed. "She was trying to help me put out the fire ..."

"Romy!" Jude cried, turning on his heels and rushing toward the fire before I could tell him she was okay.

Dad tied the horses to the post, and we all took off after Jude. The wail of the sirens screamed, piercing our ears. All of us covered our mouths, coughing as the smoke burned our lungs. We could see the fire spreading, consuming the forest and eating up every dry inch of ranch land it could touch.

"Dad, the ranch." My heart was breaking.

"I know, darlin'," he rasped as we jogged toward the flames. Every instinct in our bodies told us to run the other way.

"Romy!" Jude cried again, seeing her now holding Charli beside the fire truck while they were examined for injury.

"Jude!" She sobbed, running toward him.

They crushed each other in an embrace, Jude peppering kisses on their faces while she wept.

My lungs were about ready to give out. I stopped, bending over to wheeze.

"Lina?" Reed asked in concern, resting his hand on my

back.

"I'm okay," I said, catching my breath. I leaned against Reed. "The ranch …"

"I know, sweetheart."

More emergency vehicles started pulling up, firefighters unloading, rolling out hoses. The *whop-whop* of a helicopter overhead, hidden by the night and the thick smoke, flew in. My ears roared as I watched everyone desperately trying to save the forest … trying to save the ranch.

I intertwined my fingers with Reed's, holding on to him, drawing strength from him while I watched my land burn.

His hand flexed in mine, tightening his grip. "He's not going to get away with this." He whispered it so quietly, I barely heard him.

I pumped my hand in his grasp. "No, no he's not."

CHAPTER 42
Lina

&verything hurted. My lungs. My legs. My back. Hell, the very marrow of my bones ached, but I would have done it all again in a heartbeat.

I could sleep for a week, I was so tired, but I could feel sunlight warming the side of my face, brightening behind my eyelids.

Groaning, cracking an eye, I reached for Reed or Penn beside me, but the mattress was empty. Penn must have woken up and needed breakfast. We had all piled into bed, exhausted. There was no way in hell either of us were going to let Penn out of our sight. Scared from the ordeal, we'd both curled around her, holding her tight.

I sat up, studying the unfamiliar surroundings of the cabin we evacuated to.

One of the many perks of living in a small town was that everyone was ready to lend a helping hand. The Riggses, Christian's folks, immediately offered to help. They owned a sprawling estate near Mt. Bachelor where they bred and trained thoroughbred race horses and Norwegian elkhound hunting dogs. They had plenty of acreage to pasture our horses and open fields for the herd to graze, not to mention a vacant cabin ready for all of us to bunk up in.

Wrapping myself in the bed quilt, I padded out of the room. The floorboards creaked beneath my bare feet as I stepped out into the hallway. In another room upstairs, I could hear Charli crying while Romy spoke softly, followed by Jude's deep rumble.

The cabin was old, rustic, and looked as though it hadn't been touched since the '70s, but it was safe while we waited to go home. At least it was as safe as it could be since Junior was still on the run.

My heart just about sputtered and stopped beating, not seeing Reed or Penn where I thought they'd be. Clammy heat washed over me before noticing movement outside the front window. I clutched my chest, releasing an exhale of relief.

Reed was on the porch, leaning against the railing, his black cowboy hat pulled low, his cell phone to his ear. He had a clean white shirt on, but his arms were still streaked with dirt and soot. I knew my body wasn't much better. We'd collapsed in bed last night as soon as our boots were off, not bothering to shower.

He looked deep in conversation as he stared off toward the mountains. I opened the front door, interrupting, as he turned to look at me. His face was shaded but his lips turned up at the corners when he saw it was me.

"I appreciate all of your help with this. Thank you," he said into the phone. "Have a good day." He ended the call, returning it to his pocket, tipping his hat back to fully look at me. His eyes were sparkling. "We thought we'd let you sleep," he said sweetly, his voice still deep from the smoke inhalation.

Coffee mugs sat on the porch railing. He picked one up and handed it to me.

"I couldn't sleep anymore. Where's Penn?" I took a sip of coffee, and he pulled me to his side.

"She's with your dad." He jerked his chin across the yard to the pasture where our horses grazed.

Dad had Penn in his arms beside the fence, watching the horses eat their morning hay and oats. Seeing her there—and safe—made it easier to breathe. I took another sip, letting the warmth soothe my throat and anxiety.

"Who was on the phone?"

"My lawyer."

"Yeah?" I asked, surprised.

"Turns out with our police report about Junior, we were able to get Elise to immediately surrender full custody to me."

I sucked in a breath, feeling the news bolster me. "Reed! That's amazing!"

He nodded, the corners of his mouth twitching as if he was keeping himself from grinning. "She'll be able to have supervised visits under the condition that she gets some help, and she has finally agreed to rehab."

The relief and peace of that news seemed to wash over him, and I could feel the muscles of his arm around me relax.

"That's such good news."

I looked past him to watch Dad and Penn with the horses. Mushu walked up to the fence, sticking his nose out for pets. Penn's little hand reached out, stroking him down his stripe.

Taking another drink of the coffee, I sighed, not wanting to ask the question, but aware that I needed to know the answer. I knew not all the news was going to be good today. "The ranch … is it still there?"

Reed pulled me tighter into his side, his thumb brushing tender strokes on my shoulder. "It's still there. It may be a while before we can return, though. We lost a lot of grazing land, and there's smoke damage."

I nodded, letting my head fall and rest against his chest. That was the best I could have hoped for. The smoky haze gave an orange glow to the sky as it all continued to burn. It would be devastating to lose the ranch if they didn't get it under control, but I'd survive it. But losing Reed and Penn? That was unthinkable. I don't think I could have come back from that. "This is all I need," I said. "My family. All in one place."

He leaned down, dropping a kiss to my hair. "We smell like smoke."

I tipped my chin, letting it rest on his chest. My palm reached up to cup his jaw. His dark-brown eyes were tender and loving while I stroked his beard. "Do you think they'll be preoccupied long enough for us to go take a shower?"

Reed's eyes intensified, heating as they bore into me. "Hey, Chuck!" he called, not even looking at Dad, who turned at his name. "I'm in love with your daughter."

"That's not news, Ownstead!" Dad hollered back.

I giggled, feeling my cheeks heat. "I'm in love with him too, Dad!"

"It's about time, darlin'!"

"Could you watch Penn for a little bit?" I asked him, my eyes flicking to see Dad smirking at us while he spotted Penn as she climbed the fence.

"We got it handled here. Take all the time you need."

"Hear that, cowboy? You can take all the time you need," I teased, letting my thumb drag across his bottom lip.

He nipped the pad of my thumb. "I intend to." He leaned down to whisper, his lips brushing against the shell of my ear. "With my hands, my mouth, and my cock."

My pussy clenched. "Let's go test the water heater."

EPILOGUE
Reed

T he Columbia River Finals. The big show. The wildest crowd on the circuit. The stands were deafening. The electric guitar of Brooks and Dunn's "Rock My World (Little Country Girl)" blared through the stadium speakers while the announcer called each barrel horse and racer.

Lina sat on top of Mushu. His hooves danced with excitement. We both had to hold him back to keep him from plowing forward. She held her hat to her head, a big, bright smile on her face as she tipped her head up to bask in the glory of this moment. And she deserved to fucking bathe in it!

"Larsen, you're on deck."

Lina was next, and she turned her grin on me. "Can you have Penn meet us at the gate?"

I nodded, unable to keep myself from beaming back at her. "Chuck's bringing her down now."

She bit her lip, and I hoped she was remembering exactly how I sucked on it earlier.

"Don't choke," Paige snarked behind us.

Lina didn't even turn in her saddle or dim the smile on her face. "Eat my dust, Paige."

The other barrel racer before her raced in through the alley, her trainer catching her. Lina felt so confident, she didn't even chance a glance at her time. Fuck, it was hot.

"Larsen's up!"

She leaned down, dropping a soft kiss to my lips.

"Burn the breeze, sweetheart," I said against her mouth.

I felt her lips tip back up before she straightened her seat.

With a flirty wink, she said, "I'm going to rock your world later, cowboy."

"Is that a promise?" I called out to her as she started sidestepping Mushu.

"A guarantee!" she yelled before she let Mushu loose.

And they were off, Mushu dragging his butt around the barrels. The crowd roared. The announcer's voice blared.

"We're here, Daddy!" Penn yelled, skip-hopping to my side with Chuck wrapped around her little finger. "I got cotton candy!" A big, pink fluff was in her hand and her mouth was already sticky, but she had the happiest look on her face.

"I couldn't say no." Chuck shrugged, looking helpless.

I huffed a laugh. I'd probably be dealing with a sugar crash later. But today, of all days, it was worth it.

We barely had a chance to blink before Mushu and Lina were screaming back into the alley. She pulled up on the reins, skidding to a stop, dirt kicking up on her opponents. I had to press my lips together to keep from smiling. I rushed to her side, grabbing high on Mushu's reins to steady him. She spun around in her saddle at the same time I looked at the time clocked.

She let out a scream, then said, "13.14 fucking seconds!"

She slapped a hand to her mouth, tears springing to her eyes.

"That's your best time *ever*!" Chuck cried, clapping for her. "I'm so proud of you, darlin'."

"I did it!" Lina turned her glistening eyes on me. "I did it."

"You fucking did it, baby!"

"Drinks all around!" Lina announced as soon as we stepped into the rodeo bar.

The bar erupted into cheers and applause.

With my hand on her lower back, I ducked to whisper in her ear, "Sweetheart, are you really going to pay for everyone's drinks?"

She rolled her eyes at me, gesturing to herself. "Did I just win the fucking finals, or did I just win the fucking finals?"

I shook my head, chuckling.

Sage and Romy rushed her, drawing her into a group hug.

"You fucking crushed it!" Romy squealed.

"I've never seen Mushu run so fast!" Sage exclaimed.

Lina peeked over her shoulder, both of us remembering how fast Mushu had to run during the fire. We still hadn't returned to the ranch. Chuck was still waiting on the insurance company so we could begin smoke remediation on the properties. The Riggses had been more than generous to let us stay while we waited.

"Come on, the guys are holding down a table for us," Romy said, yanking her away from me.

Christian, Kale, and Jude were sitting back, drinking their beers. I pulled Lina's chair out, and we all found our seats—

except we were short one.

"Is there no chair for me?" Sage asked, turning to look to see if another chair was available to pull up to our round table.

"It's right here, baby," Christian said, gripping her hips and dragging her onto his lap.

"Christian!" she screeched, shoving off him.

"What?" he asked, looking innocent as she scrambled away from him and went to grab a chair.

As soon as she was free, we caught him adjusting himself.

"Pants too tight, bro?" Jude asked him, a lopsided grin on his face.

"Fuck you. You're supposed to be on my side, but yeah, I pretty much have a semi around her all the time. It's nothing new," he grumbled.

"Maybe I didn't need to know that," Kale commented, taking a big gulp of beer.

Sage pulled up a chair, surprising us all when she positioned it right beside Christian. Almost everyone hid their smiles behind their drinks as we watched her scoot up to the table. It was a little bit of a tight fit, and they were nearly touching each other.

She glanced up, noticing all of us looking at her.

"What?" she asked, her brows knit together in confusion.

"Nothing," we all muttered.

Lina leaned in, resting her hand on Sage's. "Did y'all fuck?" she whispered, but it was loud enough for all of us to hear.

Sage's eyes went wide. Even her tan couldn't hide the blush on her cheeks. "What? No! Ew! Of course not!"

I looked over at Christian, who was gazing at her with

hearts in his eyes and a crooked little smirk. But his gulp and body language were saying that maybe he wasn't just dog-sitting anymore.

Read on for a sneak peek to Book Three of the Thornbrush Ranch Series...

SADDLE THE STORM

PROLOGUE

Four Years Ago

Sage

I pushed my foot to the floor, laying on the gas. The Jeep's engine roared, accelerating with my heart rate. It was pitch black, the moon and stars hidden by thick clouds promising a storm. A storm I was trying to beat, a storm I was running away from. A storm, that if I'd stayed a moment longer would have torn me to shreds and swallowed me life and limb.

My headlights bounced across the dark country roads, illuminating only yards in front of me. My eyes shifted nervously to the rearview mirror making sure I wasn't followed.

I just needed to make it across the border. I just needed to make it to Washington.

My heart pounded in my chest. I was sweating despite the cool spring temperatures that were dropping with the approaching rain. I tried to take a deep breath, but I winced at the sudden spike of pain along my right side.

My stomach was in my throat.

His name flashed up on the center console, momentarily interrupting my "Get Away" playlist and making me feel like I was about to throw up.

Yes, I had a "Get Away" playlist. I made it for this very moment, titling it "Work Out II" so he wouldn't suspect anything. It was filled with Miranda Lambert, Shania Twain, and Gretchen Wilson. They were almost all "fuck him" songs that would keep me from turning around and going back to fawn at his feet.

"Fuck you!" I whisper-yelled, the words burning through my swollen throat, as I hit the button to ignore his call.

"Kerosene" resumed, pumping through my speakers.

Only to be interrupted again. With his call.

I growled through my teeth, but it quickly turned into more of a hiss at the way it caused my ribs to ache.

I hit the ignore button again, before bracing a hand across my aching torso.

Music blared once more.

I tapped on the breaks as I went around a curve before hitting the gas.

I just needed to get to safety. They knew I was coming and what I was up against.

A notification dinged, the music dimmed, and Siri's voice filled the vehicle.

"Clayton Creed said, *You can't run from me. I know you're going to Sanctuary Ridge.*"

"Fuck. Fuck. Fuck."

I looked back at the GPS. I was still an hour away.

He found out.

Bile stung my throat.

The bass from the stereo vibrated the speakers.

Then a drop hit the windshield. Then another one. Big, fat, drops. The sky was about to open up.

"Shit!" I hit the steering wheel with the heel of my palm. He knew where I was going. Rain would slow me down too.

Another notification ding.

New message from "Clayton Creed, *You're on highway 20. You know I can just track your phone right? Come home, baby girl, and we can talk.*"

"Hell no!" I cried out, as if he could hear me. "And wind up dead this time? No, thank you!"

New message from "Clayton Creed, *I fucked up. Please just come home.*"

Yeah, he fucked up. Glimpses of myself in the rear-view mirror showed the angry bruises scattered around my eye, fingerprints around my throat gave evidence just how hard and long he held me down. There was no way to explain this one away. He was always so careful, calculated, meticulous in everything he did because of who he was. Even in the marks and bruises there was some sort of way to hide it or explain it away. I wasn't so accident prone that I fell right into his chokehold or beat my cheek against the counter while cooking.

Headlights flashed around the corner momentarily blinding me through the rain as I turned on my whippers. I needed to get off the road and figure out what I needed to do.

I pulled off into the shallow ditch, switching on my emergency flashers so other cars noticed me in the dark and rain. If he was tracking my phone, I needed to get rid of it and fast.

I pulled up my contacts and found Susan, the woman who I was talking to at Sanctuary Ridge. It barely rang before she said, "Sanctuary Ridge, this is Susan."

"Susan, it's Sage. He knows I'm coming there and he's tracking my phone." My voice strained to get the words out. My fingers of my free hand fiddled on the steering wheel, my anxious energy building into a panic as my eyes continued to flick from window to mirror. "He could be on his way to get me right now."

"Okay. Okay. Take a deep breath. I have somewhere else safe you can go. Are you still in Oregon? Are you still on the reservation?"

I shook my head as if she could see it. "I'm still in Oregon."

It almost sounded like she was flipping through an old rolodex through the phone. "Here it is. I just have the address. Do you have something to write this down?"

Placing my phone between my shoulder and ear, I leaned over to the passenger seat where my backpack sat, unzipping it. I barely had time to throw some clothes inside before I left, but I made sure to grab my paints and charcoal pencils. The only thing I had left that was mine. Not even those clothes were mine, chosen and bought by Clayton. Nor this Jeep, a gift from him that felt more like "hush money." But those brushes and oil paint were mine well before I ever became his.

Grabbing a charcoal pencil from my bag, I scrounged through the glovebox before finding a stash of fast-food napkins.

"Okay, I'm ready."

"It's a farm just outside of the town proper of Willows on a county road."

Willows? My breath caught in my throat. Was this some sort of sign?

"Willows, Oregon?"

"Uh huh, that's right."

The last I heard, my little brother, who'd left home when he was 18, was living in Willows pursuing his dream to be a professional bull rider. I hadn't seen him since, and just like our parents, he had no idea the hell I'd endured the last two years.

"It's 5400 SW Crooked River Rd. Oregon. It's unincorporated, in Arnold County, so it may be difficult for *someone* to find. But it's between the Deschutes River and the national forest, heading toward Mt. Bachelor."

I jotted the address down. "That's okay. I'll find it."

Wheels crushed on gravel and headlights flickered behind me, making my breath freeze in my chest.

"You sure?"

"I need to go," I finally managed, folding the napkin and shoving it into my jean pocket.

"Be safe, Sage. Go directly there and please call us back to let us know you're safe."

I wouldn't be calling back. "Thank you."

Hanging up the phone, I hopped out of the vehicle, letting the rain pelt my face and drench my shirt. I looked both ways up and down the street for any other cars, but the road was dark. There weren't even streetlights on this country road. Only trees and fields lining either side. Bending over, I felt beneath the car, circling the vehicle as my fingers skimmed the cold metal surface. If he was tracking my phone, I wouldn't put it past him to put one of those GPS AirTag trackers on my car. Sure enough, a circular tag stuck beneath my bumper. Ripping it off, I chucked it onto the road hoping someone would either drive over it or it would inadvertently stick to someone's wheel and throw him off my trail.

The cold rain soaked my already frizzy hair and clumped my eye lashes together making it hard to see. I wiped my face with my sleeve, but that too was already wet. I went back to my driver's side door and grabbed my phone, positioning it right beneath the front wheel. Jumping back into the running car, I closed the door, the windshield wipers were now on full blast with the pounding rain. I was soaked water dripping on to the leather seats, but I didn't give a fuck. Putting the car in drive, I rolled over my phone, braked, shifted to reverse, and rolled over it again listening for that satisfying crunch as I threw the car back into drive and sped off into the night.

Acknowledgments

This book will always have a special place in my heart. Even though this was the first book that was stressful to write because I had a strict deadline to meet and was also releasing *Among the Willows*, it was a story that wrecked me in the best way.

The incredible patience and support of my husband and our kids while I wrote this book was more than I could have ever asked for. Part of this book was written while he drove us from Oregon to Montana, and back, during a family vacation. I don't know how I would have finished it without those hours spent in the car.

To my incredible team of editors, personal assistants, alpha and beta readers, and street team members—thank you for being the best hive! Thank you, Tabitha Bell, for coming along on this ride with me, reading and editing as I wrote to help me stay on track for the deadline. Thank you, Bri, from Dev Edits with Bri, for being the best developmental editor, taking a chance on me and sharing reactions as you read. Your insight into today's romance genre was invaluable. As always, thank you to Joyce Mochrie, my copyeditor and proofreader, owner of One Last Look, for having my back in ensuring this baby was publishing ready.

Thank you to Rose DeVault for helping me stay organized, manage the team, and making beautiful content to help promote my books. You have really taken a load off my plate, and I finally feel like I can breathe and enjoy the things I love about this blossoming career.

Thank you to my alphas and betas—Laura Pappano, Jessica Nirta, Nicole Wills, Abbie McKnight, Sarina Vega, Kristina Burt, Shay Nelson, Tiana Valdez, Kirsten Drake, Becca Schelhaas, Jorinde Pels, Jessica Snoots, Erin Sise, Casie Laughlin, Julia Halladay, Meaghan Elizabeth, Alyssa Snyder, and Crystal Gascon. A very special thank you to my barrel racing beta readers—Sanora Brewer, Dani Freeman, Deanna Webber, and Kimberly Heller. Thank you so much for sharing your expertise and helping me make sure Lina's character was done right.

To my Honeybees, both former and current, thank you for all your support and excitement around Lina and Reed. All the hard work you did to assist in promoting *Among the Willows* will forever be appreciated and remembered. Thank you for helping me get my book and name out there. I truly don't think I could have done it without you. You are my boots on the ground. Thank you, bbs.

Last, to Lina and Reed. Your story wrecked me and made me cry ugly tears. I joke that I may need to start a GoFundMe for therapy costs for my readers, but I mean it in the best way. Your story of love at first sight and redemption was just what we all needed.

Until we return to Thornbrush Ranch … thank you, reader, for picking up this book and giving this indie author a chance.

About the Author

June Lark is a romance author of steamy bygone and contemporary small-town love stories filled with tension and suspense, with strong heroines who save themselves and brooding heroes who fall first. After years of research and a career in teaching social studies, she is finally living her childhood dream.

She lives outside of Portland, Oregon with her husband, Kenny, two kids, K.C. and Skye Lynn, and their lovey-dovey Norwegian elkhound, Baldur. She loves spending time with her family, cooking, exploring the Pacific Northwest, retail therapy, and devouring romance novels. With a coconut milk latte in hand, you can find June researching and writing in her office/kids' craft room.